"The Chinese and "Malmordo"

TWO CLASSIC ADVENTURES OF

by Walter B. Gibson
writing as Maxwell Grant

with New Introductory Essays by
Anthony Tollin and Will Murray

Published by Sanctum Productions for
NOSTALGIA VENTURES, INC.
P.O. Box 231183; Encinitas, CA 92023-1183

This Nostalgia Ventures edition is an unabridged republication of the text and illustrations of two stories from *The Shadow Magazine,* as originally published by Street & Smith Publications, Inc., N.Y.: *The Chinese Disks* from the November 1, 1934 issue, and *The Golden Vulture* from the July 1946 issue. Typographical errors have been tacitly corrected in this edition.

International Standard Book Numbers:
ISBN 1-932806-52-0 13 DIGIT 978-1-932806-52-6

Series editor: Anthony Tollin
sanctumotr@earthlink.net

Consulting editor: Will Murray

Copy editor: Joseph Wrzos

Graphic production by Sanctum Productions.
Additional production by Tom Roberts.

First printing: October 2006

Nostalgia Ventures, Inc.
P.O. Box 231183; Encinitas, CA 92023-1183

Visit The Shadow at www.nostalgiatown.com

CONTENTS

Thrilling Tales and Features

Cover art by George Rozen
"The Chinese Disks" illustrations by Tom Lovell

SPOTLIGHT on THE SHADOW

by Anthony Tollin

"Your life," intoned the sibilant voice from the shadows, "is no longer your own. It belongs to me now.... I shall improve it. I shall make it useful. But I shall risk it, too. Perhaps I shall lose it, for I have lost lives, just as I have saved them. This is my promise: life, with enjoyment, with danger, with excitement, and—with money. Life, above all, with honor. But if I give it, I demand obedience. Absolute obedience."

"I accept. I promise absolute obedience."

With these words, Harry Vincent was inducted into The Shadow's service. Gifted with a persuasive personality yet capable of two-fisted action, Vincent functioned as The Shadow's advance man, usually going into the field to lay the groundwork for his mysterious chief. He became a key member in the elite band of operatives who supported the Knight of Darkness in his war on evildoers. That group eventually included reputed "mobster" Cliff Marsland, crime reporter Clyde Burke, government agent Myra Reldon and the communications wizard known only as Burbank.

To combat crime, the Dark Avenger secretly assembled an elite *Mission Impossible*-style force drawn from all walks of life. This hand-picked squad functions as The Shadow's eyes, ears and muscle in his unceasing war against the underworld. When his first major foe returns to menace society in *The Chinese Disks,* The Shadow expands his crimefighting organization to meet this unprecedented challenge.

Contributing editor Will Murray and I would like to welcome the newest addition of our team, copy editor Joseph Wrzos. Some of our readers may remember the lifelong science fiction and pulp fan from his 1965-67 run as managing editor of *Amazing Stories* and *Fantastic.* Wrzos also edited *The Best of Amazing* (as "Joseph Ross") and *In Lovecraft's Shadow: The Cthulhu Mythos Stories of August Derleth.* More recently, he edited *New Horizons,* August Derleth's last science fiction anthology for Arkham House and, with Peter Ruber, co-edited Seabury Quinn's *Night Creatures.* Wrzos is also the owner of a major science fiction and pulp collection that includes complete runs of *The Shadow* (except for #1!) and Doc Savage, which he's painstakingly comparing against our texts for accuracy.

A copy editor's work is largely invisible to readers, who take for granted the absence of typos excised *before* they get into print. His efforts are best appreciated by his co-workers as integral to the quality of any publication. Joe's professionalism and knowledge of pulp fiction will be invaluable as we launch our second ongoing series of vintage pulp classics.

The debut of *The Shadow Magazine* in 1931 triggered an explosion of single-character pulp titles. The Shadow's runaway success inspired the creation of dozens of imitators including the Phantom Detective, Operator 5, the Spider, Secret Agent X, the Green Lama and The Whisperer.

Yet only one pulp hero ever reached the pinnacle of popularity achieved by The Shadow—*Doc Savage, the Man of Bronze.* The premier issue of *Doc Savage Magazine,* dated March 1933, introduced a new breed of American hero: "Raised from the cradle for his task in life, Clark Savage, Jr., goes from one end of the world to another, righting wrongs, helping the oppressed, liberating the innocent." Doc was the world's greatest surgeon, and also a master chemist, engineer and archeologist. Doc's globetrotting expeditions blazed the way for such later adventurers as James Bond and Indiana Jones.

The Man of Bronze would have tremendous influence on future pulp heroes like Captain Future and The Avenger; and such legendary comic book superheroes as Superman and Batman. "Doc Savage and his oddly assorted team might be considered the progenitors of today's *Fantastic Four* and many other teams of superheroes—even

Sgt. Fury and his Howling Commandos," Marvel Comics-creator Stan Lee recently observed.

Doc Savage Magazine enjoyed a long and successful publishing life until Street & Smith closed down its entire pulp and comic book lines in 1949. However, the Man of Bronze made a triumphant return when Bantam Books began reprinting Doc's vintage adventures in 1964. Lightning struck twice, and Doc Savage became a paperback phenomenon. By 1971, Bantam had printed more than ten million Doc Savage paperbacks. The demand was so great that Bantam eventually reissued all 181 of the pulp novels (plus a previously unpublished epic) before publishing an origin tale by Philip Jose Farmer and new novels by Will Murray (utilizing material from previously unpublished manuscripts and outlines by Lester Dent). The Doc Savage revival also saw a Warner Brothers film and comic book series from Marvel, DC Comics, Dark Horse and other publishers.

The first of our new *Doc Savage* volumes, reprinting *Fortress of Solitude* and *The Devil Genghis,* is now available from the same retailers who sell *The Shadow* reprints. Fans may notice similarities between a recent blockbuster film and the plot of Lester Dent's 1938 novels. Both revolve around a criminal genius who steals futuristic inventions from the Arctic Fortress of Solitude of the world's greatest superhero. Clark Savage, Jr., the Man of Bronze, was a major influence on the creation and development of Clark Kent, the Man of Steel, as Will Murray explains in his introduction. This dual-novel volume reprints both appearances of Doc's greatest enemy, the diabolical John Sunlight.

In honor of Doc Savage's return, we've issued the first volume in two editions. The regular version reprints Emery Clarke's classic 1938 *Fortress of Solitude* pulp cover, while our variant edition showcases the 1968 artistry of James Bama, whose paperback covers helped make Doc Savage an iconic figure for a new generation.

We'll return next month with two more classic Shadow thrillers. In *The Red Blot*, Lamont Cranston first meets Commissioner Ralph Weston (setting up the friendly rivalry that would later be showcased in the famous radio series) and investigates a series of crimes orchestrated by a malevolent mastermind who leaves a bloody mark as his calling card. Our second tale, *The Voodoo Master,* was voted the favorite novel in a 1937 *Shadow Magazine* readers' poll and was again acclaimed as one of the top Shadow novels by pulp fans nearly a half century later.

Don't miss these exciting thrillers. Ask your bookseller to reserve your copies today.

The Chinese Disks

Tokens of crime, they lead The Shadow on a trail of danger

Complete Book-length Novel from the Private Annals of The Shadow, as told to

Maxwell Grant

CHAPTER I
COMING EVENTS

"I DON'T know nothin', Joe. I ain't no stoolie—"

The speaker was a pale, rat-faced fellow. His voice, half snarl, half whine, ended with a twitch of ugly lips. Beady eyes blinked nervously as they stared at the swarthy, firm-set visage on the opposite side of the battered desk.

"You're a stoolie right now, Duff," rasped the swarthy man. "What's more, you're going to like it. I brought you here so you could talk. No stall works with me. Get that?"

There was a pause as the two men faced each other beneath the light of a lamp that hung above the desk. Silence followed while the beady eyes tried to outblink the hard-boiled gaze that met them. Twisted lips were holding back.

The room in which these two had met was an unused office of detective headquarters. The rat-faced man was "Duff" Corley, a small-fry mobster from the underworld of Manhattan. The swarthy-faced inquisitor was Detective Joe Cardona, ace of the New York force.

Duff Corley was not the first of his ilk to meet Cardona in this little office. Detailed to special investigation in the badlands, the star sleuth forced these appointments whenever he saw fit. Few crooks had the nerve to refuse an interview when Joe Cardona demanded it. They preferred to answer the detective's summons; then try to bluff it out.

Exactly what Duff Corley was attempting. But it didn't go with Joe Cardona. His ultimatum delivered, the detective watched the twitch of the gangster's lips and waited. Duff's nervousness increased.

"Honest, Joe"—it was all whine, no snarl—"I don't know nothin' about what you're askin'. You say there's been guys duckin' out an' not showin' up again. Well—I ain't one of 'em, or I wouldn't be here. That's sensible, ain't it? There ain't nothin' I can tell you about guys that I don't know."

"Spider Mertz was one of them," put in Cardona, with a growl. "You saw him a few nights ago."

The statement jolted Duff; but the rat-faced fellow recovered quickly. Once again, he tried a whine to cover up his bluff.

"Spider Mertz? I ain't seen him." Duff's tone became pleading. "Honest, Joe. I ain't seen Spider for a couple of weeks. Not since—"

"Not since he ducked out of sight, eh?" demanded Joe as Duff caught himself in the midst of a damaging statement. "That's what you were going to say, wasn't it, Duff? Well—that just proves one thing. You did see Spider Mertz."

"Honest, Joe—"

"I'll tell you where you saw him. Down at Red Mike's. That's why I brought you here. Spider talked to you, Duff. You're going to tell me what he said."

SILENCE. Joe Cardona smiled coldly. He had scored a point; he had the opportunity to follow it with another stroke. The detective edged one elbow to the desk. Leaning forward, he gazed squarely at Duff Corley.

"The dragnet's been working," informed Cardona. "Sometimes it brings in good results. This time we hooked a couple of squealers who tried to put themselves in right. They talked. About those silk warehouse robberies. Jobs that were pulled last month. I learned a bit about you, Duff."

The mobster began a snarl. He stopped short, realizing that talk might mean new trouble. Joe Cardona resumed, in a cold tone.

"Maybe I'm not going to use what I found out," stated the detective. "You weren't in those jobs as heavy as you might have been. Six months over on the Island wouldn't do you much harm, Duff; but it wouldn't do me any good. Might be a lot of trouble, pinning it on you. Sometimes squealers get closemouthed, when the pinch hits. I figured you might be more useful where you are."

Duff winced. Cardona's tone had become mild as well as speculative; but the mobster saw the threat beneath. Duff knew that Joe could pin the goods on him. He knew that the detective would do it, in spite of the details involved, unless he found a reason to let the matter ride. Joe was leaving it to Duff to provide the reason.

"You mean you'll lay off them warehouse jobs?" asked the crook, leaning forward. "You'll let the other mugs take the rap without draggin' me into it? If I—"

"If you give me the lowdown on Spider Mertz," inserted Cardona, as Duff hesitated. "That will make you useful enough to remain at large."

Duff looked about him in furtive fashion, almost as though suspecting the presence of spies from the underworld. To the crook, headquarters was a place to be shunned. Even this secluded nook of an office made him uneasy. At last, Duff glanced toward Cardona and put a final whine.

"I ain't no stoolie, Joe," was his plea. "Maybe I'd better take the rap. When a guy turns stoolie, the dicks run him ragged. I ain't goin' to be no stoolie for—"

"Cut it, Duff," snapped Cardona. "This is a straight deal, if you deliver the goods. You'll be playing stool pigeon, right enough, but on this one job. That's all. I won't need you after you've gone through with it."

"You mean that, Joe?"

"I said it, didn't I? Come on. Spill what you know. Tell me about Spider Mertz. What's his game?"

"I don't know, Joe," began Duff. "Wait"—he raised a scrawny hand when he saw the detective scowl—"I can find it out for you. Honest, Joe. I saw Spider, down at Red Mike's, like you said. He'd been hidin' out—an' he's got some mugs workin' for him."

"Who are they?"

"I don't know their names. A crew of gorillas, that's all I know. He ain't lookin' for more, neither. Layin' low with the bunch he's got."

"Then why did he talk to you?"

"Because he knowed that I was good at spottin' the lay for a job. That's what Spider said, anyway. Told me he knew a guy that could use me."

"Who?"

"He didn't say. I'm to meet the guy and—"

"Where?"

"I don't know yet."

CARDONA shifted. These statements seemed like an evasion. Duff saw that Cardona was suspecting another stall. The scrawny crook made haste to correct the impression.

"There's somethin' big in back of it, Joe," whispered Duff, hoarsely. "There's a big shot hid somewhere. Spider's workin' for him, I'm to work for him. I told Spider to count me in. All I'm waitin' for is the tip—when I'm to meet up with the big shot an' where."

"Who'll give you the tip? Spider?"

"No. That's the part I don't know. I'm to stick around Red Mike's. See? Until some bozo shows up an' passes me the high sign."

"Yeah?" Cardona was gruff. "Listen, Duff, this kind of talk would sound natural from a hop-head. But from you it sounds like a stall. I'm telling you—"

"I can prove it, Joe!" broke in Duff, anxiously. "I ain't stallin'. There's some guy goin' to walk in on me at Red Mike's. Look at this—then you'll know I'm talkin' straight."

Fumbling in his pocket, the crook produced a small, roundish object. He dropped it on the battered table. It fell with a dull clank. Cardona picked it up. The object was a grayish disk of metal, slightly smaller than a half dollar. Engraved upon its center was a Chinese character.

"Who gave you this?" demanded Joe. "Spider Mertz?"

"Yes," responded Duff. "Spider's got one like it. He gave me this one. The guy that's goin' to meet me at Red Mike's will have one. That's how I'll know him."

"Did Spider tell you why they use a disk like this?"

"No. An' I've been wonderin' what the thing is. It ain't a Chinese coin—I've seen Chinese coins, an' they've got square holes in the center of 'em. I don't know what this thing means, outside of it servin' for a high sign."

Cardona was examining the disk. He placed it on the desk, laid a thin sheet of paper over it and took an impression by rubbing the paper with a pencil. Lifting the paper, he tossed the disk back to Duff.

"Keep it," ordered the detective. "Go down to Red Mike's. Contact the fellow that comes there. Go where he tells you. But tip me off, the first chance you get. Understand?"

"But Joe—maybe the big shot will get wise—"

"Leave that to me. Whoever I send around there won't be too close. But remember"—Joe was rising as he spoke—"play on the level with me. Or—"

Cardona had no need to complete the statement. Duff was nodding as he slouched toward the door. He waited for Cardona and watched the detective open the barrier to peer into the corridor. Joe gave a wave of his hand. Duff scurried from the little office and headed down the corridor to a secluded side door.

OUT on the street, Duff Corley looked about nervously. He seemed to fear the presence of skulkers in the dark. Hands in coat pockets, the scrawny mobster was using one to grip the disk that Cardona had returned to him. That disk was the talisman that could protect him in the underworld and with the law as well.

A man was approaching. Duff slunk into the darkness and saw the arrival enter the side door that he had left. He caught a glimpse of the man's face and recognized him as Clyde Burke, a newspaper reporter who frequently visited the underworld. Relieved, Duff shambled hastily away.

Meanwhile, Clyde Burke had entered the corridor. He strolled past the office—now darkened—where Cardona had held conference with Duff Corley. He turned into a wider passage and there stopped before a lighted doorway. Looking in, Clyde saw Joe Cardona seated at a desk. The reporter entered.

The detective looked up hurriedly. As he did, Clyde saw a sheet of paper that Joe had been examining. The dick turned the paper over and pushed it aside. Through it, Clyde could see the outline of a blackened circle that looked like the impression of a coin.

"Hello, Burke," greeted Cardona, in affable fashion. "If you're looking for a story, I haven't any."

"Too bad," mused Clyde. "You're here at headquarters; yet you don't know what's going on around the place."

"What do you mean?"

"Well—either the dragnet's working mighty good or else it's slipping. When crooks come strolling out the side door, all alone, it looks rather unusual."

"Who did you see?"

"A fellow that looked like Duff Corley. Got a bad rep, that bird. I've run into him before. But I never suspected to see him strolling around here."

"Lay off, Burke," growled Cardona. "I know what you're aiming at. A good story for the Classic—crooks dropping in to see their pals, the dicks. Well, if you run it, you'll have a black eye down here—"

"Don't worry, Joe," assured Clyde. "I just mentioned what I saw for your own information. Apparently you knew that Duff Corley was here."

"I did," returned Cardona. "I called him in here. For a little chat. That was all. But it ended nowhere, like most first interviews. So there's no story in it. But maybe, later on—"

"Corley will drop in again?"

"Yes," promised Cardona. "And that may mean a scoop for you, Burke. But in the meantime, nobody is to know that Duff Corley was around here. You get the idea, don't you?"

"Sure," responded Clyde. "I'll keep mum, Joe. I was only kidding when I came in. But remember, I'm in when it breaks."

"If it breaks," corrected Cardona. "Right now it means nothing at all."

As he spoke, the detective reached for the sheet of paper. He folded it, keeping the marked side down so that Clyde could not see the impression of the Chinese disk. The detective thrust the paper in his pocket and arose from his chair in nonchalant fashion.

Clyde Burke strolled from the office. He showed no haste in his departure from headquarters. But his footsteps quickened after he reached the street. Clyde stopped at a store a block away. He entered a telephone booth and dialed a number. A quiet voice responded.

"Burbank speaking."

Briefly, Clyde made a report of his short trip to headquarters. He told of seeing Duff Corley; he mentioned the paper that he had seen on Cardona's desk. He expressed the emphatic opinion that there must be a connection between Duff's visit and the penciled impression of what appeared to be a coin.

Report given, Clyde Burke strolled forth and headed in the direction of the Classic office. His mission, brief though it was, had been accomplished. For Clyde Burke was a secret agent of The Shadow. Through Burbank, contact man who reached The Shadow, Clyde had reported his chance discovery.

Coming events were in the making. The future smacked of crime. Mysterious doings in the underworld included Duff Corley among those concerned. The Shadow, mysterious battler of crime, had been furnished with a clue. Coming events would concern The Shadow also!

CHAPTER II
GREEN LIGHTS

THRONGED mobsters crowded Red Mike's. This dive was one of the most popular in the underworld. It had changed location on various occasions, chiefly after police raids. But the name had traveled with it. This was in deference to the brawny, red-haired proprietor who managed the improvised bar in the corner of the main room. Red Mike was a fixture in the Tenderloin.

One characteristic seemed to be the sole qualification that gained admission to Red Mike's. That was toughness. Sluggers, dock-wallopers, gorillas—these were the types that formed the habitues of the joint. Red Mike's was a meeting place for the hardest characters in slumland.

The aristocrats of the underworld avoided this dive. So did the weaklings. Petty thieves, hopheads and other small fry were not wanted. Stool pigeons stayed away from Red Mike's. That was a source of comfort to Duff Corley when he slouched into the underground den.

For although Duff was playing the part of a stoolie, he had no fear. Among the mobsmen assembled were a dozen whom he knew well. He grinned in twisted fashion as he pictured what would happen if any one challenged him as a stool. Pals would rally to his side. The accuser would be mobbed.

Duff knew that Cardona had evidence that he and "Spider" Mertz had met at Red Mike's. That was proof that one of the detective's stoolies must have been around. But as Duff recalled it, he and Spider had met outside the joint. That was where the stoolie must have spotted them.

It was inside that they had transacted their business. Over in the far corner, by the door that formed an emergency exit from the dive. Duff chuckled as he took a seat at the very table where Spider had given him the Chinese disk. It was far from the outer door. No wonder no stoolie had viewed the conference of the other night.

This table was Duff's accustomed spot when he visited Red Mike's. It was the logical place where the emissary would look for him. As he slouched at the table, Duff thrust a hand into his pocket. His clenched fist gripped the Chinese disk.

THOUGH as tough in appearance as any gorilla in the place, Duff was yellow at heart. The viciousness of his evil features offset the flimsiness of his frame; that was why he passed as a hard customer. But Duff knew his own limitations. He was a greenhorn with a gat. His punch lacked wallop.

So Duff relied on his face to get him into places like Red Mike's. He used his cunning to gain an equal rating with his associates. When he worked with crooks, Duff supplied ideas; and usually managed to get himself appointed to some duty that would allow a quick getaway when the cops showed up.

Spider Mertz thought that Duff was foxy. That was why Spider had named him for a post with the unknown big shot. But Joe Cardona had called the turn. He had spotted Duff for a yellow rat. Duff had caved when Joe had began to question him. Right now, in his usual fashion, Duff was trying to keep on both sides of the fence. In so doing, he was acting in the very fashion that Cardona had hoped.

Here in his own bailiwick, Duff possessed a cunning grin; nothing like the sickly twitch that had adorned his face at headquarters. He intended to play the fox, so far as Spider was concerned. He would horn in with the big shot and pick up some easy mazuma. But at the same time, Duff intended to play straight with Joe Cardona. That, he figured would be the only way to save his yellow hide.

A newcomer strolled into Red Mike's. Duff knew the fellow. Cliff Marsland. Here was a bird who rated a gang lieutenancy any day in the week. Yet he preferred the company of ordinary gorillas. The explanation—as Duff and others knew it—was that Cliff chose to play a lone wolf game in his dealings with the underworld.

Cliff Marsland was not of the gorilla type. Duff noted that as the arrival took a seat not faraway. There was nothing uncouth or sordid about Cliff's appearance. But his chiseled profile marked him a man of action. Tough guys edged away from Cliff Marsland. His manner meant business.

So did his rep. Cliff was known as a killer. Once he had gone gunning for The Shadow. The fact that The Shadow was still at large was no damaging factor to Cliff's underworld reputation. In fact, it only made Cliff a figure of greater prominence. To Duff Corley, it meant that Cliff had the edge on The Shadow.

For The Shadow had a way of eliminating those who declared themselves his enemies. Yet Cliff had the temerity to roam the underworld at will. He, the avowed enemy of The Shadow. Among mobsters, Cliff was unique.

Little did Duff Corley realize that Cliff Marsland, like himself, was playing a dual part. Duff, recognized by gangsters, had become the secret informant of Detective Joe Cardona. His new role had begun tonight. Cliff Marsland, on the contrary, had been playing his part for a long while. Cliff Marsland was a secret agent of The Shadow.

More than that, he was here on a mission for The Shadow. He, too, had communicated with Burbank. Clyde Burke's information had gone to The Shadow. It had come back, in the form of orders, to Cliff Marsland. His task, here at Red Mike's, was to watch Duff Corley.

EXPERIENCED at this game, Cliff kept his gaze away from the scrawny mobster. Sitting at his own table, The Shadow's agent stared toward the clustered groups between him and the outer door. But every now and then he managed a sidelong glance that Duff did not observe. Those glances enabled Cliff to watch the mobster.

Bottles and glasses were clicking throughout the smoke-filled room. Ribald mobsters were loud with oaths and jests. Cliff was watching the crowd for the moment; so was Duff. Neither noticed the husky mobster who stepped in through the little-used rear door.

The fellow moved close to Duff and nudged the scrawny crook. Duff started to turn; a growl warned him to give no sign. Glancing downward, Duff saw a grimy fist by the level of the table edge. The fingers opened. In the palm, Duff observed a disk that was identical with the one he carried.

Fumbling, Duff pulled his hand from the pocket of his ragged coat. He showed the token which he carried. He saw the other fist close and move away. Duff thrust his own hand back into his pocket. He nodded as he heard gruff orders, coming in a tone just higher than a whisper.

This was the emissary of the big shot; the messenger whom Spider Mertz had promised. Head lowered, voice muffled, the arrival was passing the word while Duff Corley still stared straight ahead. Both thought they were unobserved. They were not.

Cliff Marsland was watching. He, alone, had noted the situation. But he could get no view of the new mobster's face. He knew that the fellow was merely some underling; but he figured the meeting of consequence because of the signs that were exchanged.

The husky mobster was turned almost toward the door. The back of his right hand was toward Cliff. The Shadow's agent caught no sign of the disk that the man displayed; but he did gain a trifling glimpse of the one in Duff's hand. From where Cliff was sitting, the disk looked like an old half-dollar.

The newcomer turned. He chose the simplest action to go back through the rear door; hence his turn was away from Cliff's direction. The only impression that Cliff gained was that of a big rowdy wearing a heavy sweater and a cap pulled down over his eyes.

That mattered little. Though Cliff would have liked to keep the messenger in mind for future reference, Duff was the man whom he intended to follow. The best plan of following, Cliff decided, was to go out ahead. One minute after Duff's visitor had left, Cliff arose and strolled through the crowd until he reached the main entrance of Red Mike's. He stepped up a short flight of stone steps and gained the street.

Duff would come out this way. Cliff felt sure of that. The other fellow had ducked in and out by the rear; Duff, who had come through the front, would naturally take the same mode of exit. Crossing the narrow street in front of Red Mike's, Cliff lingered by the front of a battered, crumbling building.

Five minutes later, Duff appeared. With a quick look up and down the street, the scrawny mobster shambled away. Cliff followed. It was his job to learn Duff's destination. He was hoping for a lucky break. One came.

DUFF ducked into an alleyway and cut through to an avenue. Here he entered an old cigar store. Cliff reached the front; peering through the grimy window, he spied a door that was closing. He figured that there was a telephone beyond. Cliff entered.

The proprietor was arguing with a panhandler who wanted him to crack a pack of cigarettes and sell him six for a nickel. Cliff strolled beyond until he reached the end of the counter. Listening, he caught the sound of Duff's voice. A poor telephone connection was forcing the crook to talk loud.

"Yeah..." Cliff heard the tone. "This is Duff... Yeah, the guy showed up... Told me where to go... You know the block past Sobo's hockshop... Yeah... Well, it's in that block... House with green lights... No, he didn't say which house, except that it had green lights... Yeah, I'm goin' there... But listen, Joe. If you show up, it may queer the lay... All right... Yeah, I get you..."

Cliff swung away from the door. He was looking out through the front window when Duff passed. As Duff reached the street, Cliff turned back and approached the counter. The panhandler slouched out. Cliff bought some cigarettes. He started to the street; a quick glance told him that Duff was gone. Cliff reentered the store and headed for the room where the phone was located.

Cliff put in a quick call to Burbank. He was told to await a reply. Hanging up the receiver, Cliff remained in the back room. In the minutes that followed, he sized up the situation. The game was panning out as he had anticipated. Orders from The Shadow had indicated what might happen.

Clyde Burke had reported contact between Joe Cardona and Duff Corley. Cliff had been set to watch Duff; he had found him at Red Mike's. Duff had contacted with a mobster; orders received, he had taken time out to call Joe Cardona.

Playing the part of a stool, Duff had pleaded with Joe to stay away. Evidently the detective had agreed not to approach too close. Duff had left in satisfied fashion. His destination—unquestionably the one ordered—was a house with green lights.

The bell of the pay telephone commenced to ring while Cliff was engaged in reverie. The Shadow's agent seized the receiver. He heard terse instructions from Burbank. Cliff was to pick up Duff's trail.

That was easy. Sobo's pawn shop was only half a dozen blocks away. Leaving the cigar store, Cliff moved rapidly along the intervening thoroughfares. He was in the heart of the badlands, the district where danger lurked, despite the occasional presence of a bluecoat.

But Cliff knew this terrain. More than that, he was versed in the ways of the underworld. His pace slackened as he neared the block he wanted. Cliff lounged along as he passed Sobo's corner hockshop.

He paused to roll a cigarette as he passed beneath a lamplight. Cliff was playing a part of a chance passer; but he kept his face turned downward. He lighted the fag as he moved along; as he flicked the burnt match to the gutter, Cliff stared shrewdly through the darkness.

Houses here were dilapidated structures. There were alleyways and openings between them. All looked alike as Cliff approached; then one—across the street—displayed the distinctive difference that he wanted.

The front of the house was black. But there were dull lights shining from gloomy windows at the sides. A chance observer would scarcely have noted those rays; for they were barely visible from the opening of a narrow alleyway. To Cliff, they were a signal; the same beacon that had drawn Duff Corley.

The lights in the windows were green. Heavily shaded, they gave no idea regarding the interior of the house. There was something ominous in that fact. The dweller in the house had lights showing; but the lights revealed nothing. Open, yet secret. That was the impression that Cliff gained.

In idling fashion, Cliff crossed the street. He chucked his cigarette as he reached the curb. Pausing in his slouching gait, Cliff swung into the alleyway beside the house. Above him, more than head high, he could see the glow from the dim green lights.

Then Cliff stopped short. Crouching against the moldy brick wall, he dug hand in pocket and drew an automatic. Tensely, he waited, unwilling to make another move. Somewhere ahead, deep in the darkness of the alleyway, some unseen enemy had made a false move.

A slight footstep—just enough to reach Cliff's ears. That had been the warning. Instinctively, Cliff knew that his approach had been spotted. Danger was impending by the house with the green lights.

CHAPTER III
THE SECOND DISK

CLIFF MARSLAND had encountered many dangers in the service of The Shadow. He was not the man to fear new threats. Nevertheless, Cliff had learned that discretion could be a good ninety percent of valor.

This was a time to be discreet. With Cliff, it was not simply the risk of an encounter in the dark. He had come to this house with the definite purpose of serving The Shadow. Whatever might occur, it would be his part to strive for the continuance of that duty.

Cliff Marsland knew what The Shadow wanted. Like Joe Cardona, The Shadow had learned of sinister movements in the underworld. Some big shot had been gathering cohorts. Slowly, secretly, but with positive results.

Duff Corley had suddenly become the link. Joe Cardona had been lucky enough to spot him. The Shadow wanted to profit by the discovery. He had decided to keep close on Duff's trail. Cliff had been appointed to the task.

Why?

Because he had been close to the ground. Cliff recognized that fact. He had known it the moment that Burbank had given the instructions. If The Shadow had been close at hand, he would have taken up the trail in Cliff's stead.

Where was The Shadow?

On his way here, Cliff supposed. Instructions from Burbank had been to trail Duff until further orders. New orders would probably come from The Shadow in person. Hence Cliff, for the time, was acting in The Shadow's place. He tried to picture matters as The Shadow would see them.

First: Duff Corley was certainly inside that house. The scrawny crook had shambled away with a good head start. He had probably entered by the front door. Some countersign—perhaps the same one that he had exchanged with the big mobsman at Red Mike's—so Cliff pictured it.

Then why was someone lurking in this alleyway?

Cliff caught the answer as he waited. It was obvious. The man in the dark was a watcher, posted to make sure that no one was on Duff's trail. The alleyway was an ambush. Cliff, like a dub, had walked into it.

He had probably been heard. Just as he had later heard the movement of the lurking guard. Cliff's teeth gritted grimly. He knew that he should have waited across the street. That was too late now. He was in the mess.

Silence from the alleyway. Cliff sensed that his enemy was waiting for him to make a move. Cliff listened; he heard nothing, yet he fancied that his foe might be moving forward. More than that, Cliff began to consider a new menace—the entrance of the alley.

Had someone been posted outside? Perhaps. If so, Cliff might have been spotted back at the middle of the block. Others could be closing in. The spot was a bad one. Cliff resolved upon stealthy measures. He crouched low and began to edge toward the front of the house.

The plan was working. Each time he paused, Cliff heard no sound from the rear of the alley. Little by little, he was gaining the front corner. Six feet more—five feet—then came the unexpected.

CLIFF'S right heel kicked against a half brick that had been laid on the ledge of a cellar window. The object clattered to the cracked cement of the alleyway. Its click seemed magnified in the darkness. Cliff dropped. He was wise.

Tongues of flame stabbed the darkness; with them, the fierce bark of a revolver. The flashes came from the deep end of the alley. Leaden slugs nicked chunks from the brick wall a foot above Cliff's head.

Swinging across the alleyway, Cliff returned the fire with the automatic. His target was the blackness from which the spurts had come; the region wherein the echoes of the shots still quivered.

New bursts replied; and Cliff delivered in like fashion. His enemy was on the move. So was Cliff. Potshots failed in the dark; but the whine and spatter of bullets meant business. Cliff reached the sidewalk.

He had not forgotten the chance of enemies in the street. Safe beyond the front of the house, Cliff went hurtling for the opposite side of the narrow thoroughfare, where a blackened housefront offered temporary security. He gained his goal; wheeling, he crouched by darkened steps and faced back toward the house with the green lights. He expected his enemy to appear. The man evidently preferred the security of the alleyway.

A shrill whistle cleaved the night. It was a block away; past Sobo's pawn shop. An answer came from the opposite direction. Gazing quickly along the street, one way, then the other, Cliff saw figures approaching on the run.

Cardona's men. The shots had drawn them. Cliff was in a tight spot. Thinking quickly, he remembered the man across the way. The fellow had an alleyway through which he could escape. Would he take a look at the street before he took to flight?

Cliff decided to find out. Regardless of the approaching detectives, he arose from his hiding spot and opened fire at the alleyway. The result was spontaneous. A gun flashed from the entrance. A bullet zimmed past Cliff's head. The fellow was there; he had aimed back at Cliff's gun flash.

Cliff fired again, shifting as he did.

A fork of flame responded; a bullet whanged the steps that Cliff had left. Instantly, Cliff fired again. He found his target this trip. A cry—the clatter of a gun on the sidewalk—then the sounds were drowned by new whistles.

Cliff turned. Police were heading down from the direction of Sobo's. Half a dozen of them, in a squad. A quick look in the opposite direction showed that other officers had stopped at the corner. The purpose was plain. Crooks would flee from the raiding gang; straight into the ones who waited.

Cliff held his ground, ready to fling his gun before the police arrived. He could surrender and feign the part of a chance passer who had been trapped. But until the last moment, Cliff intended to remain on duty, watching the house with the green lights.

Then came shots from an unexpected quarter. Up by the corner, opposite the direction of Sobo's. Cliff turned in time to catch a fleeting glimpse of policemen diving for cover. Then a huge touring car came jolting around the corner; its exhaust roared as the driver gave it the gas.

A searchlight gleamed. Cliff was caught in the glare. So were the detectives who were advancing up from Sobo's. Cliff leaped for the protection of the steps. Dicks scurried for cover. Rapid flashes belched from both sides of the touring car. With those swift bursts came the rattle of machine guns.

Nothing could stop that car of death. Men had ducked for shelter; but when the car whirled by, the gunners would pick them out. Cliff's steps protected him for the moment; but he knew that the shelter would be futile when the car rode by. He was ready to give the last few bullets of his automatic, in a puny effort to ward off death. Grimly, Cliff turned toward the street.

His gaze was transfixed. Straight across the street lay the body of the mobsman whom he had clipped. But to Cliff, that figure meant nothing. What caught his eye was the apparition that had swept out from the alleyway. A new form had entered the scene.

The Shadow!

A FIGURE garbed in black. Tall, with flowing cloak; the brim of a slouch hat covering his features, the master fighter had arrived. Through the alleyway from the rear of the house with the green lights. Just in time to face the revealing glare of the death car's headlights.

Machine guns were spraying their hail ahead; for the mobsmen in the car had spotted the approaching detectives. The Shadow, as he swept into view, picked a spot uncovered by the guns. The automobile was almost upon him when he appeared.

Then, amid the typewriter clatter of the machine guns came The Shadow's thrusts. Massive automatics barked their message straight into the rear of the touring car. Oddly, The Shadow picked the gunner on the far side. Cliff, rising involuntarily, saw the man slump beside his gun. Cliff, for the moment, was safe.

A flame-belching barrel flashed as the other gunner tried to swing his gun toward The Shadow. It was a tough task, for the machine gun was pointed ahead and the speed of the car had brought it up to the spot where The Shadow stood firing. Then the attempt ended. The gunner slumped, half out of the car.

The Shadow had clipped him cleanly. Revolvers alone were barking as fuming crooks aimed wildly for their arch enemy. Moving, they failed to spot their standing target. But to The Shadow, standing, the whole car was open to his deadly aim.

Revolvers fell from nerveless hands. Men slumped beside the useless machine guns. The automatics were roaring their quick shots. Cliff joined as the car swept by and aided The Shadow by clipping a mobster who had risen.

Then came a final revolver shot from the car. The driver, alone unhurt, had yanked a gun to thrust it across the body of the man beside him. He was on Cliff's side of the street. The Shadow's agent delivered his last bullet, inches wide. But The Shadow's shots did not fail.

The driver's aim was faulty. One hand on the wheel, his foot jamming the accelerator to the floor, this ruffian had taken on too much. His bullet zimmed wide of The Shadow's hat. The automatics thundered in unison. As the car leaped forward, the driver writhed in the agony of death.

Detectives leaped from spots of shelter as the car hopped the curb and bore down upon them. Steps that had afforded safety from the machine guns were useless in the path of this hurtling machine. The car swerved toward the front of an empty house. The right wheels climbed stone steps. Then the car went toppling, crashing, over on its side; on its top and over for another quarter turn.

Wheels spinning, it lay like a fighting monster. Gunmen were sprawled on the street beside it. The machine guns had clattered to the cobbles. Detectives were bounding up to stop the motor; to drag out the gangsters who were pinned within the wreckage.

Cliff was in blackness now. The glare had passed. The Shadow's agent sprang across the street and reached the entrance to the alleyway. Detectives were hurrying up from the corner which the touring car had passed. Cliff's one avenue of departure was the alleyway where The Shadow had been.

A hiss from darkness as Cliff gained the space between the houses. Cliff uttered a response. He caught The Shadow's order to speed away through the alley. Cliff obeyed. He found a turn between two houses; a clear path after that, through to the street beyond.

A SWISH in the darkness. The Shadow had stopped at the rear of the house with the green lights. Cloaked in blackness, he ascended four rickety steps and found an old door, locked. A pick probed the keyhole.

The Shadow entered. He passed through a kitchen; then to a hallway where a dull green pervaded. It was the reflection from the lights in the side room. A darkened doorway yawned at the left of the hall. The Shadow's flashlight cut a swath into a small room.

There, on the floor, lay Duff Corley. The scrawny mobster was stretched out, with evil face turned upward. Protruding from his body was the handle of a knife. The thrust had reached the mobster's heart; a portion of the blade still showed. It glimmered slender in The Shadow's light. The weapon was a stiletto.

Crash!

The front door was giving way. The Shadow's light went out. Swiftly, the cloaked intruder swept back through the kitchen and out into the night. He passed the alleyway just before lights glimmered there. Detectives were coming through the back of the house.

The Shadow was gone. The law was on the scene. The front door broke and detectives plunged into the house. They came face to face with the others who had found the back door open. Flashlights blinked. Then came the discovery of Duff's body.

A dick pressed a switch in the little room. Members of the squad clustered about the corpse. Then Joe Cardona entered. The leader of the raiders stood silent as he viewed the body of his new stool pigeon.

Detectives watched while Joe stooped beside the body and felt through pockets. They were empty. Joe looked at Duff's right hand. It was clenched. Carefully, the ace pried fingers open. The hand was empty.

Joe Cardona grunted. He had expected to find the Chinese disk in the dead man's clutch. Instead, he had found nothing. Had the murderer made off with the disk? Or had Duff's story been a fake, so far as the disk was concerned? Cardona pondered.

A MAN arrived at the door of the room. Cardona stood up to face a panting detective. The fellow caught his breath; then delivered his message. It pertained to the gorillas in the death car.

"Just dragged another guy out," informed the dick. "I knew his mug. It was Spider Mertz. Guess he was handling one of the typewriters. Anyway, he was dying when we got him loose."

"Did he talk?" inquired Joe.

"No," returned the detective. "He didn't even try to. All he did was chuck something that he had in his hand. It didn't go far. I picked it up off the cobbles. Here it is."

Cardona shoved out his hand. The dick released a small object. It fell in Joe's palm. This was silent proof of Duff Corley's story; the absolute evidence that the reluctant stool pigeon had spoken true regarding his meeting with Spider Mertz.

For the object that Joe Cardona received from the detective was a grayish disk. Engraved in dull red on its surface was the same Chinese letter that had appeared upon the token carried by Duff Corley.

The murdered stoolie had been robbed after death. His killer had sought to keep this evidence from the hands of the law. But Spider Mertz, clipped by The Shadow's bullets, had failed to rid himself of the incriminating token.

The first disk—Duff's—was gone. Only Cardona's penciled impression remained as proof of its existence. In its place, the ace detective had gained a second disk, thanks to The Shadow's prowess in dealing with Spider Mertz.

CHAPTER IV
THE SHADOW CONNECTS

ONE hour after Joe Cardona had discovered the second Chinese disk, a group of four players were ending their bridge game at the exclusive Cobalt Club. Rising one by one, they sauntered from the private card room until a last player remained.

This gentleman was an ungainly sort of person. His head craned forward and his sharp eyes glistened through pince-nez spectacles. These features, combined with the shiny surface of his hairless pate, gave him the look of a bald eagle.

In fact, he seemed to survey the world as if from a lofty height. Even in the solitary surroundings of the little card room, his gaze was searching and his bearing filled with self-importance.

The scrawny mobster was stretched out with evil face turned upward.

Such was Wainwright Barth, at present the police commissioner of New York City.

Wainwright Barth was always the last to leave after a long session of bridge. The reason was simple; his spectacles invariably needed polishing. So tonight, Barth paused before crossing the threshold. He removed his pince-nez glasses and began to shine them with a piece of chamois.

"Good evening, commissioner."

Barth looked up as he heard the voice. Adjusting his pince-nez, the commissioner stared toward the person who had entered the card room. He saw a tall, firm-featured individual whose masklike face was turned in his direction. Keen eyes were peering from the sides of a hawkish nose. Barth recognized Lamont Cranston, millionaire globe-trotter.

"Ah! Cranston!" exclaimed the commissioner. "I did not know that you were in town. I understood that you were leaving on an exploration trip to Kashmir."

"That was postponed," returned Cranston, quietly. "I am still in New York, as you perceive. I believe I shall remain here a while, commissioner. Oddly"—thin lips framed the semblance of a smile—"one may sometimes uncover more adventure in Manhattan than in the wildest outposts of the globe."

"I agree with you," declared Barth. "When crime becomes rampant in this metropolis, more danger exists here than in an African jungle. But fortunately"—Barth chuckled—"crime has been calling for an armistice, during my tenure of office. Outside of petty robberies, there have been no real evidences of organized crime activity."

"Perhaps," said Lamont Cranston, quietly, "that may mean the coming of new efforts. Organization may be under way. Lulls are deceiving, commissioner. Let me cite an example. When I was exploring in Sumatra, we encountered a tribe of former headhunters whom the Dutch had presumably civilized. These natives were quiet, singularly passive—"

"Sumatra is not New York," interrupted the commissioner, in a testy tone. "There is no analogy between headhunters and gangsters. Furthermore, we have not attempted to civilize the denizens of the underworld. We have curbed them, driven them to cover. The proof is the fact that rogues have been disappearing from New York.

"One of my most capable men—a detective named Joe Cardona—holds to the theory that something is brewing beneath the surface. But developments have not justified his opinion. I believe that my relentless campaign is suppressing crime, that crooks realize they have met their match—"

Barth broke off as an attendant entered the card room. The man approached the commissioner and spoke in a confidential tone.

"Gentleman to see you sir," said the attendant. "He is Mr. Cardona, from headquarters. Its very important, he says—"

"Show him in," snapped Barth.

THE attendant left and returned with Joe Cardona. Barth dismissed the attendant and closed the door. He motioned Cardona to a seat at the card table; then did the same with Cranston. Barth wanted Cranston to hear what the detective might have to say.

"Well, Cardona," began Barth, as he took a chair, "I suppose you have developed some new theory regarding crime activity. What is it now? More rogues gone traveling?"

"Yes," returned the detective. "Gone where they won't come back. Plenty broke loose tonight, commissioner. Take a look at this report sheet."

Barth received the paper. He read the details that began with Duff Corley's visit to headquarters and terminated with the discovery of the man's body in the house with green lights. Then, as the commissioner looked up, Cardona laid a sheet of paper on the table. It showed the impression of the disk that Duff had displayed to Joe. With added emphasis, Joe tossed Spider's disk beside it.

"They match," he declared.

They did match. Barth discovered that when he laid the disk beside the paper and surveyed both through his pince-nez. His examination completed, Barth pushed the two objects toward Lamont Cranston. Turning to Cardona, the commissioner questioned:

"Well?"

"The case is clear-cut," returned Cardona. "It supports what I've been telling you, commissioner. These bozos have been ducking out of sight because they're needed. Some big shot intends to use them. This disk, for instance, was found on Spider Mertz. It means that he was one of the key men in the organization."

"What about the mobsters with him?"

"None of them had disks. They were just gorillas, working for Spider. The same with the dead man that we found at the entrance to the alleyway. They were covering up after Duff Corley went into the house with the green lights."

"But who killed Duff?"

"Some other member of the band. A fellow who was in the know. He stabbed Duff and took the disk. He must have made his departure by the back door. That's why Spider had his crew on duty. Just in case we landed there too soon."

"I don't quite fathom it, Cardona."

"Listen, commissioner. The thing began on the level. Spider Mertz lined up Duff Corley. Gave him a disk, so he could join with the gang. But Spider told Duff to wait until somebody tipped him where to go. Like a probation period.

"In the meantime, Duff was being watched. He didn't know it. I didn't know it. He came to headquarters to talk with me. From that time on, he was marked for death. He was told to go to the house where he went tonight. That place was a trap.

"Killing Duff was easy enough. But these crooks knew that the guy had turned stoolie—at least they figured it that way. They didn't know how close I'd be. So it was Spider's job to raise hob if anybody showed up. Well—somebody did show up."

"You and your squads!"

"Not only us. Somebody else got in ahead of us. That started the trouble. Spider and his outfit must have been around on the back street. They heard the shots and drove around the block. Meanwhile, The Sha—"

Cardona caught himself suddenly. He corrected his statement as rapidly as possible.

"Meanwhile," said the detective, "whoever it was that had trailed Duff got busy. He put some shots into that death car and crippled the machine-gunners. The rest was easy for my men."

CRANSTON had noted Cardona's pause. He knew that Joe figured The Shadow as the one who had saved the situation. But Cardona's break had slipped by Wainwright Barth. That was fortunate. The police commissioner had tabooed mention of The Shadow in connection with crime. He regarded The Shadow as a myth.

"We're up against something, commissioner," assured Cardona, in an earnest tone. "It's an organization, that works automatically. Duff Corley was lined up. He was spotted turning stoolie. He was slated to be blotted out.

"There's a Chink in it somewhere. The disk shows that. But Spider Mertz and his mob were just plain gorillas. The guy that bumped Duff must have been a wop. He used a stiletto and he knew what it was for.

"There you have it. Duff's dead. So is Spider. We've got nobody who knows anything. But we know there's an organization—a real one—of guys who carry those disks with them. We've seen what they do to a squealer."

"An organization," mused Barth. "Perhaps you are right, Cardona. Its purpose—"

"Murder," put in Joe. "That was the purpose tonight."

"Yes." The agreement came unexpectedly from Lamont Cranston. "The disk indicates agreement with Cardona's idea, commissioner."

"The disk?" questioned Barth, half puzzled.

"Yes," replied Cranston, as he passed the object to the commissioner. "I can tell you the meaning of the character engraved on it."

"A Chinese word?"

"Not exactly. The character is an ideograph, which may be applied in various fashions. It is termed a numerative. It is pronounced pa—"

"But its meaning?"

"Literally, 'something which is grasped by a handle'. That, for instance, could mean a revolver. Or a knife. Or—"

"Spider used his gat tonight," burst forth Cardona. "The fellow that killed Duff had a stiletto. Mr. Cranston has hit it, commissioner."

Barth arose and stood in pompous attitude. It was his custom, when he swung from one supposition to another, to throw full support to the new idea. He had rejected Cardona's theory, at first; now that the existence of a hidden hand seemed logical, Barth wanted to set the pace for the detective.

"Let me commend your work," declared the commissioner, turning to Cardona. "At first I considered your theory poorly founded. Events, however, have proven its soundness. These criminals who have gone from sight may all be potential members of the band which we have uncovered.

"Spare no effort, Cardona. Investigate everywhere. Inquire into the activities of the Chinese tongs. If necessary, utilize the dragnet. Search every suspect to learn if he carries one of these."

With his final sentence, Barth displayed the Chinese disk. He passed it back to Cardona, along with the piece of paper that bore the penciled impression.

"It's going to be a tough job, commissioner," declared the detective, in a dubious tone.

"Why so?" demanded Barth.

"Because," affirmed Joe, "there's something deep beneath all this. It wasn't crime tonight, commissioner; that is, it wasn't crime against the public. Those fellows were dealing with a double-crosser.

"What's more, they got Duff before he learned anything. Put him on the spot right at the start. It was just a splash on top of the water. Now its smooth again. What's more, that crowd will be foxier than ever."

"But they will have to show their hand again," objected Barth. "The rascals are planning something. That is plain."

"Sure they are," agreed Cardona, grimly. "That's what makes it tough, commissioner.

We've seen what they can do to one of their own kind. When they cut loose with crime, they'll be hard to stop."

"Therefore," asserted Barth, "we shall take measures to prevent them."

TEN minutes later Lamont Cranston strolled from the Cobalt Club. Cardona had left. Cranston had paused for a brief chat with the commissioner; then he had taken his departure. A limousine pulled up as Cranston reached the sidewalk. The millionaire entered.

Through the speaking tube, he gave a quiet order to the chauffeur. The car rolled away and twisted its course through a labyrinth of secluded streets. Finally, it stopped by a darkened curb. The chauffeur settled back behind the wheel.

A rear door opened. From the interior emerged a cloaked figure that moved away into the thickness of the night. From a bag in the back of the limousine, Lamont Cranston had produced certain garments. He had donned them while the car was rolling.

Cloak and hat had rendered him invisible after his departure from the car. His course into the night was untraceable. The role of Lamont Cranston was ended for the time. Lamont Cranston had become The Shadow.

CHAPTER V
PEOPLE OF THE PAST

TOMBLIKE darkness enshrouded a silent room. The place was filled with uncanny silence. Such was the atmosphere within the sanctum of The Shadow. A strange, unknown abode, situated somewhere in Manhattan. The sanctum seemed to await the arrival of the only being who might enter through its hidden portals.

A swish sounded in the darkness. That sound would not have been audible elsewhere. The Shadow had reached his strange abode. A click sounded from a corner. A bluish light glimmered upon the top of a polished table.

Usually, The Shadow remained at this corner. Tonight, his plan was different. His cloak swished away from the limited sphere of light. A click sounded in another corner. A second light glimmered. It was focused upon the front of a tall steel filing cabinet.

Long white hands opened a drawer. From one finger glimmered a resplendent gem. That stone was The Shadow's girasol, a rare fire opal that he wore as a sole emblem of identity. The jewel sparkled as the left hand stopped upon a folder that bore the name "Farwell."

The Shadow withdrew this folder and carried it through darkness to the table. From its interior, he drew out typewritten sheets and laid them on the table. The folder had sides like a portfolio, so that no objects could drop from it. Digging deep, The Shadow brought forth a small envelope. He tore it open. A small object fell out and plunked upon the table.

It was a Chinese disk. Its size, its appearance, its very metal was identical with the disk that Joe Cardona had shown to Commissioner Barth. The Shadow laughed softly as he noted the typed name upon the little envelope that had contained the disk. The name was "Wang Foo."

The Shadow spread out a report sheet that bore the heading "Diamond Bert." Again the soft laugh. Despite the variety of names involved, The Shadow was considering a single person: "Diamond Bert" Farwell, alias Wang Foo.

Years had passed since The Shadow had dealt with Diamond Bert. In his battles with that lawbreaker, The Shadow had faced one of the craftiest of crooks. Diamond Bert had gone in for robbery in a big way. His prizes had been rare gems.

Aided by underlings, Diamond Bert had perpetrated crime after crime. All the while, he had remained undercover. To reach him, The Shadow had been forced to fight with minions who knew no limit. Murder had meant nothing to the tools of Diamond Bert.

At the finish, The Shadow had entered the lair of the master crook. Guised as one of Diamond Bert's henchmen, he had met the evildoer face to face. Like The Shadow, Diamond Bert had been disguised. When The Shadow uncovered him, the crook was passing as a Chinaman, under the name of Wang Foo.Death would have been a fair fate for Diamond Bert. Yet The Shadow had not delivered it. Circumstances had tricked The Shadow. Joe Cardona and a squad of detectives had entered for the climax. The Shadow, to protect his own identity, had been forced to depart, leaving Diamond Bert in the hands of the law.

That had ended the character of Wang Foo. By rights, Diamond Bert Farwell should have gone to the chair. He had dealt heavily in murder; and justice should have demanded its toll. But the law had failed to pin a single death upon the slippery crook. Caught with stolen gems in his possession, Diamond Bert had taken a ten-year rap.

THESE facts appeared upon the papers which The Shadow was studying. Reports included the events of Diamond Bert's subsequent career. Up in the big house, the crook had become a model prisoner. Adapting himself to circumstances, he had gone on good behavior. His term had been shortened. According to the data on The Shadow's table, Diamond Bert was almost due for release from the penitentiary.

A clipping appeared among the other notations. It was pasted to a large sheet of paper. The Shadow scanned its lines. It told of a new experiment at the State prison. This consisted of a shop in which privileged inmates were allowed a restricted amount of freedom, as a reward for good behavior.

In that shop, their numbers were forgotten. They went by their names and worked at tables, lined up in alphabetical order. According to the clipping, the experiment was proving a success. To The Shadow, the presence of this clipping in Farwell's file meant something more. It indicated that Diamond Bert was working in the privileged shop.

Papers went back into the portfolio. Also the little envelope. One object alone remained, held between The Shadow's fingers. That was the disk of Wang Foo, the token that linked past and present. Years ago, this disk with its significant character had been the amulet carried by all who served Diamond Bert Farwell.

As Wang Foo, Diamond Bert had gained many connections. Some in Chinatown; others in the realm of crookdom. Did the reappearance of this disk mean that someone had stolen a leaf from Diamond Bert's notebook? Or did it mean that Diamond Bert was coming back to crime?

The Shadow's soft laugh gave the answer. Had the disks bobbed up a few years ago, the theory that new crooks were copying Diamond Bert's ways would have been tenable. But disks had not appeared until the present. Moreover, those who carried them were keeping undercover. Thus The Shadow took the second theory.

Diamond Bert was coming in again. Somehow, his henchmen were gathering. New recruits were being added to a hidden gang. Cardona had been right about the death of Duff Corley. The scrawny mobster had been bumped because he had double-crossed the gang.

All was to be kept undercover until the word for crime was passed. That would come in the near future, when Diamond Bert emerged from the big house.

The disk disappeared from the light. The Shadow was pocketing it beneath his coat. It would be useful should he encounter members of the hidden band. But The Shadow lingered by the table; his silence told that he was seeking a plan of action.

TO deal with Diamond Bert's scattered minions would be an up-hill task. It offered problems which The Shadow had confronted in the past. The real game was to reach the brain himself. Once freed from prison walls, Diamond Bert would be a slippery customer. The Shadow wanted to weave a web before the arch-crook gained his liberty.

That mesh required crafty spinning. It must be done so cunningly that the suspicions of the arch-crook would not be aroused. For if The Shadow entangled Diamond Bert too promptly, his minions—carriers of the disks—would be alarmed. Scurrying for cover, they would still remain a powerful band.

A group without a leader. The Shadow had encountered such organizations in the past. He knew what happened in cases of that sort. Bands of crooks did not disintegrate when the big shot was eliminated. Invariably, some new head stepped into the picture and took up where the other had left off.

This was a situation that The Shadow wished to avoid. His one course was to deal with Diamond Bert. Enmesh the big shot; then strike down upon the unsuspecting minions. Here was a plan worthy of The Shadow's craft. Yet it presented problems.

The Shadow needed an agent. One who could pass by prison walls. One who could watch Diamond Bert during the coming weeks. One who could perform his task reliably and well. Long minutes passed; then, of a sudden, The Shadow's laugh arose in sinister whisper.

Sweeping up the folder that lay upon the table, The Shadow crossed the sanctum. He reached the filing cabinet and stopped by the opened drawer. Folders were separated at the spot from which The Shadow had removed the Farwell file.

There, by remarkable coincidence, rested the answer to The Shadow's problem. As The Shadow replaced the folder that bore the name of Farwell, he lifted the portfolio that was next in line. This one bore the name of Farrow. Farrow—Farwell—the two names were right together in their natural alphabetical arrangement.

The Shadow carried the Farrow file back to the table. He opened it and let the papers slide forth. Then, in methodical fashion, he began to read the reports that concerned a man named Slade Farrow.

Oddly, The Shadow's observations of Slade Farrow had begun within prison walls. The coincidence was remarkable. Slade Farrow had been "in stir" some time ago; but crime had not put him within the confines of a cell. Slade Farrow had gone to prison to right a wrong.

Released from the penitentiary, Slade Farrow had visited the town of Southfield. Aided by

SLADE FARROW

crooks who had gone straight, Farrow had made astonishing revelations concerning big men in Southfield. He had waged war against them. He had exposed them as crooks. He had done his part for justice. Yet he would have failed but for The Shadow's hidden aid. It was The Shadow who had finally brought doom to the men of evil whom Farrow had brought to light. Slade Farrow owed a big debt to The Shadow. He was the type of man who would repay the obligation, once given the chance to do so. Here was the opportunity. The Shadow laughed softly as he found a paper that bore Slade Farrow's present address.

The folder closed. The Shadow took it back to the filing cabinet and replaced it just beyond the Farwell file. He turned out the light and went back to the table. Producing pen and paper, The Shadow inscribed a note in ink of vivid blue.

As soon as the fluid had dried, The Shadow folded the sheet and thrust it in an envelope. Using another pen, he wrote Slade Farrow's name and address in ink of a darker hue. That done, the envelope disappeared beneath The Shadow's cloak.

The light clicked out. A whispered laugh echoed through the sanctum; its rising tones broke with a quavering mockery. Echoes lisped their answer from the pitch-black walls. Then came silence. Amid the reverberations of his uncanny laugh, The Shadow had departed from his hidden abode.

CHAPTER VI
FARROW ENTERS

IT was the next afternoon. A sedan was rolling along a high road that overlooked the Hudson River. Seated at the wheel was a big, bluff-faced driver who was keeping the car at a steady speed.

Beside him was a middle-aged man whose features were hard and whose keen eyes carried a shrewd gaze. This passenger was deep in thought. At times, his lips tightened and his head gave a trifling nod. That was a habit with Slade Farrow.

One might have picked Slade Farrow as a crook. His hard face would have supported that impression. Actually, Farrow was a sociologist who had done much in the elimination of crime. He possessed one faculty, that had aided him in his work.

Farrow knew how to make crooks go straight. In his time, he had encountered hundreds of hopeless cases, which he had promptly rejected. But whenever he found a man who was on the borderline, Farrow brought the fellow back on the side of right.

The driver of the car was an example. Dave Garvell had gone crooked. He had served time. He would have remained a crook but for Farrow. The sociologist had met Dave and had put him on the right path. Since then, Dave had been one of Farrow's trusted workers.

In fact, the fellow had displayed amazing fidelity to the man who had done so much for him. Right at present, Dave was giving evidence of his concern for Farrow's welfare. Driving to an unknown destination, Dave had figured where they were going. The thought had rendered him uneasy.

"Listen, boss." Dave spoke warily as he squinted along the highway. "I've begun to get the jitters. Ever since you opened that letter this morning, you've been playing mum. What's up, boss?"

"Nothing that concerns you, Dave."

"I know that. I'm not supposed to butt into your affairs. But I've just sort of figured where we're going. Up to the big house."

"That's right, Dave. A good guess."

"I don't mind that, boss. What bothers me is a hunch I've got. The way you've been thinking things over sort of gave me the idea that you're going back in stir. It kind of makes me uneasy."

Farrow chuckled. Aroused from his reverie, he clapped a hand to the big man's shoulder.

"You're right, Dave," said the sociologist, "but don't worry about it. I'm not going to be there long. A few weeks at the most. I'm going in under my own name."

Dave looked relieved. Farrow's last trip to the pen had been a long one. He had used the name of Sam Fulwell and had remained longer than expected. But Farrow's statement that an alias would be lacking on this trip assured Dave that his chief could get out as soon as planned. Slade Farrow in prison meant a special arrangement with the warden.

THERE was something else that bothered Dave. The big driver shifted a bit before he mentioned it. He had broken the ice and felt that he could talk some more; but he hesitated before he took the plunge.

"That letter that came in this morning," said Dave, in a wary tone. "I saw it, boss. While you were reading it. I happened to see it again, after you laid it down. It was blank."

"Because I laid it with the writing side down."

"That's what I thought, boss. So I turned it over. It wasn't my idea to read it. Honest. I was clearing up in the living room of the apartment and I wasn't quite sure whether you wanted to keep the letter."

"So you looked at it?"

"Just by accident. I was going to bring it to you. When I picked it up, I turned it almost without thinking. Then was when I saw what had happened to it."

Farrow chuckled. He made no response.

"It had gone blank, boss," declared Dave, in a worried tone. "Both sides blank. But it wasn't that way when you opened it. I saw the writing when you were reading. Blue ink. But then the writing went away. That's why I began to wonder—"

"What?"

"Just who it had come from. I thought maybe it was from—from—"

"The Shadow?"

Dave nodded as Farrow, by his question, completed the name that the big fellow had failed to utter. Farrow eyed Dave carefully. He saw that the man was nervous. Farrow smiled.

"Yes, Dave," he said, "that letter was from The Shadow. Why should that fact worry you?"

"I don't how," admitted Dave. "It's just—well, it's just on account of the way things used to be. When I was a crook, there was just one person that I wanted to keep away from. That was The Shadow.

"The bulls—they didn't worry me. It was The Shadow that I was scared of. Plenty scared, too. Say—if I'd ever come up against him, I wouldn't have been able to pull the trigger of my gat."

"Probably not," observed Farrow, with a smile. "A lot of crooks seemed to have that trouble when we were in Southfield. Do you remember that night, Dave?"

"Say—can I ever forget it? Listen, boss, when The Shadow walked into that mess, I could have dived into a concrete alley if there'd been one around. I was with you—and you were on the level. That meant that The Shadow was with us.

"But I was scared, just the same. And after I saw him start with those big smoke wagons of his, I was gladder than ever that I'd gone straight. Listen, boss. You started me straight and I'm staying that way. But if you came to me and said: 'Dave, I want you to go crooked again,' I wouldn't do it. Not since I've seen The Shadow."

Farrow nodded. He had studied this effect of The Shadow's prowess. Farrow felt that his own efforts in working against crime were puny compared with The Shadow's ability. Fear, much more than reason, played its part in the mental processes of such fellows as Dave Garvell.

THE car was coming to a fork in the road. Farrow gave a terse order to Dave. The driver nodded; he took the highway that led to the penitentiary. Only a short while remained before the two men would part. Farrow gave brief instructions.

"Keep the apartment in order, Dave," he said.

DAVE GARVELL

"Get in touch with Tapper and Hawkeye. Tell them I'll be back soon. I may be needing them later."

"On account of The Shadow?"

"Possibly. Remember this, Dave. We were in a tough place up in Southfield. We were dealing with big fellows—ones that were too big. It was The Shadow who saved us."

"I know it, boss."

"Never forget it. We wouldn't be here today if The Shadow hadn't stepped in at the right moment. I've always wanted to do something in return. Now is my opportunity."

"Here at the big house?"

"Yes. That's why I want you to say nothing. Don't tell anyone where I've gone. Not even Tapper and Hawkeye. They know I make trips out of town. That should be sufficient."

"I get you, boss."

The car had swung up in front of the huge gray walls that surrounded the big pen. Dave brought the sedan to a stop. He shook hands with Farrow; then watched his chief alight. He caught a gesture that meant to depart. Reluctantly, Dave swung the wheel and turned the car about.

Heading back to New York, the ex-crook remembered Farrow's injunction. Mum was the word, so far as Dave was concerned. His boss had gone to the big house, with a promise of an early return. That was sufficient. The fact that Farrow was responding to a request from The Shadow was something that Dave was determined not to mention.

"TAPPER"

Slade Farrow, meanwhile, had passed through the huge portals. The sociologist had reached the warden's office. He was seated at one side of a desk. Across from him was the warden, a quiet-faced man who listened stolidly as Farrow spoke.

"These credentials"—Farrow laid the papers on the desk—"are ones that I always carry. I called Judge Witherspoon this morning. Doubtless, you have heard from him."

"I have," rejoined the warden.

"My purpose is a simple one," explained Farrow. "I am not the type of sociologist who seeks publicity. In fact, I shun the public eye. Once my name should become known, my usefulness would be at an end.

"I have studied prison conditions from the inside. In every case, I have delivered my compilations to the warden himself. I have given reports—anonymously—to other sociologists. Any of my findings that have appeared in print are attributed to persons other than myself."

"I understand, Mr. Farrow," stated the warden. "Judge Witherspoon's recommendation is sufficient. He told me, however, that you would state your own purpose when you arrived."

"Very well," said Farrow. "I should like to obtain firsthand information regarding your new experimental shop. The best method is for me to be placed in there, as a new prisoner."

"Under what name?"

"My own. It is not known."

"I can arrange it," declared the warden, with a nod. He surveyed Farrow's features and seemed pleased by their hardness. "In fact, I can place you there immediately. We have had occasional cases in which prisoners have been transferred here from other places. Some of them—men with good records—have been put in that shop.

"I can list you as a transfer. That will enable you to gain the confidence of the men whom you meet. As for the exact nature of the crime that cost you your liberty"—the warden paused to smile—"I think I can allow you to decide upon your own story. No one will deny it."

"I have a story all ready," replied Farrow, also smiling. "One that will make me entirely at home. I can handle that very nicely."

"Good," decided the warden. "As for your release, that can be simply arranged. The prisoners in the privileged shop are allowed to forward any written request directly to me. They do so, quite frequently.

"When you are ready to leave, prepare a note to that effect. Give it to the guard. I shall do the rest. All of the men in the privileged shop are fin-

"HAWKEYE"

ishing their terms of sentence. Your departure will cause no comment."

The warden reached out and pressed a buzzer. A secretary appeared. The warden gave him orders. The machinery was moving. While they waited, the warden chatted with Farrow regarding matters with which both were familiar; the myriad details that concerned the operation of a huge penitentiary.

Half an hour after his arrival, Slade Farrow left the warden's office. One hour after that departure, he was guised as a prisoner, gaining his introduction to the privileged shop of which Diamond Bert Farwell was an inmate.

The Shadow's plan had worked. Within twenty-four hours after crime had developed in Manhattan. The Shadow had placed a competent observer in the spot that counted most.

Diamond Bert Farwell, playing good behavior in hope of prompt release, was side by side with Slade Farrow, making the acquaintance of the very man whom The Shadow had deputed to seek the source of current crime.

CHAPTER VII
FARROW REPORTS

WEEKS had passed since Slade Farrow's self-gained incarceration. During that period, crime had lulled in Manhattan. Not one new clue had been gained since the episode of the Chinese disks. Duff Corley's death had ended the trail.

Joe Cardona had delivered new reports to Commissioner Barth. These involved investigations held in Chinatown; questionings of suspects brought to headquarters; statements gained from stool pigeons of all types. The total result was nil.

All this made Barth feel triumphant. The commissioner felt that crime had been dealt a heavy blow when Spider Mertz and his mobsters had been slain. But Joe Cardona knew that crime had gained a triumph. The murder of Duff Corley had been the accomplishment of what crooks sought.

The Shadow, meanwhile, was waiting. He had chosen the course that he had intended to follow. The clank of prison portals to announce Slade Farrow's entrance was a master stroke that The Shadow did not intend to spoil.

Facts had told The Shadow that a hidden organization existed. Duff Corley had been one of the final recruits. Perhaps others had been gained since; but to seek any carriers of the Chinese disks might mean the obstruction of Slade Farrow's work.

The Shadow knew that he could rely upon the fake prisoner. He also knew that skulking crooks—members of the hidden band—would stay away from crime until the big shot gave the word. The big shot, to The Shadow's knowledge, was Diamond Bert.

The Shadow had definite proof to back this belief. Not one word had come from Slade Farrow. That meant results were underway. Farrow was not the man to follow a blind trail. Had he learned nothing concerning Diamond Bert, Farrow would have terminated his stay at the big house. As it was, the sociologist seemed quite content to remain there.

Day after day; still no word from Farrow. Then, on a morning just three weeks after the sociologist had made his trip up the river, the change arrived. It came when Farrow, himself, entered an office high up in the Badger Building, near Times Square.

The door of the office bore a simple inscription upon its glass panel. The wording said:

RUTLEDGE MANN
INVESTMENTS

Inside, Farrow found himself in the outer room of a small suite. He saw a stenographer seated at a desk. He tendered his card and asked for an interview with Mr. Mann. The stenographer went into the inner office.

WHEN she returned, she left the door open and nodded to Farrow. The sociologist entered; the girl closed the door as she went back to the outer office. Farrow paused in mild surprise as he saw a placid, chubby-faced man seated at a desk near the window.

"You are Rutledge Mann?" inquired the sociologist, as he sat down. "I thought—"

"I understand," interposed Mann, with a smile. "You had expected to find someone else here. A person whom we both know by reputation."

Farrow nodded. He knew that Mann meant The Shadow.

"That person," resumed Mann, "is awaiting word from you. I, like yourself, am simply his agent. You received a letter some weeks ago, requesting you to perform a specialized service. The letter also stated that you should report to me when your mission was accomplished. Am I correct?"

Again, Farrow nodded.

"I presume," said Mann, "that you have a report of your findings. You may give me that report, either verbally or in writing. I assure you that it will reach the person for whom it is intended."

"Here it is," responded Farrow, drawing some folded sheets from his pocket. "I prepared a written statement while coming down to New York by train. But I would like also to give you a brief outline of my experiences. Merely to check on the details."

"Very well."

Farrow edged closer to the desk. This office offered excellent seclusion. From the window, the sociologist could see the skyline of Manhattan, a strange contrast to the towered monotone of the walls that had enclosed him during the past three weeks.

"Diamond Bert is the big shot," asserted Farrow, in a confidential tone. "I gained evidence of that two days after I entered the pen. His workbench was next to mine. I spotted him writing secret messages.

"What he did with them was a mystery at first. Finally, I gained the solution. Large boxes came into that shop. They were filled with raw goods; and they passed inspection when the materials were taken out. One day, however, I noted Diamond Bert lingering in the shop.

"Watching from a corner, I saw him reach into one of the boxes. He must have found a secret hiding place. A compartment cut in the lower frame of the heavy box. He fumbled there for several minutes. Then he brought out a bird."

"A bird?" inquired Mann, in mild surprise.

"Yes," replied Farrow, "a carrier pigeon. There was a barred window just above the box. The opening was large enough for Farwell to thrust the bird through and send it on its way. Thus I learned how Diamond Bert was communicating with his agents."

"Did the same scene occur again?" questioned Mann.

"Yes," answered Farrow. "I shall come to that. I said nothing to Farwell. I did not want him to know what I had observed. I wanted to learn how the members of his band communicated with him. I did not think that they would commit the folly of sending messages with the carriers."

"Why not?"

"Because the pigeons might have been sent to anyone. Messages would have caused trouble had guards found the birds. I watched Diamond Bert. Like the rest of us, he was allowed a certain reading time. New York newspapers were supplied. Sometimes crime news had been clipped from them.

"Diamond Bert liked to read the want ads. He made a joke of it, saying that he would soon be looking for another job. But I saw a different reason. I decided that questions concerning members of Farwell's outfit could be passed on to him through the ads."

Mann looked perplexed.

"Simple enough," explained Farrow. "Suppose an ad appeared under 'occupations wanted.' Code words could tell that some agent had performed a certain task. They could indicate that new members were needed for the band. More than that, they could be answers to questions put by Diamond Bert when he sent messages out by carriers.

"He could give orders. With them, he could state what forms of ads would tell him if his instructions had been accomplished. I decided quickly enough that Diamond Bert was managing everything on a plan that limited many of the answers to 'yes' or 'no'."

"I see it now," nodded Mann.

"Time grew short," went on Farrow. "So I resolved upon a bold course. I was friendly with Diamond Bert. I told him I was doing time for having handled fake promotion schemes. I knew that I had impressed him as being the type of man he might use.

"So I openly informed him that I had seen him taking carrier pigeons from certain boxes. I wanted to know the lay. I said that I was due to get out of stir before him. I suggested that we team up."

"What was his response?"

"This." Farrow reached in his pocket and produced a coin-like object that he dropped upon the table.

IT was another of the Chinese disks. "Diamond Bert must have some of these hidden in

his cell. He told me that by taking it, I became a member of his crew. It would be a token of identity by which I could reach him when he left the big house."

"He told you where you would be able to find him?"

"No. He simply said that when he left the pen, he would call an old friend named Yates Yocum, who runs a secondhand trunk shop down on The Bowery. Yocum, apparently, is not in the know. Merely a man whom Diamond Bert helped out in a business deal.

"I am to call Yocum. Giving no name—merely to ask if he has heard from Bert. Yocum—after he hears from Farwell—will name the place where I am to go."

Farrow paused and indicated the folded papers, to signify that all these details were present in the written report. Then, with an emphatic gesture, he leaned close to the desk.

"I know this," declared the sociologist. "Though Diamond Bert was cagey; though he postponed further talk until after our appointed meeting, he is planning crime on a heavy scale. His schemes are formulated. His workers will move when he gives the word."

"After he is out?"

"Yes. He is risking nothing until then. That brings me to the most important part of my story. The exact time when Diamond Bert will be discharged from prison—"

"When will that be?"

"Today, at three o'clock in the afternoon."

Mann opened his eyes. Momentarily nervous, he glanced at his watch. He saw that it was only ten o'clock. That allowed five hours. Mann settled back with a smile.

"I sent a note to the warden yesterday," said Farrow. "I was released at six o'clock in the afternoon. Since I could not see you until this morning, I went to a hotel in Poughkeepsie. I left by an early morning train.

"Knowing how slippery Diamond Bert might prove to be, I called Dave Garvell, who had charge of my apartment. I gave him certain orders. I told him to send a man up to watch the prison; to be ready to trail Diamond Bert when he left."

"Who was the man you sent?"

"A former crook called Hawkeye. The cleverest trailer in the business. He is stopping near the prison and will keep in communication with Dave. If Hawkeye is needed, he is ready to trail Diamond Bert. If he is not needed, we can call him off."

Mann picked up the written report. He stared from the window; then turned directly to Farrow.

"Suppose you go to your apartment," suggested Mann. "By the time you reach there, I shall have the answer. Your report will have reached the proper hands. There is plenty of time between now and three o'clock.

"It was understood that you would arrive here before the time of Diamond Bert's release. You have done so. Five hours will prove sufficient. But I feel sure"—a smile flickered on Mann's lips—"that plans have been made to keep tabs on Diamond Bert."

Farrow understood. The Shadow himself intended to take up the crook's trail. Hawkeye would not be needed. At the same time, Farrow knew that Mann—even if cognizant of The Shadow's intention—could make no further statement.

"Very well," decided Farrow. "I shall follow your instructions, Mr. Mann. But before I leave, suppose I call Dave. He hasn't heard from me since last night."

"Quite all right," responded Mann. "Use the telephone, right there beside you."

FARROW called the number of his apartment. He gained a response. He listened while Dave's voice clicked over the wire. Mann, watching, saw Farrow start. Hoarsely, the sociologist ended his conversation; then dropped the receiver on the hook.

"What has happened?" inquired Mann, quickly.

"Diamond Bert!" exclaimed Farrow. "He's out!"

"Escaped?"

"No. The warden had to go to Albany. So he made an unexpected change in his established routine. He released Diamond Bert and some other prisoners at nine o'clock this morning!"

"How did Dave learn that?"

"From Hawkeye. He must have heard that it was going to happen. He called Dave at half past eight. Then he started out to pick up Diamond Bert's trail."

Mann was making notes on a sheet of paper. Farrow was nervous as he watched him. To the sociologist, this was a catastrophe. It marked failure to the finish of his efforts. Fumbling, Farrow picked up the Chinese disk that he had laid on Mann's desk.

"Hawkeye may trail Diamond Bert," he declared, with an attempt at hopefulness. "If he fails, there's still this disk. It will give me a chance to meet with Diamond Bert. After he reaches New York."

"Don't worry about it," said Mann, completing his notations. "Go back to your apartment. Call me here or at my home, the moment that you hear from Hawkeye. Do nothing else until you receive instructions."

Farrow nodded. He arose and left the office. Rutledge Mann picked up the telephone and made a call. Burbank responded. Tersely, Mann stated that he was forwarding the report; then added the news concerning Diamond Bert's unexpected release.

That done, Mann rewrote his notations, using bright blue ink. He folded the paper along with Farrow's report and thrust all into a large envelope. He arose and went out of the office.

Mann was leaving for Twenty-third Street. There he would thrust his packet through the letter slit of a closed office in an old, dilapidated building. The Shadow, informed by Burbank, would collect the envelope himself.

From now on, decision rested with The Shadow. He had planned well; Slade Farrow had accomplished definite results. Yet chance had played an evil hand. With Farrow's information gained, The Shadow could have moved to block Diamond Bert from the time the crook came out of stir.

The Shadow had the goods. By meeting Diamond Bert face to face, he could stop the big shot without allowing time for a crooked move. Or, by staying close to the released convict, he could listen in on Diamond Bert's plans; to learn the crook's associates; to find out Farwell's schemes before delivering a thrust.

Ill luck had ended that opportunity. Diamond Bert was free. His organization was ready. Carriers of the Chinese disks were ready to aid in schemes of crime. Upon Hawkeye's ability as a trailer; upon Farrow's indefinite appointment rested the only chances that remained.

If those failed, Diamond Bert would be in the clear, ready to weave his new spell of insidious crime. A supercrook, head of a secret ring, Diamond Bert Farwell had left the toils of the law, prepared to deliver evil that would outmatch his crimes of the past.

CHAPTER VIII
TWO TRAILS

NIGHT covered Manhattan. Twelve hours had passed since Diamond Bert Farwell had left the clanging doors of the State pen. Swiftly and in expert fashion, the slippery crook had disappeared. He had headed, without question, for one objective: New York.

The metropolis, with its maelstrom of humanity, was Diamond Bert's logical goal. There his hidden organization awaited his arrival. There, lost among the teeming multitudes, he could find a place of security as headquarters for the campaign of evil that he planned.

Like a pebble dropped into a lake, Diamond Bert was gone. After him had plunked another human pebble: Hawkeye. The man upon whom Slade Farrow relied as a trailer was also missing since early that morning.

A taxi was rolling along a side street north of Times Square. It came to a halt in front of a tall but antiquated building. A neon sign, two of its letters blank, proclaimed this structure as the Hotel Rotunda. A passenger alighted from the cab, hoisted out a heavy suitcase, paid the driver and entered the hotel.

When he reached the desk, this arrival inquired for a room with bath. He scrawled a name on the register. The clerk read it as Horace Darnley. Glancing up, he viewed the new guest. The man was of squatty build; his face, though pleasant and rotund, carried a singular hardness that showed in the light.

A bellhop carried the newcomer's bag into the elevator. The man removed his hat; and the clerk caught sight of a bald head. Darnley turned toward the door of the elevator; the clerk saw his face again. This time he noted the man blink his eyes as he looked toward the light. The door of the elevator closed. That was the clerk's last glimpse.

There had been a certain oddity about Horace Darnley's manner; but the clerk soon forgot the fact. The man had appeared as desirable as most of the guests who came to this decadent hotel. So the clerk took it for granted that he was actually Horace Darnley, from Boston. He would have been quite amazed had anyone told him the true identity of the new guest.

The man who had just registered at the Hotel Rotunda was Diamond Bert Farwell. His choice of the name Darnley had been a haphazard one; but the use of Boston as his supposed home city had been governed somewhat by his day's travels. After leaving the pen, the ex-convict had headed toward the Massachusetts metropolis; but he had finally branched off, boarded a train at New Haven, changed to a bus at Bridgeport and come in from the Bronx by elevated.

In all these shifts, Diamond Bert had taken it for granted that someone might be on his trail. Crafty and alert the moment that he had retained his freedom, the smart crook had done his utmost to throw off any follower.

Yet he had failed in his endeavor. Five minutes after Diamond Bert had ascended in the elevator, another man approached the desk of the Hotel Rotunda. This arrival was a small, frail fellow, whose face immediately attracted the clerk's attention.

WIZENED in countenance, the man seemed prematurely old. His skin was colorless; only his eyes gave him expression. They were sharp and beady; as quick and certain as the eyes of a dangerous snake.

This man picked up a pen and poised it above the hotel register. His shrewd eyes spotted the name of Horace Darnley. They also saw the number of the room that the man had taken. It was 1215. The man glanced toward the clerk.

"How about a room, bo?" he questioned. "Got any that end with the number 13? That's my lucky number."

"Eight thirteen," responded the clerk.

"Not high enough," snapped the little man. "Go up a few notches if you want me to sign up. I'm particular."

"Eleven thirteen," said the clerk. "Twelve thirteen—"

"Sold," broke in the registering guest. "Twelve thirteen is my ticket. Let's have it."

He scrawled a name on the register. The clerk peered over the desk and saw that the man had no luggage.

"Two dollars for the room," he said. "Payable in advance, for those who have no baggage."

Before the clerk had finished, the new guest brought out a thick roll of bills. He peeled two ones from a batch of fives, tens and twenties. He threw the two dollars on the desk and picked up the key that the clerk presented. He headed for the elevator while the clerk was still trying to calculate the size of the bankroll that he had seen.

The clerk figured there was something unusual about the beady-eyed guest; and he was right in his assumption. This man who had talked his way into Room 1213 was a capable artist in his chosen line. This was "Hawkeye," the trailer whom Slade Farrow had put on the path of Diamond Bert.

When he reached Room 1213, Hawkeye unlocked the door with caution. He closed it softly behind him; then sneaked across the patched carpet of the floor. Already, he could hear the sound of a voice beyond the connecting door that joined this room with 1215.

Hawkeye's room was dark, save for the glow that came in from the city lights. That illumination was sufficient to show the crafty grin on Hawkeye's face. Judging from the tone of the voice that he heard, Hawkeye knew that he was close to Diamond Bert.

ALL day, Hawkeye had kept up his chase of the ex-convict. Twice he had tried to put in a long distance call to New York. Both times, Hawkeye had been forced to pass up such opportunity in order to resume the trail.

He had ridden in from the Bronx on the same car that Diamond Bert had taken in the el train. He had alighted at the same station; he had watched the ex-convict hop a cab. Hawkeye had caught the repetition of Diamond Bert's order when the driver had repeated it. He had heard the name: "Hotel Rotunda."

By rights, Hawkeye should have called Slade Farrow. But the trailer feared that the stop at the hotel might be a short one. So he had hotfooted it to the same direction. Playing hunches, he had gained the room next to Diamond Bert's.

Hawkeye could not make out what the crook was saying. Diamond Bert's call ended as he reached the connecting door. Then came another call, a mumbled number. A short interval; then Diamond Bert began to talk to someone. This time, Hawkeye made out words.

"Called an hour ago, eh?" Diamond Bert was questioning. "Wanted to know if you'd heard from me... Yes... Well, I guess he's all right, whoever he is... Yes... When he calls again, tell him to go down to Howey's...

"You know the place... Sure, the old house he used to live in, before he took it on the lam. Yes, he owned the place. I've been keeping it up for him... All right, Yocum. Tell that bird if he calls again..."

Yocum. Slade Farrow had mentioned the name to Hawkeye. He had spoken of an appointment with Diamond Bert to be made through Yates Yocum. Hawkeye had never heard of Howey; so he had no idea where the house might be.

Diamond Bert, apparently, would be going there. Perhaps not for a while yet. Hawkeye was counting upon an opportunity to slip out and call

Farrow. Then the opportunity faded. Hawkeye heard footsteps in the next room. The outer door opened. Diamond Bert was leaving.

With Hawkeye, the keeping of the trail was vital. The little man moved to the door of his own room and went out into the hall. He gave Diamond Bert enough leeway to reach the elevators. Hawkeye arrived there just as a door was closing. Two elevators were in operation. Hawkeye was lucky enough to catch the second one half a minute later.

Reaching the street, Hawkeye spotted Diamond Bert half a block away. He took up the trail and followed the crook to a subway entrance. He boarded the same train that Diamond Bert took. He alighted at the same station.

The trail led eastward. Diamond Bert proceeded on foot, heading through a dilapidated district. All the while, Hawkeye followed, turn by turn, street by street. The trailer was determined to spot the crook's destination.

WHILE Hawkeye was prowling through dingy streets, another personage was taking up the trail of Diamond Bert. A light was gleaming in The Shadow's sanctum. The Shadow was awaiting news.

On his table lay reports; with them, notations that The Shadow himself had made. The Shadow had communicated with Slade Farrow through Rutledge Mann. His orders had been simple. Farrow was to remain where he was; to make no move whatever. His one duty was to report any word from Hawkeye, by telephoning his information to Rutledge Mann.

A light glimmered from the wall beyond the table. A tiny bulb, announcing a call to the sanctum. The Shadow plucked earphones from the wall. He spoke in a whisper that echoed through the gloomy room. Burbank's voice responded.

"Report from Vincent," came the contact man's voice. "Another call to Yocum. He has heard from Bert. Directions: first alleyway below the Elite Garage on Marwell Street. Door at the end of the alleyway. Come immediately."

"Report received," whispered The Shadow.

Earphones clattered. The little bulb went out; then a click extinguished the bluish lamp above the table. A swish; a whispered laugh. The Shadow had departed from his sanctum.

Marwell Street. A short, little-frequented thoroughfare on the fringe of an undesirable district. It would be easy to find the garage that Burbank had mentioned. The Shadow was going to the appointed destination.

Diamond Bert had made a rendezvous with Slade Farrow. The in-between contact was Yates Yocum, a man to whom Farrow had been required to give no name. So The Shadow had left the job of calling Yocum to his agent, Harry Vincent. Harry had gained the required information. He had called The Shadow, through Burbank.

TWENTY minutes after The Shadow had left his sanctum, a splotch of blackness glided beneath the dull light of a streetlamp. Just ahead was the brick, windowless wall of the Elite Garage. Then came a faint swish in the darkness. Keen eyes peered into the entrance of an alleyway.

The Shadow had arrived at the location named by Yocum. Stealthily, he moved forward in the darkness. As he reached the innermost portion of the blind alley, he stopped. Unseen, he stood against a wall. Someone was entering the alleyway, stumbling through the dark.

Muttering curses, this arrival reached a spot near to The Shadow. He opened a door, the very one that The Shadow sought. A glimmer of light revealed a rough, unshaven face. It showed a sweatered figure as the man stepped through the opening. The door swung shut; but not all the way. A chink of light showed at the edge. The Shadow glided forward.

Peering through the crack, The Shadow saw the rowdy standing in a small, lighted entry. Straight ahead was a second door, sheathed with metal, that displayed a peephole in the center. The sweatered man was holding the palm of his hand toward the hole. A moment later, the inner door swung open. A second gangster joined the first.

The two spoke. The Shadow could hear their growled words. He also saw the arrival pass something to the man who had stepped out. A dull glint in the light revealed the object as a metal disk.

"The trick's yours, Hunky," said the man who had stepped from the inner door. "I'll be back in the morning. If anybody shows up, make 'em flash the coin."

This was evidently a reference to the Chinese disk. It had been the token of admission for "Hunky," the new arrival. He had given it to the man who was going off duty. That fellow would need it to identify himself in the morning.

"O.K., Luke," said Hunky. "Say—has anybody gone in tonight?"

"Only Tam Sook," returned Luke, as he moved toward the outer door.

"He shows up every night, don't he?" questioned Hunky.

Luke paused to grin.

"Sure he does," he returned. "Why shouldn't he? This is his joint, ain't it?"

"It's supposed to be. But I can't figure it. That Chink's got a place of his own, down in

Chinatown. What's he want to come up here for? With guys like us watchin' his place?"

"Search me. But what's the good of talkin' about it? You're gettin' your dough, ain't you?"

"Sure."

"Then don't squawk. When Tam Sook comes down, keep your mug shut. He's your boss. He goes in an' out when he wants."

"O.K. by me."

The Shadow drew back into darkness. A moment later, the outer door swung open and Luke stepped into the alley. The Shadow waited until the gangster had blundered through the darkness, past the old garage.

Hunky was the new inner guardian. The Shadow wanted to allow time before entering. It would be a mistake to appear too soon after Hunky had gone. Meanwhile, The Shadow was considering the case of Tam Sook.

HE had heard of this Chinaman. Tam Sook was a prosperous Chinese merchant. One whose name had never been connected with crime. But it was plain now that Tam Sook had been a secret agent of Diamond Bert Farwell. As Wang Foo, Diamond Bert had gained contacts with Chinamen during his checkered past.

Tam Sook had provided this place. He had been making visits. He was inside at present. Those facts brought The Shadow to a single conclusion. This house, with dilapidated walls three stories high, could be the hideout that Diamond Bert had chosen. Herein, Diamond Bert would meet Slade Farrow.

The Shadow had come in Farrow's place. With a reason. That would be apparent later. First, The Shadow must enter. Time had elapsed since Luke's departure. The Shadow moved forward; then halted and quickly swung back to the darkness.

The door was opening again. A squatty figure blocked the light. The Shadow glimpsed a yellow face, bland above the American garb that the man was wearing. Only for a brief instant did the face show in the light. In that moment, The Shadow recognized the features of Tam Sook.

A frequent visitor to Chinatown, The Shadow had seen the Chinese merchant several times before. He waited while the door swung shut and Tam Sook made his way through the alley. New silence came; The Shadow's laugh was a mere whispered echo.

Had Tam Sook completed final preparations for Diamond Bert's arrival? Had Diamond Bert already reached this house? If so, had Luke been instructed not to tell Hunky; or had Diamond Bert come in by a secret entrance? What if Diamond Bert had not yet come here?

These were the questions that had brought The Shadow's laugh. There was one way to answer them; to keep Farrow's appointment for him. Whether Diamond Bert had arrived or not, The Shadow could deal with the situation. Three minutes after Tam Sook's departure, the cloaked observer moved forward and opened the outer door.

The Shadow reached the inner barrier. He peeled the glove from his left hand. The girasol sparkled in the light; then the hand dipped beneath The Shadow's cloak. It reappeared, holding The Shadow's Chinese disk. This relic from the old days of Wang Foo was identical with the token that Diamond Bert had given to Slade Farrow.

The Shadow moved to the right of the door. He held the palm of his hand to the closed loophole. Only the disk showed, with its dull red character. The girasol was out of sight, behind The Shadow's hand.

With his gloved right knuckles, The Shadow rapped sharply on the inner door. The loophole clicked open; an eye spied the disk in The Shadow's palm. But Hunky, the inside observer, saw no more than the disk within the hand. The closeness of The Shadow's palm blocked further vision.

The loophole popped shut. Bolts began to click as Hunky drew them. The Shadow's left hand still remained at the center of the door. But his right hand had taken up another task. Swinging from beneath the folds of his black cloak, The Shadow's gloved fist appeared with an automatic in its clutch.

His weapon ready, The Shadow was prepared to spring a prompt surprise the moment that Hunky opened the door. The disk had worked its charm. A .45 would do the rest.

CHAPTER IX
THE DEATH TRAP

THE sheathed door swung inward. Hunky stepped aside to view the entering visitor. In his hand, as a precaution, the sweatered gangster was holding a revolver. He was ready to use it, should emergency require such action.

But Hunky, hard-faced and vicious, had expected no such arrival as the one who appeared. The gunman's bristly face quivered as his gaze encountered fiery eyes that peered from beneath a hat brim.

Directly below those burning optics was the looming muzzle of an automatic. Faced by The Shadow, Hunky lost all sense of motion. He staggered backward like an automaton, his quaking legs acting of their own volition.

Hunky was backed against the wall of a short, dimly-lighted passage. His finger had slipped from the trigger of his gun. The weapon remained in his hand solely because his loosened fist had failed to open fully. No word had been needed to proclaim the identity of the menace that stood before the affrighted mobster. Hunky had recognized The Shadow.

The girasol glimmered as The Shadow pressed the door shut behind him. Hunky did not see the flashing gem. His eyes, fixed in a helpless stare, were fascinated by The Shadow's gaze. Hunky was experiencing the hypnosis that seizes a bird trapped by the cold glare of a snake.

A motion of the automatic. This time, Hunky responded through fear. He let his revolver clatter to the floor. He raised his hands to the level of his shoulders. He quivered as he heard a whispered laugh—a merciless tone that sounded hollow in that passage.

Though his automatic remained level, The Shadow's eyes turned. They sought the inner end of the passage. There they saw another door, also metal-sheathed; but with bolts on the near side. Instantly, The Shadow discerned the purpose of that barrier.

Anyone who passed by that next door would be blocked from return. Hunky had a double duty. He could stop those who might seek exit as well as the ones who came in from outside. Had Slade Farrow come here as appointed, he would have walked into a positive trap.

Sweeping a few paces forward, The Shadow paused and turned toward Hunky. Whispered words came from hidden lips. Their hiss made the mobster cower. Hunky feared death. He did not know that The Shadow scorned unnecessary kills.

Though the mobster might prove a handicap, The Shadow intended to take him along on the path that lay ahead. Hunky, at The Shadow's bidding, was scheduled to make his first trip into the interior of Tam Sook's lair. It was a chance occurrence that altered The Shadow's plans.

THE SHADOW had passed Hunky and had faced toward him. Thus The Shadow's eyes were fixed upon the outer door. It was not from that barrier, however, that trouble came. The inkling of danger arrived from the deep end of the passage, where The Shadow had spied the door with drawn bolts.

A slight swish of air announced the opening of that second barrier. The Shadow wheeled as a second mobster stepped in view. This fellow was an inner guardian. For some reason, he had decided to enter the passage to speak to Hunky.

Under the same orders, the newcomer held a revolver. Moreover, he experienced an advantage that Hunky had not gained. This second gunman had caught The Shadow by surprise. He lost no time the moment that he saw the shrouded figure.

The revolver came up as The Shadow wheeled. Quickly, the guard aimed for the black-clad form. The revolver spurted flame. A bullet whizzed down the passage. It flattened against the door that The Shadow had closed.

For in his whirl, the cloaked intruder had performed an amazing fadeaway. Over across the passage, down toward the floor, The Shadow dwindled instantaneously. This was the instinctive trick that had served him well in combat with marksmen of the underworld. Many a killer had been astounded by that fading swerve. None who had witnessed it had remained to benefit by their discovery.

For the fadeaway was but the prelude to the deed that came a split-second later. Though his form dropped, The Shadow's right arm swung upward. The automatic thundered in the passage. The mobster staggered forward from the door.

Though clipped by The Shadow's return shot, the gunman was not finished. His body was doubled up and swaying; but his lips spat oaths as his wavering right hand loosed shots that ricocheted along the passage. With those hopeless revolver bursts came new stabs from the automatic. The mobster crumpled on the stone floor.

The sight of conflict had revived Hunky's courage. With a venomous snarl, the cowering mobster had dropped to the floor to grab his gun. While his pal's bullets sizzled above his head, Hunky made desperate aim. It was an act that The Shadow had foreseen.

With echoes still resounding through the stone-walled passage, The Shadow came upward in a rapid spin. His smoking automatic coughed as it swung. A zimming slug found Hunky's crouched body before the gangster could press the trigger of his revolver.

Instinctive aim had served The Shadow well. By incredible swiftness he had beaten Hunky to the shot. Not only that, his close-range burst was perfect. Hunky proved softer than the man at the door. A single slug was all that he could take. He rolled upon the floor and lay still.

The Shadow waited. Silence followed echoes. There was no further sound from anywhere. The whole house was like a tomb. The Shadow strode past Hunky's body and bolted the outer door. Then he turned, went along the passage and went through the inner portal, closing it behind him. He noted bolts on this side also.

THE SHADOW had formulated a swift plan. His quest was for Diamond Bert. The arch-crook might already be within this house. If so, a quick search would locate him. Should the hunt prove futile, The Shadow must make a rapid return. By taking Hunky's place behind the first barrier, he could admit Diamond Bert should he arrive and crave entrance through display of a Chinese disk.

Just beyond the second portal, The Shadow found a closed door. It was raised a short space from the floor. It indicated a stairway. Not only was this the only course that could be followed; but the presence of the door explained something to The Shadow's satisfaction. That blocking barrier told why the shots had not been heard higher in the house.

The Shadow opened the door and found a narrow flight of stairs. Dim lights showed the steps. The Shadow ascended. He reached a landing and continued upward. Past the second floor; then to the third. The stairs made short turns; and at no spot along the way did The Shadow discover any passage leading from them until he reached the top.

There, The Shadow encountered another blocking door. He opened it and found a short corridor that terminated in a steel-sheathed door. This had no loophole. Instead, its center was furnished with a square of thick glass that was evidently bulletproof. Peering through the pane, The Shadow discerned blackness only.

The light in the hallway showed The Shadow as a weird shape of blackness. Moving away from the glass panel, The Shadow brought his left hand into the light. He held it near the glass in the door, displaying the Chinese disk. Firmly, he rapped his right hand against the door.

Half a minute passed. The Shadow was holding an automatic in his right hand. He had produced it swiftly, as he had done below. Then, noiselessly, the sheathed barrier slid open. The light from the hall revealed a tiny antechamber. Directly beyond it was another door.

The next door had an opening supplied with four short vertical bars. It was through this that someone—from inner darkness—had peered clear through the glass in the outer door. The Shadow paused, pressed close against the wall. Then, from the darkness beyond the wicketed door, he heard an oddly-accented voice pronounce a single word:

"Enter."

The tone of the voice was proof that it came from a corner some distance beyond the inner door. Whoever had uttered the command, had moved away from the wicket. The Shadow was sure that spying eyes had seen the disk alone. Boldly, he stepped into the little anteroom.

A faint buzz from darkness beyond the wicket. The outer door slid shut. The Shadow was imprisoned in a tiny cell. Then came another sliding sound as the door with the wicket opened. Again, a voice from total darkness:

"Enter."

THE SHADOW was totally invisible as he stepped forward through the opening. Again a buzz gave signal to the concealed person who waited in the darkness. The Shadow paused; he heard the wicketed door slide shut. A second later, greenish lights illuminated the room.

The ghoulish glare revealed a strange scene. The Shadow was standing just past the threshold of an Oriental apartment. The smooth walls were painted with weird figures; hideous dragons, leering joss gods, grinning devils that seemed creatures of an unbelievable nightmare.

The floor was covered by a complete carpeting of blood-red hue, crisscrossed by thin lines of bright gold. Off to the left was a break that showed the surface of a metal door—a barrier that had a completely solid front. The wall on the right showed no opening.

The door through which The Shadow had entered was not in the center of its wall. It was several feet to the right. Thus, to face the center of the opposite wall, The Shadow had been forced to turn at a slight angle. He had done so in the darkness. Already, he had leveled his automatic, even before the lights had appeared. For his keen ears had told him the exact direction from which the voice had come.

Thus The Shadow, like a visitant from a tomb, was ready by dint of uncanny precision. His living form was as outlandish as any of those nightmare paintings on the walls. Blazing orbs—the eyes of The Shadow—were fixed upon a half-domed niche cut in the farther wall. For there, behind a table of solid ebony, sat the man who had twice pronounced the word: "Enter."

A Chinaman wearing a resplendent robe. A bland-faced Oriental who blinked placidly as he viewed his unexpected visitor. Though he had reason for surprise, the Mongol did not show the slightest trace of astonishment.

Yet The Shadow, too, had reason for surprise that he did not betray. For the face that he observed above that gorgeous robe was one that he had seen elsewhere, only a dozen minutes before. The Chinaman seated deep behind the ebony stand had the features of Tam Sook, the Celestial whom The Shadow had glimpsed departing by the alleyway below!

CHAPTER X
THE TRAP SPRINGS

TAM SOOK chuckled. There was dry mirth in his tone. He seemed to relish The Shadow's presence. He was unperturbed by the yawning muzzle of the automatic, though it loomed squarely before his almond-shaped eyes.

No response from The Shadow. His form became a statue; its sable hue matching the ebony of Tam Sook's table. The burning eyes; the automatic; the girasol, sparkling from the white left hand—those alone formed a relief to the blackness of The Shadow's garb.

Tam Sook's chuckle ended. His eyes blinked. Then he spoke, in perfect English, except for the slight singsong that the Chinaman had acquired from his native tongue.

"You are not the visitor that I expected," remarked the Chinaman. "The one whom I awaited is called Slade Farrow. You, however, have displayed the required token. Therefore, I shall accept you in his place."

The Shadow remained silent. Tam Sook indulged in a soft chuckle. The Chinaman settled farther back in his chair. He showed no dread.

"You are The Shadow," pronounced Tam Sook. "You have come in the place of Slade Farrow. That is good. I am here instead of the man whom you seek. He is called Diamond Bert Farwell; but there was once a time when he was known as Wang Foo."

Tam Sook paused. He placed his hands before him. They rested loosely upon the ebony table, like the hands of a musician, ready to play a piano selection. The gesture showed that Tam Sook had no weapon in readiness.

"Beneath this table," remarked Tam Sook, "is a pedal upon which my foot is resting. While I continue to press it, this room will remain unchanged. Should I lift my foot"—the Chinaman paused to blink—"the entire floor will open. You, my visitor, will fall to your destruction.

"That is why your weapon is useless. The swifter your shot—should you choose to use your gun—the more rapid will be your doom. Should you wound me; should you kill me; the result will be the same. Death to you, The Shadow.

"Therefore, I advise you to make no foolish move. It would be preferable for you to talk. If you have any entreaty that you wish to make; if you have word for our mutual friend, Wang Foo, this is your opportunity to speak."

Tam Sook paused. He fully expected The Shadow to reply. The Shadow, however, remained silent. His only motion was a slight backward glide, accompanied by a steady lowering of the automatic. Tam Sook took the hopeless retreat to be a gesture of surrender.

"PERHAPS," observed the Chinaman, "you intend to wait until I have spoken further. Very well. I shall oblige. I shall answer a question that must be in your mind. I shall tell you about our friend, Wang Foo.

"This place was prepared as his abode. I have come here, night after night, to furnish it as his stronghold. Tonight, my friend arrived. He came here as Diamond Bert. Awaiting him, I had the vestments that he required to once more assume his character of the past. The guise of Wang Foo.

"But he chose neither that guise nor this abode. Instead, he said to me: 'Tam Sook, I wish you to remain here while I fare forth. Therefore, Tam Sook, I shall go as you. I shall be Tam Sook, the Chinese merchant; not Wang Foo, whom the police have known.'

"So Diamond Bert became Tam Sook. I, Tam Sook remained. Diamond Bert, the new Tam Sook, is free. He is ready to perform his chosen tasks. His workers are everywhere here. Those who carry the disks are ready for his call."

There was cold truth in the Chinaman's singsong tone. The Shadow knew that this was the real Tam Sook. Diamond Bert had already arrived. Craftily, he had garbed himself as Tam Sook. An artist when it came to disguise, a man who had previously played a deceptive Chinese role, Diamond Bert had performed an expert job.

The Shadow had seen Diamond Bert at the alley door. The glimpse had been too short for The Shadow to discern the deception. The talk between Luke and Hunky had indicated that Tam Sook came here frequently and then departed. That had led The Shadow to accept Diamond Bert as the real Tam Sook.

"I remained here"—Tam Sook was resuming—"to greet the visitor who was expected. Slade Farrow. I stayed here to question him. To learn whether he might be friend or enemy. Instead, I have received you, The Shadow.

"You do not choose to speak. Therefore, I know that you cannot be a friend. You are an enemy. For such as The Shadow, there can be but one fate. You must die."

As Tam Sook pronounced this verdict, he settled back into his deep chair. His hands slid from the table. Then came a slight shift of his robed body. A muffled click sounded as Tam Sook raised his hidden foot from the pedal beneath the ebony table.

Splitting along its thin gold lines, the crimson floor dropped downward on heavy hinges. Except for the raised nook wherein Tam Sook was seated, the entire apartment changed into a yawning pit that formed a blackened cavern down into the cellar, three floors below. With that move, Tam Sook had blandly sprung the trap that he believed would hurl The Shadow to destruction.

But The Shadow had foreseen the move. He was acting as Tam Sook shifted. Swift in this moment of crisis, The Shadow had taken advantage of the one chance that offered. His left hand was sweeping upward as the click resounded. Just as the floor broke open, The Shadow clutched a bar of the little wicket set in the door through which he had entered.

The Shadow's form slumped downward with the falling of the floor. But his left hand held its grip. Dangling, with half his body beneath the level where the floor had been, The Shadow remained swinging before the startled eyes of Tam Sook.

THE right hand swung upward. Tam Sook slumped behind the level of the ebony table. A roar resounded through the open-floored room. A tongue of flame flashed from the automatic as The Shadow pumped a zimming slug upward through the woodwork of the ebony stand.

A scream from Tam Sook. The Shadow's deflected bullet had scored a hit. The Chinaman was wounded. His trap had failed. The Shadow was still a menace. More shots, if they came through that ebony bulwark, would spell Tam Sook's doom. The Chinaman did not wait.

Though wounded, he showed remarkable fight. He bobbed up from behind the table like a mandarin-clad jack in the box. His left hand shot out and caught the farther edge. His right hand swung forward with a long, terrific sweep as his body surged across the tabletop.

A knife glimmered as Tam Sook hurled it across the room. The deed was a swift one, performed before The Shadow could respond. As the automatic barked another bullet toward Tam Sook's unprotected body, the flashing blade was already on its murderous course.

Had Tam Sook aimed the knife for the hanging shape of The Shadow, he would have certainly gained a hit. But such a stroke, to end The Shadow, would have had to reach his heart. That was why Tam Sook had chosen a different mark.

He had thrown the knife above The Shadow's head, choosing as his target the white hand that clutched the wicket bar. Straight for the glimmering girasol. That had been Tam Sook's aim. The Chinaman's hope was to loose the hold that alone kept The Shadow from destruction.

The speeding weapon missed by the fraction of an inch. The whizzing blade breezed the knuckles of The Shadow's fingers as it flashed between two bars of the wicket and bounded from the metal door beyond the anteroom. The Shadow's clutch remained unloosened.

But Tam Sook fared less happily. In his venomous effort to dispose of his uncanny foe, the Chinaman had made himself an unprotected target. The quick response of The Shadow's automatic was a shot that found its mark.

Half across the table, Tam Sook jounced upward as the bullet reached him. Writhing in agony, the Chinaman sprawled forward. His body could not stop its lunge. His clutching claws slipped as they tried to grasp the edges of the ebony stand.

Sliding forward in twisting fashion, Tam Sook delivered a high-pitched cry as his momentum carried him clear beyond the table edge. Pitching downward, head-foremost, the dying Mongol plunged into the darkened abyss. His scream trailed as he fell. Then came a dull crash from beneath. Faint, gasping moans reached The Shadow's ears from far below. Then came silence.

Grimly, The Shadow laughed. It was the first sound that he had uttered since his arrival in this den of death. Echoed mockery was token of The Shadow's triumph over the fiendish efforts of Tam Sook. That laugh, also, was foreboding. Its hollow mirth told of the danger which The Shadow still faced.

Hanging from the bar of the wicket, The Shadow was still above the opened pit. There was no means by which he could open the door. While he remained in this predicament, The Shadow could rely upon endurance only to prolong his life. Should his firm hold weaken, he would follow Tam Sook into the depths.

THIS was an emergency for which The Shadowy was fortunately prepared. When he fared forth upon adventure, The Shadow necessarily equipped himself for obstacles. Time and again, he was forced to scale outer walls in order to gain a goal. To accomplish this, he carried special devices in the form of rubber suction cups.

While his left hand still retained its hold upon the bar, The Shadow thrust his right beneath his cloak. He left his automatic there. In its place, he brought out a greased rubber disk. He pressed this firmly against the surface of the door and twisted it in place. Carefully, he released the bar and drew his hand away. The suction cup held.

The left hand went beneath the cloak and brought forth a second disk. This clamped against the wall and showed its ability to grip. Twisting the right hand cup free, The Shadow moved along the wall.

Hand over hand, a hazardous course. The

A knife glimmered as Tam Sook

hurled it across the room.

Shadow moved beetlelike among the hideous paintings that glared from the sides of this outlandish room. Ordinarily, The Shadow would have utilized emergency disks that fitted to his feet. The difficulty of adjusting them had forced him to forego those aids to safety.

In order to reach a spot of security, The Shadow had to tour half around the room. He made the first corner. Suction cups squidged as he continued to the next. At the second turn, The Shadow paused; both disks pressed firmly to the wall.

There, he pressed his feet against the painted face of a Chinese devil and arched his body backward. The action eased the strain upon his arms. For two long minutes, The Shadow remained, swaying slightly from left to right that he might relax his muscles for a new ordeal. Then he resumed his precarious way.

Foot by foot, along the gilded painting of a Chinese dragon, The Shadow followed the final course. As he neared his goal, he moved upward on the wall. His climbing progress carried him above the arch of the half dome. The Shadow's feet settled upon the very edge of the ebony table.

The Shadow knew that the blackwood stand was firmly clamped. Hence he relied upon his foothold. He loosened one suction cup with a twist and shook it free from his hand. It bounced upon the table and rolled into Tam Sook's chair.

The Shadow did not attempt to pull away the second cup. Such a twist, without the holding force of the other disk, would have precipitated his balanced body back into the yawning pit. The suction cups had a tendency to resist release.

Holding the edge of the archway with his free left hand, The Shadow managed to pull his right from the grip-glove that covered the clamped cup. That done, he eased into the nook and gained Tam Sook's chair.

Bending below the table, The Shadow discovered the pedal of which the Chinaman had spoken. He stooped and pressed it with one hand. Rumbling, the portions of the floor came up in place. Beside the pedal was a clamp. The Shadow swung it and held the pedal down. The room was restored to its former order.

WITH a soft laugh, The Shadow climbed upon the table and pried his suction cup free from the spot above the arch. He made a close examination of the desk. There he found control buttons and pressed them. The door with the wicket slid open; also the barrier beyond the anteroom. The Shadow let them shut.

He knew that there must be other controls somewhere on the stairway up which he had come. But what means had Tam Sook used for exit from the room? Closer examination gave the answer. Above each switch was a little catch. The Shadow pressed both devices. The doors slid open.

Slowly, the catches moved like pointers on a dial. It required half a minute for them to reach their limit. Then the doors slid shut automatically. This was the means whereby Tam Sook had been wont to depart from his strange den.

On the other side of the table was a single switch with a catch above it. The Shadow knew that this must control the door that showed in the end of the room. He felt sure that Diamond Bert must have arrived here by that entrance. The Shadow decided to use it as an exit.

He found a light switch centered beneath the table. He pressed it. Darkness filled the room. Then The Shadow pressed the catch that controlled the single door. With glimmering flashlight, he saw the barrier slide open. Stepping from the nook, he made in that direction.

Passing through the portal, The Shadow found himself in a sloping space beneath a pair of steps. A click; the sliding door went shut. That did not disturb The Shadow. He found a release that opened a section of the stairway. He went through and pushed the steps shut behind him.

The twinkling flashlight showed that The Shadow had reached the normal portion of the house. This flight of steps led up to a small attic. At the bottom, where The Shadow now stood, was a heavy door, bolted. The Shadow extinguished his light and softly drew the bolt. He stepped into an outer hall.

This house fronted upon a side street. The proof was a dull glimmer from lights along the thoroughfare. By the faint glow of the windows, The Shadow was able to pick his stealthy way until he found a flight of steps that led to the ground floor. He followed them.

The Shadow reached an outer door. It was bolted. He drew the fastening and moved to a flight of stone steps, closing the door behind him. This house must have been left open for Diamond Bert. The crook, however, had bolted doors behind him.

The steps were just away from the circle of light that came from a streetlamp. They formed an excellent spot of blackness. The Shadow paused; he edged toward the wall of the house in preparation for a choice of departure. Then he made a quick whirl as a figure came upward from beside the steps.

The Shadow had closed in upon a crouching watcher. Simultaneously he and the waiting man discovered each other. An instant later, they had come to grips, staggering out to the sidewalk. There, The Shadow twisted free. His form was plain in the sphere of lamplight.

His antagonist uttered a startled exclamation, just as The Shadow swung a gloved fist toward the fellow's jaw. The blow struck. The man slumped and lay half groggy on the sidewalk. The Shadow, stooping forward, recognized a wizened face that he had seen before. The man was Hawkeye, the trailer whom Slade Farrow had dispatched to cover Diamond Bert.

Hawkeye had followed his quarry. Blocked when Diamond Bert had bolted the door of the house, the trailer had waited. In the dark, he had decided that The Shadow must be Diamond Bert, returning. Thinking himself discovered, Hawkeye had sought battle.

The Shadow plucked Hawkeye to his feet. The little fellow was groggy; his feet responded mechanically as The Shadow carried him along the way. At the end of the block, they reached a street where an elevated structure towered above dingy-fronted shops.

A cab chanced to be standing by the curb. The Shadow opened the door and hoisted Hawkeye into the rear. The driver, hearing the noise, turned. The Shadow spoke in a quiet tone, giving him the address of Slade Farrow's apartment.

The driver saw the door shut. He thought his passenger had closed it. He did not note that Hawkeye was slumped in the seat. He did not see the gliding shape of The Shadow. The driver shoved his car into gear and pulled away.

THE SHADOW faded with darkness. From then on, his course was untraceable. Only at intervals, in unfrequented spots, did a splotch of blackness manifest itself as it moved ghostlike beneath the glow of lighted patches.

This manifestation of The Shadow's presence finally occurred upon a dim, narrow street that fringed the Chinese district. Edging into darkness, The Shadow stared across the thoroughfare, toward the front of a gloomy shop. Above barred windows glittered the gilded name: "Tam Sook."

The shop of the Chinese merchant. Yet the place showed no signs of occupancy. The Shadow glided across the street; he found a side door, locked. A pick clicked in the darkness. At length, the barrier opened. The Shadow entered the silent house.

Ten minutes later, The Shadow reappeared upon the gloomy street. His search had proven futile. The house was empty. This was new evidence of Diamond Bert's cunning. The crook had taken on the guise of Tam Sook; but he had not come to occupy the merchant's shop.

A soft laugh in the darkness. A gliding shape beneath a lamp-glow. Then the figure, like the whispered mirth, had faded into nothingness. The Shadow, silent and unseen, was moving toward the lighted district of New York's Chinatown.

CHAPTER XI
CRIME BEGINS

TWENTY-FOUR hours had elapsed since The Shadow's encounter with Tam Sook. During that period, he had found no trace of the man whom he sought. Diamond Bert Farwell had closed the trail behind him.

Somewhere in Manhattan, the supercrook was at large. Crime was due to occur. The Shadow had no clue toward its location. He knew that a stroke might come as early as tonight. Yet The Shadow could do nothing more than wait.

AMID the traffic of Times Square, a limousine was honking its horn while the chauffeur fumed. Seated in the back was a restless, gray-haired man who showed impatience at the delay. At last the breaks came. Just as a huge advertising clock delivered ten clanging strokes as aftermath to discordant chimes, the traffic began to move.

Twelve minutes later, the chauffeur stopped in front of an old but well-preserved house that stood on an uptown street. This was the brownstone residence of Norris Tatson, millionaire philanthropist. It was Tatson himself who had arrived. He was the gray-haired man in the car.

There was something querulous in the millionaire's manner as Tatson stepped from the limousine and hobbled forward on a heavy cane. The chauffeur was standing by to aid him. Tatson pointed to the front of the house and spoke to the man.

"Look there, Charles," wheezed Tatson. "No light above the door. What ails Gorwin? He knew that I was coming home."

"Perhaps he did not expect you so soon, sir."

"So soon? I told him that I would be here by half past nine. This is negligence on his part."

"He never failed before, sir."

"That is no excuse. Charles. It is unnecessary for you to take Gorwin's part. I shall reprimand the fellow the moment that I see him. Come. Help me up these steps."

Charles aided. Tatson rang the doorbell. There was no response. While Tatson fumed, the chauffeur produced a key and unlocked the door. Tatson hobbled in; Charles followed. They passed through a vestibule. Then the millionaire stopped with a startled exclamation. Charles stared past the stooped form of his employer.

On the floor lay Gorwin, the servant whom Tatson had decided to reprimand. The man was stiff in death. His pale face was staring upward. The front of his livery was stained with a crimson splotch. Gorwin had been shot through the heart.

"Come, Charles!" exclaimed Tatson. "Into my study! This may mean robbery. Come. At once."

The chauffeur hurried ahead of the hobbling millionaire. He opened the door of the ground-floor study. The room was empty and undisturbed. Tatson made his way to the wall. He pressed a panel upward. The action revealed a compact wall safe. Tatson found it securely locked. He chuckled harshly.

"No one found it," he declared. "My gems are untouched. Poor Gorwin"—the millionaire clucked as he remembered the dead servant—"well, Charles, I must call the police at once."

"What about Mr. Joland?" inquired the chauffeur, in an anxious tone.

"Joland!" exclaimed Tatson. "My word! I had forgotten him. He should be here. Run upstairs at once, Charles. See if you can find him."

The chauffeur departed while Tatson made a call to the police. That done, the millionaire hobbled restlessly across the room, anxiously awaiting the chauffeur's return. Hurried footsteps on the stairs announced that Charles was descending. The chauffeur entered the study.

"Did you find Joland?" snapped Tatson.

"No," replied the chauffeur. "He is gone."

"What!"

"He left this, sir."

The chauffeur displayed a yellow telegram. Tatson pushed it aside and ordered Charles to read it.

"Not without my glasses," he explained. "Tell me what it says, Charles."

"It's from Newfield, sir," stated the chauffeur. "Addressed to Mr. Joland. Advising him that his father is quite ill. Asking him to come to Newfield at once."

"I see. What time of delivery is marked on the telegram?"

"Eight thirty, sir."

"Hm-m-m. Joland must have started shortly after that. Were his things packed, Charles?"

"Yes, sir. The room was pretty much mussed. Mr. Joland must have changed suits. There was one thrown over a chair."

"He must have had time to catch the train. Nine-twenty, wasn't it, Charles? The time you took Joland to the depot, several weeks ago?"

"Yes, sir."

A ring of the doorbell followed the chauffeur's remark. Charles hurried into the hallway, stepped gingerly past the dead body of Gorwin and answered the door. A stocky man entered. Charles nodded as the arrival flashed a badge.

"Detective Cardona, from headquarters," was Joe's gruff announcement. "Where is Mr. Tatson?"

"In his study, sir."

"Show me there—"

Cardona paused as he saw the body on the floor. He entered and stooped to examine it. Two other headquarters men came in the door. Then Tatson appeared, hobbling from the entrance of the study.

A SHORT quiz followed. The millionaire and his chauffeur told all that they knew. In conclusion, Tatson handed Cardona the telegram.

"Karl Joland is my secretary," he explained. "I left him here this evening with Gorwin. The telegram is marked eight-thirty. I suppose that Joland left before nine o'clock. Gorwin must have been murdered between then and half past."

"Why before half past?" inquired Joe.

"Because of the light over the front door," stated Tatson. "Gorwin invariably turned it on shortly before whatever time I was scheduled to arrive. I called him tonight to say that I would be in at nine-thirty. He would have turned on the light sometime between quarter past and half past."

"What time did you call Gorwin?"

"Quite early. About seven o'clock."

Cardona made notes. He was acting as inspector in charge of this case. While Joe was busily engaged, one of his men made a comment.

"Something sticking out of the flunkey's pocket," said the headquarters man. "Looks like an envelope, inspector."

Joe turned toward Gorwin's body. He spied the corner of an envelope. He removed the object, to find it unsealed. He drew out a folded paper. It proved to be a note in pencil.

"Joland's writing," commented Tatson. "I recognize it. But I can't read the words without my spectacles."

"It's to you," stated Cardona. "Signed Joland. Says that he is leaving for Newfield. Taking the nine-twenty train. Says that his father is ill; that you will get this note from Gorwin."

"That corroborates the telegram," decided Tatson.

"Let's look about a bit," suggested Cardona. "Nothing missing, Mr. Tatson? You're sure of it?"

"Absolutely nothing."

"The safe in your study?"

"Is untouched."

"Are you positive?"

"Absolutely. Of course, I can open it to make certain. But I have proof without that."

Cardona looked puzzled. Tatson motioned him into the study. There, the millionaire showed the detective the wall safe. The front of the safe was fitted with an oddly bulging knob.

"A Blefflinger safe," explained Tatson, "but

the special knob is an added device. One faulty turn will throw it completely out of gear. Then the knob will spin. As you see"—Tatson paused to place his fingers to the knob—"it is tight at present."

"But suppose someone knew the combination? Someone like Joland?"

"I alone know the combination. Furthermore, I changed it only recently."

"Hm-m-m. Well, if robbery wasn't the motive, we'll have to look for something else. Of course, maybe some crooks came here and beat it after they killed Gorwin. But in the meantime, I ought to know some more about this fellow Joland. Was there any bad blood between him and Gorwin?"

"None at all. They seemed very friendly. In fact, Joland was always willing to perform the services required of Gorwin on nights when the butler was not here."

"Was that frequent?"

"Once a week. Sometimes more often."

"I think I'll take a look up in Joland's room."

"Very well."

WHILE Cardona's men were prowling about the ground floor, looking vainly for clues, the ace went up to the secretary's room. There he discovered evidences of hasty packing. This fitted with the fact that Joland had but a limited time to make his train.

Cardona stared at the discarded suit that had been flung over a chair. He began to examine the garments. He thrust his hand into a coat pocket. His fingers slipped into a little inner pocket. They encountered something that Joe thought was a coin.

Bringing the object to light, Cardona uttered a surprised grunt. In one instant, the whole complexion of the case had been altered. It was not a coin that Cardona had brought from the pocket of Joland's suit. The object that lay in the detective's palm was a dull gray disk that bore a Chinese character.

Identical with the disk that Duff Corley had carried. A mate to the token that Spider Mertz, dying, had tried to throw away. Here was something that Karl Joland had evidently forgotten. Proof that Norris Tatson's secretary was a member of a secret, murderous band!

Pocketing the disk, Joe made for the stairs. He hurried to Tatson's study. The millionaire looked up in surprise at the detective's excited entry. Joe wasted no time. He pumped questions at Tatson.

"How much did this fellow Joland know about your affairs?" demanded Cardona.

"Why—why"—Tatson was stammering—"he knew a great deal—"

"What have you got in that safe?"

"Gems."

"Worth much?"

"A quarter of a million."

Cardona stepped back stupefied. Tatson smiled weakly. Then he spoke.

"Not much to me," he said. "I had really forgotten their value until you asked about it. You see, they are stones that I intend to sell when I am offered a proper price."

"Who has seen them?"

"Several dealers. One man—Marlin Norse—has been positive that he could find a customer. I have been keeping the gems here until I heard from him again."

"Did Joland know that the jewels were here?"

"Yes. He was present at every conference that I held. With Norse, and when I had conferences with several other dealers. Yes, he was always present."

Cardona was standing with hands deep in his coat pockets. In his right fist he was clutching the Chinese disk. The feel of that token roused him further.

"Open the safe, Mr. Tatson," ordered Joe, in a firm tone. "I've got to see with my own eyes that those jewels are safe."

The millionaire smiled indulgently, He hobbled to the wall and blocked Cardona's view while he worked the combination. Stepping slightly aside, Tatson drew back the door. Cardona was moving forward. Together, millionaire and detective stared into the interior of the safe.

Metal-lined walls alone met their view. Tatson's safe was empty. Jewels worth a quarter million had been stolen from a strongbox that was deemed impregnable. A dead butler, a vanished secretary and a rifled safe. All hinged on the Chinese disk that Joe Cardona still clutched in his tightened fist!

CHAPTER XII
THE SHADOW MOVES

IT was late the next afternoon. Joe Cardona was seated in a little office. The acting inspector was glum as he talked with Detective Sergeant Markham. Joe's voice was reminiscent.

"Remember Inspector John Malone?" he inquired.

Markham nodded.

"It was right here at this desk," recalled Cardona. "Right here that Malone was sitting. I was standing just like you are. And we were talking about a mess as bad as this one up at Tatson's.

"The Laidlow murder. Jewels mixed in that, too. And a secretary. I forget his name—Burgess,

I think it was. Committed suicide down in Florida, after we implicated him."

"Several years ago, wasn't it?" asked Markham.

"Yes," replied Cardona. "And in back of it all was a guy called Diamond Bert Farwell. A foxy egg, Diamond Bert. Passed himself off as a Chink. Used the alias Wang Foo.

"Well, here we are again. I'm behind the desk instead of Malone. You're walking around instead of me. A murder. Jewels gone. A secretary. And here's the Chinese end of it."

Cardona plunked the grayish disk upon the desk. Markham studied the object curiously.

"Chinkee Chink," growled Cardona. "Find him. A Chinaman's chance. It's the same guy back again, Markham."

"Diamond Bert?"

"Yeah. He's out of the big house. Left there yesterday and we let him slip. Shows what a guy can get away with by pulling the good behavior gag."

A shadow fell across the table where Cardona was eying the Chinese disk. The acting inspector looked up to see a tall, stoop-shouldered fellow who had entered with mop and bucket. Joe studied the dull face of Fritz, the janitor.

"Cleaning up early?" questioned Cardona.

"Yah," responded Fritz.

"He was here, too," recalled Cardona. He indicated Fritz as he spoke to Markham. "Mopping the room while Malone and I beefed away. The one guy that's sure of a job here is Fritz."

"Yah," grunted the janitor, in methodical fashion.

CARDONA forgot Fritz. He thumbed a report sheet. Markham watched Joe scowl. Finally, the acting inspector plunked the paper on the table beside the Chinese disk.

"Joland's old man didn't send that telegram," asserted Joe. "Joland didn't go to Newfield after he left Tatson's house. He beat it, Joland did. It's a cinch he's got the gems. That's the line-up I'm going to work on.

"I'm going to find out everything about that guy Joland's past. Whether or not Diamond Bert is the big shot, it's a cinch that Joland was working with him. Tatson is sure that Joland couldn't have opened the wall safe; but I'm convinced that he did.

"Somebody sent him a phony telegram from Newfield. Why? To make it look like Joland was on the level. Joland bumped Gorwin, and stuck a note in the butler's pocket, to make it look like all was on the square.

"Maybe he figured on going to Newfield. He got cold feet, that's all. Anyway, he got a cool quarter million in sparklers. Joland was around when old Marlin Norse came to see Norris Tatson. Norse was a jeweler, talking business with Joland's boss. All the while Joland was snooping, figuring out how he could grab the gems.

"And there's the proof of it. That disk. Like every smart crook, Joland made a slip. Forgot the disk when he took it on the lam. Left it in the pocket of his other suit. Where I found it. The rest of this report means nothing. Tatson, with his talk about Gorwin turning on the light night after night—Gorwin friends with Joland—nobody knowing the combination of that safe—all that got us nowhere.

"My investigation is what counted. I called up the Newfield police chief. They checked up on things there. That's how I found out the telegram was a dud; how I learned that Joland didn't come in on that train from New York.

"I'm going to dig into Joland's past like a farmer with a harrow. I'm going to find out everything he did from the time he came with Tatson. Too bad that Gorwin is dead. Well, the poor guy probably found out too much about Joland. That's why the secretary croaked him."

With this conclusion, Cardona thrust the report sheet into a drawer and locked it there. He growled something about an appointment with Commissioner Barth. Then he stalked from the room with Markham following.

FRITZ ceased his mopping. The stoop-shouldered janitor sidled over to the desk. He produced a pick and opened the drawer. He studied the report sheet that Cardona had laid aside. His eyes were keen—no longer the eyes of Fritz. They noted every item in the report. Then a hand slid the drawer shut and locked it.

The janitor shuffled from the room. He made his way to an obscure locker. There he parked his mop and bucket. From the locker, he produced jet-black garments. A cloak slipped over his shoulders; a slouch hat settled on his head.

A black form glided away along a corridor. The role of Fritz had ended. The pretended janitor had become The Shadow. He was leaving before the real Fritz arrived. Joe Cardona was correct when he had remarked that Fritz had been around headquarters ever since the days of Inspector Malone. The Shadow had been assuming the part of Fritz even in those dim days of the past. Yet no one had ever suspected the imposture.

EVENING had settled. A shapeless mass of blackness, The Shadow was wending his way through the narrow streets near Chinatown. Past the blackened front of the deserted shop that belonged to Tam Sook, the Chinese merchant.

Into an alleyway that was the last turn before the glowing center of Chinatown itself. The Shadow entered the door of a tawdry little Oriental store.

The place was empty. Evidently its owner had stepped out. The Shadow reached the wall and pressed a panel. The barrier opened. The Shadow entered a corridor and closed the opening behind him. The panel fell in place just as the Chinese shop owner came in from the street.

THE SHADOW had found steps that led downward. He followed a twisting passage that led beneath the street. He ascended steps; then edged to the wall as he neared a barring door. The portal slid open as The Shadow pressed a spot on the wall.

The Shadow came into a lighted anteroom. He pressed a knob on a huge brass door. This barrier also opened. Up a flight of steps; there The Shadow chose one of two narrow passages. Weaving his way through a labyrinth of turning corridors, he came to a final door. There, The Shadow picked up a padded stick that lay at hand. He struck the door. The signal sent a clang resounding through the passages. The door slid upward.

The Shadow entered a room where a solemn Chinese was standing, This man was clad in a robe of dull red, ornamented by dragons of dull gold. He faced his visitor and gazed with firm cold eyes. The brass door had descended; against its background, The Shadow formed a sinister figure. Yet the Chinaman showed no dread.

This Chinaman was Yat Soon, the arbiter. His name was law among the tongs, those strange secret societies that exist among the Chinese. Yat Soon, however, was a neutral. It was he to whom rival leaders came to arbitrate their differences.

The justice of Yat Soon was a legend in New York's Chinatown. There was a saying: 'When Yat Soon speaks, all must do his bidding.' Such was the power that this one Celestial wielded. And Yat Soon, being a just man, was friendly toward The Shadow.

Though ordinary visitors to Yat Soon's invariably encountered blocking challengers, The Shadow had displayed the ability to enter as he chose. Yat Soon apparently regarded this as The Shadow's prerogative; for the dark-eyed arbiter evidenced no surprise as he faced his spectral visitor. Yat Soon spoke, in quiet tone. His words indicated that The Shadow had come here two nights before.

"We have been seeking Tam Sook," stated the Chinaman. "Only I know that the real Tam Sook is dead; all others think that it is the real Tam Sook we seek."

The Shadow's tones responded. The whispered voice put a question in the Chinese tongue. Yat Soon replied in English. In these conversations, The Shadow and Yat Soon each used the other's language.

"We have found a place where the false Tam Sook has been," declared Yat Soon. "Once, long ago, the real Tam Sook had a servant. One named Loon Goy. This servant was given money by Tam Sook. He went away from Chinatown.

"Loon Goy had a laundry on a street near Sixth Avenue. With him is a man called Hoy Wen. The business, though it is seemingly theirs, truly belonged to Tam Sook. It was there that one of my watchers saw Tam Sook this afternoon.

"The word was brought promptly to me. But after that came new word, the belief that Tam Sook was no longer there. Either Loon Goy or Hoy Wen had seen my searchers. Yet Tam Sook had not been seen passing from that little store."

Again The Shadow spoke. Yat Soon nodded before responding. The Chinaman's tone was solemn:

"My watchers had seen an American man depart from Loon Goy's. He was one whom they had not seen enter. They wondered; and to me they brought that word. Then did I know that this man you seek had gone away.

"He has learned that we have watched. Hence my watchers are there no more. Chinese people are easily seen among others when they venture forth from Chinatown. Yet it may be that the man you seek—the American, Diamond Bert—will sometime come back to the laundry of Loon Goy and Hoy Wen."

Yat Soon paused. He heard a brief question in Chinese that came from The Shadow's lips. Yat Soon nodded, for the second time.

"I know that you are right," he said. "No more will Diamond Bert be as a Chinaman. Not as Wang Foo, whom he once was; nor as Tam Sook, who is dead. He will be American.

"It is wise that you should have watchers of your own to spy upon Loon Goy and Hoy Wen in their laundry. Should you find that you must deal with them, you may call upon me. I should like to give the punishment to Loon Goy and Hoy Wen."

A word from The Shadow. Yat Soon bowed. He stepped to the side of the room and pressed a switch. A panel rose close beside him. The Shadow passed through that exit. The panel descended. Through a new maze of passages, The Shadow traced a downward course. Doors opened of their own accord, apparently controlled by Yat Soon in his hidden room. The last opening brought The Shadow into a small, dingy cellar. He ascended a flight of steps and came out upon a secluded street.

SOME distance from Chinatown, yet fringing the East Side, was a district that spoke of bygone importance. Here were square-walled buildings, eight stories high, blocked close together, with only tiny passages between.

The plate-glass windows of wholesale houses were in evidence. One of these was backed by heavy metal bars. The name painted on the window declared:

MARLIN NORSE, INCORPORATED
WHOLESALE JEWELER

Eyes from the darkness observed that legend. Then a phantom figure glided through the opening between the building and the next. The Shadow had come here from Chinatown. He found bars on the rear windows; but he had no difficulty in entering the building itself, through a door that did not lead directly into Norse's.

There The Shadow found a strong door connecting with the jeweler's. The glimmer of The Shadow's flashlight showed an electrical connection in the form of an antiquated burglar alarm. This device was no trouble to The Shadow. He skillfully detached the connections; then worked on the door itself.

Soon The Shadow stood in Norse's darkened store. The bulk of an old-fashioned safe showed on the other side of the room. That box would have been easy for the average cracksman. In fact, its old fashioned style was proof that Norse must deal chiefly in quantity lots of cheap jewelry that would offer no lure to burglars.

Of greater interest to The Shadow was a doorway that led to a space behind the shop. He entered this and found a passage that terminated in a flight of inside stairs. Evidently they led up to living quarters, where Norse could stay overnight if he chose.

To the right was another door. It was locked but unprotected by alarm devices. The Shadow probed its lock. He unfastened the door and entered a little office. Here were drawn window shades that hid the bars outside the windows.

There was a small safe in the corner. Like its big brother in the outer store, this box was obsolete. The Shadow passed it and went to a desk in another corner. Using his flashlight, he began to unlock drawers and draw out record books that he found there.

These showed facts concerning Norse's business. Figures told of transactions in which the wholesaler had acted as agent. The real valuables that Norse sold never came into his possession. There were also pages of figures that concerned large quantities of cheap jewelry. These did not interest The Shadow.

The silent investigator was looking for something else; searching for a prize that he seemed sure he would find. At last, his quest was ended. Dipping deep into a drawer, a gloved hand felt among a box of paper clips. Fingers, unhampered by their thin covering, obtained another object and brought it into the light.

There, held between blackened fingers, shining dully beneath the rays of The Shadow's torch was another of the Chinese disks!

CHAPTER XIII
FARROW'S VISITOR

SLADE FARROW was seated by his living room window. Comfortable in his secluded apartment, the sociologist was reading the morning newspaper. He was particularly interested in the latest story that concerned the robbery at Tatson's.

Karl Joland was wanted for the murder of Gorwin and for the theft of his employer's gems. The police had lost the secretary's trail; but they appeared to be making a thorough investigation of his past. The sociologist studied a picture of Joland; one that Tatson had given to the newspapers. Farrow shook his head. He wondered why the law had centered on this one man. His lips moved as though framing a question.

Then, to Farrow's astonishment, came a verbal answer to the very thought that was in his mind. From somewhere close beside him, a quiet voice responded:

"Because of the disk."

Farrow dropped the newspaper and stared. A stranger was seated in a chair not five feet away. Farrow had never seen this personage before. The visitor was tall; that was apparent despite the fact that he was seated. He was quietly dressed; his features were steady, almost masklike.

A hawklike nose dominated the visage that Farrow studied. The sociologist also caught the glint of flashing eyes. Recovering quickly from his startlement, Slade Farrow felt a steady thought come drumming through his brain. He knew that this visitor was The Shadow.

Farrow was correct. Here, at ten o'clock in the morning, The Shadow had arrived to confer with him. But the disguising features which The Shadow had chosen were ones that he seldom used. He had not come here as Lamont Cranston; nor was he utilizing other physiognomies that he had worn frequently in the past. The Shadow had arrived as a nameless personage.

Farrow shifted mechanically in his chair. A flood of impressions gripped him. Dave had gone out a while before. That had paved the way for The Shadow to enter unseen. Yet Farrow, himself, was surprisingly alert. It seemed impossible that anyone could have entered without discovery.

"You were wondering about Karl Joland." The Shadow spoke in an even tone, his words slow, but clipped. "Your expression betrayed that fact. Therefore, I gave you the true reason why the police seek Joland. Because of the disk."

"Joland had a disk?" inquired Farrow, finding his voice.

"You have read the newspaper report," replied The Shadow. "It includes all the details except one. The newspaper states that Joland discarded one suit for another. It was in the pocket of the discarded suit that Detective Cardona found a Chinese disk."

Farrow nodded. He had read the facts thoroughly. The arrival of the telegram. The time that Joland's train departed. The fact that the secretary did not take the train. Even the point regarding the front light that Gorwin had failed to turn on before half past nine. The story had also included mention of Joland's note, found in Gorwin's pocket.

"I see," said Farrow. "The secretary was a logical suspect. The only trouble is that he is a bit too logical. He might have planned things better, if he were naturally a crook. He might have done worse if he were inexperienced at crime. But since a disk was found in his pocket—"

Farrow paused to stare at The Shadow. He caught the flash of the eyes that shone from the immobile face. He saw a slight smile on the almost artificial lips; an expression that seemed fixed there.

"The disk makes Joland a crook," exclaimed Farrow, suddenly. "It puts him in league with men of crime. It proves him to be capable of murdering the butler. It shows that he could have engineered the robbery."

"Then you believe," decided The Shadow, steadily, "that Joland is guilty."

"Guilty of complicity, perhaps," said Farrow. "Probably the criminal; but backed by another man. One whom we both know. Diamond Bert Farwell."

SLADE FARROW, like Joe Cardona, had reached a verdict. Yet the sociologist, after delivering his decision, began to rub his chin. Farrow realized the existence of a mysterious presence in this room; something that Cardona had not detected when Fritz had entered his office. Perhaps it was that presence; the unknown stranger whom Farrow believed to be The Shadow; possibly, Farrow possessed a keenness that Cardona did not have—whichever the case, Farrow suddenly began to reconsider his decision.

"No!" exclaimed the sociologist. "It doesn't fit! There is something missing! If Joland were actually a crook, he would not have blundered as he did."

"Name the points that impress you," stated The Shadow.

"Well," decided Farrow, "the telegram from Newfield would have been a blind to begin with. Also the note that Joland presumably gave to Gorwin. Those showed cleverness, if we assume that Joland is the murderer.

"What hits me is the matter of the suit that Joland left behind him. Suppose he changed the suit before he attempted crime. He would never have left the Chinese disk in the pocket. Anything, except that disk."

"Granted," remarked The Shadow.

"Suppose then," resumed Farrow, "that Joland had not changed his suit. Suppose he committed crime first. With time short for a getaway, the last thing he would have done would be to change his clothes. Am I correct?"

"Yes," responded The Shadow. "Your thoughts, Mr. Farrow, have paralleled my own. I also recognized another point in the Joland theory."

"What was that?"

"The matter of the outside light. The newspapers state that Joland sometimes performed Gorwin's duties for him. Had Joland—a clever crook—actually slain Gorwin, he would have certainly considered the time element."

"I begin to understand. He would have wanted the police to think that Gorwin was slain after his departure. That outside light was due to come on at about nine-fifteen. If Joland—"

"If Joland had turned it on after killing Gorwin, it would have set the time of the murder at approximately half past nine."

Farrow nodded. New theories crept through his mind. He began to have flashes of thought that came as if by inspiration. Before he could connect them, he heard the quiet voice beside him.

"The telegram was a hoax," declared The Shadow, in his even tone. "It was sent by an agent of the actual murderer. It was used to draw Karl Joland from the house. Joland had time to change his clothes. He actually gave a note to Gorwin. He left shortly before nine o'clock."

Farrow was nodding again. He was picturing the very scene that The Shadow was describing. He could see Joland packing, leaving, anxious to make his train.

"Shortly after Joland's departure," resumed The Shadow, "the actual murderer arrived. He rang the doorbell. Gorwin admitted him promptly, thinking that Joland had returned for something. The murderer backed Gorwin deep into the hall, covering him with a revolver.

"Then, deliberately, at close range, this criminal murdered the butler. A well muffled shot not only cleared the way for crime, it enabled the master crook to pin the deed on Joland."

"By planting a disk in the pocket of the other suit!"

"Precisely. The disk could have been left in a drawer, or dropped on the floor. But the murderer decided that the pocket was the best place for it. Cardona had already discovered one of those disks. There would be no use in trying to conceal the fact that the crime ring is moving. It was better to start the law upon a hopeless, blind trail."

"Diamond Bert!" exclaimed Farrow. "This is his work. He has the nerve to do it."

"Exactly," agreed The Shadow. "Now tell me what happened to Karl Joland."

The tone was not a question, yet it called for an answer. Farrow thought quickly. He knew that The Shadow had already divined the truth. Farrow got it also.

"They grabbed him," decided the sociologist. "On the street outside of Tatson's. Maybe with a fake taxi. They had to make it look as though Joland had fled."

The facts fitted. Slade Farrow was sober. He knew the power of the fiend that he and The Shadow were combating. He realized that Gorwin had been slain in cold blood, simply because the servant would have testified in Joland's behalf. It was that thought that made Farrow ask a sudden question.

"But why did they have to use Joland at all?" he quizzed. "If he wasn't needed on the inside—"

Farrow stopped short as he viewed the unchanged smile upon The Shadow's fixed lips. New thoughts popped. Set on the right track, Farrow was following the steps that The Shadow had taken hours before.

"I see!" exclaimed the sociologist. "Because someone else was the inside man. Someone else knew that those jewels were there. Someone else paved the way for Diamond Bert. That man had to be covered.

"Joland was around when dealers called on Tatson. There was one fellow who came there several times. The newspapers merely mentioned his name because it was in Tatson's testimony. I remember the name. Marlin Norse."

"Marlin Norse," repeated The Shadow. "I called at his store last night. I entered after it was closed. I knew that whatever contact Norse might have with agents of Diamond Bert would be made in his office. That would be the only place where Norse would require a Chinese disk."

"You found one?"

"Yes. In a box of paper clips. I left it there. Norse may need it later."

"It's all clear now!" cried Farrow. "Norse was a better bet than Joland, all along. Dickering with Tatson, he talked the millionaire into keeping the gems in his home. Ready for Diamond Bert to come and get them!"

"By opening the safe!"

Farrow stopped short. He began to stroke his chin. He looked steadily toward The Shadow.

"How did Diamond Bert open it?" inquired Farrow. "I understand that safe was just about crack-proof."

"Someone accompanied him," replied The Shadow.

"Even then it was a job," said Farrow. "I don't believe that anyone could have accomplished it without the combination."

"Perhaps Tapper could have."

FARROW'S eyebrows furrowed. For a moment, he was worried. Tapper was one of Farrow's reformed crooks. Cracking safes was his specialty. Did The Shadow think that Tapper had turned crooked to aid Diamond Bert? The Shadow caught the troubled thoughts that had gripped Slade Farrow.

"Tapper did not aid Diamond Bert," stated The Shadow. "I mentioned his name merely because I should like to borrow him."

"Borrow him?"

"Yes. Norris Tatson has closed his house because of Gorwin's death. The wall safe is empty. No one will be watching it. It would be interesting to have Tapper experiment with it."

"It would. Most certainly. I can assure you that Tapper could open that safe as quickly as any expert in the country. Unless—"

Farrow paused; then smiled, "Unless you consider yourself an expert," he said. "I believe that you could do the job."

"I could," declared The Shadow. "Very effectively. Too effectively. It would be an unfair test. I should like to match a skill such as Tapper's with that of the man who aided Farwell. I believe that the results would be illuminating."

"Very well. You shall have Tapper."

"And Hawkeye, also. I have work for him."

Farrow chuckled. He felt at ease by now. He was thinking of Hawkeye's arrival at this apartment a few nights ago.

"Hawkeye knows who jolted him," laughed Farrow. "You should have heard him talk about The Shadow. He's still a bit worried, even though I have reassured him. When will you need Hawkeye?"

"Later to-day," declared The Shadow. "You will hear from me. As for Tapper, you may give him the proper orders yourself."

"Very well." Farrow reached for the newspaper. He began to scan the columns. "I think Norris Tatson's address is given here. Let me see. Not there—ah! Here it is. One hundred and ninety-eight West—"

Farrow paused abruptly. He had raised his head as he turned toward The Shadow's chair. To his amazement, the spot was vacant. Silently, mysteriously, in full daylight, Farrow's visitor had gone!

CHAPTER XIV
AIDS TO THE SHADOW

NOT long after The Shadow's surprise visit to Slade Farrow, a young man entered the lobby of the Hotel Metrolite. The bell captain nodded as the arrival passed. So did the elevator operator, when the young man entered his car.

"Good morning, Mr. Vincent," was the operator's greeting.

Harry Vincent was a resident guest at the Metrolite. For several years, that hotel had been his New York headquarters. He frequently went away on business trips; but he always returned to the Metrolite.

At present, Harry was living in Suite 1010, which consisted of a small living room and bedroom. When he reached his suite, Harry sat down at a writing desk and drew an envelope from his pocket. It was a large envelope, quite bulky. In the upper left corner, it bore the return address:

RUTLEDGE MANN
INVESTMENTS
NEW YORK CITY

Harry had received that envelope from the investment broker only a short while ago. He had gone to Mann's office in response to a telephone call. Mann had given him the envelope with orders to return promptly to the Metrolite.

Harry opened the envelope. Inside, he found four smaller ones, each of a different color. Red, yellow, green and blue. To Harry, this meant a definite progression. The envelopes were to be opened in turn; the red one first.

From the red envelope, Harry produced a folded sheet of paper. It proved to be a note, inscribed in code words of bright bluish hue. Harry read the message with no effort. Immediately afterward the words began to fade. The paper became blank.

Harry Vincent was sober as he stared from the window. New York, in daytime, seemed a city of safety. Yet Harry could sense insidious evil, hidden dangers that lurked in Manhattan. As an agent of The Shadow, Harry knew that his chief was waging a new campaign against crime; but until today, Harry had not learned the full details of the case.

DIAMOND BERT FARWELL! Harry remembered the crook. He had encountered Diamond Bert when the fellow was masquerading as Wang Foo. Harry had fallen into the hands of the pretended Chinaman. But for The Shadow's timely aid, Harry would have suffered death within those toils.

Diamond Bert at large! Harry could appreciate the struggle that The Shadow faced. In that faded codeword note, Harry had learned brief details of The Shadow's recent adventures. In taking the role of Tam Sook, Diamond Bert had acted true to form. His disappearance from the laundry of Loon Goy and Hoy Wen was but further proof of his slippery ability.

Harry tore up the empty red envelope. He placed the other three envelopes in his pocket. Leaving his suite, he descended to the street and headed for an East Side subway station. He rode to Fourteenth Street. There he hailed a cab and gave the driver a destination. Riding in the cab, Harry produced the yellow envelope and opened it.

A new note with coded instructions. Harry's eyebrows lifted as he read the orders. Here was something new in Harry's experience. Contact work which he had not previously performed for The Shadow. Harry was meditative when the note faded. Then, his lips set in a firm smile. He tore up the yellow envelope and the blank paper. He tossed the fragments from the window.

The cab stopped at its destination. Harry alighted, paid the driver, and looked about. He was on a narrow street lined by dilapidated tenements. To his right was another thoroughfare that was only a block in length.

There was no traffic on the short street. The block had been transformed into an open-air market. Wheel to wheel, projecting from the curbs, were pushcarts that displayed all types of merchandise.

A babbling tumult filled the air. A motley throng of purchasers filled street and sidewalks. Buyers were walking from wagon to wagon, haggling, bargaining with these outdoor merchants. Troublesome gamins were sidling about, waiting for opportunities to pilfer from the stands. But the curb merchants were wary. No matter how eager they became to make a sale, they invariably kept a watchful eye on the juvenile pests.

Harry strolled along the street. He looked at the carts as he passed them. The block was like a bargain basement on wheels. But Harry had no eye for purchase. He was noting the license plates on the push wagons. He reached the end of the block before he found the one he wanted.

This wagon was a fruit stand. It was presided over by a keen-eyed Italian, whose chief duty was watching out for petty thieves. Fruit offered most inducement to the roving gamins. It was a commodity too frequent to attract many purchasers. Almost last in the line-up, the Italian was doing very little business; and his glumness showed it.

HARRY stepped up to the Italian. The fellow turned in his direction, eager to make a sale to this well-dressed customer. But Harry's inquiry did not concern the wares that were heaped upon the stand.

"Is your name Pietro?" inquired Harry.

The Italian stared suspiciously; then nodded.

"I want to talk to you," stated Harry.

Again a suspicious stare. Then Pietro was reassured. Harry's appearance passed his inspection. The Italian knew that this questioner was neither gangster nor detective. Those were the only two types of interrogators whom Pietro was anxious to avoid.

"I poosh da cart around da corner," suggested the Italian. "Disa place, too many da keeds. All time dey grabba da banan. One time dey grabba three beeg bunch. What you wanta say?"

The question came as Pietro, wheeling the cart, reached a spot beyond the corner. Harry was following. He looked about; seeing that no one was close, he spoke in a confidential tone.

"Remember a fellow named Tony Cumo?" questioned Harry.

"Tony Cumo?" returned Pietro. "Sure—Tony, he's dead. What you wanta know about Tony?"

"He was a counterfeiter."

"Sure. I know. He giva me da bad nickel. I getta myself in wrong. I tella da cops all about."

"And after that?"

Pietro hesitated. He eyed Harry with new suspicion. He saw friendliness in Harry's gaze. Pietro spoke:

"Tony, he have the friends. One friend, he aska me why I tella da cop. I say da cop aska me. Quattro uomini—four men—dey grabba me. Wanta keel me, Pietro. Dat's all."

"Who stopped them?"

Pietro shrugged his shoulders. Apparently, he did not care to answer the question. He shot a glance at Harry; then prepared to push his cart along the street. Harry spoke in a low tone, close to Pietro's ear.

"The Shadow stopped them."

Pietro paused. He darted a swift sidelong look; then listened as Harry spoke three short words in Italian. These were words that had appeared in The Shadow's message. Pietro understood.

"He tella me sometime he needa me, maybe," declared the Italian, in a low tone. "You come from heem. You know what he spoka to me. Da Shadow. When he helpa me from da friends of Tony.

"You tella me what Da Shadow want. I do whatta you say. You giva me da right word. I worka da way you want—"

Harry broke in. Quietly, he gave Pietro definite instructions. The Italian nodded his understanding. He repeated Harry's name when the agent stated it; also the telephone number that Harry added. The pushcart was in motion. Pietro shoved it along the street while Harry walked upon the curb. Then, as they neared a corner, their paths separated.

Harry boarded an elevated train. He chose one of the central, facing seats in the almost deserted car. Unobserved by anyone, he opened the green envelope and read its message. Paper went blank. Harry tore it with the envelope. When he alighted from the train, he let the pieces of paper flutter from the platform.

Glancing at his watch, Harry hastened down the steps. He hailed a taxi and rode westward. Leaving the cab, he strolled along Ninth Avenue until he reached a little restaurant. A cab was parked by the curb. Harry smiled as he noted its license number. He entered the cab.

IMMEDIATELY, a hunch-shouldered taximan came from the restaurant. He delivered a friendly grin as he sprang to the wheel.

"Where to, boss?" he questioned.

Harry gave a destination. The driver nodded. Looking downward, Harry spied the driver's card that showed through a celluloid pocket just in back of the front seat. It displayed a picture of the taximan; and gave his name: Moe Shrevnitz. Harry leaned to the front.

"I just had time to catch you, Moe," observed Harry. "You usually leave that restaurant at twelve thirty, don't you."

"Yeah," returned the driver, in surprise. "I was just finishin' a cup of Mocha when you hopped aboard. But say—how'd you know I ate there?"

"Turn over to Seventh Avenue," responded Harry, ignoring Moe's question. "Go up past Brindle's restaurant. I want to take a look at the place."

Moe's hands shook. He nearly lost the wheel as he turned to deliver a troubled glance.

"Remember the night those gorillas stopped you in front of Brindle's?" questioned Harry. "Made you drive them up into the Bronx? Going to rub you out and take your cab?"

"Say"—Moe's teeth chattered—"what are you? A dick? Or a newshawk?"

"Neither," replied Harry. "Neither detective nor reporter. Just a friend of yours, Moe. A friend who wants to know how you stepped out of that mess in the Bronx."

Quietly, he gave Pietro definite instructions. The Italian nodded his understanding.

"The gorillas got scared," bluffed Moe. "They was yellow. That's all."

"Scared of what?"

"Nothing that I know of."

"Then who clipped them?"

"The bulls, I guess."

"Not The Shadow?"

The question startled Shrevnitz. He yanked the cab over to the curb. His face showed pale as he turned to stare squarely through the window. He eyed Harry's countenance.

"You ain't no pal of them gorillas," decided Moe. "I can tell a gunman when I see one. You're a guy that's workin' for—for—"

Harry nodded. Moe knew that he meant The Shadow.

"Say," acknowledged Moe. "That guy gave me the creeps. But he's an ace. If he wasn't, Moe Shrevnitz wouldn't be drivin' no cab today. Tell me what he wants. I'm game for it."

Briefly, Harry spoke. Leaning from the wheel of his parked cab, Moe Shrevnitz nodded his understanding. When Harry was through, Moe shifted squarely behind the wheel. He was ready to start. Harry withheld him.

While the driver waited, staring straight ahead, Harry opened the blue envelope. He read the instructions that he found within.

"Take me over to the Broadway subway," ordered Harry, through the front window. "Then follow the instructions that I gave you. Remember: call the number I mentioned at two o'clock."

Shrevnitz nodded. The cab rolled from the curb. Pieces of paper, blue mingled with white, drifted from the side window as Harry tossed the fragments to the street.

FORTY minutes later, Harry Vincent was in Harlem. He entered a small, but well-kept office building and walked up to the second floor. He stopped before a door that bore the statement:

JERICHO DRUKE
EMPLOYMENT AGENCY

The door clinked a bell as Harry opened the barrier. Inside was a little waiting room with a rail. Beyond it, the door of a small inside office. That door opened; then the entire portal was blocked by the figure of a huge African.

"Jericho Druke?" questioned Harry.

"Yes, sah," smiled the African. "At your service. What kind of help do you need, sah?"

"You used to be doorman at the Club Galaxy, didn't you?"

"Yes, sah."

"Remember the time you stopped those two killers who had rubbed out Heinie Walbo? While they were trying to make their getaway?"

Jericho's face became solemn. The African nodded.

"It was a good job, Jericho," observed Harry. "Then that third yegg bounced in and cracked you with a blackjack—"

Instinctively, Jericho thrust his hand to the back of his head. Then realizing that the gesture was a giveaway, he dropped his massive paw and stared while Harry continued.

"It knocked you cold for half a minute," added Harry, "and the stage was set for you to go the voyage like Heinie Walbo. But when you came to your senses, you heard shots. You saw—"

Jericho was shaking his head in denial. Harry smiled; then continued:

"You saw The Shadow."

Jericho stared. He made no comment. Then, in a whisper, he repeated a brief sentence which made Jericho's eyes open.

"He sent you here?" questioned the African, in an awed tone. "The Shadow?"

JERICHO DRUKE

Harry nodded.

"This office is hereby closed," pronounced Jericho, with a sweep of his big arm. "Whatever you say goes, sah. Ah's the man for any job you want. Ah's never forgotten that night, sah."

Briefly, Harry repeated new instructions. They brought a series of nods from Jericho. Then Harry made his departure. Ten minutes afterward, Jericho left his office, carrying a huge suitcase. The African locked the door and pasted a note upon it, announcing that the employment bureau was temporarily closed.

Through Slade Farrow, The Shadow had gained the services of Tapper and Hawkeye. With Harry as his representative, The Shadow had added Pietro, Shrevnitz and Jericho. Five new aides had entered The Shadow's service.

Harry Vincent considered those facts as he rode southward on his way to report to Rutledge Mann. Harry knew that The Shadow was facing tremendous odds. Diamond Bert, with an unknown number of hidden minions, was the center of a secret organization that furnished him with almost unlimited power.

Strategic points must be watched. The Shadow needed aides who could remain unsuspected. Workers upon whom he could depend; men who could outmatch the underlings of Diamond Bert. The Shadow had gained those aides. It would be war to the finish against Diamond Bert Farwell and those who carried the Chinese disks.

CHAPTER XV
GENTLEMEN OF CRIME

THREE days had elapsed since Harry Vincent's trip about New York. A huge man in gorgeous uniform was standing by a doorway near Sixth Avenue. It was Jericho, the ex-employment agent from Harlem.

On the second floor above where Jericho stood, the large-lettered announcements of an advertising dentist were plastered in the window. Jericho, as he bowed to passers, was handing them cards that bore the dentist's name.

Jericho had walked into this job. He had visited the dentist, shown him the uniform, and had offered to work for a surprisingly low wage. Jericho's broad smile had clinched the job. The perfect teeth that the African displayed were as good advertising as the cards that he passed out.

The dentist had been rather surprised that Jericho had pressed him for the job. There were other dentists with larger businesses who would have paid more. Yet Jericho was satisfied with this spot. There was a reason that his employer did not suspect.

From the doorway outside the steps that led to the dentist's offices, Jericho commanded a perfect view of a Chinese laundry across the way. Hour after hour, the big African could spy the activities of two Celestials who kept bobbing back and forth between the front room of the laundry and the back.

Those two Chinese were Loon Goy and Hoy Wen. Formerly the tools of Tam Sook, they now served the master who had taken the merchant's place. They were underlings of Diamond Bert Farwell, who had visited them in the guise of Tam Sook and who had left their place as an American.

Patiently, Jericho watched. This was the third day that he had kept tabs on the medley of customers that came in and out of the laundry. Loon Goy and Hoy Wen appeared to be doing an excellent business. Most of the persons who visited their place either brought laundry or left with packages.

There were a few who had come and gone empty-handed. Jericho had eyed such persons carefully; but all had passed his inspection. By this time, Jericho felt convinced that any persons who communicated with the Chinamen would certainly be bringing or taking laundry as a blind.

From his post, Jericho had fair opportunity for observation. Nevertheless, he could not see as closely as he wanted. Sometimes persons spent several minutes in the shop; but Jericho had not yet gained suspicions of any one individual.

FIVE o'clock passed. The big African lost his smile as he kept on handing cards to passers. Then, suddenly, Jericho's grin returned. He saw a solemn-faced man enter the laundry. The fellow's sober gait and severe garb marked him as a serving man of a well-to-do master.

This man had left a package of laundry two days before. He was obviously returning for it. But Jericho, sighting through the window, saw him pause and speak to one of the Chinamen. The solemn man held his hand cupped, as though displaying some object in his palm.

The Chinaman stopped as he was about to hand the fellow a package. Taking the bundle with him, he went to the back room; then returned and gave the package to the customer. That was enough for Jericho.

The African let a card fall to the sidewalk. In picking it up, he dropped others. He stepped forward to gather them. Finding them grimy, he stepped into the doorway, ostensibly to get replacements. But Jericho did not ascend the steps to the dentist's office.

Instead, he thrust the gathered cards into an ample pocket of his uniform. He produced a new packet, these cards of various colors. Upon a blue card, he scrawled a few words of direction, with a short lead pencil.

As Jericho stepped back to the street, the customer was leaving the laundry. Jericho did not gaze in that direction. Instead, he spread a fan of advertising cards, flaunting them so that passers could reach for them.

Jericho's dropping of the white cards had been a signal. A man had spied it from the corner, more than one hundred feet away. As Jericho reappeared, a figure came sauntering along the street. The arrival was Hawkeye.

Like other passers, the little spotter paused to grasp a card. But Hawkeye did not take one of the upper cards, those that were most readily available. Farther down in the fan, he spied the lone blue card. He plucked it from the group. Glancing at it curiously, Hawkeye kept on.

He had turned the card over in his hand. He was reading the penciled writing that he found on the under surface. Thrusting the card in his pocket, Hawkeye threw a shifty glance across the street. There he saw the solemn-faced man with the laundry bundle. Hawkeye took up the trail.

DOWN on the old-fashioned street where Marlin Norse's wholesale establishment was located, an Italian fruit vendor was doing business along the curb. It was Pietro. He was finding business fairly good in this locality. Other venders had chosen the same street. There was nothing odd in Pietro's appearance.

PIETRO

But the Italian had business of his own. With the same wary glance that he had used on pilfering street boys in the East Side, Pietro was keeping an eye upon the jewelry store. He had seen a well-dressed customer enter. In natural fashion, Pietro pushed his fruit stand past the front of the store.

The man was not inside. Pietro paused to make arrangements among the piles of fruit. Turning, he glimpsed the well-dressed stranger coming from a door at the rear of the store. Evidently, the man had been in the office. As he pushed the cart along, Pietro saw a stoop-shouldered man following the other from the office door. He knew this fellow was Marlin Norse.

Past the building, Pietro gave the cart a jolt. A box of oranges toppled. Some of the fruit went rolling in the street. Pietro scrambled after the oranges and collected them. It was a signal, like the dropping of Jericho's cards.

From a far corner, a taxi shot forward. Moe Shrevnitz was at the wheel. He came cruising up to the curb near the front of the jewelry store. The well-dressed customer arrived from Norse's. Pietro purposely dropped an orange that he was replacing on his wheeled stand.

"Taxi?" growled Moe.

The man from the jewelry store gave a nod. He entered Moe's cab. The taxi driver saw that his passenger was a man of about thirty-five, handsome and evidently prosperous. But the passenger did not spy Moe's face. The collar of Moe's coat was turned up.

Nor did the card behind the front seat enlighten the passenger as the cab pulled away. The photograph at which the fare stared was that of a fat-faced man. It bore the name of Tobias Coyle. Moe had planted that phony card.

"Castellan Apartments," ordered the passenger.

Moe nodded without turning his head. The passenger added the exact location, which was not far from Times Square. Amid gathering dusk, the taxi speeded toward its destination.

THE Castellan Apartment Hotel was an imposing structure north of Times Square and just east of Seventh Avenue. While Moe Shrevnitz's cab was on its way there, a man entered the lobby of the pretentious building. This fellow was the solemn-faced individual who had Hawkeye on his trail.

With the laundry package under one arm, the man stopped at the desk and inquired for the key to Room 1420. The clerk handed it to him. Hawkeye, who had followed into the lobby, heard the request as he stood at the newsstand, looking over magazines.

The little spotter was well-dressed. Moreover, he had a way of rendering himself inconspicuous when he chose. He lounged about a few minutes after the man had entered an elevator. Then he started for the outer door.

At that moment, Moe Shrevnitz pulled up in front of the Castellan. Hawkeye, about to go through the revolving door, gained a glimpse of the alighting passenger. Acting on a hunch, the spotter strolled back to the newsstand. He was buying a magazine when Joe's passenger entered.

"Fourteen twenty," said the man, as he approached the desk. "The key, please."

"Just gave it to your man," replied the clerk. "He went upstairs, Mr. Agland."

"All right," responded the arrival. "Thanks. I hadn't expected Hubert back so soon. I sent him out on errands this afternoon."

Hawkeye took a good look at Agland as the man swaggered to the elevator. Then the spotter moved from the lobby. He had a call to make; he decided to use an outside telephone. He wanted to report to Slade Farrow that Hubert, a suspicious visitor at the laundry, was in the employ of a man named Agland, who lived in Suite 1420 at the Castellan.

When Hawkeye went by, a taximan was talking to the door attendant. It was Moe Shrevnitz; but Hawkeye did not know him. As yet, Hawkeye had contacted only with Jericho. Hawkeye kept on his way. Moe, remaining, made an explanation to the doorman.

"That guy that just went in," said Moe. "He had half a buck comin' to him in change. He walked away before I could give it to him."

"He must have meant it as a tip," replied the doorman. "He has plenty of money."

"It ain't everybody who hands out half a buck these days," observed Moe. "I'd like to carry that bird in my cab again. Who is he, anyway?"

"His name is Monte Agland," replied the doorman, responding to the casual question. "A gentleman of leisure. He lives here at the Castellan. Mr. Agland and his valet, Hubert."

Moe stepped back into his cab. He drove away, turned a corner and parked in front of a cigar store. From there, he called the number that Harry Vincent had given him. He put in his report to the quiet speaker that replied. Receiving new orders, Moe reentered his cab, circled the block and drew up within view of the Castellan Apartments.

Meanwhile, Hawkeye was returning. Spying a cheap eating house across the street from the Castellan, Hawkeye went in and took a table by the window. It was dinner time. Hungrily, Hawkeye ordered a meal. He stalled with his food; and while he dawdled, he kept a watchful eye on all who came and went from the apartment hotel.

UP in Suite 1420, Monte Agland was talking to Hubert. He was questioning the valet about the errands that he had performed that afternoon. Strolling into his living room, Agland noted the package of laundry.

"The laundry," he remarked in a casual tone, "I had almost forgotten that it was on your list, Hubert. By the way, do you have that disk I gave you?"

"Certainly, sir," replied the valet. "Here it is. I showed it to the Chinaman as you told me. May I ask, sir, just what was its purpose?"

"Just a business custom among the Chinese," laughed Agland. "I've dealt with a great many of them. They give these disks to good customers. No Chinaman will ever overcharge any one who carries such a token."

"An odd custom, sir. I recall now that the Chinaman added a special ticket to your package. That red strip of paper on the bundle. Maybe you noticed it, sir."

Agland nodded. Hubert went into another room. Agland opened the package. He dropped the slip on a desk, picked up two blotters and laid them like ruled edges, to hide portions of the Chinese characters. He chuckled; then crumpled the slip and tossed it in the wastebasket.

THERE was a ring at the door of the apartment. Hubert answered the call to admit a well-dressed visitor. The man removed a muffler that was about his chin. He took off a hat with low-turned brim. He stepped into the living room, where Monte Agland greeted him. Agland dismissed Hubert and closed the door.

In routine fashion, Agland and his visitor displayed a common token. Agland showed the disk that he had taken back from Hubert. The visitor also produced a Chinese disk.

"This mug that works for you," he said. "You haven't told him anything at all?"

"Hubert?" inquired Agland, with a laugh. "Not a chance. The less he knows, the better."

"He doesn't even know who I am?" asked the visitor.

"Not a chance," chuckled Agland. "Say—wouldn't I be a dub to let him know that Ruke Perrin came up here to see me."

"Think he'd recognize my name?"

"Probably. You're pretty well known, Ruke, even though you do keep your rackets undercover.

But there's not many people who have ever seen you—outside of those in the rackets—so it's safe enough for you to come here anonymously."

"You're right, Monte," agreed Ruke. "There wouldn't be any gorillas hanging around this swell joint. But let's get down to business. Any word from Diamond Bert?"

"Yes. The job is set for tonight."

"Good. I'll have the mob there."

A pause while they lighted cigarettes. Then Ruke made a casual remark.

"Diamond Bert is smart," said the racketeer. "I can't figure yet how he pulled that job at Tatson's."

"You were there, weren't you?" inquired Monte.

"Sure," replied Ruke, "but not on the inside. Diamond Bert had a fellow with him, but I didn't get a good look at the guy. I was outside with the mob, grabbing Joland."

"You took Joland away?"

"Yeah, but Diamond Bert picked him up afterward. I guess he's got him now. Say—Diamond Bert is a slick customer when it comes to picking hideouts."

"Agreed. I haven't an idea where he is located. I send him messages in laundry bundles and get them back the same way. That's all I know."

"Not quite," put in Ruke, with a grin. "You've seen the fellow who gave you the dope on Tatson; and on this job tonight."

"You mean Norse," returned Monte. "Of course I've seen him. I put those ads in the newspapers, so Diamond Bert could read them while he was in stir. But that's all I've done. You had your job, too."

"Shipping him those pigeons?" quizzed Ruke. "What of it? I didn't know where the birds came from, did I? They were shipped to me first off. When Diamond Bert let them out from the big house, they flew back to the starting point.

"Say—you and I may be big wheels in the machine that Diamond Bert's got, but there's plenty of other wheels turning us. That's the way I like it. I'll bet there's not one guy in the whole works that could queer the racket if he squawked.

"Take that safe at Tatson's. How did Diamond Bert bust it? Don't ask me. How's he going to crack this box at Lewkesbury's tonight? I can't guess. It's a hundred percent straight through, this racket. I'm for it. All I was figuring is—what happens after tonight?"

"I don't know yet," admitted Monte. "All I can tell you is that Norse is out of the picture. He's got nothing else worthwhile. But I'm playing a bet of my own. If it comes through, it will be the best of the lot."

"Here's hoping," grinned Ruke. He tossed his cigarette in a stand. "Well, I'm on my way. I'll see you later, Monte. Unless you want to phone me."

"Meetings are better," decided Monte, "unless things get hot. I'll let you know if we have to lay low. But if it keeps on smooth like it has been, we won't have any worries."

Ruke Perrin arose and strolled from the apartment. Monte Agland called Hubert. The valet appeared, bringing tuxedo, shoes and shirt. He carried the garments into a dressing room. Monte Agland changed attire with a swiftness that showed he was accustomed to formal dress.

Ten minutes later, Monte left his apartment. He descended to the lobby, whistling softly as he rode down in the elevator. The tips of Monte Agland's fingers were in the pockets of his vest. Whistling ceased and a smile showed on the man's lips as his right fingers encountered metal.

Safely in Monte's pocket was the token that marked him as a man of crime. But to him, it was a talisman that brought wealth and luxury. A willing underling of Diamond Bert, Monte Agland was as dangerous a crook as any who carried a Chinese disk.

CHAPTER XVI
CRIME'S TRAIL

HAWKEYE was not at the restaurant window when Monte Agland reached the street. From his vantage point, the little watcher had spied Ruke Perrin when the racketeer had entered. Despite Ruke's muffled garb, Hawkeye had recognized his features beneath the light of the marquee that fronted the Castellan Apartments.

Hawkeye had put in another telephone call. He had received orders to trail Ruke Perrin. When the confident racketeer had reappeared upon the street, Hawkeye had followed him. Hence this crafty trailer was not available when Monte appeared.

But there was another of The Shadow's new aides on duty. A cab swung across the street, cut in front of a second taxi and was the first to reach the curb when the doorman gave a signal. Monte Agland stepped into the cab and named his destination as an uptown nightclub.

Monte did not see the face of the muffled driver. Hence for the second time, he failed to spy the features of Moe Shrevnitz. Monte had no idea that he was riding in the same cab that had brought him from Norse's. The card in back of the front seat did not enlighten him. Moe had changed the card again.

This time the license showed a long, dark face. The name printed on the card was Pedro Aldaban. Monte noted the name; then forgot it. He settled back in the seat and lighted a cigarette.

In recounting this story, The Shadow illustrated his method by showing me the message, reproduced above. By holding a blotter over the right half of the Chinese characters, the word "Tonight" is readily deciphered. A copy of this message appears as part of the cover of this issue of *The Shadow Magazine*.

Maxwell Grant

BACK at the Castellan, a new arrival was entering the lobby. It was the same personage whom Slade Farrow had met a few days before. The unknown stranger with the immobile visage, whose discourse had marked him as The Shadow. Clad in light overcoat and wearing a soft gray hat, this arrival passed as a visitor who might be calling upon any of the many dwellers in the Castellan.

The Shadow stepped from the elevator when he reached the fourteenth floor. Moving into a gloomy end of the hallway, he underwent a strange transformation. His light overcoat dropped away, to reveal a tuxedo-clad figure. The gray hat rolled into a compact bundle; then deft hands twisted the overcoat about it.

From beneath The Shadow's coat had appeared a flexible bag, shaped like a briefcase. Its snap came open. Cloak and hat appeared. Stooping, The Shadow swept these garments to his shoulders and head. He dropped his light overcoat and briefcase into a space behind the hallway radiator.

As he donned black gloves, The Shadow moved toward a corridor. A creature of invisibility, he arrived at the door of 1420. Here, he produced a blackened pick and probed the lock. He opened the door and stepped into a little anteroom.

The Shadow knew that Monte Agland had left. He had seen Moe Shrevnitz pick up a passenger who answered Monte's description. Until another report came from Moe, The Shadow could best use his time investigating this apartment.

Keen eyes saw Hubert walking across the living room. The servant was carrying out the contents of the laundry package. He did not return to the living room. The Shadow entered. He examined the wrapper that had contained the laundry. It passed his inspection.

Keen eyes glanced toward the wastebasket. There The Shadow saw the crumpled paper. He produced the Chinese laundry ticket and smoothed it out upon the desk. The Shadow's eyes gleamed as they studied the characters. These were not genuine Chinese, though the ordinary observer might have taken them as such.

Promptly, The Shadow duplicated Monte Agland's action with the blotters. He obscured portions of the fake Chinese characters. Those that remained spelled an English word from top to bottom. The oddly inscribed letters stated: "Tonight."

With a gloved hand, The Shadow crumpled the paper. He wheeled away and with a sweeping gesture sent the wadded paper toward the wastebasket. It was still in air when Hubert entered. The servant failed to see the wad as it dropped lightly into the basket, tossed from a distance of eight feet.

Nor did Hubert see The Shadow. With his whirl, the intruder had reached a gloomy corner of the room. He became completely motionless, a strange, blackened shape that the valet failed to observe. Hubert picked up the ash stand and carried it into the kitchenette, intending to empty it. The Shadow glided across the living room.

Knowing that Hubert might return, The Shadow saw no time for further search. Moreover, he had learned the most important news that he could have gained. The Shadow knew that "Tonight" meant coming crime. He had learned of Ruke Perrin's arrival at the Castellan. He knew that Ruke was gone, even though he had not yet received Hawkeye's next report.

For The Shadow had divined that Ruke's business here was with Monte Agland. Both were agents of Diamond Bert. Both had been trailed and must be watched. That work could belong to The Shadow's aides. Tonight, crime was due; and at the first inkling of its location, The Shadow must head for the spot.

By the elevators, The Shadow reclaimed his coat, hat and briefcase. He completed another rapid change. He was standing in wait for an elevator when other persons put in their appearance. Reaching the street in his guise of an ordinary person, The Shadow strolled a half block and entered Lamont Cranston's limousine. Through the speaking tube, he ordered the waiting chauffeur to take him to another part of the city.

THE next manifestation of The Shadow's presence came shortly afterward, in the sanctum. There, The Shadow received prompt reports from Burbank. Moe Shrevnitz had dropped Monte Agland at the Taussig Cafe, a small but prosperous nightclub on Seventh Avenue.

Hawkeye had trailed Ruke Perrin. The racketeer had made a telephone call from a cigar store pay station. Hawkeye had caught a few words by listening in from the adjoining booth. He had heard Ruke tell some one to pick him up near Brindle's Restaurant, in twenty minutes.

BURBANK had handled each of these matters in accordance with an emergency schedule which The Shadow had provided. The contact man had called Harry Vincent, dispatching him to the Taussig Cafe, there to observe Monte Agland, while Moe Shrevnitz remained parked outside.

Then Burbank had called Cliff Marsland, ordering him to drive his coupe to the vicinity of Brindle's, whither Hawkeye had gone to keep on Ruke Perrin's trail. Hardly had Burbank finished giving this information to The Shadow when he announced that a new report was coming over the wire. There was a pause. Then Burbank's steady voice resumed; but its tempo had become swifter.

"Car has picked up Ruke," announced the contact man. "Hawkeye, close by, heard instructions. Ruke told the driver to drive to the home of Nicholas Lewkesbury, on Long Island. Marsland has contacted with Hawkeye. Instructions awaited."

"Report received," whispered The Shadow, by the blue light of the sanctum. "Instructions: Marsland and Hawkeye to follow. Await further orders at Lewkesbury's."

"Instructions received," came Burbank's answer.

The blue light clicked out. The Shadow's cloak swished in the darkness of the sanctum. Crime tonight! Through Hawkeye's craft, The Shadow had learned the location. He had dispatched Cliff and Hawkeye, knowing that they could reach the place before him. But The Shadow, too, was departing for the common goal.

SOMETIME after The Shadow's departure, a speedy coupe was rolling along a boulevard on Long Island. Cliff Marsland was at the wheel of the car. Beside him was Hawkeye. The little trailer was chuckling.

"Say, Cliff," he said. "I've knowed you off an' on for a long while. But it never hit me that you was playin' straight. I got a boss that's a prince—fellow named Slade Farrow—an' when he told me to be on the lookout for you, I thought he meant to look out for you.

"You could have blackjacked me with a toothpick when the boss says that I'm to work with you, that you're in this game to nab Diamond Bert. Then after I call the boss up by Brindle's, to tell him where Ruke Perrin is headin', you pop up with this buggy an' say to climb in.

"But listen, Cliff. There's four gorillas in that bus with Ruke. An' I figure that ain't all. I'll bet there'll be another boatload of 'em when we get to this place of Lewkesbury's. We can't crack an' outfit like that—just you an' I—"

"We'll do our share," interposed Cliff.

"Listen," rejoined Hawkeye. "Don't think I ain't game. I can handle a rod when you're ready. What I was thinkin' is we ought to pile in on 'em as soon as we get there, if we get a chance."

"We'll see," said Cliff. "I know you can use your gat, Hawkeye. Leave it up to me."

"O.K."

Cliff made a turn. He came to the gates of a large estate. Nicholas Lewkesbury's was one of the showplaces in this part of Long Island. Iron fences stretched from either side of the gate. Cliff picked a vacant space among some trees on the other side of the road. He drove the coupe in there and parked. Hawkeye followed Cliff to the ground.

"Where d'you think them mugs went?" inquired Hawkeye, from the darkness. "Inside the gates?"

"I doubt that they went through the gates," responded Cliff, in a whisper, "but it's a safe bet that they're on the other side of the picket fence. That's where we're going."

They climbed the fence and made their way up through shrubbery along a slope. They approached the side of a lighted mansion. Though the night was cool, it was evidently warm inside the house, for windows were open and voices could be heard. Nicholas Lewkesbury was entertaining guests.

There was no sign of Ruke Perrin and his mob. Cliff and Hawkeye crept forward toward the lighted windows, which were at the front of the house. As they approached, laughter ceased beyond the opened windows. Cliff caught the sound of suppressed cries. Then came silence that was broken only by a muffled, incoherent growl.

Before Cliff could stop Hawkeye, the little man had scrambled forward. He had gained the edge of the porch and was up it like a monkey. Cliff could see him peering through a window; then Hawkeye dropped and came scudding back.

"Ruke an' the outfit," whispered Hawkeye. "Eight of 'em, I counted. They must have come in from the front. They got about twenty people covered, includin' the servants. All in one great big room."

"Any action?"

"No. Just holdin' the crowd there. I don't get it, Cliff. Say—if we came up on that porch, we could bust in on Ruke an' his mob. Give it to 'em good an' hard—"

"Two against eight?"

"We could smear 'em." Hawkeye flashed a revolver in the gloom close by the house. "You an' me, Cliff—"

"But what about the people in the house?" interposed Cliff. "Some of them might get bumped."

"That's right," admitted Hawkeye. "Say—"

He paused and gripped Cliff's arm. Off by the rear of the house, Hawkeye had caught the sound of an opening door. Other intruders were on these grounds. A minute passed. Suddenly, Hawkeye detected a glimmer from above. He pointed upward.

"Look, Cliff!" he whispered. "Right over us. Light comin' through barred windows. You know what that means? I'll tell you. It's a strongroom!

"I know who just sneaked in from the back. Diamond Bert, an' maybe somebody with him. They're after swag, workin' on their own, while Ruke an' his outfit is keepin' the folks in order. That's the lay, Cliff—sure enough—"

Hawkeye rose to his feet. He was starting toward the rear of the house, expecting Cliff to follow. Suddenly, Hawkeye realized he was alone. Stopping, he fancied that he heard a sinister hiss from the spot where he had left Cliff. Hawkeye paused longer. Someone was speaking to Cliff Marsland; someone whose shape Hawkeye could not see.

The Shadow!

SEIZED by a weird spell, Hawkeye crouched. From close beside him came a faint swish, as of a moving cloak. Hawkeye, who had once boasted that he could spot The Shadow, was numbed by the sense of a mysterious presence. Something was passing him in the dark—something that he could not discern; that he could no longer hear.

Hawkeye realized suddenly that The Shadow had taken up the task of trapping Diamond Bert. The Shadow had made for that door just past the edge of the house. Lingering, Hawkeye could hear Cliff's whisper from the side of the porch. Hawkeye crept in that direction.

"We're going up on the porch," Cliff told him, in an undertone. "New orders. We're to hold back; to see that nobody gets hurt in there."

"I get you," muttered Hawkeye. "Somebody else is gettin' Diamond Bert."

"Right," responded Cliff.

He was climbing the porch. Hawkeye followed. They reached a pair of double doors that were ajar. Crouched, with guns in readiness, they could see the entire situation.

From the front end of the room, Ruke Perrin and his mobsters were covering Nicholas Lewkesbury and the guests. Ruke and his crew were masked; but Cliff and Hawkeye knew the leader by the tuxedo he was wearing. The guests, huddled in the rear end of the room, were standing fearful. Men in evening clothes were pale, clenching their upraised fists. Gowned women were trembling at the sight of mobster guns.

"I'd like to plug that egg," mumbled Hawkeye. "It's Ruke Perrin, the dirty louse—"

"Easy," whispered Cliff. "You'll get your chance, maybe."

The words were prophetic. At that instant, one of the covered men looked upward. A portly, baldheaded fellow, he had heard sounds from the floor above. Closest to a side door of the room, the portly man moved in that direction.

"Hold it, there," ordered Ruke, in a growl. "If you move, Lewkesbury, we'll fire. At the whole bunch—"

The warning went unheeded. Almost at the

door, Lewkesbury made a lunge. Ruke Perrin barked an order and loosed a shot at the millionaire. The bullet sizzled wide. Yet that one shot had touched off a miniature arsenal.

With Ruke's order; with the burst of his gun, venomous mobsters directed their weapons at the helpless crowd before them, ready to pour a leaden hail into a score of unprotected victims!

CHAPTER XVII
HALF A MILLION

RUKE'S gorillas were merciless killers. To these villains, slaughter was a pastime. They felt no qualms at following their evil leader's bidding. To a man, they were cool and calculating as they aimed their guns. Speed was unnecessary with these helpless victims.

But where mobsters saw occasion to deliberate, there were two men who had cause for hurry. Cliff and Hawkeye, too, had heard Ruke's command. Their time for action had arrived. They were dealing with armed gorillas. They acted on the instant.

As Ruke blazed a second shot at the scrambling form of Nicholas Lewkesbury, two reports burst as one from the opened doorway to the porch. Cliff and Hawkeye, simultaneous in their fire, beat all of Ruke's gorillas to the shot.

Two mobsters staggered. The others wheeled, fingers on the triggers of their guns. Again, the outside marksmen fired. This time the mob responded. Cliff had clipped another gorilla. But Hawkeye had failed. Too hastily, the little sharpshooter had taken aim at Ruke.

Mobsters leaped for cover as they fired. So did Ruke. Cliff and Hawkeye dropped to the level of a stone step that formed an entrance from the porch. Flashing guns produced a cannonade as bullets sizzled in both directions through the open doors.

Cliff and Hawkeye were firing rapidly, with no thought of further aim. They wanted to draw the mobster fire in their direction. From within, the gorillas were blazing away at low-lying men whom they could not see.

The odds were against The Shadow's marksmen. Outnumbered, five to two, their cause would have been lost; but for an attack which came from another quarter. Nicholas Lewkesbury had staggered back from the side door of the room. That portal had yawned black when the quick fight began. Now, in the midst of the fray, came thunderous roars from that inner doorway; powerful shots that were accompanied by tongues of flame.

The Shadow, en route to the second floor, had turned back at the sound of gunfire. Arriving to find his aides pressed in their battle, he had opened with two automatics. The result was immediate. The flanking fire did its work.

Two of Ruke's four mobsmen sprawled. The other pair turned and boomed quick shots at the doorway, while Ruke, in a front corner of the room, kept up the fire toward the porch.

The mobsters who aimed in The Shadow's direction were hasty. Their first shots splintered the woodwork of the doorframe. Their second efforts might have been more damaging, had they gained the opportunity to follow their improved aim with gunfire. But those smoking revolvers were doomed to sudden silence.

The Shadow's automatics roared. Slugs from the .45s found human flesh. The last gorillas rolled to the floor, snarling futile oaths. Only Ruke Perrin remained for combat. Ruke turned yellow. As the last of his henchmen sprawled, the racketeer hurled an empty gun toward the porch door and dived from the big room into the front hall.

Cliff and Hawkeye came to their feet. They dashed along the porch and fired parting shots as they saw Ruke legging it from the house. The range was too great to get the racketeer. Guns emptied, Cliff and Hawkeye stood side by side. Cliff shrugged his shoulders and began to reload his automatic. Hawkeye did the same with his revolver.

MEANWHILE, The Shadow had turned for his original goal. With smoking automatics in his fists, the master fighter whirled from the rear doorway and made for the stairs to the second floor. Halfway up, he heard men dashing across the house. Weaving his way through a gloomy hall, The Shadow found an empty room and spied an open window on the farther side.

This was the course that Diamond Bert and his companion had taken. They had leaped from the window to the ground below. The upper slope of the hillside had lessened their jump. The Shadow peered from the window. He saw no one.

Shots came from off beyond the housefront. The Shadow knew the course that the crooks had taken. Cliff and Hawkeye were pursuing them. Wheeling from the window, The Shadow found a front room. Dull moonlight showed two figures running along a quarter mile driveway, spurting shots at two others, fifty yards ahead. The fleeing men dashed off through a clump of trees. Cliff and Hawkeye kept up the almost hopeless chase.

Footsteps were pounding up the stairs from below. The Shadow turned. People were coming, but not in his direction. They were headed for a side room of the house; the spot where Hawkeye

The last gorillas rolled to the floor, snarling futile oaths.

had seen the lights. The Shadow moved out into the hall.

Peering from a corner, he saw Nicholas Lewkesbury and three male guests entering the strongroom. At the far side was an alcove. This was protected by a triple-locked grille, a most formidable array of ornate bars.

"The locks are all right," Lewkesbury was gasping. "I—I knew they would be all right. They—they're fitted with alarms. The rogues—didn't—didn't get in."

Guests were clattering the heavy bars. Drawing closer, The Shadow saw that the barrier was unscathed. Lewkesbury, nevertheless, was working the combinations of the door in the center of the grille.

The millionaire swung the door wide. He entered the alcove and advanced to a small vault that showed in the wall. The Shadow was closer than before, waiting. It seemed certain that no robbery had been effected, with the short time involved. Nevertheless, he lingered.

"They couldn't crack this vault," decided Lewkesbury, speaking proudly to his audience. "It's one I had built specially. A Blefflinger. Just the same, I'm going to open it. There's a half a million dollars' worth of gems inside this vault!"

The announcement brought startled comments from the guests. It told the reason for the armed attack. Apparently none of the guests had known that Lewkesbury had such wealth in his home.

"Half a million," repeated the millionaire, as he worked the combination. "That's the estimate of the experts. There was a wholesaler among them, too—old Merlin Norse—and he said the same as the rest. Half a million doll—"

The vault door opened. Light glimmered into it from a bulb that shone at the top of the alcove. A hoarse cry of dismay came from Lewkesbury's lips. Papers were strewn upon the floor of the vault. Upon them were emptied sliding drawers. Vacant spaces in the back of the vault showed that the massive strongbox had been rifled.

"Call the police!" blurted Lekesbury. "I've been robbed—robbed of half a million. The police—"

The Shadow had turned. He was on the deserted stairway, sweeping downward. He reached the floor below, picked a hallway, and moved out into the night. There were guests about; but most of them were in the big room, or close to the house. None saw The Shadow make his silent departure.

TWO hours passed. A light glimmered in the sanctum. A white hand made inked notations as The Shadow talked with Burbank. The contact man was delivering reports. Diamond Bert and his companion had escaped, following Ruke Perrin. They had apparently fled in two automobiles, leaving a third behind.

Clyde Burke had supplied a brief report from Lewkesbury's. This agent, as a reporter for the New York Classic, had visited the scene of crime. Various gorillas had been identified. Some were dead; the others, badly wounded, had refused to talk. Joe Cardona had expressed the opinion that they knew nothing.

Footprints of two men had been found in the soft ground outside the opened window. Those and the automobile were the only physical clues. Vault and grilled door had been locked after the burglary. The car, Clyde added, was a stolen vehicle.

Then came the last report. This one was from Harry Vincent. Harry had spotted Monte Agland at the nightclub. The young man had dined and wined with a convivial group who were evidently habitues of the place. Harry had learned the names of several men in the group.

One, a bearded Frenchman, was named Gautier Ranaud. Harry had learned from the headwaiter that Ranaud was the representative of some concern in Paris. More than that, Ranaud, himself had talked, loud enough for Harry to hear from a nearby table.

The bearded man had spoken of jewels. He had stated that he had made purchases through the International Mining Syndicate; that a supply of uncut diamonds would be in the syndicate office by tomorrow night, so that Ranaud might take the gems to France.

No mention had been made of money. Harry had gained no idea concerning the value of the diamonds. Ranaud, at Agland's suggestion, had suddenly nodded and decided to talk no further. The bearded Frenchman seemed on friendly terms with the suave young American.

THESE reports concluded, The Shadow produced two envelopes that he had gained from his secret postbox on Twenty-third Street. He opened them and read fading messages from Rutledge Mann. Both envelopes contained enclosures.

The first was from Slade Farrow. It concerned Tapper. The ex-crook had encountered difficulty in entering Tatson's; he had made too much noise on his first attempt. So he had waited until a later night. Then he had entered.

The wall safe had proven too formidable. Tapper had never struck a box like it. He admitted that his ability had failed him and he was high in his admiration of Blefflinger safes. What puzzled Tapper was how anyone could have cracked the box.

The second enclosure was a message from Yat Soon. It was written in quaint Chinese characters, which The Shadow read quite easily. The message must have contained suggestions, for the soft laugh that came from The Shadow's lips was a quiver of appreciative mirth.

Plucking earphones from the wall, The Shadow put in a call to Burbank. He delivered instructions for the morrow; word that must be passed to waiting agents. Methodically, The Shadow made his whispered statements. The orders were of his own making; yet among them came a repetition of the name "Yat Soon."

The earphones clicked. Burbank's bulb darkened. The blue light went out. A final laugh rose through the sanctum; then faded into strangely ebbing echoes, as though unseen beings were joining in The Shadow's mirth.

Diamond Bert had committed new robbery, with double gain. But this time, murder had been averted. The supercrook had fled with pursuers close upon his heels. Barely had he eluded The Shadow.

Safe in his hideout, Diamond Bert would deliver a new challenge. Crime had not yet ended. But when Diamond Bert again fared forth, The Shadow would be ready with a snare. Such was the meaning of The Shadow's departing laugh.

CHAPTER XVIII
MOVES ON THE MORROW

AFTERNOON. A huge limousine was rolling along a West Side avenue. Seated in the car was a personage who wore the guise of Lamont Cranston. Deft fingers were opening envelopes; keen eyes perused the messages contained within.

Reports. A new contact point had been established for the day. Harry Vincent had received calls from agents in a little office that he had rented for the purpose. After dark, Burbank would again take up the duty.

There had been no emergency calls. Harry had given his reports to Clyde Burke, who had carried them to Rutledge Mann. The investment broker had left them in the deserted office on Twenty-third Street, along with a report of his own. This was the one that most interested The Shadow.

It concerned one Gautier Ranaud. Through wealthy clients of his investment bureau, Mann had learned more about the Frenchman. Ranaud was unquestionably the representative of foreign interests. He was here in New York on a bona fide mission; to make purchases of diamonds.

Apparently, the Frenchman had been waiting a favorable condition of foreign exchange. The past two weeks had been slightly to his advantage. The dollar had lulled during its upward climb. Ranaud had gained his opportunity to spend French francs, or English pounds. But Mann had gained no data concerning any actual transaction.

Investigating the International Mining Syndicate, Mann had learned that the corporation was doing an active business. By direct inquiry, he had found that the syndicate could not promise delivery of uncut diamonds for several weeks to come. The inference was that Ranaud had bought all the available gems.

THE limousine stopped in the middle of a block. Stanley, the chauffeur, sprang to the curb and opened the door. Lamont Cranston alighted. He entered a building, noted a name on the list by the elevator and ascended to the fourth floor. There he arrived at the offices of the Blefflinger Safe Company.

When he announced his name, the visitor was at once conducted to a private office. There he met a pudgy, heavy-jowled individual who proved to be Maurice Blefflinger, the president. Blefflinger had just returned from Buffalo; he expressed his regret that he had been absent in the morning when Lamont Cranston had telephoned him.

The visitor was prompt in stating his business. It concerned safes of special construction. Lamont Cranston was apparently in the market for a built-to-order article. Blefflinger shook his heavy head.

"Can't supply you, Mr. Cranston," he declared, "We're only making standard models at present."

"Odd," remarked the visitor, "I was informed that you specialized in safes and strongroom equipment made to individual design."

"We did," admitted Blefflinger, "but the idea didn't work out. It depended too much on one man. He had entire charge of the department. Used to work on each order like a sculptor with a statue. He'd stay here half the night, after the mechanics had gone."

"He must have been a remarkable craftsman."

"He was. Throckton Rayne was his name. Made his own designs for safes and vaults. Turned out the most remarkable grilles that you could ever see. He was an artist in his line."

"What became of him?"

"His health went bad"—Blefflinger shook his head sadly—"and the doctor told him to retire. Too bad; Rayne wasn't much more than forty. He left us a year ago and took a place in the country."

"Have you seen him since?"

"Once. Funny thing"—Blefflinger paused to chuckle—"you know I popped in on him, just by accident. What do you think he was doing? Last thing you'd ever expect. He was raising pigeons. But I guess he quit that, too."

"You saw him again?"

"No. That's just it. It was early in the summer when I dropped in on him up in Connecticut. I came by the place a month later. Rayne was gone. Just packed up and left. I inquired about him; none of the natives knew what had become of him. They thought he'd gone out West."

A nod from Lamont Cranston. The visitor was rising. Blefflinger, also coming to his feet, spoke in a serious tone.

"I'd like to recommend you to another concern," he said, "but I honestly don't know who to name. What's more, I advise you strongly to forget this idea of a made-to-order vault."

"Why?"

"We did about a dozen special jobs while Rayne was here"—Blefflinger stooped to open a drawer and take out a typewritten sheet of paper—"and there's the list of the purchasers. Notice anything about it?"

"Some of the names appear familiar."

"They ought to," Blefflinger grunted. "Tatson and Lewkesbury. Both of their places were robbed during the past week. Maybe I sound like a poor business man, mentioning this fact. But I can tell you for certain that if Tatson and Lewkesbury had bought our standard safes, right out of stock, they wouldn't have had this trouble."

"What was the fault with the special ones?"

"I don't know," admitted Blefflinger, shaking his head in puzzled fashion. "They ought to have stood the test. But they didn't. It's my opinion that putting so many tricky devices on a safe is the worst thing you can do. Weakens it. Lays it open to a smart cracksman.

"Rayne took all his plans along with him when he left here. I thought we had duplicates; but it appears we didn't. So I can't figure what was wrong at those two places. It beats me. But there's one lesson I've learned, Mr. Cranston. I'm out of the special-made business. Anybody that wants Blefflinger safes or strongroom equipment will have to buy out of regular stock."

Lamont Cranston left. He entered his limousine and ordered Stanley to drive him to the Cobalt Club. Drawing a small pad from his pocket, Cranston used a fountain pen to write a column of names. From memory, he copied the entire list that Maurice Blefflinger had shown him.

The writing faded. The names were perfectly impressed upon The Shadow's memory. He had learned another phase of Diamond Bert's game. He had discovered the identity of the slippery crook's chief aide. Throckton Rayne.

DIAMOND BERT had made many contacts during his checkered past. Marlin Norse, Tam Sook, Monte Agland, Ruke Perrin—these and others had done his insidious bidding. But the master stroke of his ingenuity had been the acquisition of Throckton Rayne.

Working for Blefflinger, Rayne had unquestionably made definite use of the time while Diamond Bert was in the penitentiary. Employed to design special strongroom apparatus and to superintend the construction, Rayne had added his own secret devices.

With a dozen formidable safes ready to be opened by Rayne's ingenuity, the stage had been set for Diamond Bert's return from Sing Sing. His work accomplished, Rayne had retired; ostensibly for his health; actually to raise carrier pigeons that could be shipped to his chief.

The quick and efficient robberies at Tatson's and Lewkesbury's were now explained. Rayne had accompanied Diamond Bert on those raids. Other strongrooms would yield should Rayne enter them.

Only, however, if the owners of the special vaults chanced to have jewels stored there. Gems were Diamond Bert's best bet. He had agents who could fence them. Two of twelve potential victims had been robbed. Which would be the next?

A soft laugh came from the lips of Lamont Cranston. It was like an echo of The Shadow's mockery. For The Shadow knew where crime would strike. Tonight. He knew it from Blefflinger's list. Among the customers who had been supplied with special vaults, The Shadow had read the name of the International Mining Syndicate.

CHAPTER XIX
AT THE LAUNDRY

THE SHADOW'S visit to Blefflinger's had necessarily been late in the afternoon. Dusk was approaching as the limousine neared the Cobalt Club. Time would soon bring word from The Shadow's agents. It would be phoned to Lamont Cranston at the club.

Already events were in the making. Moe Shrevnitz, cruising about under his right name, had stopped his cab near Chinatown. He had chosen an appointed spot. There, two solemn-faced Orientals had entered the taxi. The men were dressed plainly, in American clothes.

Moe had taken orders. They had given an address near an uptown corner of Sixth Avenue. Arrived there, the two had left the cab to enter a Chinese restaurant. They had given instructions when they left. Instructions that were almost a query. Moe had nodded his understanding.

Parked in front of the restaurant, the taxi driver

could see a full block ahead. Off beyond an elevated structure, he made out a uniformed figure standing in a doorway. It was Jericho. Moe kept his eyes fixed upon the distant man.

Upon Jericho's actions depended Moe's next step. Moe, in a sense, was a contact between Jericho and the two Chinese who were lingering in the restaurant. A signal from Jericho; Moe would stroll into the chop suey house to ask the Celestials if they still wanted his cab. They would then return to the taxi. After that, Moe's duties would be definite.

Yet two hours had passed since Moe's arrival here. The taxi driver was getting impatient. It seemed as though the signal would never come. Jericho was still visible, but dusk was gathering. Soon Moe would have to count on the streetlights to make out the shape of the huge African.

Meanwhile, Hawkeye was also waiting at an appointed spot. The little man was in the vicinity of the Castellan Apartments. He, like Moe, was becoming anxious. But his impatience ended when he saw a solemn-faced man come from the big building, carrying a bundle under his arm. It was Hubert, the valet.

Hawkeye took up the fellow's trail. Hubert reached Sixth Avenue. He took a turn at the corner of the street where the laundry was located. Hubert's destination was obvious. Hawkeye moved ahead, sidled through a passage between two buildings and reached the back of the house where the laundry was located.

Stepping into a recessed doorway, Hawkeye found a locked portal. He produced a skeleton key and shoved it into the keyhole. An inner key twisted loose and fell. Hawkeye opened the simple lock with his skeleton key. He entered a dingy hallway.

A door on the right proved to be unlocked. Opening it a trifle, Hawkeye gained the view he wanted. He was looking into the back room of the laundry. Almost immediately, a Chinaman appeared from the front. The Mongol was carrying a bundle that looked like Hubert's. Hawkeye saw him open it. From the folds of a tuxedo shirt, the Chinaman produced an envelope.

A message from Monte Agland. One that was to be forwarded. Positive that Hubert had gone out again, Hawkeye decided upon prompt action. Moving into the rear room, the trailer produced a revolver and shoved its muzzle against the Chinaman's ribs.

YELLOW hands went up. The Chinaman made no outcry. Helplessly, he stood there until Hawkeye gave a low-voiced order. Then the Chinaman turned around to face his captor. Hawkeye grinned. This Chink had been easy. The man's helplessness was ludicrous. Hawkeye backed him toward the wall. He intended to hold him there; then wait for the other Chinaman to appear.

Suddenly, Hawkeye's prisoner sprang forward. He grabbed for Hawkeye's wrist. Taken by surprise, the little man twisted away. He swung to aim his gun; but he was too late. A form came leaping toward him. It was the second Chinaman. Hawkeye went down in a heap. His gun clattered on the floor.

The Chinamen leered as they made Hawkeye prisoner. To the invader, both Celestials looked alike. He could not tell Loon Goy from Hoy Wen. Nor did their chatter tell which was which. It happened that Loon Goy had been the first whom Hawkeye encountered. Hoy Wen had been the one who had remained out front. But this distinction did not concern Hawkeye for the present. The two were just Chinamen to him; and he liked neither of them.

Hoy Wen drew a long-bladed knife and held it above the half-huddled form of Hawkeye. He looked to Loon Goy for an order. The second Chinaman was about to speak when a clink came from the front of the shop. With a motion that meant for Hoy Wen to wait, Loon Goy went out through a curtained door.

There was a counter just beyond. Loon Goy came face to face with Jericho. The uniformed card-passer was holding a bundle that he had brought from the doorway across the street. Loon Goy had observed the African during the past several days. He suspected nothing.

"The doctah's laundry," remarked Jericho. "Open it up and tell me how much you want to charge. Doctah's particular about the price."

Loon Goy complied. That was the simplest way to get rid of this customer. But as he was opening the bundle, the Chinaman suddenly looked up. Jericho had raised the hinged portion of the counter. He had stepped through to reach the Chinaman's side.

With an evil grimace, Loon Goy shot his hand beneath his coat. He was after a knife; but he never reached it. Jericho's huge arms shot forward and caught the Chinaman in a powerful grip. Then, with unconcern, Jericho twisted Loon Goy underneath his left arm and dragged the struggling Celestial into the back room.

Hoy Wen, knife in hand, was poised above Hawkeye. Coming up as Jericho dragged Loon Goy into view, Hoy Wen leaped forward, with the flashing blade in motion. Jericho's massive right paw swung through the air. As one would catch a mosquito, Jericho plucked Hoy Wen's driving wrist and twisted it upward.

Hoy Wen delivered a sharp outcry. The knife

dropped from his fingers and fell upon an ironing board. Hoy Wen twisted his wrist free. Loon Goy pulled one hand out from under Jericho's arm and clawed at the African's face.

Viciously, Hoy Wen leaped forward, thinking that Loon Goy could aid him. It was just what Jericho wanted. Hoy Wen's clawing hands reached the collar of Jericho's heavy uniform; then the second Chinaman found himself struggling in the grip of a powerful right arm.

Hawkeye, half-dazed, came to his feet to aid. Then he sprang from a corner of the room as three milling forms came lurching toward him. Jericho's arms were loosening. Four Chinese hands were at his throat. His case looked bad. Backing away, Jericho was gripping each Chinaman by the back of the neck.

It seemed a futile process. Hawkeye, diving across the floor, found his revolver and turned toward the three fighters. He saw the face of Jericho, wearing a broad grin, framed in the wildly driving arms of the Chinese. He saw the powerful grip that the African's hands had gained upon the back of each Oriental neck.

Then, as Hawkeye stared, the finish arrived. Laughing as he leaned back to avoid swinging fists and clawing fingers, Jericho brought his outstretched hands together. Two Chinese pates cracked sharply as they met. Jericho's hands relaxed. Slumping, the released Chinamen rolled side by side at Jericho's feet.

"Boy!" exclaimed Hawkeye, in admiration. "That was somethin'. Bouncin' their conks together. Say—both of them Chinks is out cold!"

Jericho grinned as he surveyed Loon Goy and Hoy Wen. He saw that there would be no trouble from either of them for a while. He nudged Hawkeye's gun, indicating that it would not be needed. Then, with a chuckle, he strolled out through the front of the laundry.

When he reached the street, Jericho removed his long-visored cap and mopped his brow with a rainbow hued silk handkerchief. He strolled back to his post across the street. He had given the signal that the job was done. Two minutes later, Jericho was passing out cards when Moe's cab pulled up in front of the laundry.

MOE'S Chinese passengers alighted. Blandly, they entered the laundry. They looked like two visitors coming to see Hoy Wen and Loon Goy. Actually, they were; but they had no friendship for the two crooked Chinamen. These new Celestials were agents of Yat Soon, the arbiter.

Hawkeye knew that they were coming. He received them with a grin when they entered. He pointed to the bodies on the floor. The new Chinese spoke together in their native tongue. Then one of them went out to the front of the laundry, while the other began to bind and gag Hoy Wen and Loon Goy in turn.

Hawkeye watched the process in admiration. The Chinaman was as capable at his job as Jericho had been at his. Using thongs that he produced, Yat Soon's agent made short work of trussing up the Oriental crooks.

In the course of his work, he fished out two Chinese disks that Hoy Wen and Loon Goy had been carrying. Leaving the two men bound, he went to the front of the shop. Hawkeye, peering through the curtains, saw him give one disk to his companion and keep the other for himself.

There were boxes in the back room. Large ones. When the agent of Yat Soon returned, he called on Hawkeye to aid him. They loaded Hoy Wen in one box; Loon Goy in another. Hawkeye nailed lids on the boxes while the Chinaman used the telephone to make a call.

This done, the Chinaman found brush and ink. He painted Chinese characters upon the boxes; then added a name and address in English. The name was that of Yat Soon. This careful work required nearly ten minutes, for the Chinaman was deliberate. Hardly had he finished before there was a pounding at the rear door.

The Chinaman admitted two truckmen. They carried out one box; then came for the other and removed it also. Seated in a corner, Hawkeye looked on in wonder. He had heard of Yat Soon. He wondered what punishment would come to Loon Goy and Hoy Wen when they were delivered to the arbiter.

To Hawkeye, the two new Chinese looked exactly like the pair that had been shipped away. He realized that these men of Yat Soon were taking over the business. As a reminder of that fact, the Chinaman who had addressed the boxes suddenly handed Hawkeye the envelope that had come with the laundry left by Hubert.

The envelope was sealed. Hawkeye hesitated to open it. The Chinaman settled the matter when he observed Hawkeye's dilemma. Over in one corner was a washing machine. All this while it had been bubbling with boiling water. Steam was coming from beneath the lid.

The Celestial took the envelope. Deftly, he passed it back and forth in the escaping steam. The flap of the envelope loosened; the Chinaman peeled it open and removed a sheet of paper which he handed to Hawkeye. Hawkeye stared at the message that he found. It was printed in capital letters:

IMSOK

"Imsok," read Hawkeye. "What does that

mean? Sounds like Russian, don't it?"

"You writee him down?" questioned the Chinaman, standing with a laundry slip and a pencil.

"Sure," replied Hawkeye. "Imsok."

He copied the word and handed the paper back to the Chinaman, who replaced it carefully in the envelope and closed the flap. Hawkeye watched the Chinaman run an iron over the envelope. The neat job killed all traces of the envelope having been opened.

Hawkeye picked up the telephone and made a call. It was to a number that Slade Farrow had given him. Hawkeye was calling Harry Vincent. When Harry responded, Hawkeye reported. He told the contents of the note. When he repeated the word "Imsok," Harry asked him to spell it. Hawkeye complied; then, in response to a new question, stated that all the letters had been capitals. Harry's tone denoted satisfaction.

The Shadow's agent had promptly understood the meaning of the message. This was because Harry had overheard Monte Agland talking, last night, with Gautier Ranaud. "I M S" meant "International Mining Syndicate." "O K" signified itself: the slang expression "O.K." It was Agland's tipoff to Diamond Bert that the job could be worked tonight.

HAWKEYE remained in the rear room. Darkness had settled over Manhattan; evening was underway. Stolidly, Yat Soon's men were running the laundry in place of Hoy Wen and Loon Goy. Hawkeye was watching through the curtains. He saw a middle-aged man enter.

The arrival laid a laundry ticket on the counter. One of Yat Soon's agents picked it up. Instantly, the customer raised his hand, holding it cupped so the Chinaman could see an object in the palm. Hawkeye caught a flash of a Chinese disk.

The Chinaman promptly displayed the token that he carried. He found the customer's package and carried it into the rear room, passing Hawkeye who drew back from the curtains. Picking up the ironed envelope, the Chinaman thrust it into the overlapping edge of the package.

He went back to the customer. A clink announced that the man had gone with his package. The Chinaman appeared at the curtains and beckoned to Hawkeye; then pointed to the door. Hawkeye nodded. He strolled out to the street.

A cab rolled up. It was Moe's. Hawkeye sidled into the rear and stared out through the front window. He saw the man with the package turn the corner. Moe started the cab. As it turned the corner, Hawkeye caught sight of the man ahead. The fellow was springing into a cab.

The chase began. A cab ahead, with Moe following. Moe's craftiness gave Hawkeye the jitters. Moe would linger far behind, so that the man in the front cab would not know that he was being followed. Yet Moe did not lose the trail.

Hawkeye settled back in the rear seat. He tried to relax; to leave the chase below. He thrust out his arm. It encountered something in the darkness of the rear seat. Hawkeye turned to stare squarely into burning eyes that stared from solid blackness.

A soft laugh whispered in the cab. Hawkeye shivered and stared straight ahead. He was not alone on this chase. With him was another, a master trailer. One with whom Hawkeye must work tonight.

A personage whom Hawkeye feared, even though he was an ally with that being. Hawkeye was riding with The Shadow!

CHAPTER XX
THE DOUBLE SLIP

THE cab ahead had stopped. It had reached a destination close to the East River. The glow of city lights showed the structure of the Brooklyn Bridge looming high beyond low-lying buildings. Boat whistles were sounding from the mist that rose above the channel.

A weirdly whispered voice was ordering Hawkeye to continue the pursuit. Nodding as he stared through the front window of Moe's cab, the little trailer prepared to open the door. Moe stopped by the curb. Hawkeye spied a man leaving the cab ahead.

The fellow edged into an alley. Hawkeye started in that direction, as the discharged cab pulled away. Then, phantomlike, The Shadow alighted also. From the darkness, he whispered orders to Moe. Startled by The Shadow's presence, the driver could only nod.

Then Moe pulled away as The Shadow took up Hawkeye's trail. Through the alleyway, he followed the spotter's path until he found Hawkeye waiting in front of an old, brick-walled building that appeared to be deserted.

The quarry had entered that house. The Shadow knew the fact from the way Hawkeye was prowling. In a little court beside the building, Hawkeye was testing a heavy door, only to find it locked. The Shadow gave no order. He saw that Hawkeye intended to wait. Stealthily, The Shadow passed Hawkeye in the darkness.

Manhattan's low-hanging red glow showed above the house, giving the building a silhouetted effect. The old structure was three stories high at the front; but the top floor did not extend clear to the rear. Jutting back from the side was a brick wall; in it, a tightly-nailed gate.

While Hawkeye was moving from the side court, going to examine the front of the house, The Shadow scaled the wall. He peered down into the cracked cement of an inner court. There he saw a back door that might afford a mode of entrance.

But The Shadow had another choice. He took to the wall of the house itself. In limber fashion, he reached the flat roof that topped the rear second story. There, he discerned iron-shuttered windows that were evidently barred on the inside.

That was not all. The Shadow observed the outline of what appeared to be a large, coffin-shaped box close by the wall at the front of this low roof. Coos sounded as The Shadow glided close. The white forms of pigeons appeared beyond a wire-fronted door in the box.

Diamond Bert's carriers! This house was the residence of Throckton Rayne. Here was the headquarters to which Diamond Bert had dispatched his messengers. The slippery crook had evidently decided to use it as a hideout also.

STEPPING upon the high pigeon box, The Shadow gained a hold upon jutting bricks above the shutter level. Beetlelike, his blackened shape moved upward until it reached the upper roof. Here, above the third floor, The Shadow appeared as a fantastic phantom, his form outlined by the glow above the housetops.

A trapdoor was set in the roof. It was firmly fastened; but The Shadow loosed it. Using a jimmy, he wrenched the slab from its moorings. He dropped down into the complete blackness of a third-story room.

A tiny flashlight blinked. The Shadow found a door. He opened it and spied a dim light coming up a pair of stairs. He moved down to the second floor. There his keen ears detected buzzing voices in a front room. The Shadow approached a half-opened door.

Though the barrier obscured the men within, The Shadow could tell them by their voices. One, who spoke in a harsh, firm tone, was certainly Diamond Bert. The other, whose voice betokened caution, could have only been Throckton Rayne.

"Don't worry," Diamond Bert was growling. "This job'll be the last. Why shouldn't it be? It means more than a million in one trip."

"But last night—"

"I know what you're going to say. We ran into a mess. But that was just a bad break—and anyway, we got the swag, didn't we?"

"Yes. But The Shadow—"

"Say, Rayne, I was a dub to talk to you about The Shadow. If I had kept mum, you wouldn't be scared tonight. Listen. I've slipped The Shadow so far. I'll keep on slipping him."

"He eluded Tam Sook's trap—"

"Yes. But he didn't get me, did he? No. I was wise enough to go to that laundry instead of to Tam Sook's place."

"But there were Chinese spies—"

"Up at the laundry, yes. Sent there by that smart Chink, Yat Soon. Well, I moved out of that place. The spies didn't learn a thing. Listen, Rayne, I've been taking no chances. Those fellows that you paid to take laundry bundles up to Hoy Wen and Loon Goy looked just like ordinary customers. They couldn't have been spotted. That's a sure bet."

"I know; but I—"

"You were scared today. That's why I let you go yourself. You brought back the message we wanted, didn't you? And what did you find in the laundry? Who was there? Two Chinamen. Hoy Wen and Loon Goy."

"I saw two Chinese"—Rayne was speaking slowly—"but I could not swear that they were Loon Goy and Hoy Wen. All Chinese look alike to me. Besides, I never had previous contact with Loon Goy and Hoy Wen."

"The Chinks had disks, didn't they?" demanded Diamond Bert.

"One of them did," admitted Rayne.

"All right." There was a scuffling sound as Diamond Bert arose. "Let's get going then. I'm not going to do this job alone tonight."

"Perhaps I ought to stay here," pleaded Rayne. His chair was grating on the floor. "One of us ought to watch the jewels that we took from Tatson and Lewkesbury."

"Yes?" There was irony in Diamond Bert's tone. "Well you won't be the one to watch the swag, Rayne. It will be safe enough here. I need you tonight."

"Why? You know the secret yourself—"

"I know what you told me; but I'm not going to look for secret catches that you already know. You can do the work quicker than I can—"

Diamond Bert stopped short. He had reached the door. To his amazement, it was swinging inward. The squatty crook blinked as he stared forward. There, just inside the door, was a figure garbed in black. Burning eyes flashed from blackness; below them loomed the muzzles of The Shadow's .45s.

DIAMOND BERT blinked. He was trapped and he knew it. Though his fists clenched, the crook made no move. Throckton Rayne, staring also, began to quiver. A gaunt, pale-faced man of middle age, Rayne was pitiful as he faced this master foe.

The Shadow had trapped Diamond Bert. Trapped him in the hideout on which the crook had relied. Diamond Bert was in a spot which he had not provided with secret snares. Outguessed, outwitted, he was hopelessly caught.

A laugh came from The Shadow's hidden lips. It was a burst of foreboding mockery; mirth that marked the end of a long trail. It spelled doom for Diamond Bert Farwell; yet even as The Shadow laughed, the situation took a sudden turn.

To most men, the sound of that shuddering mirth brought terror. There were a few in whom it inspired madness, also. Throckton Rayne was one of these. As The Shadow's sinister taunt echoed through the room, Rayne delivered a frenzied cry and hurled himself upon the being in black.

There was incredible swiftness in Rayne's wild attack. It came with an impetus that only madness could have inspired. It came with a suddenness that was unexpected, even by The Shadow. With insane power, Rayne clutched the tall cloaked figure and sent The Shadow spinning back against the wall.

His right hand automatic thrust up by Rayne's swift arm, The Shadow fired at Diamond Bert with his left. Rolled back by Rayne's attack, The Shadow shot wide. Diamond Bert dived for a table by the door. He grabbed a suitcase as a second shot sizzled past his ear. Then, with a mad scramble, he fled for the stairs.

The Shadow fired again. This time, Rayne destroyed the aim. Battling like a demon, the man grabbed the barrel of the automatic and jerked it as The Shadow fired. Diamond Bert dodged down the steps. Gaining The Shadow's gun, Rayne delivered a fierce hammerlike blow toward the head beneath the slouch hat.

The Shadow twisted. The butt of the automatic split the woodwork of the door frame, so vicious was Rayne's blow. Then the frenzied fighter made another swing to sideswipe The Shadow's weaving head. It was a murderous attempt; but it failed.

In his twist, The Shadow had freed his right hand. His automatic boomed as Rayne swung. The butt of the second gun swept the top of The Shadow's hat. Then Rayne went sprawling, gasping to the floor. The automatic clattered from his grasp.

From out in front of the house came distant shots. Diamond Bert had reached the street. The Shadow knew that he was exchanging bullets with Hawkeye. Then came silence. Rayne coughed from the floor, writhed and lay still. He was dead.

Though belated, The Shadow was about to take up the pursuit of Diamond Bert. No use for a search here; the bag that the crook had grabbed most certainly contained the stolen gems. Then The Shadow paused. He heard a low moan from beyond a side door of the room.

That barrier was bolted. The Shadow opened it. His flashlight showed a man lying on a cot. The Shadow aided the fellow to his feet. As he brought him to the light, he knew that the man was drugged. More than that, he recognized this victim of Diamond Bert's. The man was Karl Joland, the missing secretary.

Aiding Joland to the stairway, The Shadow descended. He took the side door to the courtyard. As he reached the front of the house, The Shadow could hear clubs clicking on the sidewalk beyond a corner of the alley. From the distance came police whistles.

The Shadow spied a stooping figure. Hawkeye. The man was clutching a wounded shoulder. The Shadow was right; Hawkeye had tried to intercept Diamond Bert. But the crook had beaten him to the shot.

The Shadow whispered an order. Hawkeye grunted a response. He could see Joland's figure staggering along the alley, supported by what appeared to be a pillar of blackness. The Shadow was guiding the drugged secretary to the nearest corner.

A cab popped into view just as The Shadow reached his goal. It was Moe's taxi. The Shadow hoisted Joland aboard; then dropped away as Hawkeye stumbled up. Hawkeye gained the cab and slumped in beside Joland. Moe heard a whispered order from The Shadow. The cab shot away from the curb.

Shots sounded from across the street. Policemen had spied the cab and were trying to stop it. From the entrance of the alley, The Shadow fired his automatics, high above the heads of the bluecoats. He wanted to divert their attack. He succeeded.

Police bullets zinged toward the alleyway, flattening against brick walls, ricocheting from the curb. The Shadow responded twice from deeper in the alley. Again, his shots were purposely high. Officers advanced on the run.

But by the time they flashed their lights along the alleyway, The Shadow had swept far from view. Moving rapidly through, he was heading for the street beyond. He had sent Hawkeye and Joland to a place of safety. His task was to resume the trail of Diamond Bert.

HALF an hour later, a tiny flashlight glimmered on the glass-paneled door of an office. It showed the name of the International Mining Syndicate. It moved downward and spotted the brass lock. The Shadow's pick came into action. The door yielded.

Entering a darkened office, The Shadow paused. He knew that Diamond Bert could not yet have reached this destination. The lock would have shown some sign; moreover, The Shadow had come here with the utmost speed.

Yet The Shadow was also positive that Diamond Bert would not desist from his attempt to gain the uncut diamonds. This crime was to be the crook's master stroke. Moreover, Diamond Bert had much reason to believe that The Shadow did not know where tonight's crime was to fall.

The note had come intact from the laundry. Diamond Bert and Throckton Rayne had made no mention of the place where they were going. There was every reason why Diamond Bert should attempt this robbery as soon as possible. Delay was not part of the slippery crook's game.

The Shadow reached an inner office. Beyond it was a little room. The doorway was blocked by a massive metal grille. Half of this contrivance was hinged to open. The fastenings consisted of three formidable locks, evidently equipped with an alarm.

The Shadow knew that Throckton Rayne had designed the contrivance and that Diamond Bert knew its secret. While he awaited Diamond Bert's approach, The Shadow began an inspection of his own. He discovered that a heavy cross piece ran along the middle of the upright bars. This was decorated with an ornate scroll. It was there that The Shadow looked for the secret. He found it.

The scroll was loose. This was natural, for it had no protective value. But as The Shadow shifted it with his gloved fingers, he found the combination. Up—then to the left—a click and the iron cross piece moved with the scroll.

The vertical bars now formed two sets, a little off-line. Those below the cross bar were slightly to the left of those above. The Shadow pressed the bars upward. They arose together, forming an opening beneath. The Shadow edged through this space, on the side of the grille which apparently had no door.

Within the little room, The Shadow discovered a vault built in the wall. It bore the name Blefflinger. Like the grille, it was heavily decorated around the edges of the door. The Shadow pressed portions of the metal molding.

At last he found the secret. After intricate manipulation, sections of the molding began to slide apart. From between them, halfway up either side of the door, metal rods slid out automatically. These thin pieces were each three inches high. They were provided with finger holes.

The Shadow drew them toward him. Working on ball bearings, the entire front of the vault slid outward, the door coming with the frame. Stepping to the side, The Shadow saw that the vault was double-walled, with these drawerlike segments between. A wide space yawned in the side of the sliding inner wall. Through it, The Shadow stooped into the vault.

He had found the mode of opening which had enabled Diamond Bert and Throckton Rayne to do quick work at Tatson's and Lewkesbury's. This vault, though different from the other safes, had operated on what must be the same principle, a sliding front.

Now The Shadow's task concerned the uncut diamonds that were being held for Gautier Ranaud. He intended to remove them; to leave an empty vault for Diamond Bert. Then could the arch-crook be trapped, while seeking for treasure that was not here to gain.

THE interior of the vault, though high, was not deep. The Shadow's search was rapid. Boxes, files, other objects were moved aside by the gloved hands. At last the search had narrowed to a single compartment at the bottom of the vault. The Shadow opened the little door. His blinking flashlight showed total emptiness!

The diamonds were already gone! Who had taken them? Diamond Bert? The Shadow's hollow laugh was a denial. The crook could not possibly have come here and gone by this time. Stooping, The Shadow left the vault. He pushed the front shut. He made his way out through the grille and closed the tricky barrier.

Reaching the outer office, The Shadow paused to listen. No sound of any approach. Yet by now, Diamond Bert should be close at hand. The Shadow found a switchboard; he plugged in and used the telephone. He gained his connection. A quiet voice responded:

"Burbank speaking."

"Report," ordered The Shadow.

"Report from Burke," stated the contact man. "Cardona has left headquarters. Destination, Hotel Wildebrand. Purpose unknown. Cardona accompanied by Markham."

"Report received."

Ending the call, The Shadow laughed. He remembered an item in one of Rutledge Mann's reports. That was a statement concerning Gautier Ranaud. The Frenchman was stopping at the Hotel Wildebrand.

Some new development had occurred since Monte Agland's message had been dispatched to Diamond Bert. It concerned the uncut gems. Diamond Bert, after eluding The Shadow, must have made contact with Monte. He had learned the news.

Crime was not due in this office. The place where it would strike was at Ranaud's hotel. Again, Diamond Bert had slipped The Shadow; but the master sleuth knew where the crook would be.

A soft laugh echoed within the office. Then came echoes, finally a hush that arrived with the soft closing of the outer door. The Shadow had fared forth toward another goal.

CHAPTER XXI
CRIME STRIKES

FIVE men were in the living room of a suite at the Hotel Wildebrand. Seated in the center of this group was Police Commissioner Wainwright Barth. To his right was Gautier Ranaud. Leaning back in his chair, the bearded Frenchman was smiling as he smoked a cigar.

Standing beyond Ranaud was Monte Agland. Attired in tuxedo, the debonair young man seemed quite at ease. Tall, of rather slender build, Monte formed a contrast to Ranaud, who was short and chunky.

On Barth's left were two representatives of the law. They had arrived but a short while before: Acting Inspector Joe Cardona and Detective Sergeant Markham. Barth had introduced them; now, in exacting fashion, the police commissioner was summarizing the events that had brought them here.

"Monsieur Ranaud," stated Barth, "has completed a purchase of very valuable uncut diamonds. He is leaving for France in a few days, aboard the Steamship Burgundy. The stones will be placed aboard that vessel at midnight."

"Where are the gems right now?" inquired Cardona.

"Here," replied Barth, "in Monsieur Ranaud's possession. He values them in excess of one million dollars."

"And he's got them here!" exclaimed Joe.

"Yes," said Barth, with a serious nod. "Locked in the drawer of that table."

"Let me explain, M'sieu," interjected Ranaud, with a motion of his hands. "You have not tol' our frien' the inspector what I have tol' you, M'sieu Barth. It was not because I wish that I bring those jewel here. Non, M'sieu.

"I have bought them from a syndicate"—Ranaud turned to Cardona—"an' I ask that they keep them in the safe, until tomorrow. But they say: 'Non, M'sieu. Those diamon', they are too valuable. You mus' take them to the bank.

"But it was late, M'sieu. So I say: 'Poof! No one can know if I have the diamon' with me. It was good that I should take them.' So I bring the diamon' here. Then I arrange that the armor truck shall come to get them for the boat. Comprenez-vous, M'sieu?"

"I get you," returned Cardona. "But why haven't you sent the diamonds down to the steamship already?"

"I mus' tell you, M'sieu," returned Ranaud before Barth could make a response. "I call to the steamship from here. They say: 'Non. We cannot take les bijoux—those jewel—until Monsieur le captaine, he is aboard. That will not be until after midnight, so I see that I mus' wait. I am much worry, also, about the armor truck.

"So I say what shall I do? Then I pretend that I am in France; in Paree. I know what I mus' do. I call M'sieu le Prefect; he will be my good frien'. Here, you call him the commissioner. So that is what I do. I call M'sieu le Commissionaire"—he indicated Barth—"an' I say that I must talk to him about one million dollar. That is all I say. So he come here."

CARDONA grinned in spite of himself. He could picture Wainwright Barth speeding in response to Ranaud's cryptic request. Barth, finding opportunity to speak, put in his added explanation.

"Monsieur Ranaud was not at all specific," he declared. "From his conversation, I knew there had been no crime. So I came here to learn what was at stake. Mr. Agland had arrived only a few minutes before me.

"I saw at once that the diamonds should be guarded. So I sent for you and Markham. In the meantime, while you were on the way here, Cardona, I called the Gotham Transportation Company. They will have an armored truck here at midnight.

"I see no occasion for a squad. That would only attract attention. Having no engagement for this evening, I shall remain here with you and Markham. Mr. Agland has decided to remain also. He is a friend for whom Monsieur Ranaud has vouched."

Cardona nodded. He looked toward the table. Seeing his action, Ranaud lumbered to his feet and produced a key. The Frenchman unlocked the drawer, brought out a small leather bag and opened it. Cardona could see the uncut stones within. Ranaud smiled and placed the little bag upon the table.

"Who else knows about these diamonds?" questioned Joe, turning to the commissioner.

"No one," replied Barth. "Except the offices of the International Mining Syndicate."

"No word went out from here?" inquired the detective. "No telephone calls?"

"None," responded Barth.

"I made a call," remarked Monte. "Before you arrived, commissioner. But it did not concern the diamonds. You see, I just happened to drop in to see Ranaud. When he told me that he had the equivalent of a million dollars, entirely unprotected, I thought it best to remain in case he needed me.

"So I called my apartment at the Castellan, to tell my valet that I did not expect to be in. I remained here; and a few minutes later you arrived, commissioner."

"Very good," decided Barth.

"We'd better talk to the house dick," suggested Cardona. "Put him wise to the situation. He's probably down in the lobby."

"Very well," agreed Barth.

"Where is the telephone?" asked Joe.

"Through there," replied Monte, pointing to a door.

Cardona went into a little hallway. He noticed three doors. One was open. Cardona saw that it was a bedroom, with a telephone on the table. He called the lobby, inquired for the house detective and ordered the man up to 1228, the number of Ranaud's suite.

JOE recognized the dick when he arrived. The fellow's name was Lennis and he was an experienced man at hotel work. Briefly, Cardona explained the situation. Lennis started back for the lobby, after promising to keep watch on all who entered.

Just as the detective's elevator reached the lobby, the door of another car clanged. Thus Lennis failed to glimpse a face that he might possibly have recognized. Ruke Perrin, missing racketeer, had gone aboard that car.

At the desk, Lennis inquired concerning new guests. There had been an influx during the past half hour. Some twenty persons had registered. Three had been placed on the twelfth floor. The clerk recalled that one man had specifically wanted a room on the twelfth. But he did not remember which of the three it was; and he had noted nothing suspicious about any of the three.

Lennis studied names on the registration cards. He decided that nothing was wrong. Taking a position where he could view the revolving doors on two separate streets, the house dick waited and assumed a wise expression.

MEANWHILE, Ruke Perrin had reached the door of Room 1216. He rapped softly. The door came ajar. The racketeer thrust his hand into the opening and displayed a Chinese disk. The door opened; Ruke stepped into a dim room and closed the door behind him. He stood face to face with Diamond Bert.

"Quick work," commended the crook. "Looks like we're all set. But let's get it straight before we start. Monte called you right after he got here. Is that right?"

Ruke nodded.

"Then I happened to call you to say that I'd ducked The Shadow. He got the guy that was with me. Never mind who. Down at the hideout. You told me Monte was here and that Ranaud had the sparklers."

"Right," agreed Ruke, "and the next thing I hear is when you called me to say you were in Room 1216 at this hotel. Say, Bert—you work swift."

"I was over by Grand Central," chuckled Bert. "Checked one bag there and took another out. I've got other bags planted places, too. Didn't have time to bother with a disguise. All my makeup is in other bags. Just wanted a big suitcase to check in here with.

"But here's the lay"—the crook blinked, then became harsh—"and it's a tough one. As soon as I'd checked in, who showed up but Joe Cardona and Markham. I spotted them through the transom. I heard what they said, too. Commissioner Barth is in there. He was the fellow that sent for them."

"Three of them, eh?" commented Ruke.

"Four," replied Bert, "counting Ranaud. But we've got Monte. And what's more, we've got a real bet. The house dick came up and then went down again. I guess they wouldn't be surprised if he came back."

"That might mean more trouble for us."

"Not a bit of it. That's our bet. We'll tap on the door; they'll think it's the house dick, coming up to tell them something. Get the idea? But before we start—what about the mob?"

"All set, unless I make a call to Jigger. He's the lookout, planted over at a hash house, across the street."

"How long did you give them?"

"Fifteen minutes."

"We'd better move."

Diamond Bert produced a .38. Ruke did the same. Bert unlocked the door of the room and motioned Ruke to follow him into the hall. They crept to the door of Ranaud's suite. Diamond Bert tapped, copying the knock that Lennis had given.

INSIDE the room, men exchanged sudden glances. Since Lennis had left, Joe Cardona had made a new suggestion. He had formed a plan to be used should anyone knock at the door. Wainwright Barth had approved the suggestion. He was the first to act.

The commissioner strode to the door and rested his hand on the knob. Cardona and Markham produced their revolvers and aimed for the doorway. With a dramatic gesture, Barth yanked open the door, stepping back as he did so.

FACE to face, muzzle to muzzle, two detectives were facing two crooks. Cardona and Markham were ready; so were Diamond Bert and Ruke.

Both sides were momentarily startled. It was a stalemate for the instant. Then, before anyone could fire, Monte Agland snapped a brisk command.

"I've got you covered, Cardona," he announced. "You too, Markham. Drop those rods before I plug you."

The tone was businesslike. Turning, the detectives saw that they were covered. They were forced to release their guns. Monte kept a drawn revolver toward them, while Bert and Ruke took charge of Barth and Ranaud.

Diamond Bert Farwell chuckled. His tone carried an evil sneer. He closed the door and made the prisoners back over to a corner. He spied the bag of diamonds on the table and was about to reach for the prize when a sound deterred him.

The telephone was ringing from the bedroom. Diamond Bert hesitated; then motioned to Monte. The young man nodded. While Bert and Ruke covered the men in the corner, Monte started for the telephone. He closed the door behind him. The ringing ceased; then Monte returned and poked his head from the door.

"It's the house dick," he informed, in a whisper. "Wants to talk to Cardona. Says a couple of tough looking mugs just came up in the elevator."

"Some of your mob, Ruke," growled Diamond Bert. "Sort of clipped that fifteen minutes short, didn't they? Where are they going? To my room?"

Ruke nodded.

"Go back to the phone," said Bert to Agland. "Tell the dick that Cardona wants him up here. Tell him to make it snappy."

Monte nodded. Diamond Bert was growling when he returned to say that Lennis was starting up.

"All right," decided Diamond Bert. "Stick that bag in your pocket Monte"—he paused while his minion plucked the bag of diamonds—"and slide over to 1216. Flash the disk on those mugs of Ruke's. They'll be in the room. I left the door open.

"Have them grab the house dick when he comes by. Tie him up and gag him. Then bring the mob over here. We'll let them hold these cuckoos while we move out with the swag. I'm letting you hang on to it for the present, Monte. It's better in your pocket than in here."

The big shot nudged his thumb toward the door. Monte hastened out into the hall. Diamond Bert, with only occasional blinks to mar his steady gaze, maintained his close watch on the captured men. Ruke Perrin did the same.

MONTE had closed the door behind him. He had reached 1216 and shown his disk to a quartette of mobsters. One gorilla was watching through the transom. He announced the approach of Lennis and scrambled down from the chair on which he was standing.

Monte opened the door, just as the house dick passed. Two gangsters grabbed the detective, muffled his shout and drew him back into 1216. Monte closed the door while the gorillas bound and gagged the dick.

The corridor was gloomy and deserted. Then, amid the brief interlude came the clang of a distant elevator door. Half a minute passed. Something appeared within the corridor. It was a shape of blackness that materialized into a swiftly stalking form. The Shadow had reached his destination.

The spectral arrival passed the door of 1216. He reached the door of Ranaud's suite and paused. Slowly, almost imperceptibly, The Shadow turned the knob. He pressed the door a fraction of an inch, so that the knob remained unlatched. Bringing two automatics from beneath his cloak, he pressed the door with his foot and sent it inward with a rapid swing.

Diamond Bert and Ruke Perrin turned. Their guns were still covering the men in the corner; but their eyes saw The Shadow. Confronted by this unexpected menace, they wheeled to fire their revolvers. It was then that things happened.

Automatics thundered. Ruke Perrin swayed; his revolver wabbled in his hand. But Diamond Bert Farwell managed to zim a quick shot past The Shadow's shoulder. For Diamond Bert, in whirling, had ducked beyond Ruke's body. The racketeer had proven a human shield.

Both of The Shadow's bullets had clipped Ruke. The racketeer was toppling and Diamond Bert, with one shot fired, was a target. But others unwittingly saved the arch-crook's life as they intervened, intending to give aid.

Cardona and Markham were pouncing upon Diamond Bert. They downed the crook and tried to snatch away his gun. The Shadow could not fire into that milling trio. Moreover, he sensed new foes coming.

Shots burst from the door of Room 1216. The Shadow sprang into Ranaud's living room as bullets whistled their opening message. Howling mobsters followed, four in a squad, thinking that The Shadow had fled. But as they swept up to the open doorway, they learned their error.

The Shadow had wheeled. Just as the mobsters arrived, he came swinging from the room. His automatics pumped hot metal squarely into the group, so close that the spitting flame singed the clothing through which the bullets passed.

Meeting the impact of the four-man horde, The Shadow was hurled backward in the corridor. Surprisingly, he sprawled beneath the heap of lunging gorillas, whose trigger fingers were still acting though guns had fallen from their hands.

The Shadow, literally, had been downed by a squad of dead men! His guns were still roaring as he lost his footing. Rolling forms, convulsive bodies, those were the forms that he had met en masse. Piled high upon The Shadow were enemies whom he had banished from the ranks of the living, but whose plunging corpses had kept on coming as a result of the maddened charge!

THE SHADOW had met four—not five. Monte Agland had not joined the wild rush. He had sped in the opposite direction, heading for the elevators, anxious to get away with the swag. He had resolved upon that course the moment that the first shots resounded.

Now, from Ranaud's living room, came another fugitive. Diamond Bert, fighting like a fiend, was dragging Cardona and Markham out into the hall, before Barth or Ranaud could render aid.

Breaking free, the crook dashed madly down the corridor, while Joe and Markham, gunless, traveled at his heels. At the turn, Diamond Bert fired a shot that clipped Markham in the shoulder. As Cardona knocked the crook's gun from his hand, Farwell delivered a haymaker to Joe's jaw.

The Shadow was coming to his feet, hurling aside two dead men who had pinned him to the floor, by weight alone. Diamond Bert, grabbing his gun from the floor, made a lucky dive for cover, just as The Shadow opened fire.

Dashing to the elevators, the crook was just in time to find a car door open. He leaped aboard, covered the operator and told him to let the elevator drop. The doors clanged just as The Shadow arrived in quick pursuit.

Another car stopped three seconds after The Shadow pressed the button. Like the first it was empty, except for the operator. The startled elevator man obeyed as The Shadow gave the order to descend.

Again, Diamond Bert Farwell was at large. Once more, luck had been with the super-crook. Though The Shadow was close at his heels, Diamond Bert had gained the start he needed.

CHAPTER XXII
THE LAW MOVES

MONTE AGLAND had reached the lobby. There was no haste in his manner as he strolled toward the outer door. He was in advance of the news that would soon be broadcast. Word of the battle on the twelfth floor had not yet reached the lobby.

As Monte reached the sidewalk, he was spotted. A crafty-eyed taximan—one who had driven Monte before—was watching from a space up the street. Moe Shrevnitz had delivered Hawkeye and Joland to a physician. Reporting, he had been ordered to cruise about the Hotel Wildebrand.

There was a cab parked in front of Moe's; but the shrewd driver had allowed for it. His wheels were turned away from the curb; Moe had edged back just far enough to allow quick starting space. He was ready when Monte appeared.

Moe's cab shot out from the curb. An approaching sedan squawked its brakes. The cabbie in front of Moe had also seen the wave of the hotel doorman as Monte had called for a taxi. That fellow was starting, too; but Moe cut in ahead of him.

As Moe wheeled up just beyond the door, the other driver rammed his bumper. Moe's foot slipped from the brake; the crash sent his cab ahead a dozen feet before he could stop it. Turning in his seat, Moe saw Monte about to enter the other cab.

At that instant, a bellhop came dashing from the hotel. Monte sprang into the cab and shouted an order to the driver. The startled jehu wished that he had let Moe take this passenger. Monte was wielding a revolver. The driver cut away in back of Moe's cab.

The door was still open. Two men sprang into view. They were agents of The Shadow: Harry Vincent and Cliff Marsland. With one accord they bounded upon the running board of the fleeing cab, just as Monte Agland slammed the door.

Moe swung out to block the escaping taxi. The wildly excited driver, frightened by Monte's gun, swept wide of Moe. Then came shots. Not from Monte; but from spots along the other side of the street. Jigger, the lookout in the hash house, had seen the escape. He figured Monte as a friend of Ruke's.

A bullet stung Harry's arm. Only a flesh wound; but it caused him to lose his hold. Cliff, about to thrust a gun in Monte's face, grabbed Harry to keep him from falling into the street. Harry toppled. To save him, Cliff leaped also. He broke Harry's fall as they struck the street. Monte's cab swerved the corner.

Bullets crackled on asphalt. The Shadow's agents were targets for the firing mobsters. But Moe was at hand. Almost at the corner, he jammed the brake and wrenched open the door. Cliff hoisted Harry into the cab and dived in afterward. Moe shot around the corner, grazed a trolley car and sped up the avenue while pedestrians scattered.

No chance to follow Monte. The crook had made a getaway. Moe's effort had been to save Cliff and Harry. He had done well. Guns were still barking when his cab swerved from view. Jolted

MOE SHREVNITZ

by their drop to the street, both Harry and Cliff had needed this prompt aid.

MOE had seen a rakish touring car coming slowly along the street. He had feared this vehicle, suspecting it was filled with mobsters. That was why Moe had kept on his rapid way. He wanted to avoid pursuit and he succeeded. The touring car did not take up the futile chase.

Police on the avenue had witnessed the mad flight of two cabs. They had heard the shots; suspecting that they came from within the hotel, three bluecoats dashed in through the avenue entrance. They arrived just as Diamond Bert Farwell came dashing from an elevator.

An officer grabbed the crook. Bert shook him off. Guests scattered for cover as the fugitive dived for the entrance to the side street. As cops pulled their guns, two gorillas stepped in to cover Diamond Bert's flight. Revolvers barked. Bullets whined past bluecoats.

Caught in the center of the lobby, the policemen would have been victims of this new gunfire, but for the arrival of a new marksman. The lobby of the Wildebrand was high. A balcony topped it, a full story above the ground level.

The Shadow, hoping to cut off Diamond Bert's escape, had stopped his elevator on that upper level. Too late to stop Farwell, he dealt with these gorillas instead. From above the balcony rail, he delivered a shot that clipped one mobster. The other, hearing the echo from above, raised his gun and fired twice. His frantic shots missed the high target. The Shadow, however, responded. The gorilla sprawled wounded beside his pal.

OUTSIDE, Diamond Bert had seen the touring car. Flashing a Chinese disk before the driver's eyes, he clambered aboard. The car shot away. Revolvers spat hasty shots to ward off pursuers. Safe with the remnants of Ruke Perrin's new mob, Diamond Bert was speeding to new shelter.

Cops in the lobby were looking toward the high ceiling, anxious to find out who had fired those timely shots. They never learned. The Shadow had vanished. Cutting back from the balcony, he found a flight of service steps. He descended toward the hotel kitchen; then turned and gained the street.

Pandemonium reigned throughout the lobby; and the excitement was carried to the twelfth floor when police headed there. They found Commissioner Wainwright Barth and Joe Cardona. The two were taking care of Markham. His wound was serious enough to require a prompt trip to the hospital.

Barth descended to the lobby. Like a field marshal viewing a battlefield, he took charge of police proceedings. Orders went out to patrol cars. A manhunt was on. But it was belated. The crooks had made good use of their head start.

Joe Cardona, remaining on the twelfth floor, was the man who obtained the real results. Entering Room 1216, Joe discovered Lennis, bound and gagged. Joe released the house dick. He sent Lennis in to see if Ranaud had been hurt. The dick came back to report that the Frenchman was all right but moping over the loss of his diamonds.

"The Frenchman says he's sick," stated Lennis. "He looks it, too. Wants to be left alone. I don't blame him. A million bucks is plenty to lose. He's calling it twenty million. Guess he's gone goofy."

"He's thinking of francs," explained Cardona. "Well, let him figure it out for himself. I'm going to get those rocks back. Here, Lennis. Go through this suitcase with me."

The bag contained an odd assortment of clothing. But beyond the fact that the articles belonged to Diamond Bert Farwell, there appeared to be nothing that might mean a clue. It was only when Cardona ran his fingers deep into a pocket in the top of the suitcase that he found something. It was a card.

Joe produced the article. He recognized the name as he read it. The card gave the name of

Marlin Norse, wholesale jeweler. It also carried Norse's address.

"Huh," grunted Joe. "I guess that double-crossing secretary gave this to Diamond Bert."

"Who was he?" questioned Lennis.

"Fellow named Karl Joland," replied Cardona. "We figure him in on the jewel robbery at Tatson's. Norse—this is his card—was a dealer that Tatson had business with. Come to think of it, Lewkesbury mentioned Norse, too. Said the guy was one of the bunch that appraised his gems. Say —"

"What?" inquired Lennis.

"What," replied Joe. "That's just what I'm asking. What. What did Diamond Bert want with Norse's card? He couldn't be going to crack that guy's place, could he?"

"Norse is a jeweler, isn't he?" put in Lennis.

"Sure," replied Joe, "but from what I heard, he handles cheap stuff. When he goes in for real sales, he acts as agent. I was sort of worried about fellows like him, on account of these robberies. So I checked up on them.

"Say—maybe I've got it! I've been wondering who tipped off Diamond Bert about that swag at Lewkesbury's. It could have been old Marlin Norse! What's more, he could have passed the word about Tatson's. Maybe that's why we've found nothing on the secretary, Joland!"

Holding the card in his right hand, Cardona began to nod. He was seeing through the game at last. Lennis was lost in admiration. To the hotel dick, this had been a process of masterful deduction.

"Give me that phone," said Cardona, suddenly coming from his reverie. "I'm going to get the commissioner up here. You can stay, Lennis. You'll have your chance to listen in on something. I know where that bird Agland beat it to. Maybe we won't get him; maybe we won't find Diamond Bert. But we'll get those rocks!"

NORSE'S jewelry store. That was the place that Joe Cardona had picked as a goal. Figuring Norse in on the racket, the detective had decided that the wholesaler's safe would be the logical place for Monte Agland to store Gautier Ranaud's diamonds.

But already, a super-sleuth had chosen the same objective. The Shadow had arrived at the building where Norse's store was located. He was working on the door that he had entered on a previous night. The door yielded once again.

The Shadow entered. He reached the passage that led to the jeweler's office. He picked the lock and stepped inside. At that moment, The Shadow heard a muffled buzz from somewhere above. He waited. Footsteps came from the stairway at the rear of the passage. The Shadow closed the door just as Marlin Norse pattered by in his slippers.

The Shadow locked the door from the inside. His flashlight glimmered. It picked out an old showcase, caticornered near the front of the room. The Shadow extinguished his light and moved behind the high case. He crouched there. A key clicked in the door from the passage.

Two men entered. One turned on a light. The glare showed Marlin Norse, in dressing gown. The old jeweler was wearing tortoise-shell glasses that gave him an owlish expression. With him was Monte Agland. The two sat down. Norse was nervous.

"Here's the rocks," declared Monte, abruptly, as he passed the bag of uncut diamonds to the jeweler. "They're going in your safe, see? Until the big shot wants them."

"But—but"—Norse paused in his protest—"I—I thought I had done my share. I'm—this is dangerous. What if the police—"

"The police?" jeered Monte. "Say, they'd never think of looking here. Listen, Norse, I'm going to take it on the lam. In a hurry. All you've got to do is hold the swag."

"Until someone comes with a disk?" inquired the jeweler. "Like the one you showed me? Like the one in the desk? You mean that I should give these diamonds to whoever shows the token?"

"Sure," returned Monte. "If any fellow comes with a disk, hand them over. But you won't need to see the disk, the way I figure it."

"Why not?"

"Because Diamond Bert will be here himself. He was up against it, but I think he made a get-away. I hopped a cab myself; after I left it, I doubled back by the hotel and then took the subway."

"You mean there was much trouble at—"

"Forget it, Norse. I want to see you put these rocks in your safe. Or anywhere else that you know is good. Then all you've got to do is wait for Diamond Bert—"

Monte broke off. He grabbed Norse's arm. He had heard faint prying sounds from somewhere outside. He stole toward the door and listened. He came back hurriedly.

"The police," he whispered. "Quick, Norse. Stow me somewhere. When they come in, you act blank. See?"

The jeweler trembled.

"Hurry!" ordered Monte.

NORSE pointed to a closet at the back of the room. Monte entered it. At that instant, an outer door began to crack. It was the side entrance to the jewelry store. Alarms started ringing.

Norse scrambled to his feet and hurried into the hall. He made for the steps; then turned. He was doubling back when he encountered Joe Cardona.

"What—what's the trouble?" blubbered Norse. "Who are you? Breaking in? Starting my alarms?"

Joe was flashing a badge. Norse moved into the office, faltered about to find the alarm control. Then he turned off the bells. He sank into a chair behind his desk.

"Who's been here?" demanded Cardona.

"Nobody," pleaded Norse. "Nobody was—"

"Take a look around the store," ordered Joe, turning to two plainclothes men who had followed him to the office door. "Say, Norse"—this to the jeweler—"where were you when we broke in?"

"Upstairs," quavered the jeweler. "I heard the alarms. That is the truth."

Cardona was on the point of believing the jeweler. Norse looked pitiful; too helpless to be a minion of Diamond Bert. Then Joe had a hunch.

"Upstairs, eh?" quizzed the acting inspector. "With a light burning in this office?"

Norse capitulated. He began to talk incoherently. The Shadow could hear Cardona asking new questions. He could see the detective leaning forward, glaring at the jeweler. But beyond, The Shadow saw something else.

The shining muzzle of a revolver was creeping from the crack of the closet door. Then the barrel. The gun was turning toward Joe Cardona. Low by the edge of the old showcase, The Shadow aimed an automatic straight across the desk, between Cardona and Norse. The Shadow fired.

Cardona leaped to his feet as the shot burst and a bullet whined close in front of him. But before he could turn to locate the source of the shot, his attention was turned in another direction. The closet door had opened. Monte Agland was staggering forth.

The Shadow had clipped the barrel of the crook's gun. The slug from the .45 had knocked the .38 from Monte's hand. Numbed from fingers to wrist, Monte had instinctively tumbled from his hiding place. Recovering, he threw himself upon Joe Cardona, endeavoring to seize the police revolver that Joe was drawing.

Cardona fired. Monte did a sprawl in the air. He flopped to the floor; the bag of diamonds clattered from his pocket. Joe grabbed the prize. The other detectives pounded in from the hall.

The Shadow had dropped behind the showcase. As he waited there, the sound of new shots burst from outside the building. Cardona waved the two detectives in that direction. Holding the bag of diamonds, he stood above Monte Agland's gasping form. Norse was cringing.

None saw The Shadow as he moved across the room. Outside firing had dwindled. The Shadow paused in the passage. He saw Monte Agland raise his head and utter dying words.

"You fool!" snarled the smooth crook. "Maybe—maybe you got the rocks. But you—you didn't get Diamond Bert. He—he was due here. Those shots—outside—were on his account. But you've missed—missed out on—"

Monte Agland gasped and died. The Shadow faded with blackness. He knew that the dying crook had spoken the truth. Joe Cardona, unwittingly, had aided Diamond Bert Farwell in another getaway. Had The Shadow remained here alone, he would have trapped the arch-crook with the others.

Yet The Shadow, traveling through outer darkness, delivered a soft, eerie laugh. He was not yet through with Diamond Bert; because he knew that the crook had not completed crime. Those uncut diamonds that Cardona had recovered would still remain a lure.

Diamond Bert Farwell would never rest until he had gained a chance to recover the gems that he had won and lost. Upon that fact, The Shadow was counting for the finish.

CHAPTER XXIII
MASTERS MEET

MORNING newspapers headlined Cardona's triumph. The ace had recovered a million dollars' worth of stolen gems. A manhunt was on for Diamond Bert Farwell.

Up in his suite at the Hotel Wildebrand, Gautier Ranaud was reading the story of last night's fray. The day was dull; light was poor in the living room. The bearded man was seated by a floor lamp.

A rap at the door. Ranaud arose and answered it. He bowed to Police Commissioner Wainwright Barth; then thrust forth a hearty handshake to Joe Cardona, who was with the commissioner. A third man was present. Barth introduced him as Lamont Cranston. The bearded Frenchman faced a tall personage whose countenance seemed stern and hawklike.

"But these, M'sieu?" questioned Ranaud, waving his hand toward the hall, where half a dozen men formed a squad. "Are these detectives?"

"Yes," replied Barth. "Close the door, Cardona; the detail can wait outside. You see, Monsieur Ranaud, we intend to give you absolute protection."

"Ah! You have brought my diamonds?"

"As you requested. Also to complete the case. The diamonds were stolen from you in this suite. We are returning them intact."

Barth produced the bag and placed it upon the

table. Ranaud seized it and let the uncut stones trickle into his hand with the air of a child admiring shiny pebbles. Lamont Cranston leaned forward. The Frenchman stepped back as he poured the diamonds into the bag.

"Mr. Cranston is a friend of mine," said Barth, seriously. "He is a millionaire. He wanted to see the uncut diamonds. But of course, without your permission—"

"Ah, oui, M'sieu." Ranaud obligingly shook the diamonds into his hand and held them before Cranston's eyes. "You wish to see them longer?"

"No," rejoined Cranston. "I understand that these stones are to be taken to the steamship. I do not wish to cause a delay."

"There is much time, M'sieu," replied Ranaud. "The ship—she do not sail for two days. I send these gems to the ship. I go for a trip to Philadelphia."

Ranaud had lowered his hand to the lamplight. Cranston examined three stones that particularly attracted his attention and replaced them carefully upon the Frenchman's hand. At that instant, the telephone rang from the bedroom.

"I answer it." Ranaud poured the diamonds back into the bag. He went into the other room.

"Ah, no, M'sieu," they heard him on the wire. "I have already say that I do not wish to keep this suite. I have told the maid to wait until I have gone. Do you understand? I leave soon... Yes... Yes... I check out. That is the way I say it... Yes, I check out..."

A minute later, Ranaud reappeared, carrying a small, but heavy metal casket. He was dangling a key from a ring on his finger. With a bow, he placed the coffer in the hands of Wainwright Barth.

"I have placed the diamonds in here, M'sieu," said Ranaud. "It is large—this box—so it can be kept safe. You have the big truck? With the armor?"

"Yes."

"This is to go in it. To the captain of the vessel. It is to you that I trust this box, M'sieu."

"Very well."

BARTH nodded to Cardona and Cranston as witnesses. Joe opened the door. The detail of plainclothes men snapped into attention.

"I shall come to the ship," declared Ranaud, to Barth. "I shall see the captain. After that, I go to Philadelphia. Tomorrow—perhaps I see you, M'sieu?"

"Certainly," replied Barth. "You will be quite welcome at my office."

Cardona received the box from the commissioner. Surrounded by the detail, Joe marched down the hall. Barth and Cranston followed. Gautier Ranaud went into the bedroom. The living room remained empty. Minutes passed.

A soft click from the door. The barrier opened. Into the gloomy living room stepped Lamont Cranston. He closed the door softly behind him, then moved easily to the little passage. He noted that of the three doors, only one was open. That was the entrance to the front bedroom.

Gautier Ranaud was muttering to himself as he packed clothing in a heavy traveling bag. Lamont Cranston, fingers resting loosely in coat pockets, stepped into the room. His shadow fell across the white shirts in the suitcase. Ranaud looked up.

"Pardon the intrusion," Cranston spoke these words in a steady, even tone. "You did not hear my knock when I returned. I thought that I should like to speak with you, Monsieur Ranaud."

"Ah, yes!" exclaimed the Frenchman. "You were the gentleman who came with the commissioner. What do you wish, M'sieu?"

"To make sure that your gems are safe."

"But they are, M'sieu! They have gone to the ship."

"Are you sure?"

Ranaud stared. Cranston's voice resumed.

"Diamond Bert Farwell wants those diamonds," came the steady tone. "He is a crook who usually gains whatever he goes after."

"But not my diamonds, M'sieu!" Ranaud spoke triumphantly. "They have been put where they are safe."

"In the armored car? I hardly think so. I should think that you would prefer to carry them in that traveling bag."

Ranaud blinked. For a moment, he seemed concerned. Then lips formed a smile through the heavy black beard. The squatty Frenchman chuckled.

"Ah, oui," he laughed. "You are a friend of the commissioner, M'sieu. You are very clever, You have guessed my little joke. These New York police! Bah! I do not trust them. So I have kept the diamonds here and you have guessed it. When I reach Paree, M'sieu—"

"Paris?" came the quiet interruption. "You do not intend to go to Paris, Diamond Bert!"

Two figures stood motionless. Master of vengeance was face to face with master of crime. The Shadow, as Cranston, had penetrated Diamond Bert's disguise. But not until this moment had the crook realized that the visage of Lamont Cranston was no more than a mask for The Shadow.

"I knew you would come back." Cranston's lips were uttering a weird, taunting whisper that Diamond Bert recognized. "That is why I stayed close to the diamonds. Then I met you. I knew that you were not Gautier Ranaud. He is alive, I suppose, like Joland."

"In the back room," snarled Diamond Bert, through his false beard. "I grabbed him last night. I came back here"—the crook seemed defiantly proud—"because it was the last place they would look for me.

"I had my other bags. I checked in and came to see Ranaud. He let me in. I knocked him out and doped him. It was a cinch, this makeup. I had plenty of whiskers in my bag."

"But your knowledge of French was limited."

Diamond Bert snorted. He shrugged his shoulders as if in surrender to a superior foe. This was his first move; his next was to scruff the shirts that lay on top of the bag.

"Call it quits," suggested the crook. "You're The Shadow; you've licked me. Take the diamonds. They're here. I stuck them in the bag when I came in for that box."

"And Tatson's jewels," hissed The Shadow. "And Lewkesbury's."

"They're yours too," growled the crook. "Here in the bag. All yours."

"And the men who died because of your crimes—"

Diamond Bert paused. He knew that there could be no compromise with The Shadow. But he seemed to hold to hope as he pawed another shirt aside. He stopped, his right hand still, and stared at the form before him.

"I'm giving you all the swag," he pleaded. "Take it and call it quits. I'm playing fair. Here's the rocks—"

The crook's hand came up; with the motion, Diamond Bert swung back from the suitcase. Out from the clothes he was sweeping a big .45. Pulling the gun toward him, he aimed the smoke wagon toward The Shadow.

A runner can travel one yard in the tenth of a second. The Shadow's right hand, which had edged down into his pocket, had less than ten inches to come up, In that short space, it equaled as fast a pace as any human being could make.

A pocket automatic snapped into view, in the tenth of a tenth of a second. Simultaneously a finger pressed the trigger and held it. Shots drilled forth with the rapidity of machine gun bullets while The Shadow's hand moved slightly from side to side.

The Shadow had brought a snub-nosed .32 in place of his huge .45s. He had left the heavy artillery to Diamond Bert. Before the super-crook could fire his big .45, he had received the full quota of The Shadow's weapon.

Girdled with bullets, Diamond Bert collapsed. His smoke wagon thumped the floor. Murderous to the last, treacherously trying to spring a double cross, the killer had received no mercy from The Shadow.

One life or the other. The Shadow had won. A solemn laugh came from his immobile lips as this mighty fighter viewed the dead form of Diamond Bert Farwell. Then, pocketing his emptied automatic, The Shadow turned. Quietly, in the manner of Lamont Cranston, he strolled from the suite and closed the door behind him.

DOWN in the lobby, Commissioner Wainwright Barth was looking about for Lamont Cranston. His friend had disappeared. Suddenly the commissioner spied him. As he spoke to Cranston, Joe Cardona entered.

"The diamonds are on the armored truck," announced Joe. "Ready to pull out—"

Joe turned as a man hastened up. It was the house dick, Lennis. The man buzzed excited words in Joe Cardona's ear. The acting inspector whirled to Commissioner Barth.

"Shooting up on the twelfth floor!" he exclaimed. "People trying to locate it! They think it may be from Ranaud's suite. The door's locked—he doesn't answer—"

Barth was heading for an elevator. Cardona followed with Lennis. Lamont Cranston strolled in just before the door closed. The car shot upward. On the twelfth, the arrivals found a group of frightened servants outside of Ranaud's door.

Lennis produced a passkey. He opened the door. Cardona bounded through the living room, gun in hand. He stopped when he reached the passage and waved the others back.

"It's Ranaud!" he exclaimed. "Drilled clean! Diamond Bert must have got him—for revenge—"

Cardona turned toward the door at the end of the passage. Grimly, he sprang forward and thrust the barrier open. He found a second bedroom. Shades were lowered; a figure was huddled on the bed.

"Got you, Diamond Bert!" cried Joe, clicking on the light, "One move and I'll—"

He stopped short. The figure was not that of Diamond Bert Farwell. It was Gautier Ranaud, bound and gagged. Amazed, Joe wrenched the bonds from the Frenchman. He helped Ranaud to his feet.

"Two of you!" Cardona exclaimed. "Say—"

"Ah, m'sieu," gasped Ranaud, dopily. "The other—he have take my place. Las' night, m'sieu. He have come in to mock me, this very day. Ou est le prefect—the commissioner—"

"Out here," replied Cardona, grimly.

He dragged Ranaud along. "Look at this, commissioner!"

Barth had reached the front bedroom. He was looking at the body on the floor when Cardona arrived. The commissioner gaped when he saw the second Ranaud. Releasing the Frenchman, Cardona stooped and seized the black beard that covered the dead face on the floor. He yanked away the disguise.

"Diamond Bert," asserted Joe. "I don't know who got him. But whoever did—well, it was a good job."

On a hunch, Joe swung to the suitcase. He scattered shirts aside. He grabbed out a bag—the one with the diamonds—and passed it to Barth. Then he found a large box, buried deep. Jewels glittered as Cardona cracked it open.

"All the swag!" exclaimed Cardona. "The stuff he got at Tatson's and Lewkesbury's! He foxed us, commissioner, sending out that dummy box to the armored truck!"

Barth was nodding. He had opened the little bag and was shaking out the uncut diamonds. Gautier Ranaud, recovered from his grogginess, was reaching for the stones, counting them. The Frenchman was excitedly gasping in his native tongue, declaring that every stone had been recovered.

Joe Cardona tossed a bundle of shirts back in the suitcase. He stared. Upon the white surface came a splotch of blackness, the outline of a weird silhouette. A hawk-faced profile; one that brought sudden understanding to Cardona's brain.

The profile glided away. It was gone. Yet Cardona stood staring. When he looked up, he saw Barth and Ranaud still busy with the diamonds. A third person had joined them: Lamont Cranston.

Joe Cardona never connected the quiet-faced millionaire with the profile that had faded. For Joe's stare had become distant. The star detective had found the answer to the deserved death of Diamond Bert.

Joe realized, who, alone, could have trapped the super-crook. He knew whose hand had waged the strenuous battle that had finally brought triumph to the cause of justice. Voiceless, Joe Cardona's lips phrased a silent name:

"The Shadow!"

THE END

ALPHA AND OMEGA by Will Murray

When the Nostalgia Ventures editors first began discussing how best to reintroduce the Master of Darkness to 21st century readers, our biggest challenge was to select one classic novel that not only reacquainted a new generation with The Shadow and his far-flung network of agents, but was also a sizzling suspense story that would cause readers to clamor for more.

The selection came down to *Crime, Insured*—arguably the best Shadow novel ever written—which showcased The Shadow's crime-busting undercover group at top efficiency, or *The Chinese Disks,* a direct sequel to *The Living Shadow* which featured the return of one of the first foes the Knight of Darkness ever battled, prompting him to first organize his urban spy ring.

Ultimately, the most electrifying adventure won out over strict chronology. *Crime, Insured* had the added advantage of depicting as no other story did, how The Shadow's undercover organization operated.

And so the pivotal *Chinese Disks* leads off our second volume.

It's amazing to reflect that 62 novels passed before writer Walter Gibson had assembled his core cast of characters. The Shadow had been collecting agents since Harry Vincent was plucked from certain doom in *The Living Shadow.* Over time, others followed. Some appeared only once or twice. Others went on to see long deadly service.

In this striking story, Gibson reached back into earlier novels and revived several half-forgotten Shadow allies to form the nucleus of The Shadow's secret network. It also features an appearance by Police Commissioner Wainwright Barth, substituting for the familiar Ralph Weston.

Recurring villains were rare in the formative 1931-34 period. Diamond Bert Farwell was one exception. After *The Living Shadow,* he was sent to prison, from which he goaded another enemy into taking on the Master of Darkness in the classic *Shadow's Shadow.* But Farwell had evaded true Shadowy retribution. For The Shadow was not in the gentle business of sending crooks to prison. He usually executed them in the heat of battle. Farwell was a loose end that Gibson decided to finally tie up in *The Chinese Disks.*

Asked how this novel came to be, Walter Gibson confided: "I kept an actual card index of all the characters that The Shadow met, and then suddenly we said, 'What's the deal with this? We're not going to use them again. They either get shot, or else get reformed, or they get out.' But we did keep a few of them. And there was one, Diamond Bert Farwell. After I'd gone about five years, I said, "Gee, this guy's in jail. It's time to get him paroled.' So we got him paroled and he made trouble. So after that, we killed them all."

Thus, *The Chinese Disks* is not only one of the most significant Shadow mysteries, but also one of the most satisfying.

Stories set in New York's Chinatown had been a Shadow tradition ever since the start. A less frequent locale was foreign capitals. The Shadow usually operated in the United States. From time to time, he went international in *The London Crimes* and the celebrated Parisian mystery, *Zemba.*

Our second Shadow selection draws upon that tradition of foreign intrigue. And it has a curious history. Early in 1946, Gibson was awaiting a new Shadow contract and, frustrated that Street & Smith appeared to be dragging its feet, sat down in a foul mood to tackle *Malmordo.*

"I got up Sunday morning," Gibson recalled, "and it was a case of going ahead with the story or else. I said, what the hell. I'll just wait and do some on Monday and say I won't get it in 'til Tuesday or Wednesday, and where's the contract? I was feeling in that kind of a mood after all these years.

"Well, I started to hit some off on Sunday. I said, I'll get a leg up on it, and then I got mad and I said, I'll just go right with it. And I just kept right on it. I didn't quit until five o'clock on Monday morning, And I finished the whole story. I did 20,000 [words] that day."

Malmordo has the distinction of having been completed in a 24-hour fugue state. By a strange coincidence, Gibson turned in the tale almost 15 years to the day that he had completed *The Living Shadow.* Street & Smith did not renew that disputed contract, and Gibson became estranged from the characters he created for two years, returning in 1948 to pen five final stories. But in a very real sense, the series that had finally come together in *The Chinese Disks* culminated with *Malmordo,* one of Gibson's most atmospheric tales of the 1940s.

In 1981, Gibson reread the latter story with an eye to reprinting it in hardcover, and recorded the following candid assesement in his diary:

"Malmordo is fine on action—great surprise finish—but not much variance in crime sequences, as I did the last 80-odd pages in a day!"

We happen to feel this creepy crime thriller represents the best of all the post-war Shadow novels. After years of having to write pseudo-Shadows that mirrored the urbane radio incarnation of his own character, Walter Gibson reverted to the mysterioso pulp crimebuster that made creator and creation a legend.

MALMORDO

by Maxwell Grant

A daffodil as a symbol of danger; a creature with a rodent face; a menu card with the circled message: "Midnight—Morte—Monday" send The Shadow in pursuit of the world's most desperate criminal.

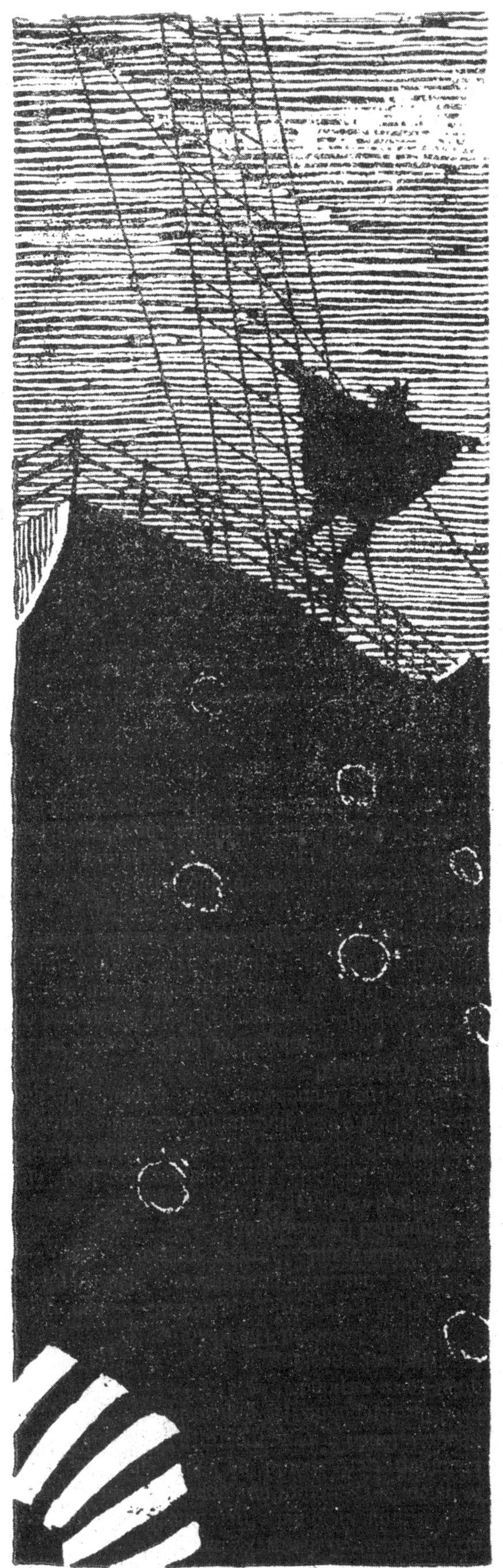

CHAPTER I

LIKE some weird creature from the deep, the crawling fog enveloped the Steamship *Santander* as she lay at her North River pier. From the grimy blackness that represented the river came the deep-throated blares of steamship whistles and the shrill squeals of tugboats, like voices urging the thick mist forward.

The fog was kind to the *Santander*.

For one thing, the fog hadn't arrived until the banana boat had docked, so now its hemming mass was harmless. And now, artistically speaking, the drizzling mist was giving this floating junk-pile both grace and proportions that had never belonged to such a ship.

The dim, dewy pier lights scarcely reached the side of the *Santander.* Her hulk, fog-painted a whitish gray, seemed to be undergoing the swathes of an invisible brush that produced a streamlined effect of motion. Magnified by that blanketing gray, the *Santander* literally towered out of sight, creating the illusion that this squatty tub had the bulk of a leviathan.

Between the varied blasts of the frequent river whistles came silence, broken only by an occasional splash. An angler might have mistaken those sounds for jumping fish, except that fish didn't jump in the oily, ugly water flanking these piers.

Then, like a warning all its own, came a slow, flat beat of footsteps tramping inward from the pier end in slow, methodical rhythm. As those footsteps neared a light that was hanging from a post, they were accompanied by a creaking from dried, warped boards that formed the surface of the pier.

Out of the fog loomed a burly policeman who, like the *Santander,* looked three sizes bigger. His footbeats stopped as he heard a movement beside him; bringing his swinging club to his fist, the officer turned sharply. The stir had come from a batch of packing cases stacked near the post. Hearing it again, the patrolman crouched and began a slow-motion approach to the pile of boxes.

Again the stack wobbled, to the accompaniment of a creak. The officer straightened with a short laugh. A loose plank had jiggled the packing cases, that was all. After testing it a few times, the officer continued his patrol toward the shore.

Whistles sounded intermittently, punctuated by those curious, recurrent splashes from alongside the *Santander.* Then, from back where other lights formed glowing dots and nothing more, came the plodding beats of the patrolman's footsteps, making their return.

This time those beats halted at short intervals. Close to the post-light, the patrolman showed his face in the murky glow and his expression was troubled. He took a few more paces, stopped and listened. From behind him he heard a slow *creak-creak* like something governed by remote control. It couldn't be the echoes of his own footsteps; echoes didn't act that way, nor footsteps either.

He couldn't have been as clumsy as he looked, this cop, for at the end of half a dozen paces he made a neat, deft shift beyond the packing cases. There, crouching, he put away his nightstick and drew a revolver instead. There wasn't any guessing about those creaking sounds, not any longer. They were approaching and with them bringing cautious footsteps.

The crouching officer shifted upward, forward. He elbowed one of the packing cases and then grabbed at it. The box didn't fall, although the cop's clutch was limited to his fingernails. It must have struck a propping box beyond. But the sound was heard by that other man, approaching through the fog. The creaky shuffle did a sidestep and halted.

There was only one place where the newcomer could have located himself; that was behind the post, beyond the glare of the already muffled light. Pointing his revolver at the post, the patrolman demanded hoarsely:

"Who's there?"

A voice returned the challenge with, "So it's you, Moultrie!" and a stocky man edged into sight around the old wooden post. Moultrie, the patrolman, slid away his revolver and fumbled for the nightstick, trying to change his sheepish look to match the poker-faced expression that showed on the swarthy face of the stocky man.

"I didn't know who you were, Inspector—"

"That's all right, Moultrie," interposed the stocky arrival. "You're on duty to question people. I wasn't sure who you were, either, the way you kept halting your patrol. Notice anything special back there?"

"Only—well, only that I must have heard you following me—?"

There was an interrupting nod. Inspector Joe Cardona, despite his deadpan manner, could sympathize with a slight case of the jitters. In fact, though he didn't mention it publicly, his years of experience had convinced Cardona that a certain amount of nerves rendered a patrolman alert and therefore made him a good patrolman.

This applied to Moultrie. Cardona gestured to the stack of packing cases.

"Think there's anything in there, Moultrie?"

"I don't think so, Inspector," returned the cop, glad that his shift behind the stack had been interpreted as a performance of duty. "Those boxes wobbled when I was going past, but it may have been on account of this."

To illustrate, Moultrie stepped over to the right board and pressed his foot on it. The boxes wobbled accordingly and the tilted one threatened to topple, but didn't. Then, approaching the boxes, Moultrie added:

"I—looked through them earlier. Maybe I ought to do the same right now, Inspector, even though they're empty—"

By way of illustrating the final point, the patrolman thwacked one of the packing cases with his club and automatically modified his statement. Something bounced from beneath the empty box, scudded across the planking and disappeared between the pier edge and the moored *Santander,* concluding its trip with one of the sharp splashes that had been featuring the entire evening.

Even in the gloom, Cardona and Moultrie didn't fail to recognize the creature as a sizeable rat, which didn't require the magnifying effect of the fog to class it as an unusually large specimen.

"Whoof!" exclaimed Moultrie. "That was a big one!"

"Not as big as the kind we're looking for," returned Cardona, "nor as slimy. Human rats, those stowaways that have been slipping into port, from where and how we don't know."

Cardona's lips kept moving along that line of talk but Moultrie didn't hear him. The *Queen Mary* was speaking from somewhere in the fog, the grand diapason of her whistle threatening to rip the mist asunder. Even the planking of the old pier quivered under such vibration and the topmost packing case began toppling, only to tilt back the other way as though hoisted from within.

It would have taken a dozen rats to have accomplished that, but Cardona and Moultrie were both turned away, hence they failed to witness the phenomenon. Then, when the ear-shattering blares from the *Queen Mary* ended, Cardona managed to get some parting words across to Moultrie.

"The police boats take over at midnight," declared the inspector. "Until then"—Cardona's hand made a sweeping gesture meant to include the pier as far as its invisible outer end—"it's yours."

With that, Moultrie resumed his outbound patrol, much bolstered by Cardona's visit, plus the fact that there was less than a half hour remaining to midnight. Cardona watched the pacing patrolman disappear into the fog; then turned shoreward. But at the first post with its foggy light, the inspector halted. In mentioning the time limit of Moultrie's patrol, Cardona had brought to mind an appointment of his own.

From his pocket, the inspector produced a folded piece of cardboard and opened it in the light. It was a half a menu card, which had measured about six by nine inches until someone had torn it across the middle, the short way. What Cardona held was the upper half.

The heading of the card read as follows:

MIDNIGHT REVEL
at the
CAFE DE LA MORTE
in
Greenwich Village

MENU FOR MONDAY

Part of the menu list remained but most of it had been torn away, reducing the card chiefly to an announcement, accentuated by the upper portions of a pair of skeletons that stood at each side like heralds, pointing to the heading. But there was something else that interested Cardona more.

Three words of the heading were circled with a thick black ring, made by an artist's crayon. Those three words were "Midnight," "Morte," and "Monday." Right now, midnight was approaching, the word *morte* meant death, and today happened to be Monday.

Probably a hoax, this card, like many other such trophies that the police received, but Inspector Cardona wasn't passing it by. As an anonymous communication, it was terse and to the point; it showed intelligence behind it, which wasn't usual with a crank note.

And thinking further in terms of the unusual, Cardona had heard that the newly-opened Cafe de la Morte was a most unusual place, worthy of a visit during one of its midnight revels. Having intended to go there anyway, Cardona could think of no more fitting occasion than tonight.

Timed to the fading beat of Moultrie's plodding march, Cardona's creaky footsteps dwindled in the opposite direction, leaving only the thickening swirl of fog upon the gloom-laden pier.

CHAPTER II

MINUTES until midnight.

Slowly, those minutes were ticking by, broken as before by the weird whistle blasts and those maddening splashes which now meant rats. Choked more than ever by the fog, the light from the pier post failed even to reach the bulking side of the *Santander.* Glowing downward, that light barely disclosed the warped planking of the pier beneath it.

Then even those boards were obscured, but not by fog.

Something that swirled more fantastically than the mist was cutting off the gleam. A figure, shapeless at first, had moved up beside the post to appear only as a darkened smudge of enormous size. Then, momentarily revealed in a fog rift which its own arrival produced, the figure showed as a human form cloaked in black, with a slouch hat above.

Gathering as if by command, the fog shrouded the mysterious arrival, whose disappearance, as much as his brief disclosure, marked him as that legendary personage known as The Shadow.

At least it wasn't strange that The Shadow should have put in an appearance here. The setting was of his choice, the situation intriguing, particularly because it had already attracted the attention of the police, whose interests were The Shadow's also.

The uncanny part was that The Shadow should arrive, as usual, just as the situation was taking an important turn. Hardly was The Shadow at his chosen post, before the mass of packing boxes stirred.

From that stack emerged a darkish man wearing old, ill-fitting clothes. His teeth gleamed white as he turned his grinning face and even the dull light produced the glitter of gold earrings from beneath the shaggy black hair that made the man's old straw hat appear two sizes small.

The Shadow observed that this man's baggy trousers, frayed jersey, even the strawhat, were all dark in color, giving him an advantage in the night fog. For when the darkish man completed a slink to the side of the *Santander,* he became quite inconspicuous against that background.

There was a sharp, low hiss, like a signal. It came from the grinning lips of the darkish man. A pause, then the signal was repeated. This time it brought a response. A man in the gray working clothes of a sailor appeared several feet above, like something floating in the fog, until a slight swirl revealed that he was leaning over the rail of a lower deck of the *Santander.*

The sailor spoke, in foreign accent:

"That you, Panjo?"

From below, the hiss turned to a snarl, then became words.

"Give no names, please." Panjo spoke it more like an order than a request. "You tell me, you bring birds?"

"Tried to bring them," replied the sailor, "but no luck this trip."

Panjo didn't seem to understand.

"I come for birds," he snarled. "You let me have them now, see? You let me have them quick."

"No luck, I tell you. They're all dead."

"You kill them? Why?"

The sailor laughed at Panjo's query.

"You want to know what killed them?" asked the sailor. "Listen, if you want to hear."

Whistles throated through the fog, then ceased. The sounds that supplanted them were those same, startling splashes from the water beside the ship.

"That's what killed them," informed the sailor. "The rats. They flattened the cages to get at them I mean it, Panjo."

Again, Panjo delivered a half-snarled hiss. It wasn't just a reminder that he didn't want his name mentioned. It was a warning, too, induced by the returning pound of Moultrie's footbeats. The sailor slid down behind the solid rail of the deck, while Panjo crouched low against the background of the ship. They remained that way while the patrolman passed, bound toward the shore end of the pier. The figures reappeared and the conversation was resumed.

"You bring no birds," rebuked Panjo, in an ugly tone, "so why do you bring rats?"

"Because we take food to Europe," the sailor explained. "The rats know it comes from the ship, so they come on board to get their share."

"But no food they find. So why they stay?"

"They want to get to the place where the food came from. Rats are smart that way."

Panjo thought that over. Then, sharply he asked:

"You bring birds from Europe?"

"Parrots, macaws and such?" queried the sailor. "We picked them up in South America, on the way back, where we unloaded surplus military supplies."

"If rats so smart," conjectured Panjo, "why they not go ashore then?"

"Because the South Americans were smarter. They took the supplies and left us the rats. We unloaded onto little boats—lighters they call them—outside the harbor!"

"And then you pick up birds?"

"That's right. We took on a cargo of mahogany logs that they towed out on barges, because they're too heavy to float by themselves." The sailor leaned well over the rail, as though to become confidential. "That's how I made the deal for the birds, Panjo. The men on the lighters fixed it with the barge men."

Panjo was still obdurate. There was something sullen in the darkish man's snarl:

"Maybe something more big than rat kill bird."

Their faces were sharply etched, Panjo's and the sailor's, for there wasn't much distance between them. Panjo was glaring upward, the sailor staring downward, so neither noticed the shape that glided to the side of the *Santander,* somewhat toward the bow. In fact, the shape couldn't be seen at all, though it manifested its presence by the eddy it produced in the fog.

In a sense, The Shadow was surrounded by a ghostly wrapping that finally dissipated itself as he reached the ship's side and began an upward climb toward the higher bulwark near the bow.

Meanwhile, the sailor was parrying with Panjo.

"Something bigger than rats?" The sailor's face scowled down at Panjo. "Like what for instance?"

Before Panjo could specify, there came a louder splash from near the ship, a sound which by comparison with those earlier plops could represent something of human size. The sailor turned quickly and Panjo, giving his head a quick tilt to make sure the patrolman wasn't near, traced a rapid course back toward the stacked packing cases.

Hardly had Panjo reached there, before another man-sized splash was heard off the bow of the *Santander.* It was then apparent that Panjo hadn't wheeled away just to hide. He was turning again, to get a better look at the *Santander,* to see what was happening on its upper decks.

Panjo made only one mistake. From this range, he couldn't hope to see much through the soupy fog. The sailor's plan was better; he was racing up a companionway, shouting for other crew members to join him and find out what was happening on board. Nevertheless, Panjo did see something, thanks to a brilliant light which suddenly arrived atop a stumpy mast near the bow of the *Santander.*

Some crew member had turned on the light just in time and at the wrong time.

What Panjo saw was a figure like a monstrous bat, rising above the bulwark of the *Santander,* spreading what seemed to be gigantic wings for a forward swoop. The thing was human-sized and Panjo, terror stricken by the very sight of it, shrieked wild words that stabbed like a warning through the fog.

"Vourdalak!" screamed Panjo. *"Vourdalak! Nosferadu! Vampyr! Vampyr!"*

Those last words struck an echoing note. From the far side of the *Santander,* near the bow which none of the sailors had yet reached, came a high, frantic shout:

"Vampiro! Vampiro!"

Moultrie was arriving on the run. The patrolman saw the thing that Panjo mistook for a vampire and fired three shots at it, all much too late. The figure was gone, swallowed by blackness below the high rail of the upper deck. And Moultrie was glad that he had missed for he was realizing that the creature was more human than batlike.

To Moultrie came recollections of a strange personage that he had heard about, but never before had seen—The Shadow!

Savagely, the patrolman turned to deal with the malefactor who had led him into firing shots at the law's best friend. The malefactor that Moultrie had in mind was Panjo, who by now was diving deep into his nest of packing cases. The boxes were wobbling, toppling, and Moultrie used the remaining three cartridges in his police positive to riddle them. Then he scrambled on board the low deck of the *Santander,* dropping to shelter in order to reload his gun.

Panjo hadn't halted among the packing cases. Sounds of the first shots had spurred him right on through. The darkish man was speeding shoreward; all Moultrie had riddled was an empty nest.

What covered Panjo's flight completely was the excitement on that high deck of the *Santander.* Following the cry of *"Vampiro!"* there had been two loud smacking splashes from the water alongside, indicating that a pair of men had jumped there, rather than combat the formidable unknown.

But there was another, who had taken a different route. He was scurrying down a companionway, heading for a hatch, dodging crew members in his wild flight. Rather than cross the deck and make himself a target in the light, The Shadow was following that last man, knowing that one stowaway, if captured, could give details concerning the rest.

When three sailors cut across The Shadow's path, he gave them precedence. They knew this ship better than The Shadow did and they were competent to make the capture. Nevertheless, The Shadow followed them, ready to remain in reserve. The chase proved as short as it was rapid.

The chase ended in the hold.

There, dull labored sounds told that the fugitive was seeking shelter among great piles of mahogany logs that banked clear to the ceiling at one end of the hold. Armed with improvised clubs, the sailors were moving in that general direction. Hearing the clang of arriving footsteps, The Shadow merged with the darkness at the fringe of the hold, just as Moultrie arrived.

The sailors were voicing admonitions:

"Don't let him out of there!"

"Watch him or he'll get out through the hatch over those logs!"

"He can't manage it. That hatchway is clamped on the deck!"

A fierce bellow came from among the logs, half challenge, half terror, a man's voice so strained and frantic that it was impossible to define. To settle the question, Moultrie fired above the heads of the sailors, ploughing his bullets deep into the mahogany.

The result was stupendous.

With a great heave, the huge pile of logs came tumbling, rolling, sending the sailors dodging along with Moultrie. Out of that melee, rolling like one of the logs, came the fugitive stowaway. Clambering over the logs, sailors and patrolman reached him, only to find him limp, almost lifeless.

The reason was plain when they turned him over. The man's body was contorted, crushed. It was horrible, but not surprising, considering that he'd been carried in the midst of that unexpected avalanche of huge logs, from the moment the pile had given away.

He was an ugly, rattish man, this stowaway, and his eyes glared up from beneath the twisted visor of his shabby cap. Then, with gasps that marked his death throes, the man panted these singular words:

"Malmordo—morto—noktomezo—"

Those words were all. Having gasped them, the man sank back dead. Like the other listeners, The Shadow heard them, for he had drawn close. Now The Shadow was on the move again, to reach a layer of logs against the bulkhead, the only portion of the stack that had not toppled.

Swiftly, silently, The Shadow scaled that layer like a ladder, nor was his route interrupted at the top. The hatchway that the sailors had mentioned was wide open; its cover lying beside it, ripped from the big clamps that had held it. The top log gave way as The Shadow used it to propel himself up through the hatchway. It came banging down, bringing Moultrie and the sailors to the alert, leaving them wondering as they stared upward and saw the wide gap leading to the deck.

By then, The Shadow had reached the rail and his keen eyes were probing the blackened water below. No figures were visible there, but The Shadow could trace a thin, undulating line in the oily scum, fading off from the side of the *Santander.*

Crossing the deck, The Shadow dropped to the lower rail on the dock side, then to the dock itself. A low, whispered laugh stirred the hovering mist as the cloaked figure flitted past the hanging light and took the shoreward route that Panjo had so recently followed.

"Malmordo—morto—noktomezo—"

Unintelligible words to others, but to The Shadow they formed a link to something far more sinister than the chance death of a fugitive stowaway on board the Steamship *Santander!*

CHAPTER III

IT was nearly midnight when The Shadow left the North River pier and midnight was the hour for the usual revel that took place at the new but already popular Cafe de la Morte, Greenwich Village's latest screwball attraction.

With his head start from the pier, Inspector Cardona had reached the cafe just before the appointed hour. He was reluctantly checking his hat and coat in a cloakroom painted all about with imitation flames and presided over by a somewhat timeworn check girl who looked anything but cute in a devil costume adorned with imitation horns.

The hellfire *motif* persisted into the cafe itself, then gave way to walls painted to represent tombstones with hovering ghosts all about. The waiter who conducted Cardona to a table was dressed in an outfit decorated with skeleton ribs and over his head he wore a hood painted to represent a skull.

Cardona noted that the other waiters were similarly attired, which gave them excellent opportunity to cover their identity, a fact which the inspector intended to put in his notebook at an early moment. The one man who was not so disguised—and therefore worthy of a separate notation—was a stolid bartender over at one side of the cafe, behind the inevitable bar.

Maybe the barkeep objected to such a costume or was too busy to be encumbered by one. At any rate, he had nothing to conceal, for Cardona recognized him as a veteran bartender who had served at several Village spots. With a further eye to detail, Cardona noted that the bar was well-stocked, both in quantity and variety of liquors. Behind the barkeeper was a rack of shelves, divided in three vertical sections, all loaded to capacity with fancy bottles of imported goods.

The patrons next.

Studying the customers, Joe Cardona decided that they represented the usual sprinkling of Villagers and the customary majority of out-of-towners who would patronize a freakish place such as the Cafe de la Morte. Business was always good when such establishments opened and generally sustained itself until some other novelty supplanted it.

Many of the customers were drinking beer, the chief reason being that the beverage was served in big mugs shaped to resemble skulls. Quite a thrill, such sport, but it wasn't showing big profits for the house. The popularity of beer in skull-mugs could account for the untouched stock of much more expensive elixirs on the shelf behind old Jerry, the squatty bartender who looked as though he didn't have enough to do.

In Cardona's opinion, the Cafe de la Morte wouldn't begin to make profits until it stopped serving beer in bizarre mugs; and when it stopped that practice, people wouldn't come here anymore.

But people were here tonight, that was the important thing. Moreover, the menu card lying on Cardona's table was a perfect match for the half-card that Joe had in his pocket. If death happened to be due at Monday midnight, it was Cardona's business to pick the persons who might be involved.

So far, Cardona could only pick the waiters, with their disguising skull hoods. Ordering a beer, Joe not only kept a close watch on his waiter, but all the others who came within his scope.

The policy brought results.

One waiter, passing another, whispered a word that Cardona overheard, a word that sounded like a name:

"Malmordo."

The second waiter repeated it to a third and Cardona caught the word "Malmordo" plainly. He also saw both waiters throw worried glances toward the rear of the cafe and when men in masking hoods could give the impression that they were worried, it was obvious that they must be worried indeed.

Joe's trouble was that he couldn't see the rear of the cafe at all. Ignoring his beer, he rose from his table and sauntered over toward the bar, then changed course and found a good observation spot along the same wall. The spot was particularly good because it was beneath a stretch of sloping ceiling, about four feet wide, that slanted down behind the bar and cut off old Jerry's view of the place that Cardona had chosen.

From his new vantage, Cardona saw that the rear of the restaurant opened into an outdoor garden and through the connecting door, the slight breeze wafted the strains of wild exotic music, played by a violin.

Wondering who the musician might be, Cardona took a casual stroll out to the garden.

From the moment that he made his advent into the al fresco setting, Joe Cardona was spotted. The man who pegged him was a rather handsome young chap named Harry Vincent. Parked at a rather obscure table alongside the green board fence that served as boundary to the garden, Harry immediately concerned himself with the remaining contents of a skull mug, rather than have Cardona see his face.

As a rule, persons who didn't want to be noticed by Joe Cardona were fugitives from justice. Harry Vincent happened to be a rare exception.

Harry Vincent was an agent of The Shadow.

Through channels peculiarly his own, The Shadow had ways of finding out about things and places that aroused the suspicion of the police. There were times, too, when The Shadow anticipated a growing interest on the part of the law. Though The Shadow's data might be incomplete, he seldom let such a condition continue.

The Shadow had ways of building up his own statistics. One of those ways was Harry Vincent.

This evening Harry had been told to cover the Cafe de la Morte. He had picked the outdoor garden as the best area, because it had attracted the majority of the patrons. The weather was warm and the garden was therefore cooler than the cramped indoors. Though the high board fence cut off passing breezes, there was compensation in the fact that the garden had no roof.

Running from the building to the fence were a series of well-spaced iron rods intended as a support for a huge canvas canopy that served in rainy weather. At present the canopy was rolled up and parked against the building wall, above the down-slanting rods.

The garden's chief attraction was the violinist, who answered to the name of Gregor. He wore a Hungarian costume of boots, baggy trousers, fancy sash and ruffled shirt. He was a good-looking chap despite his frequent scowls which seemed the result of concentration on his music, which constantly approached a tumultuous staccato and always ended unexpectedly. However, it had taken Harry less than an hour to observe that Gregor's gripe concerned something other than his music; namely, Madame Thalla.

According to the little cards that she distributed at tables, Madame Thalla was a gypsy palmist and she certainly looked the part. Though young, Thalla had a wise face that befitted her colorful gypsy costume. It wasn't always possible to see her face, because the brilliant handkerchief that she wore as a headdress drooped down beside her cheeks like the blinders on a horse.

At least those blinders helped Madame Thalla concentrate on the person whose fortune she was telling. There was another point that interested Harry quite as much. Though she advertised herself as a palmist, Madame Thalla told fortunes by playing cards instead. The particular type of cards she used were the old-fashioned tarots, with curious pictures embellishing their faces.

At present, Madame Thalla was dealing the tarots for a blonde young lady who wore a white dress. Since Cardona was noticing Gregor, Harry decided to look at the blonde instead. In fact, he shifted his chair so he particularly gained a ring-side seat to the conference between Madame Thalla and the girl in white.

What Harry heard made him forget the hazard of being observed by Cardona.

"Your name," Madame Thalla was saying, in a low, sharp tone. "I can read it here in the cards."

"My name?" exclaimed the girl. "But that's impossible."

"It is not impossible," declared Thalla. "It is Janice. Wait, I can read the rest! Your full name is Janice Bradford."

From the way the girl drew her breath, Harry knew that Madame Thalla had scored a ten-strike. Then:

"That is my name," the girl admitted, soberly. "But surely, the cards could not tell you."

"The cards tell everything," asserted Thalla. "Most of all, they warn of danger. The danger that comes to those who wear the yellow flower."

Janice Bradford went tense. Harry Vincent saw her hand creep to the lapel of her jacket, where a daffodil was pinned. A rather unusual flower, thought Harry, and apparently Thalla was of the same opinion.

"Three nights now you have worn it," the gypsy told the girl, "and each night brings more danger. I warn you, it is not safe to come here!"

"But I have come here safely—"

"And you may not find it safe to stay." Thalla pointed a shapely finger to one of the tarot cards. "This is the sign that tells your future."

Janice stared at the card, much puzzled.

"But that card is blank!" she exclaimed. "How did it come to be among the others?"

Thalla shrugged as though she didn't know.

"But since it is blank," persisted Janice, "how can you read it? What does it tell?"

"Your future." Thalla intoned the words solemnly. "No future. Blank, like the card!"

Thalla could say no more, for Gregor was drowning all sounds with the maddened shriek of his fiddle. Then, with a burst that seemed to strain the violin's strings, the wild music ended.

The sudden silence seemed sharp. It made ears keen, too, for Harry could hear a peculiar sound from somewhere along the wooden fence. The more he listened, the more that sound reminded him of something gnawing at the wood. Immediately the thought of rats sprang to Harry's mind, though it seemed unlikely that rats would try to chew their way into as populated a spot as this outdoor garden.

And then, from within the Cafe de la Morte came the strokes of a strange gong, announcing the beginning of the midnight revel.

A revel that tonight spelled death!

CHAPTER IV

JANICE BRADFORD was rising before the gong strokes ended. Madame Thalla was saying something to the girl and again Harry Vincent caught the words, when the gypsy repeated the admonition.

"Your future will be blank," Thalla stated, "unless you heed my warning. Go, before the message of the tarots can be fulfilled. The blank is one that allows you another choice." Sweeping the cards from the table, Thalla held them as though about to deal, then shook her head. "But tonight, we have not time to continue. Go!"

Deciding to go, Janice was nevertheless reluctant. As she left the table, she looked for her waiter in order to pay the check and was rather bewildered when two skull-hooded men ignored her as they passed. Finding your waiter wasn't easy at the Cafe de la Morte.

As yet Cardona hadn't noticed Janice, nor was it likely that he would. The inspector was concentrated upon Thalla as the gypsy woman strolled past his table. Watching Thalla, Cardona picked up one of her table cards without letting his eyes leave the fortune teller.

Shuffling her tarot cards, Thalla was moving past Gregor and the wise look she gave him brought a fresh scowl from the violinist. This time, Cardona didn't miss it and if he had, Gregor's action would have been enough to declare the spite that existed between him and the fortune teller.

Tossing his head, Gregor brought his chin down upon the violin and immediately broke forth with a fanfare of barbaric music that denoted anger in every chord. So fierce, so frenzied was the music that it drowned every other sound. Among those sounds was an unheard clatter that came from the wooden fence.

A portion of that fence, approximately three feet square, opened like a thing of cardboard and through it writhed a loathsome creature so far from human that any resemblance seemed completely coincidental.

The thing that twisted itself into sight looked like a rat of man-sized proportions that had borrowed somebody's clothes simply to disguise the fact that it was a rodent, not a human.

It was the creature's face that made the impression most convincing.

No face could possibly have been so ugly, so vicious in its own right alone. Its owner must have purposely misshapen it, or practiced facial contortions to the limit, in order to acquire such grotesque, inhuman features.

If the arrival looked like a rat, he was even quicker.

With a snarl that drowned the high notes of the violin, the thing from the fence reached Gregor. In its course, the contorted creature flung tables right and left; their crashing froze Gregor in the midst of his wild rhapsody. Recoiling, the musician flung his arms, violin, bow and all, in warding off fashion as he tried to crouch for shelter.

From Gregor's lips came a shriek of higher pitch than his violin had ever reached, as he screeched the name:

"Malmordo!"

In his effort to escape the terrible creature he called Malmordo, Gregor made one great mistake. It was a natural thing, to go diving away from a huddly creature that had launched itself from a self-made man-sized rathole. Natural too, for both Joe Cardona and Harry Vincent to lunge toward Malmordo, stretching as they drew guns, intent upon aiming downward. But they were as mistaken as was Gregor.

The thing called Malmordo unlimbered, lengthening itself in an astounding fashion. With his left hand, the unkempt creature flung a light table sideward, sending a shower of skull mugs with it. Cardona dodged the missile; it skimmed him and forced Harry to duck it too. By then, all was up with Gregor.

Malmordo's right hand had whipped out a long, thin-bladed knife and was overtaking Gregor with it. The long, hooking thrust of the knife point seemed to carry Malmordo after it. If Gregor had turned or straightened, he could have at least coped with his attacker, but his instinctive crouch and mad effort to escape were his undoing.

The thin knife buried itself in Gregor's back and stayed there. The musician sprawled, his violin and bow flying ahead of him, while Malmordo, now unarmed, wheeled to meet other foemen.

Cardona and Harry were aiming their guns upward, straight at the leering face that was Malmordo's. Even the intensity of the moment could not lessen the hideous impression that those grotesque features gave. Indeed, the situation accentuated the appearance of Malmordo.

A livid face, all out of shape, from its bulging teeth to beady eyes, a face that seemed uglier than the snarl that spat from a mouth that looked lipless. Above the face was shaggy hair, strewing down upon a forehead whose lines seemed continuations of the misshapen grimace which was fixed on Malmordo's visage.

Again, this human monstrosity showed the cunning that went with Malmordo's rattish looks. From his stretched position, Malmordo telescoped into his former pose, dwindling so suddenly that for the moment he appeared to be plunging himself, corkscrew fashion, down through the flagstone paving of the garden.

This was illusion, nothing more, but it completely fooled both men who were trying to drop Malmordo in his tracks. Two guns blasted in unison, their shots whizzing high. Then, before Harry or Cardona had a chance to fire again, Malmordo was flaying them with a new deluge of tables that he scooped up during his flinging whirl.

And now Malmordo was a gone rat indeed, a rat scampering in maddened flight. He was cutting a swath among tables and chairs, apparently in search of some outlet. He couldn't regain the hole that he had literally gnawed through the fence, for from hands and knees, Harry and Cardona were starting over to block that outlet. Nor could he scoot into the cafe itself, for the skull-hooded waiters were coming from that direction, some of them with revolvers. They were the ones who dodged the next tables that Malmordo threw, until he found another use for the furniture.

Feinting with a table, Malmordo suddenly planked it on top of another table that was standing by. Grabbing a chair with his other hand, he sprang upon the first table, planting the chair on the table above. At the same time, his free hand deftly whipped a clasp knife from a pocket of his baggy trousers, flipped it open, and cut a taut rope that slanted by his shoulder.

That rope was the control line for the canopy that sheltered the patrons of the garden on rainy days. With a sudden rumble, the canvas came rolling down along the metal rods that formed a track above Malmordo's head. Even before the canvas reached him, Malmordo was clambering to the chair above the upper table and his long-bladed clasp knife gave another slash that met the canopy when it arrived.

Guns roared upward, too late. Everybody was aiming for the chair, but Malmordo was no longer there.

He'd gone, with a leap, right through the opening in the canvas that his handy knife had ripped, using the nearest slanted rod to help him complete the rapid hoist. In a trice, Malmordo had staged as spectacular a getaway as The Shadow's departure from the hold of the *Santander,* and under conditions far more pressing.

Except that here, Malmordo lacked the benefit of a solid shield like a ship's deck. Beneath him was canvas, nothing more. As he went through the slit in the canvas, he flung his clasp knife at one waiter who was aiming a revolver and the man in the skull-hood had to dodge. But there were others with guns, who were shifting to drill the canvas and ferret out the rattish Malmordo with bullets.

Malmordo must have expected it, for hardly had the first guns talked before a roundish figure came rolling down above the canopy, marking its progress by the way it sagged the canvas. A clever trick, this, rolling straight for the back alley behind the green fence. It explained why Malmordo had gone to such exaggerated measures in the first place. Here he was slipping the men who had tried to round him up, gaining the very outlet from which they had blocked him off!

It was a long chance though, taking a roller coaster trip above the heads of the very men who sought to stop him. Before the trip was over, guns were blasting at the traveling bulge that followed down the canvas and although they were again belated, it was largely luck that caused them to miss the object they sought.

Over the edge of the canopy, just ahead of frantic bullets, even then, Malmordo wasn't out of danger. There was a terrific clatter of a landing in the rear alley, indicating that Malmordo must have overturned a waiting ashcan and before the clangor ended, Cardona was through the gap in the rear fence, aiming for Malmordo in the darkness.

The alley ran parallel to the fence and shots responded from both directions, shots fired by distant, crouchy men, who were obviously leagued with Malmordo. But the killer himself couldn't have headed in either direction. There was only one place where Malmordo could have gone, into a deep, dark courtyard across the narrow alley.

That space represented a connection between two sections of a storage building that rose windowless above. Cardona knew that Malmordo must have gone there, because he heard the ashcan rolling that direction; therefore, it followed that Malmordo must have taken it along to serve as an improvised pillbox.

Putting a whistle to his lips, Joe Cardona blew a signal that would bring all the police from blocks around, for on the way here, he had instructed various patrolmen to be on the alert.

Whoever this Malmordo was, whatever his purpose in Manhattan, the law was prepared to eliminate him on the scene of his first crime!

CHAPTER V

THE shrill of Cardona's whistle roused Harry Vincent from the excitement of the chase. Abruptly, Harry put away his gun, realizing it wasn't good policy to be brandishing one unofficially, even after siding in behalf of the law.

Looking about at the waiters, Harry saw that they had already adopted the same notion. They were not only gunless, some of them had peeled away their skull hoods to reveal their faces. A few looked tough, but most of them appeared to be scared. This left Harry wondering as to how many had been in on the gun work.

Cardona at least was giving the waiters benefit of doubt, for he was ordering them to quiet the customers, to keep the place closed, and to admit only arriving police. Since Malmordo had chosen to play rat, Cardona right now was acting the cat, for he was watching the hole where the murderer had gone and did not want to be disturbed.

Dropping back, Harry crossed to the doorway that led into the cafe proper and halted there beside some black-draped curtains. A hand emerged suddenly from the darkness and gripped his arm; before Harry could take action, a voice intoned for silence.

It was The Shadow, just arrived, for from his hidden lips came the one word: "Report."

Before Harry could do more than point out Gregor's body and name Malmordo as the murderer, there were voices from the front of the cafe. The first of the police were arriving and taking over in characteristic style. The Shadow pressed Harry in among the black curtains and blotted himself against another wall. Observation at this moment was more important than a report. But Harry noted to his satisfaction that the spot The Shadow had chosen, slightly away from that slanted roof leading down to the side of the bar, offered a good outlook to the rear garden where Cardona was still playing pussy cat at Malmordo's rathole.

It took the police only a few minutes to learn that no one had fled the Cafe de la Morte by way of the front door, or for that matter, by any route other than the garden. They learned this from the stammering red devil who minded the cloakroom and from a helpless looking manager. Old Jerry, the bartender, corroborated everything with nods while he calmly polished the bar glasses and Jerry, being a well-known character of unimpeachable quality, was the sort whose word would stand.

Then, brushing past the curtains where Harry was hidden, and totally failing to notice The Shadow blacked out against the opposite wall, the police reached the garden to find Inspector Cardona. By that time, Cardona was already gaining further aid, consisting of a few detectives who had come in from the side alleys.

These men were reporting that several ratty looking characters had scurried away as soon as they appeared, which to Cardona meant that Malmordo's followers had been forced to abandon their chief. Nevertheless, Cardona wasn't taking chances on a counterthrust.

"Don't come through here," Joe warned the detectives, referring to the hole in the fence. "We've got a rat trapped in the court across the way and he might start shooting. Go around to the front of the place, where you'll find a patrolman on duty. He'll let you in.

"Then round up all the customers and the waiters, so I can quiz them. Nobody is to come in or go out. As for you fellows"—this was to a pair of patrolmen who were in the garden, crowding up to Cardona's shoulders—"keep watching that courtyard. I'll send for some tear gas and tommy guns. They'll be good rat poison."

Harry could hear all this, though it was around the corner from him. At the same time, he was watching blackness glide out to the garden. The Shadow was on his way to study the Malmordo situation at close range, which left it to Harry to check on matters inside the cafe proper.

Waiting until the detectives appeared at the front door and talked to the brawny patrolman stationed there, Harry did a quick shift among the curtains to see how the customers and hired help reacted. First, the police were lining up the waiters, listing their names; then, having tallied them, they told the waiters to assemble the customers.

For a few moments, the waiters were moving here and there; during that period Harry noticed that one of them had put on his skull hood. Harry was shifting to watch where the waiter went, when something else attracted his attention. Hearing whispered voices nearby, Harry leaned among the curtains to eavesdrop.

The voices belonged to Madame Thalla and Janice Bradford. Apparently the gypsy fortuneteller had discovered the blonde girl crouched in an alcove.

"You must go from here!" Thalla was telling Janice. "You believe me, when I say there is danger!"

"I did believe you," began Janice, "but I should be safe, now that the police are here."

"They will ask you questions," asserted Thalla. "They will not tell you answers, like I did. Do you want to answer questions?"

"No," admitted Janice, "but if the police merely consider me a regular customer—"

"It is not what the police think! It is what Malmordo will think. You understand?"

"In a way, yes—"

"And in a way is enough. Even the police can not protect you if Malmordo knows where you are! Come!"

Footsteps shuffled away and when Harry managed to peer from beside a curtain, he saw Thalla, stooped beside a counter in the corner, lifting a trapdoor. The gypsy woman gestured Janice down into the cellar, spoke some reassuring words, then lowered the trap.

Did this mean that Thalla was double-crossing Janice? The idea struck hard through Harry's mind, particularly when he saw the fierce, vengeful expression that registered itself on Thalla's wise features. Then, the gypsy woman was stalking along the wall, peering everywhere, as though looking for someone else.

Perhaps Thalla was seeking that lone waiter who had put on the death hood. But now, for some reason, others were doing the same. It was impossible to tell which was which and Harry gained the sudden impression that some new trouble was about to start.

Then, from the other side of the curtains came The Shadow's low tone. Harry shifted over to report to his chief. Instead, it was The Shadow who opened the discussion.

"The wall above the canopy," stated The Shadow. "You saw it before the curtain rolled down. Describe it."

"It was just a building wall," expressed Harry, "with two small windows."

The Shadow undertoned a laugh.

"The ceiling over there," he spoke. "Part of it is slanted, ending down in back of the bar."

Harry had noticed that stretch of ceiling before. It was the slant four feet wide, that hadn't much impressed him at the time. Now suddenly, he realized what it meant.

"An inside stairway!" Harry's whisper was excited. "Coming down from the second floor. If that rack of bottle shelves could open, it would bring you out right behind the bar!"

At that same moment, Harry was noticing that the bar was singularly empty. Old Jerry, the bartender, had disappeared. As Harry still stared, Cardona came stalking into the cafe and the place the inspector looked first was toward the bar. Striding over, Cardona took a look across the bar, then turned and bellowed at his men.

"Who let this happen?" demanded Cardona. "Here's old Jerry slugged and unconscious, down in back of the bar!"

"The hooded waiter!" Harry told The Shadow. "He came from that direction. I didn't watch him, the only man who was still wearing his hood, because I was listening to Madame Thalla and Janice Bradford. Thalla was steering Janice down into the cellar, through a trapdoor over there!"

As Harry pointed from the curtains, he saw Thalla again. The excitement over finding Jerry had caused the gypsy woman to change her mind about remaining in the cafe. Thalla was at the trap again, this time using it for her own departure.

The trap was dropping above Thalla, just as Harry pointed, and before The Shadow could do a thing about it, Cardona heard the trapdoor slam. Instantly, the inspector was on the pounce, calling upon the detectives to follow him.

A singular circumstance, this. True to police practice, Inspector Cardona was accepting the situation close at hand, forgetting the greater issue of Malmordo, trapped in the courtyard behind the alleyway. Yet by that freakish shift of judgment, the law was actually on Malmordo's trail.

Such was The Shadow's analysis, and once again The Shadow was right!

CHAPTER VI

THE rush for the trapdoor brought with it three of the hooded waiters and Cardona did not order them to stay behind. In fact, he gave them precedence over his detectives, because they knew these premises and would therefore be helpful in the pursuit of the unknown who had gone into the cellar.

Madame Thalla knew that cellar too.

There wasn't a trace of the gypsy woman when Cardona and his human bloodhounds reached the cellar. All they saw were crates, casks and other impedimenta of the sort commonly found in the cellar of a restaurant.

Standing beside a door that he had flung wide, Cardona ordered the searchers to fan out and find the person who had fled by this route. The waiters were to shift the crates and casks, while the detectives stood by with ready guns.

Upstairs, The Shadow was profiting by the changed situation. In drawing men to the cellar, Cardona had left the cafe guarded, so far as the door was concerned, but the men there were so occupied with such duty that they were unable to watch elsewhere.

Telling Harry to join the other patrons and glean any details that might arise, The Shadow started on a foray of his own. Even if the police at the door had been looking The Shadow's way, it was unlikely that they could have seen him. For Harry, who could guess what his chief was about, found it difficult to trace The Shadow's progress.

Gliding blackness seemed to fold itself fantastically as it streaked along the slanting width of ceiling that marked the blocked-off stairway down from the second floor. Yet only eyes like Harry's, looking for such a token, could have observed it, for the background itself was dark and absorbed the moving silhouette.

Somebody had propped old Jerry in a chair behind the bar to give him air and he was showing signs of recovery. It might have been Jerry's own shadow that moved along the bottle-racked wall behind him, to be swallowed by darkness further on.

Then came the ticklish portion of The Shadow's expedition. Slowly, blackness moved upward, until it obscured the center row of shelves. Next, those shelves moved outward, door-fashion. Harry saw the motion, but realized that the very fact he could discern it meant that The Shadow was cutting off the line of vision from the front of the cafe.

The shelved door closed and the blackness was gone. The Shadow was using the hidden route to the second floor.

From those little windows at the rear of the building it was easy to look down above the slanted canopy and study the rear courtyard where a clumpy shape awaited the attack by the police. The Shadow could make out the form that represented Malmordo, something impossible for the men at the hole in the fence, due to the lack of visibility at that lower altitude.

Waiting for tear-gas and tommy guns seemed a wasteful delay to The Shadow. He preferred to settle the question of Malmordo by a rapid probe with bullets. Drawing a .45 automatic, The Shadow planted bullets into the huddly object.

Every bullet brought a clang.

There were echoes from the courtyard, as sharp as shots themselves. The patrolmen at the fence thought that Malmordo was shooting back at the unknown marksman up above. They opened fire at the courtyard, too, whereupon The Shadow ceased his fire and declared himself with a weird, challenging laugh, which the men below recognized. Realizing that The Shadow was on their side, confident that his taunt represented triumph, the patrolmen charged through the fence shooting as they went, intent upon taking the courtyard by storm.

The Shadow saw the blue-coated cluster surge into the court. Thrusting himself through the window, he rolled himself down the canopy at an angle, his feet reaching the lower edge first. There, The Shadow dropped adroitly to the now-deserted alley and landed cleanly in its darkness. Instead of joining the attack, he moved swiftly toward the street at the alley's end.

Having found his own means of departure from the Cafe de la Morte, The Shadow was taking his own measures toward the capture of Malmordo. Not only was The Shadow undeceived by Malmordo's methods, he was informing the police that they had chosen a blind trail.

This latter point was proven when Inspector Cardona reached the yard, attracted up from the cellar and out through the garden fence by the sounds of repeated gunfire. In the courtyard, Cardona found the patrolmen staring stupidly at an ashcan which was lying on its side, the contents of said ashcan being a pair of baggy trousers and an oversized blouse which had been Malmordo's costume.

Then did Cardona guess Malmordo's ruse.

"That's what rolled down the canopy!" The inspector kicked the bullet-riddled ashcan. "Malmordo must have had it rolled up in the canvas. We thought it was Malmordo and when it landed, we thought it was something he'd knocked over!

Turning, Cardona stared up at the little windows above the canopy.

"There's where Malmordo went!" Joe added. "He came down in back of the bar and slugged old Jerry! Then he must have ducked down through the trapdoor to the cellar. That was his trail, so let's follow it!"

Speedily, Cardona led the chase back through the cafe, down to the cellar, past the open door at the bottom, and through to a deep corner where the detectives and the hooded waiters were lifting a grating beyond a stack of crates. They had found the final exit, an outlet leading up to the front street.

With one accord, the group poured up through, to resume the belated rat hunt.

There were others besides Malmordo who knew of that front street outlet. One person was Janice Bradford and she had learned about it from Madame Thalla. Already, Janice was well away from the Cafe de la Morte, but her escape was by no means complete.

In fact, Janice was fearful that she had not escaped at all. At least there had been security in a place that the police dominated, Thalla's arguments to the contrary; but here, among the helter-skelter streets of Greenwich Village, danger seemed very rife.

In her dash from the cafe, Janice had lost her sense of direction and now the streets were not only unfamiliar, they all seemed to lead into darkness, perhaps back to the Cafe de la Morte itself. The blocks were brief, the streets crossed at diagonals, and their silence made Janice think of lurkers in every doorway. Nowhere could she spy the distant glimmer of an avenue, where she might find a cab.

Then, as if Janice's own fears had hatched it, the menace became real.

From somewhere came a snarled hiss, like a vicious command. Doorways showed the very figures that Janice had imagined would be there; slinky, dark-clad men who moved into sight like whiskered rats, boldly showing themselves in the open.

Each way Janice turned, a lurker blocked her off and despite the darkness, the girl could see the ugly grins they gave her.

They numbered at least half a dozen, these rat-men, and all seemed lesser editions of the murderer, Malmordo, who had slain Gregor while Janice watched. They moved in crouching fashion and Janice could tell from the way their hands were buried in their jackets that they, like their monstrous overlord, preferred the knife as a quick and silent death weapon.

Again, that snarly voice, repeating a strange, unintelligible command, at least unintelligible to Janice, though her stalkers seemed to understand it.

With a shrill, desperate scream, Janice darted for the nearest corner, realizing that doom would probably overtake her on the way, which well it might, but for the fact her terrified cry brought immediate results.

Janice's shriek was answered by a mocking laugh, but its taunt was meant for the slinky men, not for Janice. The street seemed to fill with snarls as the rat-men whipped back into their doorways, putting away their knives and drawing guns instead. Looking across her shoulder as she reached the corner, Janice saw a cloaked figure weaving into sight, purposely choosing a streetlight as a background.

Guns spoke from the doorways, all aimed in the direction of The Shadow. Those hasty shots were wide and they were answered by a rising laugh that echoed eerily from surrounding windows as though The Shadow were everywhere. With that peal came the staccato bursts of The Shadow's own guns, his shots probing the doorways, too close for the comfort of the occupants.

In picking revolver spurts as targets, The Shadow could come closer than his opponents, when they had his shifting form to aim at. And as he fired, The Shadow was no longer there. He had faded into darkness so swiftly, so surprisingly, that his blending with that element had all the effect of an instantaneous vanish.

Malmordo's tribe didn't wait to argue further. They scattered amazingly, traveling every direction except toward The Shadow. Janice was traveling too, her high heels clattering the sidewalks, until she found herself blocked anew. Other shooters were entering the general fray, Cardona and his detectives, but Janice didn't recognize them as such for with them were men who wore the skeleton jackets that featured the waiters at the Cafe de la Morte.

Instinctively, Janice turned toward the shelter of a corner doorway, set in the narrow angle of the junction of two diagonal streets. She recoiled suddenly as she saw a man step out; then, his hand

was gripping her arm, and he was pressing her into the shelter that he had just left.

The man was tall and in the slight light, Janice could see his face, blunt, square-jawed and quite unperturbed. The man was wearing a dark-gray suit, which was a helpful contrast to Janice's white attire.

"Stay in the doorway," the man ordered, in a low but forceful tone.

"Those fools will shoot at anything they can see." His eyes, a clear gray in the darkness, studied Janice intently. Then he added. "What are you doing around here, anyway?"

Janice started to say something, then tightened her lips. The gray man's eyes fixed on the yellow flower that sprouted from Janice's dress.

"You came from the Cafe de la Morte?"

Again, Janice decided not to answer. The man, quite unalarmed by the shots that were echoing around this very corner, drew a notebook from his pocket, wrote something on the lower portion of a space, tore off the half sheet and handed it to the girl.

"There is the best clue to Malmordo," the man said, coolly, "but be careful when you follow it. Now go straight down this street"—he thrust Janice out the other side of the doorway—"and you will reach the avenue."

Crumpling the unread note in her hand, Janice turned in the direction indicated and saw the lights of the avenue, only half a block ahead. This street was silent, but Janice wasn't taking chances that it would remain so. She headed for the avenue on the run.

As for the man in gray, he turned in another direction and walked along a street where shots still echoed, but did not perturb him, because they were moving away. Within half a block he turned into a side street where all was quiet.

Complete silence soon gripped that little corner doorway where Janice had met the man who knew about Malmordo. It was then that another figure arrived there, emerging so suddenly that he seemed to come from nowhere.

The new arrival was The Shadow. He saw the lights of the avenue and seemed to know that they must have spelled safety to Janice Bradford.

With a low, strange laugh which seemed to link the future with the past, The Shadow glided into the all-enveloping night.

CHAPTER VII

POLICE COMMISSIONER WESTON was staring at the exhibits that lay upon his desk. They formed a mass of evidence, those exhibits, even though they had the symptoms of a hodgepodge.

The exhibits tallied as follows:

A long, thin knife, defined as a Borgia stiletto.

A large, crude clasp knife of the variety preferred by Parisian Apaches.

A man's costume consisting of a pair of baggy trousers and an oversized blouse.

A waiter's costume from the Cafe de la Morte, comprising a skeleton-painted jacket and a skull hood.

A wallet and its contents, formerly the property of a Hungarian violinist, one Gregor Shaksha, deceased.

Several tarot cards of European manufacture, including one blank.

Announcements bearing the name of Madame Thalla.

A sample menu card from the Cafe de la Morte.

The top half of a menu card, with crayon circles around three words, producing the message: "Midnight—Morte—Monday."

Along with these were copious reports provided by Inspector Joe Cardona, who was present in person to amplify them. Arms folded, stolid as usual, Cardona was watching Weston mull over the items on the desk in what the commissioner probably considered to be an official style.

Commissioner Weston was a broad-faced gentleman with a short-clipped but pointed mustache. For years he had carried a military bearing which he had acquired during the First World War. Just when Weston had been about to forget that he'd once been an army officer, the Second World War had come along to remind him of the fact. Since then, Weston's manner had been more military than ever.

Finished with his survey, Commissioner Weston leaned back in his big swivel chair, waved his hand brusquely at the exhibits and ordered:

"Add them up, Inspector!"

"All right, Commissioner," said Cardona, "but there are some loose facts that go with them." He gestured to the report sheets. "Facts mentioned in there."

"Include them as you proceed."

Cardona proceeded.

"The case seems to revolve around a character named Malmordo," the inspector declared. "He has a face like a rat and he acts like one. He murdered Gregor. I saw him. He used that stiletto."

Weston eyed the Borgia dagger with its wicked blade of ice-pick proportions. It was the kind of weapon that could deal sure death with a single stab. Then the commissioner gestured to the Apache knife.

"And this?"

"Malmordo cut the canopy rope with it," returned Cardona, "and slashed his way through the canvas. He slung the knife at somebody and found time to dump these things"—Joe was gesturing to the baggy costume—"into an ashcan that was parked up above the canopy. It rolled down to the back alley and we thought it was Malmordo."

Weston set his chin in his hand.

"About that costume," he inquired. "Why did Malmordo get rid of it?"

"So he could double as a waiter," replied Cardona, promptly, pointing to the skeleton jacket and the skull hood.

"Malmordo doubled down through the cafe, by means of a blocked-off stairway. He'd been wearing the jacket under the blouse he'd discarded, so all he had to do was put on the hood. He slugged old Jerry the barkeep and slid across to a trapdoor leading down cellar. That's how he got out to the front street."

"And all the while," put in Weston, crisply, "you thought he was a waiter."

"I did," acknowledged Cardona, "until I found the outfit afterwards, parked behind a crate in the cellar."

Weston picked up Cardona's report and riffled its pages. Then:

"Your report mentions some other waiters," remarked Weston, "who helped you hunt for Malmordo."

"Three of them," Cardona admitted. "They went out through the front grating with us."

"Wearing their hoods?"

"Yes."

"Didn't that strike you as suspicious?"

"No. We thought they didn't want Malmordo to recognize them if they ran into him."

"And what became of them?"

Cardona drew a long breath before answering Weston's question. This part of the story bothered him.

"We spotted some ratty looking characters," explained Joe, "not far from the cafe. They looked like second-rate editions of Malmordo and we naturally linked them with him, particularly when they started shooting. So we opened fire on them, and next thing the waiters who were with us pulled guns and began shooting too."

"You should have placed them under immediate arrest," chided Weston. "They had no right to be carrying guns."

"We were glad they had guns, right then," returned Cardona. "They helped us send those rats to cover. Except that would probably have happened anyway. Because when the shooting kept on, we kind of realized that the waiters and the rats weren't shooting at each other."

Weston gave a stiff stare.

"At whom were they shooting?"

"Take it or leave it, Commissioner," replied Cardona, "they were shooting at The Shadow."

Cardona expected an outburst, but none arrived. Officially, The Shadow was not supposed to be mentioned in police reports because an identity such as his, based on the evidence of a cloak and hat, might technically be assumed by anyone. In this instance, however, there was a counterbalancing factor in Malmordo, whose own attire, trousers and blouse, were about the only proof that he existed as a personality.

So Weston let the question ride.

"And then, Inspector?"

"Next thing, the waiters were gone," declared Cardona, "hoods and all. They'd scattered just like the rats in the baggy clothes."

"You checked on them at the cafe?"

"Yes. There were half a dozen legitimate waiters still there. The ones who had helped us chase Malmordo and then skipped were trading under phony names."

"Any good descriptions of them?"

"None. But it's a safe bet they were an inside mob planted there by Malmordo."

Weston raised his eyebrows at the word "bet" and then lowered them. The word that Weston really regarded as horrid, whenever Cardona used it, was "hunch" because the commissioner didn't believe in hunches.

"Malmordo had another plant back at the cafe," continued Cardona. "A gypsy fortune-teller named Madame Thalla. We haven't been able to find her since."

"And how," inquired Weston, "did Madame Thalla slip away?"

"By the cellar route," explained Cardona, ruefully. "We found out later that she'd ducked down there. She must have hidden until we went through; then she was free to follow."

"But where could she have hidden? You searched the place, didn't you?"

"Everywhere except behind the door. I didn't remember until later that hiding behind a door is an old gypsy trick. But we weren't looking for Thalla at the time."

Cardona paused, awaiting questions, but none came, so he brought up another factor.

"There was a girl mixed in the thing," declared Joe. "A girl in a white dress, wearing a yellow flower. Some of the waiters remembered her. She'd been at the Cafe de la Morte for the last three evenings."

"Her name?"

"Nobody knew it." Joe scowled. "Nobody, except maybe Madame Thalla. Or Gregor."

"Why would they have known?"

"Because Gregor had his eye on the girl," explained Cardona, "and Thalla didn't like it. People at the cafe think Thalla was sweet on Gregor and therefore jealous, the way gypsies are."

"Gregor was a gypsy too?"

"No. Hungarian. We checked over the cards in his wallet."

"Then you think Madame Thalla was working with Malmordo?"

"Very likely. She spoke to Gregor several times and acted rather angrily. Only Malmordo wouldn't have killed Gregor just to please Thalla. Unless Thalla trumped up something against Gregor, to make Malmordo think he was dangerous."

"Thalla would have preferred to make trouble for the girl, wouldn't she, Inspector?"

"You can't tell," concluded Cardona. "Nobody can figure out gypsies. Thalla was telling the girl's fortune, though, and she may have threatened her then. The girl certainly disappeared in a hurry."

"How?"

"We don't know, unless she skipped through the cellar too."

"That might link her with Malmordo."

"Yes, Commissioner, it might."

The discussion having reached a temporary impasse, Weston began drumming the desk as though it might bring him an idea. Finally he reached for a slender report that lay at hand.

"The stowaway on the *Santander,"* recalled Weston. "Patrolman Moultrie reports that he said something about Malmordo just before the logs fell and crushed him."

"Malmordo and *morto,"* nodded Cardona. "Whether morto meant death or the cafe, we don't know. There was another word, but we aren't sure what it was. The important thing, though"—Cardona was becoming emphatic—"is that there were other stowaways on board that ship. There's been a lot of stowaways coming into port lately, human rats we call them, and they tally with the tribe that Malmordo had around last night."

More drumming from Weston, but it produced no new opinions. So Cardona supplied one.

"Our best clue is this." Joe picked up the half menu from the Cafe de la Morte. "This was a tip-off, Commissioner. Somebody is working on our side and whoever it is, wanted us to block what happened last night."

Hesitating a moment, Weston inquired:

"The Shadow?"

"I don't think so," replied Cardona. "He was with us, one hundred percent, but this isn't the kind of message The Shadow would send. If I could only—"

A knock interrupted at the door. Weston recognized it as belonging to his secretary and pressed a buzzer, giving the word to enter. The secretary, a dapper man, reached the desk and turned apologetically from Weston to Cardona.

"Beg pardon, Commissioner," the secretary said, "but there's a gentleman outside who says he must speak to Inspector Cardona."

"If he's a gentleman," blustered Weston, "tell him to send in his card!"

"He did," began the secretary, "but it's a most unusual card—"

The card was unusual. Cardona snatched it the moment the secretary showed it. The card was the lower half of a menu from the Cafe de la Morte.

Eagerly Cardona matched it with the half-card he already held. The two fitted, proving that the visitor was the unknown informant who had tipped off the law to impending murder at the Cafe de la Morte!

CHAPTER VIII

THE visitor was shown in promptly.

He was a blunt-faced man with square, solid jaw, short-clipped hair with a trend toward iron gray, about the same color as his dark suit.

This was the same man who had been blocked off from the Cafe de la Morte the night before, after bullets had begun to dominate the streets nearby. The same man, in fact, who had met Janice Bradford, drawn her to shelter, and then pointed her to the avenue.

However, Cardona was not thinking in terms of subsequent events, particularly as he knew nothing about them. Joe was still concerned with the tip-off. Separating the halves of the menu card, he gestured at the top portion and demanded:

"You sent me this?"

The visitor supplied a short, stiff bow, then declared in a precise tone:

"That fact should be apparent."

"Good enough," snapped Cardona. "Now tell us who you are and what you know about Malmordo."

Quite unperturbed, the visitor seated himself and looked slowly from Cardona to Weston. The gray man had a deliberate way that impressed his viewers. Cardona, for one, was ready to concede that this stranger would be a tough nut to crack.

Coolly, the visitor announced:

"I must request your absolute confidence before I speak. No word of this conference can be given to anyone."

Terms like that went against Cardona's grain, but before Joe could protest, Commissioner Weston gave the nod. For once, Cardona realized that the commissioner was right.

If the visitor preferred to remain silent, there would be no way of making him talk. Charges against the gray man would be very slender on the mere strength of the menu card. Indeed, he could rest on his dignity, with the fact that he had really aided the law being something in his behalf. It was best to hear him out.

At Weston's nod, the gray man ran his thumbnail down the lapel of his coat. The cloth spread apart and from between, the visitor drew out some thin papers, which he unfolded on the desk. In matter-of-fact tone, he stated:

"My credentials."

The credentials bore an official stamp from Scotland Yard. They named the gray man as Trent Stacey, of the C.I.D., or Criminal Investigation Department. A thin photograph was with them; it tallied with Stacey's features. In routine style, he matched his approved signature, as shown on a document, using Weston's desk pen. Finally, he called special attention to a brief order accompanying his credentials.

This order was from Scotland Yard, informing all law enforcement officers throughout the British Empire that they were to maintain strict secrecy regarding Stacey's presence, wherever he might be.

"I am aware," put Stacey bluntly, "that your jurisdiction is outside of such limitations, Commissioner. But I trust in your judgment to honor this request so long as we both deem it expedient."

"Quite right," agreed Weston, only to add sharply: "Provided you can prove the existence of such expediency." A bow from Stacey. Then:

"I can," he declared, "and in a single word. That word is the name—Malmordo."

Weston and Cardona sat right back to listen. Their visitor needed no further go sign.

"Malmordo is a notorious criminal," asserted Stacey. "In fact, until recently, he was the most notorious criminal on the European scene. He would still be—if he happened to be in Europe."

"His name would indicate that," stated Weston. "I take it that the name is derived from *mal* and *morte,* words signifying "evil death" or its equivalent."

Slowly, Stacey shook his head.

"You are wrong," the gray man declared.. "The term *mal* means opposite and *mordo* means something that gnaws or bites. Hence the term is a corruption—"

"In what language?" put in Weston. "Spanish?"

"In Esperanto," replied Stacey, "an international language. Malmordo's activities were so far flung, that before the war, the police officials in various countries used Esperanto in their interchangeable reports, in order to puzzle Malmordo's followers."

"And did it work?" asked Weston.

"It worked well at first," replied Stacey. "Quite a few of Malmordo's workers were trapped. But then they began using Esperanto too. At that time, Malmordo was known to the police in European countries as *"Mordetbesto"* which in Esperanto means a rodent. That angered his followers who called him "Malmordetbesto" meaning just the opposite of a rat. They shortened it to "Malmordo" and there it stands." Stacey gave a shrug. "So we accepted the term too."

By "we" Stacey obviously meant more than just Scotland Yard. He was including all the law enforcement agencies of Europe.

"If Malmordo made such a stir in Europe," inquired Cardona, "how come we never heard of him in America?"

"The war intervened," explained Stacey. "The Nazis hired Malmordo and his fellow rats to squirm into every occupied country. There, they not only fomented vicious trouble; they destroyed all records pertaining to themselves."

"But why have they come here now?" inquired Cardona.

Stacey took that question blandly and put another as its answer.

"Why have other rats come to America?"

"Because it's the only place where they can find what they want," conceded Cardona. "They're after food and Europe has gone short of it."

"And Malmordo's rats are after loot," specified Stacey. "Europe has gone short on that commodity too."

It made sense to Cardona and with it, the inspector remembered something. He plucked up Moultrie's report and read the words of the dying stowaway:

"Malmordo—*morto*—*noktomezo*—!"

"That's Esperanto," acknowledged Stacey. "It means Malmordo—death—midnight. I heard those words spoken yesterday afternoon, Inspector. That's why I sent you the marked menu card."

"And a patrolman heard them just before midnight," declared Cardona, "spoken by a dying stowaway in the hold of the Steamship *Santander.* I get it now: the fellow must have thought Malmordo double-crossed him."

The news interested Stacey.

"There is your link," he declared. "Malmordo has been bringing his riffraff into port. Until yesterday they were around the Black Star Warehouse, but today they are gone."

Cardona gave Stacey a sharp eye.

"Why didn't you let us in on that?"

"Because I had too much consideration for your very fine police," returned Stacey, coolly. "It would be suicide to invade a fortress belonging to Malmordo unless you first stopped every human rathole connected with the place. I was still checking on the place when I saw some of Malmordo's rats slink away and I followed them to the Cafe de la Morte."

Weston was taking time out to call the Black Star Warehouse. He held a brief conversation, then hung up abruptly.

"That's odd," announced the commissioner, "but it fits. At the Black Star they say they were going crazy on account of rats—they meant the usual kind—but today, they've begun to disappear."

"Because Malmordo's men are gone," nodded Stacey. "They are no longer there to feed the rats."

"Why should they feed the rats?" Cardona demanded.

"So the rats won't feed on them," Stacey explained. "They could never hope to drive the rats from the miserable places that both breeds prefer, so they befriended them. Then they get along comfortably together."

Such solid knowledge of Malmordo and his ways was giving Trent Stacey an invaluable status in the eyes of Commissioner Weston. Folding the credentials, Weston returned them to the C.I.D. man and announced:

"We shall give you full cooperation, Mr. Stacey. In return, I want you to tell us everything else you know about Malmordo. Tell us what crimes you think he intends to attempt, what measures you believe he will employ, and most of all—"

The commissioner paused; then repeated himself for emphasis:

"And most of all, tell us how we can trap him!"

CHAPTER IX

IT took Trent Stacey half an hour to cover the full subject of Malmordo, though it wasn't all continuous talking on Stacey's part. Weston and Cardona had numerous questions, all apt ones, that they inserted at intervals.

Stacey's summary was this:

Before the war, Malmordo had adopted aggressor tactics of his own, including the Fifth Column system. He and his ratty followers slipped into countries, established themselves in the most detestable of hideouts, which were therefore the most difficult to search, and from such headquarters, made deals with local criminals.

Crimes were accomplished and the greater percentage of the stolen goods reached Malmordo and his followers, like water seeking the lowest level. Malmordo preferred objects such as rare paintings and famous jewels, because he disposed of them in other countries. Always, Malmordo and his tribe filtered out as remarkably as they had arrived.

Stacey had the explanation for this: Malmordo and his human rats used gypsies as accomplices. Traveling gypsy tribes were common throughout Europe. In going from country to country, their wagons were thoroughly inspected, but customs men seldom cared if gypsies carried odd items through, particularly as the gypsies could get away with it, anyway.

There were thieves among gypsies, but they were an individual clan and they strictly avoided local criminals. Therefore nobody looked upon them as carriers of highly valued property; indeed, no criminal of any sense would have entrusted such stolen goods to gypsies in the first place. So Malmordo had instituted something novel and unexpected, when he mingled his followers among gypsy troupes. Malmordo's rats had carried their own loot with them.

Then war struck.

Instantly Malmordo and his despicable followers commanded high premiums from the Nazis. No longer were gypsies fronting for the human rats; now, refugees were the cover-up. Poland, France, the Balkans all suffered from the same infiltration process. According to Stacey, they were responsible, Malmordo's men, for many of the most outrageous robberies that brought the treasures of occupied countries into Nazidom.

Stacey's descriptions sounded like a digest of a casebook. When he had finished, he delivered added facts that gave still higher value to his account.

"Malmordo came to England," stated Stacey, "at the time of the Blitz. In fact, we are sure that some of his tribe, perhaps Malmordo himself, mingled with the troops that were rescued from Dunkirk. Malmordo started operations in London, expecting the Nazis to arrive. They never did, and Malmordo gave his game away.

"Unfortunately, Malmordo and most of his rats escaped in fishing boats across the Channel before we had time to unearth them. We discovered, though, that they had plans for supercrime and that they intended to use pressure upon important men who had been engaged in subversive dealings with the Nazis.

"When the war ended, we expected them to filter back into England. They failed to appear, so we decided to look for them in various British dominions. I was assigned to Canada and began my search in Montreal. There was no sign of Malmordo in that city, but I gained a lead that brought me to New York."

That summed Stacey's account. He sat back, ready for questions and received some. "This Malmordo," asked Cardona. "What does he look like, or haven't you ever seen him?"

"I have seen him," replied Stacey, solemnly. "He is so hideous, so grotesque, that it would seem impossible for any human face to be so contorted. In appearance, he is twisted and deformed, yet singularly agile."

Cardona nodded. That fitted his impression of Malmordo.

"How did you happen to see him?" inquired Weston. "And where?"

"I was born, raised and educated in Canada," explained Stacey, "but I lived in Montreal and learned French along with English. I spent three years among German settlers in Canada and learned their language too. Among other languages"—for the first time Stacey smiled, but barely—"I—learned Esperanto."

"Which made you useful in trailing Malmordo," suggested Weston.

"Exactly," acknowledged Stacey. "That was why Scotland Yard took me on."

"And what would you suggest now?"

"That you give me a few days to trace Malmordo" requested Stacey. "It is imperative that I operate on my own, as I always have, but I can report at stated intervals directly to Inspector Cardona."

Weston pondered, then agreed.

"Until you have actual facts as to the whereabouts of wanted criminals," decided the commissioner, "there can be no reason why you should not act in unofficial—or I might say individual—capacity. Meanwhile, Stacey, rest assured that we shall mention this visit to no one."

With that promise, Trent Stacey left.

When Commissioner Weston made a promise he kept it, but he also had an innate curiosity for things unusual. That was why, a few hours later, Weston walked into the Cobalt Club, his regular off-hour habitat, reading a pocket-sized book that interested him so intently that he almost stumbled over a chair containing a friend of his, Lamont Cranston.

Few persons could take matters more calmly, almost indifferently, than did Cranston. He was a man with an impassive face that impressed some observers as masklike and his features, viewed at certain angles, gave a hawkish appearance. Cranston's eyes were easy, but steady, a fact which characterized them now. Indeed, only by gaze did Cranston imply that he was interested in anything that could so preoccupy Weston.

The commissioner seemed to realize it, for he became apologetic, then enthusiastic.

"Sorry, Cranston," began Weston. "I should have remembered I was to meet you here. But you see, I've run across something quite fascinating. Did you ever hear of Esperanto?"

"I have made a few trips around the world," responded Cranston. "Do you think I would have started without equipping myself with an auxiliary language that is known everywhere?"

Weston hadn't thought of that. "Then you speak Esperanto, Cranston?"

"Mi parolas Esperante," replied Cranston, *"Mi trovas la elparoladon tre facila."*

Weston began looking through the book, so Cranston saved him the trouble by translating for him.

"I said that I speak Esperanto," stated Cranston. "I added that I find the pronunciations very easy."

"Do you know the meaning of the word *noktomezo?"*

"That would mean midnight."

"And what would Malmordo mean?"

"Something that doesn't bite. It sounds more like a name, though, than a word commonly used in Esperanto."

"You are right, Cranston," conceded Weston. "It is a name. The name of the world's most desperate criminal."

With that beginning, Weston reeled off all the data that he had gained from Trent Stacey, excepting of course any mention of the C.I.D. man himself. All the while, Cranston listened intently, without showing it. Behind that impassive face of Cranston's lay a keen mind, the mind of The Shadow, for the guise of Cranston was one that The Shadow adopted in the more ordinary stages of his career.

It was palpable to Cranston that Weston had acquired all this information very recently. The reason: if Weston had known all this last night, Malmordo would not have cavorted in such murderous style at the Cafe de la Morte. In his casual way, Cranston decided to seek the source.

"I suppose you learned all this at the Cafe de la Morte," remarked Cranston. "I read about a mysterious murder at that place last night."

"Malmordo was involved," admitted Weston, "but they know nothing about him at the cafe."

"Then you captured some of Malmordo's men?"

"Those rats? Impossible! They have even abandoned their hideaway at the Black Star Warehouse, they and their pets, the ordinary type of rats."

Cranston could have raised his eyebrows, but didn't. Weston hadn't mentioned the Black Star Warehouse in his run-up on the Malmordo question. He regarded it as too closely associated with Stacey. So Cranston was getting somewhere with his casual inquiry.

"I didn't mean Malmordo's regulars," corrected Cranston. "You say he enlists local malefactors wherever he goes. I supposed you might have captured some of the Manhattan contingent that was working with him."

"Some were on the job last night," declared Weston, "but they got away before we could identify them."

"I have it, then," expressed Cranston. "You've been questioning the local gypsies."

"You can't quiz gypsies," declared Weston. "They never tell the same story twice. They have a king who acts as spokesman, but he's out of town at present. King Dakar, they call him, and every gypsy we've asked says he's away. None of them ever heard of Madame Thalla, the fortune-teller at the Cafe de la Morte. They'd say the same about Malmordo."

There were a number of inconsistencies in Weston's speech, but Cranston didn't suggest that the commissioner might be something of a gypsy himself. Instead, Cranston broached a last query.

"The customers down at the Cafe de la Morte," mused Cranston. "There weren't any missing later, were there?"

"One was," recalled Weston. "A girl in white, who wore a yellow flower and had her fortune told. We don't know her name though, or anything else about her. Maybe I should have asked—"

There Weston cut himself off in his own brusque style and threw a challenging glare at Cranston. When Cranston became persistent, he made people tell things they didn't mean to say and Weston had come near mentioning Stacey. Of course Cranston couldn't have been fishing for information; he was just helpful, that was all—or so Weston thought.

Anyway, the commissioner didn't want that kind of help.

"Sorry, Cranston, but I have an appointment." That was Weston's best way to relieve the pressure of this conversation. "I'll be seeing you later."

Remembering that he too had an appointment, Lamont Cranston strolled from the Cobalt Club and out into the gathering dusk.

There Cranston became The Shadow.

CHAPTER X

JANICE BRADFORD wasn't wearing white tonight. Instead she'd chosen a dark blue sweater dress with a beret to match. Janice wasn't taking chances on dodging bullets this evening.

Or knives for that matter.

That was the part that bothered Janice, the way the slinky men seemed to be around again. What they were doing here, away from the docks and warehouses, away from the Village and the Cafe de la Morte, was something that wasn't too hard to guess.

Like Janice, they were probably looking for Madame Thalla.

Regarding Thalla as a friend, Janice was trying to find her somewhere along Gypsy Row and that was just the trouble. Thalla wasn't around, but the human rats were; at least Janice fancied that she could see them poking their imaginary whiskers out of practically every cranny.

Silent houses here, with no signs on the windows denoting fortune-tellers as Janice had supposed there might be. She realized now that gypsies wouldn't advertise such talents in their own neighborhood, just as she recognized they wouldn't talk about each other. The best thing Janice could do would be to find a cab. She'd stopped in too many stores to inquire about Madame Thalla. The people who had given her dumb looks and headshakes might not be so dumb as they looked.

It was thought of Malmordo however, that worried Janice most. And again, she made the mistake of thinking that obscurity would shield her from that Master Rat.

Turning into a side street, Janice hadn't gone a dozen paces before she saw a slinker move from a doorway, as though to sidle across the street and cut off her retreat. There was a doorway on this side and instinctively, Janice turned toward it, then shied away, only to have a firm hand emerge as on the night before and draw her into shelter.

The girl gasped; then, thinking she recognized the clasp, she breathed:

"It's you again! I thought it wasn't until tomorrow night—"

Janice interrupted herself when she saw that her present friend wasn't the blunt-faced man in gray, whose name, though she didn't know it, had today been disclosed as Trent Stacey, but only to Commissioner Weston and Inspector Cardona.

Oddly though, Janice had found another friend, a rather handsome and self-assured young man whom she remembered from the Cafe de la Morte. In the light that slanted into the doorway, Janice was looking at Harry Vincent, who in turn was getting another and more detailed impression of the girl herself.

However, it wasn't wise to stare too long, because the process required light and light was dangerous with lurkers about. Satisfied that Janice regarded him as a friend, due to his lack of resemblance to any of Malmordo's clan, Harry drew the girl deeper into the doorway.

"Speaking of tomorrow night," undertoned Harry, "I was worried about last night. I saw Thalla steer you out of the cafe, but what happened after that?"

"Why—why"—Janice stammered a moment. "I—I managed to get away, that was all."

"Somebody else helped you?"

"Well—yes."

"Somebody you were to meet near here," defined Harry, "and tomorrow night. You mistook me for him."

There was silence for a moment. Janice gave a slight shudder, worrying about the slinkers.

"Whoever he was," suggested Harry, "he found a cab for you, probably over on the avenue."

Janice remained silent.

"There will be a cab here shortly," promised Harry. "I can get you away in it, if you tell me about this other chap. After all, he and I are working toward the same purpose, to trap Malmordo."

At the name "Malmordo" Janice supplied a really appreciable shudder. Then quickly she said:

"I don't know who he was. I promised to meet him tomorrow night, but not here. Unless I know more about you, I don't think I should tell you more."

"My name is Harry Vincent," was Harry's reply. "Now who was your other friend?"

"I don't know," expressed Janice truthfully. "He didn't have time to tell me his name."

"Did you tell him yours?"

Janice tightened her lips, then said:

"No."

From the way she said it, Harry decided that the girl wasn't going to give her name now. Nevertheless, he waited patiently, confident that Janice's interest in the expected cab would make her talk. The process worked. Fumbling in her purse, Janice brought out a folded slip of paper; with a little pencil, she wrote something on it.

"There's the message," she undertoned, "and I've written my name on the back. You can have the paper when you give me the cab."

Lights were coming around the corner and lurkers were scooting for cover. Stepping out boldly, Harry flagged the cab. As it stopped, he opened the door and beckoned to Janice; as the girl hurried into the cab, Harry reminded her of the paper and Janice planted it in his hand.

Then the cab was off with Janice as a passenger and Harry was making a quick dart, openly, toward the corner, to draw attention his way. At that, Harry couldn't feel that he was taking much risk because he'd been expecting a cab piloted by a driver named Shrevvy who was to drop off The Shadow at this very corner. If any lurkers had taken potshots at Harry, they'd have received plenty more virulent bullets in return.

Apparently the lurkers had been smart enough to be on their way, but at that they'd outsmarted themselves. For Harry was scarcely past the corner before another cab pulled up and this time it was Shrevvy's. Not until then did Harry realize that he'd flagged a chance cab that had happened to swing into that side street just before Shrevvy's scheduled arrival.

A whispered voice sounded almost at Harry's elbow, out of darkness that seemed vacant. It ordered:

"Report."

Briefing his report to The Shadow, Harry finished by extending the folded paper. A hand took it and moved into the light, where Harry saw another hand join it. It was a rather astonishing effect, watching those gloved hands unfold the slip of paper and turn it over, for the hands seemed like independent creatures floating in midair.

Even more startling in a way was the slip of paper itself. Staring eagerly, Harry blinked when he saw that it was blank.

"That's the message somebody gave the girl," Harry was saying, "and she wrote her name on back of it—"

Only it wasn't the message and Janice hadn't written her name and she hadn't gone away in Shrevvy's cab. So far as The Shadow was concerned, the girl was still Miss X, which represented an unknown quantity.

Nevertheless, The Shadow's laugh came softly as though he appreciated the humor of the thing. Then, leaving Harry to figure some way of redeeming himself, The Shadow glided off into the darkness.

Better luck was waiting a few blocks away. There, The Shadow stopped in front of a dimly lighted store which proved to be a pet shop. Inside was a customer, a wizened little man, who looked normal enough for this neighborhood. The proprietor, a squatty, sleek-haired man, was warning the customer not to bother the pets and particularly the little green love birds.

The customer answered to the name of Hawkeye and he worked for The Shadow, but of course he hadn't stated either of those facts. What intrigued him about the love birds was that they would peck at odd things, like the cover of a match pack, something that the average parrot would ignore, at least after the first taste.

"Those birds not for sale," the squatty storekeeper was saying. "Customer already buy them. Closing shop now. Come back tomorrow."

The storekeeper was brushing Hawkeye away

from the cage, where one of the green birds was reclaiming the piece of cardboard that had dropped between the bars. Wrapping a cloth around the cage, the squatty man took it to the back of the shop, then returned to pull down the shades in the show window.

Shambling out in slow fashion, Hawkeye would have sped his pace the moment that he turned past the window, if The Shadow had not stopped him with a whispered signal. The result was that Hawkeye paused, then shuffled across the street in careless fashion while the blackness that represented The Shadow continued the swift glide in the original direction.

Through an alley and around to the back street, The Shadow was waiting when the squatty man came from his darkened shop bearing the covered cage that contained the green birds. After a hurried look from right to left, the storekeeper headed for an opposite alley.

The Shadow took up the trail.

That trail ended after a zigzag route through several back streets. The squatty man tapped at an obscure door which opened cautiously. A few words passed through the crack, then the door widened enough for the cage to follow. His order delivered, the owner of the pet shop waddled away.

A few moments later, The Shadow, invisible in the shrouding darkness of the doorway, was opening the door itself to cross the threshold of a new adventure.

CHAPTER XI

THE narrow hallway was pitch-black, its floor so old and creaky that it responded, though ever so slightly, to The Shadow's usually noiseless glide.

At the end was another door, which The Shadow found by a careful probe. His gloved hand muffled the rattle of the loose knob; even the groan of the rusted hinges was suppressed as The Shadow pressed the door inward.

A dim light issued from within, showing a tawdry room furnished with battered chairs and table, a turkey-red curtain hanging across a doorway beyond. If eyes behind that curtain could notice the door's motion, The Shadow's gaze was even keener. He observed the curtain's quiver.

Inching the door slowly inward, The Shadow literally baited the watcher beyond the curtain. He could sense when someone there was ready to surge; then, boldly, suddenly, The Shadow flung the door fully open and whirled through.

As he twisted, The Shadow produced an automatic from beneath his cloak. He completed a full turn that not only carried him away from the wide-open doorway, but brought him back against the door itself, clattering it against the side wall of the room so it formed the long side of a triangle which included the brief stretch of front wall between the corner and the doorway.

This peculiar double process completely fooled the man beyond the curtain. He came charging through, only to halt blankly and bewildered, not knowing how or where to aim the old-fashioned pistol that he clutched in his tawny hand. Then, as The Shadow delivered a shuddery, whispered laugh, the man's face enlarged in terror.

His face was the darkish face of Panjo, the man who had contacted the sailor on the *Santander.*

The Shadow's whisper phrased the name "Panjo." As the darkish man quivered, he saw blackness stretch to a table near the door and whip away the cloth covering of an object standing there, to reveal a cage containing two green birds. Then the whisper formed words, in accusing tone:

"Panjo! *Avakle avnas tut chirikla!"*

In gypsy dialect, The Shadow was saying: "Panjo! These were your birds," to which Panjo could only nod. Then came The Shadow's sharp query:

"Ti romni?"

Panjo broke into a wild babble.

"Mri romni odoi geyas," he pleaded, *"oi n'avel pale. Na janav so pes lake talindyas."*

The Shadow had asked about Panjo's wife and in reply Panjo was saying that his wife had gone away and not come back; that he did not know what had happened to her.

In gypsy talk The Shadow ordered Panjo to give him the gun, which Panjo did, quaking the while. Then, in sinister tone, The Shadow suggested that perhaps Panjo's missing wife might be responsible for Gregor's death. Before Panjo could chatter a denial, The Shadow wheeled, flinging the door shut to reveal a trembling woman in the space represented by the corner.

The woman was Madame Thalla. Quivering, she dropped the knife she held. The Shadow had been ready for the trick that Thalla had used to elude Cardona and had imprisoned the woman behind the door where she had hidden. And now Thalla was chattering wildly:

"Me na chinghiom les! Me na chinghion les!

Thalla was repeating "I did not kill him!" in reference to Gregor and The Shadow's laugh eased to a tone that made Thalla realize he believed her. The Shadow had accomplished what he wanted; he had linked Panjo with Thalla.

And now, in a sterner tone, The Shadow demanded:

"Kai baro kralis th'arakas?"

The Shadow was asking where he could find their great leader, which to Panjo and Thalla meant King Dakar, so lately reported out of the city. Eagerly, Panjo and Thalla conducted him past the turkey red curtain, where Panjo rapped at a door beyond. The door opened and The Shadow found himself facing King Dakar, a gentleman whose surprise diminished rapidly when Panjo, and Thalla chattered to him in gypsy talk.

"Yek Ushalyin!" Panjo exclaimed. *"Laskoro Romeskero!"*

"Ov hin Rom!" added Thalla. *"Na gajo!"*

The title *Yek Ushalyin* was Panjo's way of saying "The Shadow." Translated literally it meant 'a shadow' but in Romany, the indefinite article "a" also meant "one." In defining the visitor as "One Shadow," Panjo was seeking to confer a distinction upon so notable a guest.

Also, Panjo had added that Yek Ushalyin was of the gypsies and Thalla had supplemented the claim by declaring: "He is gypsy, not a foreigner," for the term *Rom* meant someone of the gypsy race, while gajo signified any non-gypsy.

From there on, The Shadow took up the conversation and King Dakar, hearing his speech, bowed low. To term Dakar a 'king' seemed ludicrous, for he was a drab, sunken sort of man, whose broad, droopy face was so weather-beaten that it had lost its natural color. Nevertheless, if The Shadow deserved a title, so did King Dakar.

For after he heard The Shadow declaim in pure Romany, Dakar did likewise. The language that they talked showed that Panjo and Thalla were limited in gypsy-speech to a hodge-podge of varied dialects.

It was a pleasure, Dakar told The Shadow, to hear someone speak the *lacho romano chib,* or pure gypsy, and not the *posh romani* toward which so many of Dakar's people trended. They were even forgetting their *romnipen,* or gypsy ways.

The Shadow inquired if that applied to a Rom named Gregor and Dakar was startled. When The Shadow wanted to learn the connection between Gregor and Malmordo, Thalla became terrified and even Panjo was shaken. Then, Dakar standing speechless, The Shadow calmly expressed himself in English, interspersed with gypsy terms, to clarify the purpose of his visit and how he had arrived here.

"At the pier, I learned that Panjo was Rom," declared The Shadow. "When he saw me, he cried *"Vourdalak"* and *"Nosferadu"* meaning he mistook me for a vampire, which any Rom might. *Yek Rom,* seeking birds, such was Panjo. Why should he want *chirikla?* Because birds are used for telling fortunes. Bring your *chirikla,* Panjo."

Panjo went to get the birds.

"On the boat was a *gajo* who died very suddenly," The Shadow told Dakar. "He said three words: 'Malmordo—*morto—noktomezo.'* Do you understand those words, Dakar?"

Dakar's expression had gone rigid. As it relaxed, he nodded slowly.

"I know who Malmordo is," said Dakar. "But those other words"—he shook his head—"they are in the language that we do not understand."

"The words meant death and midnight," declared The Shadow. "I knew of the Cafe de la Morte and assumed that the man might refer to it. I went there and saw Madame Thalla, a fortune-teller. A *romni* who tells fortunes"—The Shadow gestured to Thalla—"would not her husband be a Rom who would buy *chirikla* like these?"

The Shadow completed another gesture, toward the green love birds which had just arrived in their cage, carried by Panjo. Then, as if to acknowledge The Shadow's skill at deduction, Panjo took the birds from the cage while Thalla brought a little box containing rows of small cards, about the size of place cards used at a dinner party. At a signal from Panjo, one of the birds flew to the box, picked up a card with its beak, fluttered over to The Shadow and deposited the card in the visitor's gloved hand.

"Chirikli dela tuke, Yek Ushalyin," said Thalla. "He is giving you the card, the bird is, that you may read your fortune. So *kamavela?"* Thalla gave a professional shrug. "What will come? *Kon janalo?* Who knows?"

A quaint custom this, of having birds pluck cards and deliver them to customers, so that each could read an individual fortune. Traveling gypsies had trained such birds for centuries, but in recent years, palm reading and interpretations of the tarots had superseded this picturesque type of divination.

"Panjo and Thalla went in hiding," explained King Dakar. "It was then that Panjo remembered his trained birds. He sent word for them to be brought here so that no one could find him through them. But you were very wise, Yek Ushalyin."

The Shadow put a sharp question to Dakar.

"As wise as Malmordo?"

"Wiser, Yek Ushalyin. So we hope!"

"Perhaps Malmordo already knows where to find you!"

"No, no!" Dakar spoke excitedly. "That is why I am in hiding too! So Malmordo cannot find me."

"Nor have the police managed to find you," declared The Shadow. "It is curious you do not wish to talk to them."

"They could not protect us against

Malmordo!" exclaimed Dakar. "That is why we cannot talk to them."

"It has given them a singular impression," stated The Shadow. "The police believe that you are friendly to Malmordo."

That brought a storm of indignant denial from Dakar, with Panjo and Thalla joining in the protest. Every curse that could be invoked in the gypsy language was uttered and all were directed against Malmordo. To another visitor, it would have seemed that the gypsies were overdoing it, but not to The Shadow. They had called him Rom; they had termed him Yek Ushalyin. To him they would only tell the truth.

"We Rom have suffered much from Malmordo," asserted Dakar when the hubbub ended. "We have been called many names in many lands, such names as heathen and outcasts. But in only one land, Egypt, were we called robbers. They gave us the name *Harami* there. And now today, Malmordo would have us called *Harami* everywhere."

"I have heard," affirmed The Shadow, "that Malmordo and his *gaje* traveled with your comrades in Europe."

"Because we thought them poor strangers," argued Dakar. "Malmordo! Bah! The other name they called him, Mordetbesto, was a better name for him. It sounds like the beast he was. So low did he sink that he was taken as a freak to be exhibited for copper money by the foolish Rom he deceived. A *divio gajo,* a wild man they thought he was and others of his kind posed as the same. They learned our customs, *romnipen,* to help them on their way."

"You should have learned more about them," reproved The Shadow. "You avoided the criminals with whom they dealt. Why did you not avoid them?"

"But Malmordo and his *gaje* never dealt with others!" protested Dakar. "We would surely have known if they had."

King Dakar meant it, but as a gypsy leader it was his part to claim he knew everything. His statements did not tally with what The Shadow had learned from Commissioner Weston. Dakar might give the gypsies benefit of doubt where connections with Malmordo were concerned, but he would not extend the courtesy to common criminals. However, The Shadow had a way to test King Dakar further.

"You have said that Gregor once was Rom," The Shadow asserted. "But Gregor called himself a *gajo* and he was at the Cafe de la Morte—"

Madame Thalla babbled an interruption and King Dakar halted her. With all the dignity of his office, Dakar declared:

"As Rom, we both hate and fear Malmordo. But I have ordered my people that if they do neither, Malmordo may not harm us. None were to speak to Malmordo once he arrived here, nor to watch him. Gregor was one who would not obey and when I chided him, he said he was no longer Rom, but *gajo.*

"What Gregor learned about Malmordo, we do not know. How he learned it also puzzles us. But since Gregor was watching for Malmordo, it was necessary that we watch Gregor. I chose Thalla for that duty because she could tell fortunes at the Cafe de la Morte. Because her husband, Panjo, often bought birds from the sailors, I told him to watch the ships. That is all."

Dakar had put it well. The Shadow could have queried what the gypsy king intended next, but such a question was unnecessary. The Shadow simply waited, knowing that Dakar would declare himself. And Dakar did.

Across Dakar's weather-beaten face came a vengeful expression inspired by the demand for justice.

"Gregor was Rom." There was finality in Dakar's tone. "Gregor was murdered by Malmordo. Whoever may ask me to help destroy Malmordo will have the services of any Rom I can supply. I, King Dakar, have so sworn, and I can be found here whenever I am needed."

That promise was meant for The Shadow and it ended the interview. Turning, the cloaked master, whom the gypsies styled Yek Ushalyin made his exit through the red curtain. Only the whispered echoes of a parting laugh remained, as The Shadow went out into the night.

The Shadow needed no further pledge from King Dakar. Already the gypsy leader had provided him with a trail, through Madame Thalla. The card that the trained bird had given The Shadow was not inscribed with some trivial fortune.

Instead it bore a name, one which Madame Thalla had learned and knew that The Shadow would want.

The card read: Janice Bradford.

CHAPTER XII

It was late the next afternoon when Inspector Cardona looked up from his desk to meet the steady gray eyes of Trent Stacey. It was rather startling, the way this visitor had arrived, though Cardona's office wasn't difficult to enter unannounced.

However, whatever annoyance Cardona might have felt he instantly suppressed. Stacey was a special case, by mutual agreement. This was the right way for him to appear here.

In his cool style, Stacey inquired:

"Any reports on rats, Inspector?"

"Plenty," assured Cardona, "but not the sort we want, though they may be a lead. I've been checking with the warehouses around the waterfront to learn how badly they are infested by rats. I haven't forgotten what you said about Malmordo's gang making pets of the pests."

Stacey's straight forehead formed a frown.

"You may arouse Malmordo's suspicions—"

"Not the way I'm handling it," interposed Cardona. "I'm working through the health department. The trouble is the rats are bad news everywhere, big fighting rats, so big they kill some of the cats that are planted to kill them."

"The boldest rats would be where Malmordo is. His men would see to it that they spread out from ordinary hiding places."

"I figured that. You were right about Black Star. It's really free of rats, that warehouse, so we're no longer bothering with it."

Stacey gave a short, pleased nod. His gray eyes were reflective for a moment; then he brought up another subject. Spreading a sheet of paper on the desk, Stacey pointed to a rough diagram that he had drawn.

"Malmordo's present headquarters," he declared. "There is a chance we may trap him there tonight."

"This isn't a warehouse," remarked Cardona, studying the chart. "It looks more like some old residence."

"Malmordo never stays with his tribe," explained Stacey. "He doesn't want them to know too much about him."

"Then how did you find out about this place?" demanded Cardona. "By staying away from Malmordo's mob?"

Stacey smiled and nodded.

"In a sense, yes," he stated. "I overheard a few roustabouts talking in that doggerel form of Esperanto that Malmordo's followers use. They mentioned his headquarters, because naturally they have to contact him. He will probably go there tonight."

Cardona began to study the chart more intently.

"At dusk, I can go in there," suggested Stacey. "Give me at least a half hour's leeway before any of your men even approach that area."

"But suppose you meet Malmordo, in the meantime?"

"I should like to meet Malmordo," replied Stacey, grimly. "It would be a pleasure to take him by surprise. However, I don't expect him there that soon."

"What if some of his men are on guard?"

"I talk their language. I can pose as a representative of the local talent that Malmordo is lining up. But I don't expect them either. What I want to do is get at any loose evidence that may be lying around."

That part pleased Cardona immensely. He could foresee that some sort of a case would have to be built against Malmordo to make the public believe that such a vicious and fabulous criminal existed. So Joe asked:

"After I post my men—what then?"

"If Malmordo appears," returned Stacey, "let him through. Then close in and box him. I can work from the inside and drive him right back into your hands."

Cardona thought that over. Then:

"We might nail him going in."

"Malmordo won't come within a block of that house," objected Stacey, "if you are any nearer. You are dealing with a Master Rat and don't forget it. Outdoors, Malmordo has a way of keeping just beyond a good marksman's range. You can sight him, but never hit him."

"You're right," Cardona agreed, remembering how elusive Malmordo had been, even in the restricted area of the dining garden at the Cafe de la Morte. "The only game is to turn that house into a rattrap, which judging from the address, it probably is already."

Methodically, Cardona made a brief time sheet with a carbon copy which he gave to Stacey. Then, as the C.I.D. man was about to leave, the inspector asked:

"One matter I meant to mention yesterday—were you in the Cafe de la Morte before Malmordo appeared there?"

"Not on the night he murdered Gregor," replied Stacey. "I was on my way there at the time. But I was in the place on previous evenings."

"Did you see a girl in white, wearing a yellow flower? The blonde who talked to Madame Thalla?"

"Yes. I saw her after the murder, too."

"Where?"

"A few blocks from the cafe. She was dodging the shooting. I realized that something must have happened at the Cafe de la Morte and I took it that she had fled with other patrons. I directed her to the avenue."

"And did you learn her name?"

"Unfortunately no, but I would recognize her again."

"That's what everybody else says," declared Cardona, grimly, "but we haven't been able to find her. If you should see her anywhere again, be sure and let me know."

Pausing at the door, Stacey gave a slow, emphatic nod and said:

"I shall."

Though it wasn't dusk yet, Cardona's office was getting dark because it had an eastern exposure through a none-too-ample window. Several minutes after Stacey left, Joe decided to turn on the lights. When he did, a new surprise was staring him in the face.

The surprise was a gentleman named Lamont Cranston.

And a real surprise this.

Cranston's usual contact with the law was Commissioner Weston. Though he knew Cardona well, Cranston had rarely visited the inspector's office, at least not as himself.

There was a special reason for Cranston's visit. He hadn't been able to find Weston. The commissioner had slipped away somewhere to study his Esperanto. This in turn meant there was little use in trying to interview him, because when Weston concentrated on one thing, he dropped others. Cranston had gotten the hint that Weston was leaving the case of the Cafe de la Morte to Inspector Cardona.

There was someone else that Cranston hadn't been able to locate: Janice Bradford. That was why Cranston had come here, to sound out the law as represented by Joe Cardona.

Almost immediately Cranston discovered something; namely, that Cardona was fidgety. This was so unusual that it showed, even though Joe managed to keep his usual deadpan expression. So Cranston, ever calm, immediately became calmer than ever. He had something to chat about, he said, but it could wait. So Cardona's eyes went to the rough chart on the desk and Joe decided to act as Weston had in Cranston's presence the day before.

Cardona simply said as much as he could without saying too much.

Using his phone, Cardona called a couple of special men and told them to bring certain others. He summoned one detective to his office, showed him the rough chart and drew a larger plan, pointing out where all hands would be stationed. All the while, Joe tried to make it look like mere routine.

"There's been a little trouble in that neighborhood," the inspector told the detective. "I'll make the rounds after you're all posted."

All the while, Cranston was sitting by indifferently, getting occasional glimpses at the chart and hearing the detective's queries. He took in something that the detective didn't; namely, that a certain house marked on the diagram could well be the center of the whole thing.

Next, Cardona glanced at his brief time chart, then turned it over and pushed it to one side, among some loose papers. Here Cardona copied a bit of Cranston's indifference.

"Don't post yourselves too soon," Cardona told the detective. "You might be noticed. It will be dusk about seven o'clock, so make it seven thirty."

Glancing at his watch, Cranston remarked that it was already seven o'clock, which pleased Cardona.

"Get started," Cardona told the detective, "and take the others along." Then, as the detective left, Joe added: "Sorry, I'll have to be leaving in a few minutes, Mr. Cranston."

"Very well." Cranston arose in leisurely style then paused. "I just wanted to ask about a girl named Janice Bradford."

"Never heard of her."

"She seems to be missing," continued Cranston. "Maybe she just went away for a rest."

Cardona shrugged as though that didn't belong in his department.

"She might need a rest," decided Cranston, "after experiencing a lot of excitement. Some of her friends say that she was very fond of the Cafe de la Morte."

That brought Cardona around.

"What does she look like?" Joe demanded. "Is she a blonde?"

"I didn't think to ask," replied Cranston. "I simply thought you might be interested. Only her friends know nothing more."

"What about her family?"

"She has a father, but he is missing, too, which is the oddest part. They seem to have moved from one hotel to another and stopped giving forwarding addresses. The father's name is Andrew Bradford and the hotels—"

Pausing, Cranston reached for a loose sheet of paper and added: "Here, I'll write out the data for you."

Cranston wrote the names of the persons and the hotels, folded the sheet of paper and laid it back upon the desk. Cardona didn't observe what happened during the folding process for he was on the wrong side of the desk. In folding the paper toward himself, Cranston brought a smaller slip into view, his own view. It was Cardona's time chart and it automatically came with its writing side up.

The list was as follows:

Stacey—7:00 p.m.

Cardona—7:30 p.m.

Malmordo—? ? ?

In putting the folded paper on the desk, Cranston turned it downward so that the list dropped beneath it, writing side also down. He gave the folded paper a slight slide, so it glided toward Cardona, who picked it up and creased it again as he put it in his pocket. Seeing the blank side of the sheet that bore his list, Cardona picked it up too, keeping the writing away from Cranston's sight. Poker-faced, Joe hid the grim satisfaction that he felt at thus outwitting the astute Mr. Cranston.

Cardona didn't know that Cranston had swapped one name for another, that of Janice Bradford in return for Trent Stacey or at least the Stacey part of it. Nor did Cardona begin to guess what Cranston would do about those other facts he had learned, once he discovered their importance.

In the dusk that was heavy outside police headquarters, the departing Mr. Cranston hailed a waiting cab and once inside it merged with darkness. For the cab was Shrevvy's and from a secret drawer beneath its rear seat, Cranston produced and put on the regalia of The Shadow.

The address that Shrevvy heard his chief give was very close to the old house that Trent Stacey had defined as the probable headquarters of a supercriminal called Malmordo.

CHAPTER XIII

SIGHTSEERS wishing to view the house that Malmordo used as his headquarters can find it by looking for the most decrepit house in the most dilapidated section of Manhattan south of Forty-second Street and west of Fifth Avenue.

The house had to be about that bad because it was empty and during the housing shortage in New York practically any house that still stood of its own accord was remodeled in some fashion or another so that it could be occupied.

To say that this house was standing of its own accord at first sight seemed an exaggeration. Its brick front was falling apart in such chunks that it looked as though it were propped between the two adjacent houses that formed part of the solid block. But those houses were so ramshackle that they couldn't have supported more than their own weight; therefore Malmordo's house must have been standing on whatever trifling merit it still possessed.

This block and those surrounding it were gloomy and quiet when Cardona's men put in an appearance on the fringes. They managed to keep out of sight without trouble, taking advantage of the very gloom which had probably attracted Malmordo to this area. There was one fault, however, which worked against Malmordo and pleased Cardona immensely as he began his rounds to tell his detectives what this was all about.

A grimy streetlight stood directly opposite the empty house, making the building perhaps the most conspicuous in the block. It probably annoyed Malmordo, that light, but since this was the only empty house in the neighborhood, or for that matter about any neighborhood, he had to make the best of it.

Cardona now understood why Trent Stacey had chosen dusk as the right time to enter and had also wanted a reasonable leeway. Stacey had probably waited while it grew dark, until just the time when streetlamps began to flicker. That was his cue to get into the house in a hurry, before the glow appeared from across the street.

How long Stacey had been inside was a question but a rather important one. The really important question was how soon Malmordo would arrive, if at all.

It happened sooner than the ace inspector had hoped.

Out of the surrounding gloom that might have harbored a few dozen lurkers came as grotesque and distorted a figure as any freak show ever boasted.

The term human rat was hardly adequate for Malmordo. He had the writhe of a human snake.

Malmordo's figure, clad baggily as at the Cafe de la Morte, seemed to grow right out of the grimy sidewalk and coil itself up the front steps. Watching from nearly a block away, Cardona started to move in, his men copying his example, but as he did, Joe realized how right Stacey was in saying that long-range fire couldn't reach Malmordo. The human monstrosity was safely in the shelter of his own doorway before anyone could have aimed a gun.

And then, as if to tantalize anyone who happened to be watching, Malmordo poked his head and shoulders into sight. The streetlamp opposite gave a full but fleeting view of those misshapen, vicious features that were so unmistakable. Only one man could have displayed such an ugly, twisted visage: Malmordo.

He fitted the rat definition as he peered up and down the street, in a quick double take. Then, rat fashion he was gone again, into the house itself.

There was proof that Malmordo had really gone.

A long streak of blackness that sliced from across the street began to take on line. A shadowy stretch, that was all, and its waver could have been due to a flicker of the streetlamp. But there was solid blackness moving in the streaky gloom that shrouded it.

Solid blackness called The Shadow.

At the steps, The Shadow did a curious sidle, up toward the edge of the doorway.

Malmordo had been misshapen; The Shadow was shapeless.

Growing blackness, that was all, like something unreal, which evaporated, smoke-fashion before anyone could define it. The fade took place when

The Shadow deftly twisted himself into the doorway, from which, unlike Malmordo, he did not take a last quick look.

Even Inspector Cardona was deceived. On the move, he thought that the rise of darkness and its curious fadeaway were due to the changing angle of his vision. Besides, Cardona couldn't picture even The Shadow as part of a scene which had been unearthed exclusively by Trent Stacey, a man whose own ways were exceptionally undercover.

Inside the house, The Shadow was hearing creaks.

The house was a three-story affair; by this time the creaks were going up beyond the second. They represented footsteps, though they were not distinguishable as such. Rather they were a cross between a creep and a snaky progress which defined them as Malmordo's. What The Shadow was hearing were the transcribed sounds of Malmordo's ascent as reproduced by the old beams and shaky flooring.

A tiny flashlight spotted its glow along the hall, shrouded by the folds of The Shadow's cloak. With that light The Shadow picked out the stairs and began a climb of his own, a trifle slower than Malmordo's but considerably more efficient. For as he reached the second floor, The Shadow could hear the creaks upon the third, which wouldn't have been possible had The Shadow been producing such sounds himself.

As near noiseless as was possible in this old house, The Shadow was betraying no token of his presence. But now, hearing a pause in the sounds that meant Malmordo, The Shadow slackened his climb to the third floor, practically feeling each step ahead, shifting his weight by degrees, so that not even the slightest token of his approach could be sensed.

Almost at the third floor, The Shadow heard the muffled closing of a door. He was conscious next of creaks that must have come from a hallway, moving toward the rear. It was as if some eavesdropper were stealing away, eager for haste, yet anxious for silence. The closing of the door, however, indicated that Malmordo had isolated himself in a room; therefore whoever was sneaking along the third floor could do so without too much risk of being heard, at least by Malmordo.

In turn, The Shadow increased his speed, knowing that Malmordo could not hear him and recognizing that the interloper was making enough sounds of his own to drown any that The Shadow made. That interloper, of course, would be a man named Stacey, who had been listed at seven o'clock on Cardona's schedule. Right now, The Shadow was summing the whole arrangement between Stacey and Cardona, though he had already assumed that it might be something of this sort.

Had Stacey boxed Malmordo?

Hardly, not in so short a time space. Rather, Malmordo had boxed himself, though certainly not too solidly. As The Shadow reached the third floor he could hear creaks in the rear of the house and below, indicating that Stacey had found a back stairway as a better way down.

What Stacey should do was obvious. By promptly summoning Cardona and the detectives, Stacey could lead them up to the room where Malmordo was, with little chance of being heard. Then Malmordo would be really trapped, provided he remained in that room.

There was another proviso.

Could half a dozen men or more come up the front stairs and the back without multiplying those creaks to such a degree that Malmordo wouldn't hear them? The Shadow doubted that such a mass invasion could be muffled; yet he knew Cardona well enough to realize that the inspector would attempt it. Cardona believed in using men when he had them and tonight he had them.

The solution was simply for The Shadow to trap Malmordo first and hold him until the police arrived.

Licking along the hall, the flashlight picked out a closed door halfway to the back of the house. It fitted with the location of Malmordo's final creaks and the muffled sound of a closing door; it also explained why Stacey would have taken the back way down. The back stairs were nearer and toward them was an open doorway from which Stacey might have watched Malmordo enter the room which now was closed.

Silently, swiftly, The Shadow reached the closed door. He placed one hand on the knob while his other drew an automatic. Expertly, The Shadow turned the knob with a squeeze. He eased the door inward and saw a room with a tiny, shaded window; a room lighted by a single candle that was burning on a table beside an old trunk.

The trunk was opened and its tray was strewed with envelopes and papers. More important, in front of the trunk was the crouched figure of Malmordo, huddled as though reading something by the candlelight. There were no chairs in the room, but its floor was covered with a frayed carpet, which came clear to the door.

In fact, the door, in opening inward, had lifted the edge of the rug, scruffing it just enough to show the glint of a wire that ran beneath. The Shadow, ever alert for detail, was quick to note that item. For already, as he lunged across the threshold, The Shadow had sensed something wrong with the bunched figure of Malmordo.

It seemed to be swaying, that crouched form, but the reason was the waver of the candlelight. In order to produce such an illusion, the figure had been set between the light and the trunk; therefore Malmordo couldn't be reading anything at all. The figure itself wasn't Malmordo, it was a dummy. The lack of chairs in the room was an indication of the structure on which the dummy was formed.

Malmordo had simply planted his baggy garb upon a chair. The wire, running straight toward the trunk, was obviously connected with a booby-trap. Half into the room, The Shadow could lose more time by turning than he would in completing his surge. So he turned his drive into a dive, hitting the chair shoulder first.

A tiny flashlight spotted its glow along the hall, shrouded by the folds of The Shadow's cloak.

It was a cushioned armchair, the kind it had to be to give sufficient bulk to the improvised dummy. Taking the chair with him, The Shadow somersaulted at an angle past the trunk, to a corner of the room, where he landed, chair uppermost.

And just in time.

As the chair legs kicked toward the ceiling, the trunk exploded with a sullen blast that filled the room with a pungent white smoke which echoed with the rattle of flying metal fragments, ricocheting from the walls!

CHAPTER XIV

VIEWED from the street, the old brick house seemed to jolt and shake itself under the force of the blast. If the charge had been planted in the cellar, the structure might have given way, but as it was, the building settled back to normal, except for a flying shower of broken windows that burst from every floor.

Curiously, the crash of the windows was like a sequel to the explosion and another follow-up occurred a dozen seconds later. The front door came flying open, disgorging a plunging figure that righted itself at the bottom of the steps and arose to reveal itself as Trent Stacey.

At least Cardona recognized the man as Stacey, though the detectives didn't know who he was. Except that they were sure the man couldn't be Malmordo, the writhy thing that had entered the house only a short while before.

Stacey looked bewildered for the moment, then hearing the pound of approaching feet, he knew that they must mean Cardona's squad. With an eager wave of his arm, Stacey gestured the detectives into the house and led them in a rush up the front stairs, with Cardona pressing to the fore.

Meanwhile, the smoke was clearing in the third floor room that Malmordo had designed as a death trap. From the corner came a whispered laugh, a battered chair came flinging through the air to land where the trunk had been. Enveloped in the remnants of the smoke, The Shadow appeared as a ghost as he arose and surveyed the damage all about him.

The room was really wrecked. Chunks of plaster had fallen from the walls, along with portions of the ceiling. On the floor lay a broken square of wood; above it, a similar hole in the ceiling, indicating that the thing was a trapdoor. Malmordo's papers had vanished in a puff of brilliant flame, accompanying the blast. If The Shadow had been caught unshielded in the midst of that explosion, he would have been hurt badly and perhaps permanently.

As it was, he remained unscratched, thanks to the protecting chair which had taken the brunt of the blast.

And now, with footbeats pounding on the stairs, The Shadow needed the quickest exit that would keep him in active circulation. One loomed above, the gaping hole where the trapdoor had been. Using the now unsteady chair, The Shadow reached the hole with his hands and chinned himself through, fading like the drifting smoke, just as Stacey arrived with Cardona and the crew of detectives.

The devastation amazed them, so much that Cardona's men weren't surprised to see the inspector talking things over with a total stranger, which was what they regarded Stacey to be.

"Malmordo was here!" asserted Stacey. "I was looking at some papers in the tray of a trunk that was right in the center of the room, when I heard him coming up the front stairs. So I sneaked down the back way."

"You saw him come in here?" queried Cardona.

"Yes," replied Stacey, "and he closed the door. It was open when I first came here."

"What about the papers?"

"I snatched a few that looked important." Stacey tapped his inside pocket. "I didn't want to disturb too many, not after I heard Malmordo coming. He might have noticed it."

"Looks like he did notice it," gruffed Cardona. He was looking along the carpet, scorched by the blast, and now showing the line of the wire. "That's why he rigged this room into a trap. Unless—"

Joe had glanced up. He saw the open gap above the rickety chair.

"That's where Malmordo went!" exclaimed Cardona. "Out through that trapdoor! We'll go after him!"

On the theory that what goes up must come down, Cardona was too smart to take his whole squad to the roof. He sent men to the ground floor to cover the front door and the back, gesturing Stacey along with them. The detectives were to spread, while Stacey was to stay across the street and watch the front door. From there, he could signal up to the roof as needed.

This was decided amid the sweep of flashlights, for the explosion had snuffed Malmordo's candle. It was during one of those sweeps that Cardona had spotted the open trapdoor, but now Joe was using a flashlight to bore straight up through that space as two detectives gave him a hoist and then prepared to follow.

Sweeping the flashlight around the flat roof, Cardona saw only blackness, so he turned off the light and laid low while one detective boosted the other, who promptly leaned back through the opening and helped his companion up to join him. Then, as the three men spread, they began to slice everywhere with their flashlights, producing prompt results.

From behind a chimney, where only blackness seemed to dwell, an automatic opened fire.

Those shots weren't directed at Cardona and the detectives. They stabbed toward the roof of one adjoining house, then at the other, in quick, alternating precision. They brought wild yells and even wilder fire.

The Shadow fired those initial shots. He was aiming at crouched gunners who were entrenched on each side of the empty house. Catching them unaware, The Shadow had broken up an ambush that would have been ruinous to Cardona and his men. As it was, the return fire was hasty and most of it directed at the chimney. This gave Cardona and his two companions time to flatten and start jabbing at the ambushed crooks.

Those gunners were ambushed no longer. They heard a fierce, strident laugh from behind the chimney, a taunt that mocked their futile gun fire. Recognizing that laugh as The Shadow's, the crooks turned and fled down through trapdoors in the adjoining houses, peppered by gunfire as they went.

From their appearance and the fact they shouted in English, it was apparent that these were hired hoodlums of the breed that had served as waiters at the Cafe de la Morte. Since Malmordo was gone, it seemed obvious that he was using this crew to cover up his flight instead of employing his own band of slinky rats. This fitted with Stacey's data regarding Malmordo and the alliances he formed with local criminals wherever he operated.

The Shadow wasted no time in going after one batch of fleeing hoodlums. Hearing the laugh trail in that direction, Cardona recognized the fact and motioned his men to pursue the other half of the fugitive tribe. People living in the houses adjoining the empty building were startled and cowed by what seemed human stampedes coming down the stairways.

All was quiet on the street until suddenly two doorways gushed a divided human tide. Three men poured from each exit; those from the house where The Shadow had headed were staggering, the reason being that two were literally carrying along a third. He was coughing his last, that thug, so they dropped him on the steps.

Across the street, Trent Stacey dropped away from the light and into shelter just as a rakish car came roaring from the corner. Five hoodlums should have hopped on its running board, but only four did. The fifth man had a wounded arm that dangled so that its hand couldn't grab, so he dived for shelter in the darkness in front of Malmordo's house.

In the wake of the rakish car came a speeding cab and as it passed the doorway just beyond Malmordo's, a cloaked figure whirled down the steps, cleared the dead thug lying there, and sprang into the cab as it briefly slackened speed. All with one twist, The Shadow opened the cab door and closed it with himself inside; then was off to the chase.

There was an interval between; in fact, the car had turned the corner before the cab arrived. During that interval, Stacey emptied his revolver after the fleeing car, but its speed carried it beyond range. By then, Cardona and his two detectives were piling from the other house; from both corners came other headquarters men who had spread themselves too far.

Stacey shouted to them that one of the thugs was still at large; then, looking up, he waved his arms in a mad warning. The detectives looked up to the roof of the empty house, as Stacey sprang into the shelter of its doorway.

The shout that Stacey gave was this:

"Look out! Malmordo is still up there!"

Cardona bellowed for his detectives to dive to cover instead of standing flat-footed in the middle of the street. They did and thereby cleared the way for the crippled thug to make a rush for it. The fellow popped from the darkness of an areaway in front of the empty house, but that lunge was his last. Hardly across the sidewalk, he sprawled as something overtook him and planted itself between his shoulders.

The thing was a long-bladed throwing knife that had whizzed down from the dark. Its glinting handle told what it was and instantly Stacey leaped down the high steps from the doorway of the empty house and turned to aim his replenished revolver straight upward.

Stacey's stream of bullets did nothing more than nick the cornice along the roof front and the same applied to the leaden deluge that spurted from the guns of Cardona's squad as they sprang out to copy Stacey's example. Cardona bawled for some of them to race up through the empty house again and find Malmordo on the roof, but Joe didn't go along; he knew it would be useless.

With dozens of adjoining houses to choose from, in this block and the next, Malmordo would be sure to reach the ground. The only thing was to spread out through the neighborhood and try to spot him, but knowing the elusive qualities of the Master Rat, Cardona doubted that he could be snared.

More imperative at the moment was the questioning of the dying thug who had received the blade of Malmordo's uncannily thrown knife. With Stacey, Cardona stooped above the man and recognized him as a freelance thug named Kirky Schleer. Seeing that Kirky was nearly gone, Cardona lost no time in trying to make Kirky talk.

"Hello, Kirky," put Cardona. "We know you were working for Malmordo. He double-crossed you when he saw you couldn't get away. We'll square it for you if you tell us all you know about Malmordo."

"Malmordo." Kirky repeated the name parrot-style, with a spread of ugly, leathery lips, "Double cross. You want to know about Malmordo. I'll tell you—"

That sentence ended with a grimace, Kirky's last. Kirky Schleer sagged back and the facts that were on his lips died with him in an unintelligible groan.

CHAPTER XV

SHREVVY'S cab pulled over to let a patrol car shriek by with its siren going full blast. There was no use in going further. The carload of crooks had made its getaway, despite Shrevvy's efforts to overtake it.

Inspector Cardona had calculated too well. In hope of trapping Malmordo, he had brought in police from everywhere. With its head start, the rakish car that had made away with a load of gunzels had found the clear, while The Shadow's cab in hot pursuit had been snarled by the incoming traffic.

If Shrevvy expected criticism, he didn't get it. Instead, a low, whispered laugh sounded from the darkened backseat of the cab. Low spoken orders; then the slight slam of a door. The Shadow had left, after telling Shrevvy to report in order to be available later, if needed.

This was over on the East Side, well remote from the house where Malmordo had stirred up so much chaos. In a slight way, however, Malmordo had done The Shadow a favor, or rather the fugitive car had. The Shadow was in a vicinity where certain information awaited him, information which the pressure of other business had prevented him from gaining earlier.

On foot, The Shadow covered several blocks in rapid, phantom style. He reached an obscure doorway in a row of silent houses and paused there. From his lips, came an unexpected sound, a chirp much like a bird's.

The signal was answered.

From a darkened window beside the door came an answering chirp, a genuine one. Then, barely discernible in the darkness, a green love bird fluttered from a slightly opened window and placed a fortune card in The Shadow's hand. The bird flew away and The Shadow focused his concentrated flashlight upon the card.

Instead of a name, this card bore a drawing. It was simple and hand-colored in crayon. The sketch showed a tiny yellow lantern.

The Shadow's whispered laugh was whimsical. He had come a long way to learn where he could have gone immediately after leaving Malmordo's house. The Yellow Lantern was the name of a small, obscure cafe over on the West Side. It had taken a trip to the East Side to acquire the necessary facts.

So The Shadow set out upon what was a trail in reverse, confident that the gypsies had learned something about the Yellow Lantern which would develop when he arrived there.

Something was already developing at the Yellow Lantern.

The little restaurant was quiet and not too crowded. Nobody seemed to notice the girl who had slipped in from the side street. She was wearing dark clothes again tonight, but just for luck—good or bad—she was wearing a yellow daffodil.

The girl was Janice Bradford.

Quiet though the place was, Janice felt nervous.

From her purse, the girl had taken a folded slip of paper, half of a larger sheet. She kept reading the brief message that was written on it. The message said:

"The Yellow Lantern, Wednesday evening, eight o'clock."

A yellow lantern—a yellow flower.

The connection was enough to bring Janice here. She felt no danger, rather a sense of assurance. However this message might relate to Malmordo, it had been given to her by someone who had helped her, the gray man with the blunt square features whom she had encountered after her flight from the Cafe de la Morte.

That was why Janice kept looking up from her table, hoping that the gray man would arrive. Suddenly her hopes were realized. Strolling in from the front door came the very man she wanted to meet again.

The man was Trent Stacey.

In his bland fashion, Stacey came over to Janice's table and sat down. From his pocket he produced a batch of papers and glanced through them. Then, looking at Janice, Stacey smiled slightly and said:

"These belong to the police, but I won't have to deliver them until later. Meanwhile, suppose we introduce ourselves. My name is Trent Stacey. And yours?"

"Janice Bradford."

Stacey's gray eyes fixed steadily.

"You are Andrew Bradford's daughter?"

The girl nodded.

Putting away the papers that he had brought from Malmordo's, Stacey produced the compact credentials that he carried in his lapel and presented them to Janice. The girl's eyes widened when she saw their reference to Scotland Yard.

"We nearly trapped Malmordo tonight," stated Stacey. "The police are searching for him now. I couldn't help, so I excused myself, because I remembered my appointment with you. I should like to hear your story."

"Very well," Janice decided. "My father had a partner named Lucien Thorneau, who handled business here while my father and I were in Mexico."

"I know," nodded Stacey. "An oil business."

"Correct," said Janice. "Then Thorneau died and we came to New York. Everything was wonderful until a man named Malmordo sent word to father that he wanted a mere quarter of a million dollars to hush up a slight scandal that involved the business."

"And your father told you about it?"

"No. I found out for myself. I saw the letters that came and I overheard some phone calls. It seems that Thorneau faked a deal with some Nazi agents and wrote off a half a million dollars profit as loss."

"Your father knew about it?"

"Of course not!" Janice's tone was indignant. "Now Malmordo is trying to collect half of that money. He said he would suggest a way that would be mutually satisfactory."

"What way was that?"

"I don't know. Father was to meet Malmordo at the Cafe de la Morte, wearing a yellow flower to identify himself. He decided not to go, so I went there instead."

"Were others to do the same?"

"I think so. But since father, an innocent man, refused to go there, it's not surprising that guilty parties wouldn't. I was just foolish enough to want to see what would happen. I waited three nights for Malmordo to arrive and when he did come, he murdered Gregor."

Stacey gave a slow, understanding nod.

"Gregor was the reason," he decided. "Malmordo must have known he was on the watch for him. That was why Malmordo wouldn't talk to you. Has your father heard anything since?"

"Not yet."

For a while, Stacey pondered. As he did, he brought a half-sheet of paper from his pocket and matched it with the torn note he had given Janice.

"Just my way of positive identification," explained Stacey. Then he added, emphatically: "I think, Miss Bradford, that you should await further word from Malmordo."

"But I can't!" Janice objected. "You see, father, has been moving from hotel to hotel, so there is no way of tracing us. I'm not afraid of Malmordo." The girl set her chin defiantly. "In fact, I want to meet him. If you know where he is, tell me!"

Stacey pointed from the window. Across the street, Janice saw the looming bulk of an old warehouse that bore a huge black star painted on its wall.

"That's where he was," expressed Stacey. "In the Black Star Warehouse, living with the rats he called his followers. That's why I wanted you to come here."

"So I could meet Malmordo!"

"Quite the contrary," declared Stacey, coolly. "I knew that Malmordo would be avoiding this neighborhood. By present calculations, his human rats are now infesting the building owned by the La Plata Grain Storage Company, four blocks north of here. I intend to report that to the police tonight."

Still wearing that determined expression, Janice opened her lips, then closed them. What she was about to say, she didn't say, but it would have been another defiance of Malmordo. Perhaps Stacey realized it, because his tone was serious when he said:

"Believe me, Miss Bradford, you must avoid Malmordo. Whatever I can do to help your cause, I shall. If you will tell me where I can reach you—"

"At the Azalea Plaza," interposed Janice. "Anytime you care to call there, Mr. Stacey. Father is registered under the name of Howard Gantry."

Stacey arose with a bow.

"It would be better if we left separately," he decided. "If the coast is clear, as I am sure it will be, there will be no reason for me to return. Allow about five minutes and if I do not come back, you can go"—he paused and gave Janice a steady look—"directly home to the Azalea Plaza."

Janice nodded that she understood. She watched Stacey leave and waited the full five minutes in accordance with his instructions. But from then on, Janice decided to act upon her own. Instead of leaving by the front door, as Stacey had, she went out the side way. Then, instead of hailing a cab, Janice turned directly north for a four-block walk.

Despite Stacey's advice, Janice was determined to meet Malmordo, the archfiend who would at least recognize the token of the yellow flower.

Or would he?

Debating it, Janice could see no reason why he wouldn't. Yet as she walked bravely northward, Janice felt worried. Looking back to see if anyone were following her, the girl saw only blackness.

There were wavers in that blackness as though some phantom figure had picked up the trail that Janice Bradford hoped would bring her to Malmordo.

Such wavers could not be real. In forced fashion, Janice laughed them off as she trudged onward.

CHAPTER XVI

FINDING a way into the La Plata Storage Building was a problem in itself. The place appeared to have only one door, big enough to drive the biggest truck through, and blocked by a steel barrier that would have stopped a Sherman tank.

Going around the building, Janice looked in vain for other entrances and in her hunt, she was annoyed when her high heels caught in a steel grating that looked like the opening of a culvert. Stumbling onward, Janice decided to be more careful, so she looked back at the grating to check it in case she encountered another like it.

That was when footsteps shuffled up beside her. Turning, much startled, Janice found herself confronted by a pair of leering faces that looked yellow and apish in the dim light. Instantly, she knew that these two men must belong to Malmordo.

They proved it by the deft quick way they laid their slimy hands upon Janice's arms. So tight was the grip that the girl was afraid to resist. She felt that if she did, those hands would go to her neck and strangle her on the instant.

Now, swiftly, these fiends were sweeping Janice back to the broad grating. They lifted it, slid her through, and the bars dropped with a clang, against the sidewalk above. Bent forward by the gripping arms, Janice was rushed through a low, pitch-black tunnel, where she heard things scurrying ahead.

Those things were rats and big ones.

Janice saw the rats when she emerged into the dim light of a lower cellar that they reached by a downward slope. But the rats—and there were dozens of them—were not the worst sight that Janice faced. In fact, the rats were scurrying for cover, as though they dreaded something.

That something could well have been Malmordo.

He was standing there beyond the brink of a slimy pool that ebbed in a corner of the slanted cellar. The pool was composed of stagnant water that had accumulated as the result of a stopped drain and it looked deep and sullen.

So deep that Janice shuddered. Somehow, she felt as though that Stygian pool had been gathered to receive her. For at sight of Malmordo, Janice found herself wishing that she had never wanted to meet him.

The other night, Janice had no more than glimpsed Malmordo's face. He had been in action and murderous, but he had seemed more like a fighter finishing a feud than something belonging to an actual realm of fiends. Now, snakish, his body practically coiled, his face as twisted as his contorted frame, Malmordo was his most terrible self.

The words that Malmordo mouthed were unintelligible to Janice, but the fiend's followers understood them. Dragging Janice along, they brought her past the far end of the pool, to a ledge that ran along its brink. As they passed Malmordo, he whipped a knife from a frayed jacket that he wore and Janice, her gasp stifling the scream she wanted to give, found herself staring at the deadly blade, raised to the level of the ugly fangs that were Malmordo's bared teeth.

All this was by wavery light, the glow from ship's lanterns hanging along the low ceiling. The recoil that Janice gave brought a happy snarl from Malmordo and it was echoed by similar glee from other ratty throats. For now, as Janice's two captors pressed her against the wall at the ledge, the girl could see a dozen or more of Malmordo's ugly clan, peering from niches and other openings in the cellar wall.

Small wonder the rats had scurried away, when this fiendish assemblage was about to hold court! This was no feeding time for the pets kept by Malmordo's followers. Malmordo, champion of injustice, was about to deliver some evil verdict.

It dawned on Janice then what Malmordo intended. The two men were starting Janice along the ledge, dragging her between them in what could best be described as a sideward single file. From further along came a sucking sound and as Janice turned her head, mostly so she wouldn't have to look at Malmordo, she saw where the sound came from.

There was a gap in the ledge, crossed by a plank, which was at the mouth of a small, low archway, no more than waist high. The sound came from that arch; it was an outlet that sucked the overflow from the stagnant pool which was being gradually replenished by water seeping from the walls about.

And it was down through that black, forbidding arch that Malmordo's two followers intended to thrust Janice!

"Ni mortigos la malliberulo senpere!" announced Malmordo. *"Morgau la laboro estos finita!"*

Those final words echoed: *"La laboro estos finita"* as if uttered by the leering lips that showed from every crevice. Yet it was not Malmordo's men who added that shout. The echoes were from Malmordo's voice alone.

The very tone made Janice shudder. If she could have translated that statement, she would have realized that it was her epitaph. What Malmordo had announced was this:

"We shall kill the prisoner immediately! Tomorrow the work will be finished!"

The pair who were working Janice along the ledge understood what Malmordo meant. The man on her left was already on the plank that bridged the open arch, hauling at Janice to bring her along, while the man on her right was pushing from his side. A few feet more and Janice would be on the plank alone, ready for a tilt that would carry her back and down into that flowing depth that emptied into some pit from which there would be no return.

And then, as if picking up the echoes of Malmordo's pronouncement came a shivery laugh that rose to a sharp crescendo which ended in these words:

"Mi estas malgusta, Malmordo! La laboro komincegas nuntempe!

That pronouncement was The Shadow's. He was saying, "You are wrong Malmordo! The work is beginning at this moment!" Those words, understood by Malmordo's followers, produced a consternation that proved his statement. Whatever Malmordo's idea of work, The Shadow's was rapid action. Instinctively, Malmordo's men swung into it thereby playing into The Shadow's hands, since they were complying with his wish.

Guns spurted everywhere—at echoes.

The Shadow's tone, caught up by the walls, was quite as elusive as Malmordo's. The shots that were fired at him never found him, but they formed a camouflage for his own. For among the numerous gun bursts, there was no way of identifying which The Shadow supplied. Malmordo's men began to reel among their niches, but which shots produced that result, nobody knew.

Not even Malmordo.

At least the Master Rat realized the futility of combating The Shadow.

"Zorge!" came Malmordo's shout. *"Venu! Rapidu!"*

He was telling his followers to look out, to come along, and to hurry. Like the rats they were, they dived among the crannies. They fired parting shots at the only targets they could see, the lanterns, hoping to black out The Shadow's marksmanship with them.

Only two remained, deserted by their fellow rats. They were the pair who held Janice captive. One lantern had been missed in the general barrage; it was the lantern hanging near the planked ledge. Its glow showed one man hauling, the other shoving, in a last effort to get Janice on the plank; to hold her fate in their own hands as a threat to The Shadow, or at least a compromise.

But already, blackness was gliding into that lamplight, along the ledge itself, like an encroaching mass of doom; not for Janice but her captors. And with it came The Shadow's sinister tone telling Malmordo's stranded malefactors that they were too late:

"Tro malfrue!"

The man on the near side of the plank let go of Janice, whipped out a knife and flung it into blackness, shrieking: *"Prenu la ponardo, Ombrajo!"* but The Shadow did not take the knife as the hurler hoped. The blade flicked into blackness only and from below its line of flight came well-placed gun stabs that toppled the chunk of human scum into the shallow slime of the unsightly pool that flanked the ledge.

Next, The Shadow was gripping Janice's arm as he sidestepped as far as he could to aim at the man still on the plank. But before The Shadow could fire what would have been a certain shot, Janice's other captor released his hold.

The plank swayed and heaved as Janice left it, hauled to safety by The Shadow. The girl heard a wild, incoherent shriek behind her and turning, she saw her late captor writhing in a strange fantastic twist that carried him away from sight, down through the arched opening. With him went the plank, crackling as it disappeared, as though some superhuman force had carried it along with its occupant.

The walls quivered with solemn echoes. This time, The Shadow's laugh was like a knell, in appreciation of justice singularly delivered. Whatever it was that produced that sudden climax, snatching a foe from the very muzzle of his gun, The Shadow seemed to know its source.

But now The Shadow was rushing Janice up through the grating, where on the sidewalk, he paused long enough to deliver bullets, turret-style, at scattering creatures who represented some of Malmordo's human rats, fleeing their underground lair. Next, police cars, with whining sirens and slicing searchlights, were roaring into the scene, but by then, The Shadow had rushed Janice well away.

There was a cab around the corner and The Shadow pointed Janice to it. Stumbling ahead, the girl was sure that her cloaked friend was in the background, ready to aid her in case of last minute complications. She thought she was meeting such when a man sprang suddenly from the curb and gripped her arm. Then she recognized his voice:

"Miss Bradford! Why did you come here?"

It was Trent Stacey, chiding Janice on the fact that she had come to this vicinity against his advice. In her turn, Janice was stammering that she was all right, that she was sorry, that all she wanted was to get away. They were at the cab door; the driver was opening it, and Stacey saw that the cab was empty. He helped Janice inside and closed the door.

Then to the driver, Stacey said:

"Take this young lady wherever she wants to go—and forget where you took her."

To remind the driver to forget, Stacey handed

him a five dollar bill and the cab wheeled swiftly away. Turning, Stacey went to look for Inspector Cardona, who by now had probably reached this area.

If Trent Stacey thought that he was really Janice's rescuer, he was wrong. He was mistaken, too, if he thought that the cabby would purposely forget the address the girl gave him. For the cab driver happened to be Shrevvy, The Shadow's standby.

Back by the corner a whispered laugh denoted The Shadow's satisfaction as Janice's real rescuer faded into the thickness of night.

CHAPTER XVII

"Kion vi demandis?"

"Nenio."

"Pri kio estas?

"Mé tute ne scias."

"Kion vi volas?"

"Parolu pli laute."

The little man who had been asking the questions gave a nod and mopped his forehead with a handkerchief. Commissioner Weston, who had given the answers, leaned back in his chair and beamed across the desk.

As a chance visitor, Lamont Cranston looked puzzled. The Commissioner gave a gesture to the little man.

"This is my Esperanto teacher," defined Weston. "He has been giving me questions and I have answered them."

As proof, Weston handed Cranston a list of questions and answers. The first three, which were checked, ran thus:

What did you ask?

Nothing.

What is it about?

I haven't an idea.

What do you want?

Speak louder.

"A few more lessons," decided Weston, "and I can question any of Malmordo's men we capture. In fact, we nearly captured some last night."

Cranston's expression remained unchanged, so Weston decided he was interested.

"They had a quarrel among themselves," explained Weston, "in the cellar of a warehouse where they made their headquarters. One of them was killed."

"Too bad you didn't have a chance to quiz him," remarked Cranston. "Where did the rest go?"

"To some other warehouse," returned Weston. Then, glumly, he added: "We don't know which. We shall have to wait until we learn where the rats are the thickest."

Cranston gave a nod as though he understood and Weston in turn was quite surprised. Then Weston demanded:

"How would you know, Cranston?"

"The same as you would, Commissioner" Cranston replied. "From our mutual friend Mr. Stacey."

"You mean you know Trent Stacey?"

"Of course I know Trent," returned Cranston, picking up the first name instantly. "I met him in Europe."

The Shadow was playing a good hunch that Stacey had recently come from Europe in order to know so much about Malmordo. Weston, nodded, then said dubiously:

"Odd that Stacey didn't tell me you were a friend of his."

"Not odd at all," declared Cranston. "He doesn't know you are a friend of mine. He wrote me he was coming here on business and would look me up later. I assume he is still busy."

"He is," said Weston. "How long ago did he write you?"

Cranston pondered, as though trying to recall the exact time. Weston put a prompting question:

"Was it after he came back to Canada?"

"It was" replied Cranston. "Not more than a week or two ago."

The Esperanto teacher having left before this conversation started, Commissioner Weston decided he could speak quite freely. And since Cranston, in whom Weston usually confided important matters, knew so much about Stacey already, it wasn't long before the commissioner detailed the remaining facts.

All those details interested Cranston. Stacey's Canadian background, the fact that he had gone to school there, the way he had acquired other languages, gone out to see the world, and finally become invaluable to Scotland Yard in the widespread search for Malmordo—all marked Stacey as the one important key to quick results.

Which in turn meant that the sooner Cranston contacted Stacey, the better. Indeed, Cranston expressed that point in a calm, casual way, when he spoke:

"Morgaula laboro estos finita."

"What's that, Cranston?" Weston looked up to see his friend glancing at some of the language sheets. "Did I hear you saying something in Esperanto?

"I was trying to pronounce the words in this lesson." Cranston laid one of the sheets aside. He stared at some papers Weston had taken from the desk drawer. "But what do you have there, Commissioner?"

"Some odd papers Stacey picked up in Malmordo's place," Weston declared. "They give something of an insight into Malmordo's ways, but not enough. Here is evidence that Malmordo was recently in Algeria, under the name of Pierre Dubroc. More references to certain notorious New York criminals, at present in Sing Sing Prison. Apparently Malmordo wanted them to operate with him here, so I have sent some detectives to Ossining to question them.

"This European police report"—Weston tossed another paper across the desk—"proves that some of the gypsies there were leagued with Malmordo. The same may be true here"—Weston gave a frown—"because that local leader of theirs, King Dakar, has been dodging me consistently."

Gathering the incomplete papers, Weston thrust them back in the drawer and brought out a large-scale street map. While he was doing this, the phone bell rang; Weston lifted the receiver, found that the call was for Cranston, so passed him the receiver and continued to open the map.

Cranston's call was brief. He spoke in monosyllables, then finished the call abruptly. By then, the map was spread and Cranston was watching Weston point out certain buildings, each marked with an X.

"We have checked this map with Stacey," stated the commissioner. "All these are warehouses where Malmordo's band may be hiding, but there are too many of them."

"Of which, Commissioner? Warehouses or rats?"

"Of both," affirmed Weston. "Now we have learned this: there are underground connections between some of the warehouses. Stacey suggested that fact, through having observed the way Malmordo's men appeared in various unexpected places. We made a brief check to prove the fact, but it would have been suicide to send men probing further or deeper."

Remembering the arched pit that had swallowed one of Malmordo's men as substitute for Janice, Cranston could have certified the commissioner's statement, but didn't. Instead he broached a theory of his own.

"There could be other passages," suggested Cranston, "leading to the river. They would account for the fact that stowaways disappeared so remarkably along the waterfront."

Cranston was harking back to that first night when, as The Shadow, he had witnessed the disappearance of stowaways plopping overboard from the *Santander*. However, Weston, though he approved Cranston's theory with a nod, also found reason to smile.

"Stacey has already analyzed that situation,"

declared the commissioner. "But he added a point to prove it."

"I can do the same," declared Cranston. "There must be connections between the river and the warehouses because of the rats. They wouldn't have traveled above ground as Malmordo's men might."

"You've struck it exactly!" exclaimed the commissioner. "Stacey's proof to the dot. But you see what would happen, don't you, if we invaded the warehouses wholesale, to capture Malmordo's human rats?"

"They would take the quickest route out to the river."

"Precisely. But where would that outlet be?" Weston shrugged hopelessly. "We would need all the available men to stage the warehouse raids, but that leaves too few to watch the piers. Nor do we have enough police boats to do more than patrol the waterfront. However, we are ready, because if we drive those human rats from the warehouses, we will have accomplished half the job and can then concentrate on the rest."

Cranston let the discussion end there, since he had an appointment elsewhere. But as he left the commissioner's office, Cranston did something rather rare for him. He smiled.

Doing things by halves did not satisfy Cranston, either as himself or The Shadow. He could foresee that if Malmordo's men were driven from some warehouse out to the river, only to be allowed to scatter, they would assemble again and reoccupy a warehouse as soon as the police had left it.

However, there could be a way of finding the right warehouse and, after that, the outlet which belonged to it. But first, the person to find was Malmordo. Cranston had hinted that to Weston by saying *"Morgau la laboro estos finita"* which Weston, if he'd progressed enough in Esperanto, would have interpreted as "Tomorrow the work will be finished."

Malmordo's words, and today was the tomorrow that Malmordo had meant!

Yet there was still time for Lamont Cranston to act as The Shadow. Like Trent Stacey, The Shadow had a single lead that could prove vital. That lead was Janice Bradford.

Like Stacey, Cranston was following the lead. The call that Cranston had received in Weston's office was from Burbank, his contact man. Hawkeye had just reported seeing a man who looked like Stacey entering the Azalea Plaza, the hotel where Janice and her father, Andrew Bradford, were living incognito. Hawkeye had been watching the Azalea Plaza ever since Shrevvy took Janice there last night.

Whatever Trent Stacey learned from Andrew Bradford, The Shadow intended to be on hand to learn it too!

CHAPTER XVIII

IT was only afternoon, but the day was rainy and the low clouds made it as gloomy as dusk.

And such gloom made Janice shudder, even though she was safe in a hotel suite, in the company of her father, Andrew Bradford, and her good friend, Stacey Trent.

Andrew Bradford was a man of elderly appearance but Janice could testify that his age had begun to show only recently. Even his broad, rugged features were sagging through worry and his eyes, usually keen, had become hunted when not listless.

It had taken Janice half an hour to convince her father that he should meet Trent Stacey. Once Bradford had agreed and had seen Stacey face to face, the result was like a tonic. They had come right to business, these two, and Stacey's blunt insistence on settling the Malmordo question once for all, had given Bradford the real lift he needed.

"The situation is plain," declared Stacey. "Obviously, Mr. Bradford, you are not to blame because your business partner, Lucien Thorneau, wrote off half a million dollars to business losses on account of South American shipments which were purchased but never delivered."

"Those shipments were to come from Nazi firms," declared Bradford, seriously. "Thorneau gave the orders just before the firms were blacklisted."

"Which left the whole case legal—"

"Except that Thorneau knew the inside facts," inserted Bradford. "The shipments were never even planned. Thorneau paid a quarter million to a Nazi agent who represented those firms and received a receipt for a half million. Each profited equally. Thorneau thought the deal ended there."

"You found evidence of this among Thorneau's papers?"

"Not enough to matter. Here is the real evidence." Bradford brought some sheets of photostats from his pocket. "Exact copies of papers that the Nazis kept. The originals are in the hands of Malmordo; he sent me these to prove it."

Stacey nodded.

"Quite simple," Stacey decided. "Now Malmordo wants the other quarter million for the originals."

This time it was Bradford who nodded and Janice gave another shiver, but not from repressed fright or harrowing recollections. It happened that

Janice was seated by the door to a connecting room and she felt a draft from an open window.

This was odd in itself, because she was sure the window was closed. Getting up from her chair, Janice went into the other room to see and found that the window really was closed. What she didn't observe was the blackness that glided away from that window just before she arrived. In the dusk of the room, the blackness followed unnoticed around the wall and stationed itself behind the open door through which Janice had come.

There the blackness stayed while Janice went back to join Stacey and her father; living, shrouded blackness that Janice would have welcomed had she seen it. For the arrival was her cloaked rescuer of the night before, The Shadow.

"My dilemma is this," Bradford was telling Stacey. "Malmordo wants to pin Thorneau's guilt on me. Given time, I can assemble facts that will uphold my innocence. Then I can turn all the data over to the government and let them decide the case."

"At a cost of a quarter million dollars," put in Janice, as she resumed her chair. "They will probably demand its repayment."

"The government may demand a half a million," declared Bradford, "but Thorneau's estate will be forced to pay it, once I can prove that the claim belongs to his account, not mine. I believe, however, that Malmordo's original documents, which include some that he did not copy, will clear me completely. But I cannot gain them without paying Malmordo for them."

From his listening post, The Shadow could well appreciate the dilemma which confronted Bradford. It was up to Stacey to provide a solution and Stacey set to work.

"About the yellow flower," said Stacey. "Malmordo wanted you to wear one to identify yourself."

"Yes," replied Bradford. "I was to come to the Cafe de la Morte and bring the money with me in cash or securities."

Janice gasped at that and Stacey heard her.

"That must have been your mistake," Stacey told the girl. "Malmordo picked you as a substitute or a decoy. He was sure you wouldn't have the money."

"But why," asked Janice, "did he kill Gregor instead of me?"

"Because Gregor was watching for him. Maybe Malmordo was tipped off by Madame Thalla. He uses gypsies, Malmordo does, and Gregor was no gypsy."

Stacey's analysis was good, a good one hundred percent wrong, since it was based on the mistaken notion that the gypsies were leagued with Malmordo. The Shadow made a mental note of that and waited to check Stacey's further theories.

"Since you did not contact Malmordo," Stacey told Bradford, "it is obvious that he needed some stronger threat against you. When Janice acted against my advice and fell into his hands last night, Malmordo must have decided that by holding her a prisoner, he could make you come to terms."

"Janice is always acting against people's advice," declared Bradford. "That is why I didn't want her mixed in this situation at all. You see, Janice?" Bradford turned to the girl. "Where would I be now, if you were Malmordo's prisoner?"

"You mean where would I be!" exclaimed Janice. She swung to Stacey. "You're wrong about Malmordo wanting to hold me as a hostage. His men were trying to kill me!"

"Dead or alive," stated Stacey, coolly, "you would still have been a hostage, or a *garantiulo* in Malmordo's language. Did you hear him use any word like that?"

"No. He called me a *malliberulo* or something of the sort."

"That means a prisoner. But whether he intended to keep you as such or kill you, he would have told your father that you were still alive and redeemable at a cost of a quarter million dollars. Since you managed to escape, you can be sure that Malmordo will attempt some new move."

Stacey's statement brought a worried look from Bradford who inquired:

"How soon?"

"Very soon," replied Stacey in a positive tone. "The police are pressing Malmordo hard and from the way his scurrying rats were shouting *'Ombrajo'* they were unquestionably having trouble from an enemy called The Shadow."

"I'll say they were!" expressed Janice. "So that's what *Ombrajo* meant!"

"And in your case, Mr. Bradford," continued Stacey, "Malmordo must know that any delay is in your favor, which is not true where the others are concerned."

Bradford's expression went surprised.

"What others?"

In reply, Stacey reached to the right lapel of his coat and zipped it open, to produce some thin papers from a hidden pocket, much as he had once brought his own credentials from the other lapel. Going through the papers, Stacey queried:

"Did you ever hear of Jerome Ghent?"

"The rubber wholesaler!" exclaimed Bradford. "Why, Ghent had a regular black market in that commodity. We even heard about his operations in Mexico, but nobody could prove anything against him."

"Malmordo could," declared Stacey, "at least where dealings with Nazi agents were concerned. Next"—Stacey thumbed to another paper—"we have Clinton Waybrook."

"An exporter." Bradford nodded slowly. "With a reputation beyond reproach. That is why he could have covered any Nazi dealings, but it is not for me to judge. Waybrook may be as innocent as I am."

"I don't think so," declared Stacey. He came to the third paper. "Felix Kelfert, the jeweler is most certainly involved. We have already traced false sales of diamonds that were shipped from Amsterdam and they lead to Kelfert through Nazi channels."

"Who has traced all this?" inquired Bradford.

"Scotland Yard," explained Stacey. "You see, there were British blacklists of firms with Nazi inclinations, differing from the American. This is confidential data, not final evidence. Unless certain facts are admitted by the persons involved, I have no right to make such cases an international matter."

"But why should guilty men admit anything?"

"Because by now they must fear Malmordo. The fact that they were afraid to contact him is proof. They are even afraid to contact each other, but if one man were bold enough to suggest it, I believe the others would agree."

Even before Stacey finished, Janice caught the logical conclusion. She turned to Bradford and exclaimed:

"You, father!"

Half-bewildered, Bradford stared at his daughter, then turned to Stacey, who nodded.

"She is right," Stacey declared. "Your position is enviable, Mr. Bradford. Since you are innocent, you would be inclined to regard others as the same. If you called any of these men, told them your predicament and said that you had heard them mentioned in the same connection, they would be only too glad to come here for a conference."

Rising, Bradford became his old strong self, as he announced with ringing emphasis:

"I shall call all of them!"

Call them Bradford did and with the result that Stacey had predicted. The very mention of the dread name Malmordo was enough to make men like Ghent, Waybrook and Kelfert listen. Bradford, a man of strict integrity, whose very tone expressed his indignation, was the perfect man for such a mission. Through his whole discourse ran a challenge that he wanted others to accept and in one brief speech he expressed it thus:

"Together we shall find a way to end the menace of Malmordo, once and for all!"

Grandly though Bradford handled it, the effect was a strain. Finished with the phone calls he sank back in his chair, turned to Stacey and said wearily:

"They will all be here at nine o'clock. But what shall we do then?"

For answer, Stacey picked up the telephone and made a call of his own. The call was to Inspector Cardona.

"Hello, Inspector," said Stacey. "Yes... This is Stacey... I've arranged for another try tonight... Yes, we'll need a squad and a cordon... No, not too tight... We can go over the details together and profit by previous mistakes.

"I can tell you the location now, so you can check the neighborhood... It's a hotel, the Azalea Plaza... No, not Aurelia. It's Azalea... A-Z-A-L-E-A... Not C... Z as in Zenith... P-L-A-Z-A... That's right... Azalea Plaza..."

The phone call finished, Stacey turned to find both Bradford and his daughter facing him in amazement and Janice, for one was quite pale.

"Do you mean"—Bradford's voice came with a falter—"do you mean you expect Malmordo here tonight?"

"I do," returned Stacey, in a positive tone. "He had local criminals covering for him last night, but the police lost track of them. You can be sure that Malmordo is using some of those crooks to keep tabs on Ghent and other men whose names the police don't even know."

"Then when Ghent and the rest come here—"

"Malmordo will show up, expecting it to be the payoff; and it will be, but not in the way Malmordo expects. Don't worry"—Stacey was putting on his hat and opening the door—"I'll be here before nine o'clock."

As the door closed behind Trent Stacey, Janice Bradford thought she felt a draft of air from the hallway. She was wrong; it came from the window in the other room. That window had opened and closed again, to let a cloaked figure slide out and find a rubber-soled footing on the rain-drenched cornice.

Obscured by the settling dusk, The Shadow delivered a whispered laugh that was anything but a parting token. It meant as much as Stacey's stated words, that mirth.

The Shadow, too, would be here by nine o'clock, prepared to deal with Malmordo!

CHAPTER XIX

IT was really pouring rain when nine o'clock approached. From the doorway where Inspector Cardona had posted them, the detectives could scarcely see the dim lights that represented the windows of the sizeable Azalea Plaza. It was a bad night for the police, which made it a good night for Malmordo. Perhaps Stacey had taken that into consequence when predicting that Malmordo would appear.

Cardona had compromised by moving the cordon in a trifle closer, but it still wasn't close enough. Joe could see better hiding spots nearer to the hotel, but decided not to use them. They were the sorts of places that might be noticed by anyone entering the hotel. Remembering how well Malmordo had taken the bait the night before and realizing how capably Stacey had functioned as the inside man, Cardona was resolved to play the game as Stacey wanted it.

Cars were stopping in front of the hotel and some had the lights of taxicabs. Which were bringing whom, Cardona didn't know, except that Stacey was among the visitors. If Joe had let his men move to closer posts, they might have identified some of the arrivals, but it didn't seem important.

Perhaps it was more important than Cardona supposed. At any rate, watchers were at those posts, having reached them easily in the rain, by keeping clear of the hotel lights. Those watchers were the crooks who had fled from Malmordo's roof the night before, hoodlums like Kirky Schleer and the other thug who had been left dead on the battleground in front of Malmordo's house.

Again, those hoods were here to cover, without the knowledge of the police!

Tonight, however, there were others.

Figures were snaking into the Azalea Plaza right through the outer cordon of detectives and the inner circle of crooks. Figures that emerged from culverts and manholes, wriggled to the gutters and gave the effect of swimmers as they moved through the torrents that flowed there. That was, they would have looked like swimmers, if anyone had seen them, but no one did.

They were Malmordo's own breed of human water rats. They'd left the warehouses that the police were watching, to infest this fancy hotel. Arrived beside the Azalea Plaza, they wiggled in by side passages and delivery entrances, found cellar windows to their liking and plopped into the preserves of the hotel itself.

Whether he noticed any of these snaky figures when he stepped from Shrevvy's cab, Lamont Cranston gave no sign. At least he had provided for future developments, because over his arm he carried what looked like an opera cape but wasn't. It happened to be a black cloak, neatly folded, with a slouch hat beneath.

Crossing the lobby, Cranston didn't go to the fifth floor by elevator. The fifth was Bradford's floor but Cranston preferred to use the stairway. Hardly past the first turn, he paused, put on his cloak and hat and became The Shadow. From the hat, he removed a small, waterproof bundle which he tucked beneath his cloak.

Cranston's guns, the automatics which were The Shadow's, were already packed beneath his well-fitted evening clothes in special holsters. So now, in the evasive, almost invisible style that characterized his black-clad self, The Shadow continued up to Bradford's apartment. Choosing a side hall, The Shadow paused outside a door which had a lighted, half open transom above it. From a small box that he produced from a fold of his cloak, The Shadow released a little green bird that promptly flew through the transom.

In her own room, Janice Bradford gave a sharp start and a little cry as a bird fluttered to her hand and dropped a fortune card from its beak. On that card was a silhouetted profile of a hawkish face topped by a black hat, with cloaked shoulders beneath. Looking toward the door, noting the open transom, Janice hurried there and admitted The Shadow.

It was hardly necessary, this form of entrance, for The Shadow could have easily unlocked that door, but he was sparing Janice's well-shaken nerves. Besides, he had instructions to give the girl and along with those instructions, a revolver.

"Stay here," The Shadow undertoned to Janice. "If anything happens, go there"—he gestured to a closet in the corner—"and if you need to use the gun, do so. I can assure you that any danger will be brief."

Then, moving to a far door, The Shadow inched it open. There was a short passage beyond so he went through to the next door and handled it in the same style. This time, however, The Shadow halted the door after the first few inches. He was looking into the main room of the suite, where Andrew Bradford was receiving his guests.

Ghent, Waybrook, Kelfert—all three could be defined by their faces as men of guilt.

They had no reason to hide that guilt, rather they were proud of it, although their situation made them tense. But it was plain that Ghent, a man with a big-jawed, overbearing face; Waybrook, of bloated visage with a triple chin; Kelfert, sallow and scheming in expression, regarded themselves as comrades in a cause that included Andrew Bradford. In fact, this was their way of congratulating Bradford for his smart work in arranging a rendezvous with Malmordo on a common meeting ground.

Yet honest Mr. Bradford hadn't tumbled to a thing. He wasn't even surprised by the fact that these visitors had brought well-padded briefcases with them. Charitable at heart, Bradford was hoping that they, too, were innocent and he felt the briefcases might contain documents to prove it.

A knock sounded at the door of the apartment and the visitors became alert, Ghent's hand, for one, going to a pocket of his coat. Bradford stepped over, opened the door and admitted Stacey, who stepped into sight wearing evening clothes. At sight of such a visitor, Ghent relaxed, thinking perhaps that Stacey was another member of the subversive brotherhood, come here to discuss terms with Malmordo.

Then Bradford made the introduction:

"Gentlemen, this is Mr. Trent Stacey of Scotland Yard. He has data that I think will interest all of you."

Stacey did have. From his pockets he produced it, separate bundles, small ones, yet much larger than those tissue paper reports he had shown to Bradford that afternoon. Stepping behind a table, Stacey laid the packets in a row and his viewers noticed that his right hand had gone to his hip.

And Stacey's eyes were watching Ghent so coldly, so steadily, that the big-jawed man let his own hand move free from his pocket. Then, in a blunt tone that carried the hardness of flint, Stacey said:

"Let me see what you have brought."

Three men opened their briefcases and brought out the contents.

"Securities," said Ghent. "All negotiable."

"Cash," declared Waybrook. "Large denominations, but I suppose you can find a way to pass them."

"Diamonds." Kelfert presented a square package. "Good anywhere."

There was still suspicion in their eyes and noting it, Stacey laughed. With his free hand he picked out a packet from the four that he had laid on the table and tossed it to Bradford.

"I have already settled with Bradford," declared Stacey. "His case was rather special. He will assure you that he is receiving the documents he wants."

Beyond the door, The Shadow was removing his hat and cloak. Hanging them on a hook in the passage, he stepped into the conference room quite calmly, just as Bradford gave an amazed exclamation.

"Why, these are the originals of Thorneau's papers!" exclaimed Bradford. "They clear my case entirely. Why—why, you must be—"

Bradford was looking up at Stacey, ending the sentence in a gasp. It was Cranston's calm tone that completed the statement.

"Yes," announced Cranston. "Stacey is Malmordo."

Although ready to admit the fact himself, Stacey couldn't repress a snarl at hearing it from this unexpected quarter. He was drawing his revolver as he wheeled back from the table, but he stopped the draw halfway. Cranston was already covering him with a very convincing .45.

"I heard about you from my friend the Police Commissioner," Cranston told Stacey, in an even tone. "You knew a great deal about Malmordo, so much that you should have been right on all the facts. For instance, such points as Malmordo using local criminals and inducing gypsies to serve as his accomplices. I was quite sure that Malmordo did neither."

The snarl that Stacey gave in reply belonged distinctly to Malmordo.

"It was remarkable how well you set the stage," continued Cranston. "Too well in fact. As Malmordo you slipped from the Cafe de la Morte; as Stacey you met Janice soon after. When you told the police to give you leeway in order to enter the empty house, you did not go there at all, until you arrived as Malmordo. Then you came out as Stacey."

This time Stacey's snarl became an off-key laugh.

"Very well," he conceded. "I fooled the police, didn't I? Particularly when I knifed that crook, Kirky Schleer, from the doorway and then took potshots at the roof, claiming Malmordo was still up there. They were making trouble for me, that gang, and Gregor was spying for them. I had to make the police think they were part of the Malmordo setup."

These statements were bringing a narrowed look from Ghent, the most aggressive of Stacey's victims. Ghent's left hand was moving now, not to his coat pocket, but to his vest, and only the forefinger and thumb were on the creep.

"I warned Bradford's daughter about a trap," added Stacey, "because I knew that would make her walk into it. I was in and out of it, acting as Malmordo in between. I suppose The Shadow guessed it and told you, whoever you are."

"You told me yourself," stated Cranston calmly. "I happened to overhear the phone call you made to Inspector Cardona this afternoon." From the way he spoke, Cranston gave the impression he had heard it from Cardona's end. "You had told Commissioner Weston that you were educated in Canada. Your phone call disproved that you were a Canadian."

Stacey, his face showing an ugly scowl that suited Malmordo, was staring at Cranston, puzzled.

"In Canada," declared Cranston, "the letter Z is called Zed. When you spelled Azalea Plaza, you used the letter Z twice, even terming it 'Z as in Zenith'—an odd thing for a person who would hardly know that Zed is sometimes called Z."

It was Jerome Ghent who supplied a short laugh of approval. He turned to Cranston with a bow.

"Very good," asserted Ghent. "The little details are the sort that crack big cases. But what about these local criminals you mention? Who could have hired them?"

"You did," returned Cranston. "They fit with your black market operations. You were using them to trap Malmordo. He called in the police to counteract them."

"Correct," acknowledged Ghent, "and the police are always prompt to respond to a whistle. That is a little detail which also could work two ways."

With a sudden twist behind Waybrook and Kelfert so that their bodies shielded him from Cranston's gun, Jerome Ghent flipped a whistle from his vest pocket and gave it a shrill blast that could be heard for blocks around.

It was Ghent's summons for his waiting mobsmen to appear and deal with both The Shadow and Malmordo!

CHAPTER XX

GHENT'S act produced chaos.

Before Cranston could shift and produce a second gun to cover the black marketer, Bradford made a spring to grab Ghent and inadvertently blocked Cranston's drawn gun, which was aimed at the man who called himself Stacey. Already Malmordo had begun to drop the Stacey pose, now he was acting in full Malmordo style. Hurling the table ahead of him, Malmordo sent its papers and its wealth scattering everywhere, then dropping behind it with a writhe, he swung his gun upward, and blasted at where he thought Cranston was. Except that Cranston was no longer there; he had wheeled back through the door to become The Shadow.

Outside, whistles were blaring everywhere and guns were barking in response, which left Jerome Ghent frozen in horrified surprise. Ghent's great stunt had backfired the moment he staged it, for his cordon of crooks had been surrounded by a larger cordon of police.

The moment Ghent's men had risen from cover and surged toward the hotel, Cardona's sharpshooters had sprung out to chop them down. Even Malmordo couldn't have figured out a better trap for Ghent's doomed crew.

Tonight, Malmordo had figured out a device all for his own immediate benefit.

Just as blackness swung from the connecting passage, skirted the group of men and came with a surprise lunge toward Malmordo, doors buckled everywhere and slinky men with baggy clothes and drawn knives took over the apartment.

Malmordo had lost sight of Cranston and was receiving The Shadow instead. The Shadow, in his turn, was to become the focal center of a mass drive delivered by this tribe of murderers who, as humans, did the term 'rat' an injustice.

Janice's gun was popping from the closet in the other room, but Malmordo's men weren't stopping on account of it. Bradford was flinging Waybrook and Kelfert to an isolated corner of the big room and both were taking the hint, thoroughly willing to escape with their lives and take whatever other consequences followed.

Ghent, hauling out his gun, was lunging at Malmordo, who was now completely his writhing distorted self, his evening clothes rendering him the uglier and more incongruous than ever. All Ghent gained for his effort was a deluge of knives that came in response to Malmordo's snarled order:

"Mortigu!"

And then, as Ghent sprawled, Malmordo, twisting half to his feet, met the cloaked figure of The Shadow in a sudden surprising grapple. In all that chaos, Malmordo's arriving followers had scarcely seen The Shadow's launching form until the tangle came. Now from the whirl that followed, they heard Malmordo's call:

"La Ombrajo! Mortigu lin!"

The Shadow! Kill him! Unnecessary orders to these fiends. Their question was how to manage it as The Shadow spun about with Malmordo in his clutch. All they could really see were snatches of Malmordo himself, in the midst of a kaleidoscopic whirl, his hands and face disappearing and reappearing like a blinking light.

The Shadow held the upper hand in that grapple, but to finish Malmordo would have been suicidal. Any letup in the struggle would define The Shadow clearly enough for Malmordo's men to strike with their regained knives. In fact, some were already preparing to hack at The Shadow as he whirled past them with Malmordo in his grip.

Whatever The Shadow might have done on his own account—and he had turned the tables on enemies like these more than once before—delay was imperative to protect Bradford and the two men who had now become his willing prisoners: Waybrook and Kelfert. Janice too would be in danger if any of Malmordo's crowd returned, to seek her. Right now, all of Malmordo's followers were in a sense immobilized, since they were concentrated on the question of The Shadow.

And The Shadow himself settled that question by changing it, producing a new bewilderment among his foemen.

A slouch hat scaled across the room; next, a black cloak went flapping after it, as two fighters sprawled apart, then came to hands and knees, facing each other. Somehow, The Shadow had lost his identifying garb and was now unmasked. To pick him from Malmordo would be easy, so it seemed. Ready to spring with their knives, Malmordo's followers paused briefly, then retained their pose like statues.

Writhing from the floor were two Malmordos, each contorted and vicious. They were pointing at each other and their faces registered all the venom that belonged with their snakish postures. And from each pair of lips came the selfsame snarl:

"La Ombrajo! Mortigu lin!"

The man who was known as Malmordo had encountered an actor whose skill was equal to his own. That actor was The Shadow. He was able to distort his features, those of Cranston, as capably as Malmordo could twist the face he used when he styled himself Stacey. As they were now, there was no choice between them.

How could Malmordo's followers kill when they saw no one to be slain except Malmordo?

Both figures were in disheveled evening clothes. Each spoke the language that the murderous rat men understood. If Malmordo had straightened and let his features snap back into joint, he would have identified himself as Stacey, whereas The Shadow, doing the same, would have answered to Cranston.

Still there would have been no choice.

There lay Malmordo's weakness. His followers knew him only by that forced appearance which made his features hideous. To show any other face would have been a symbol of weakness on Malmordo's part. As Stacey, he would be accepted as the false Malmordo, just as The Shadow would if he reverted to the looks of Cranston.

Snarls passed back and forth and the listeners understood them. Accusations, but always in the language that Malmordo had taught his followers to use. All was at a standstill and the longer it remained so, the more to The Shadow's advantage it would be. And so it remained.

As moments turned to minutes, the time limit ended. Footsteps came pounding from the hallway, announcing the arrival of the law. One Malmordo snarled *"Foriru!"* telling his followers to go away and the other gave the same word in the next breath. With that, the police appeared.

It was then and only then, that the situation broke. One of the writhing figures turned, scooped up the slouch hat and the black cloak and made a dive straight for the window. As the window crashed, knives followed, but they flew wide, for the police were pumping shots at the men who threw them.

Half-cloaked, the Malmordo who had thus declared himself The Shadow, made a landing on an adjoining roof a floor below. His rival, left on the scene as the real Malmordo, straightened in a swift lunge for the door, reaching it despite the grabs of the detectives, shouting *"Venu!"* as a call for his men to follow, which a few managed to do.

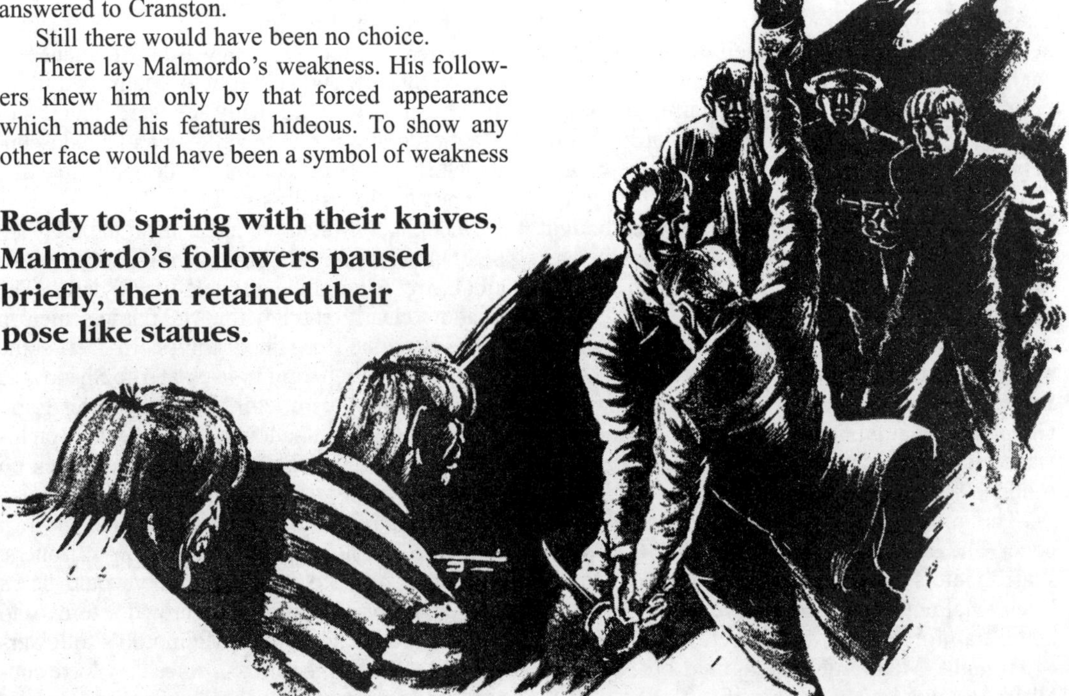

Ready to spring with their knives, Malmordo's followers paused briefly, then retained their pose like statues.

Down the stairs and out to the street went the man in tattered evening clothes, the last of the rat men dashing with him. Swallowed by the rain, they were on their way to the warehouse area, with a slender chance of beating the roundup planned by the law. Elsewhere, his course unknown, a figure garbed in black was bound for the same destination.

So far at least, The Shadow had scored. For up in Bradford's apartment, the law was taking over in a thorough way. Bradford was safe, so was his daughter Janice; while two men who had traded with foreign enemies, Waybrook and Kelfert, were prisoners, along with their funds and the papers that proved their guilt, all abandoned by Malmordo.

They were glad to give up, that pair, rather than share the fate of Ghent, who lay dead on the floor, with the evidence of his transactions spread about him.

The Shadow had cracked Malmordo's game. The next task was to settle scores with the Master Rat himself!

CHAPTER XXI

POLICE whistles were shrilling in the warehouse sector when a little cluster of men came tearing from a side street toward a bulky brick building that bore a big sign saying:

WESTERN CORN EXCHANGE

Sweeping searchlights picked out those fugitives, scrawny men in baggy clothes followed by a loping figure that wore the remnants of a dress suit. Police guns barked, but as they did, a grating came flying up and the fugitives dropped through it with all the speed that characterized Malmordo's rats.

By the time police reached the grating it was clamped and guns were shooting up from among its slats. If the police intended to enter the corn warehouse, they would have to find some other way.

There were other ways. Around the corner, a cloaked figure was already using one. He was climbing the fire escape of an adjoining building to reach a little window that led into the warehouse. He was gone by the time the police came around the corner.

Sirens screeched announcing the arrival of more police cars. From one sprang Inspector Cardona, ready to take command. Informed that Malmordo had gone into the corn warehouse, Cardona urged his men to continue their present plan of invasion and hunt crooks down to the last rat.

The police were smashing doors leading into the warehouse when someone thrust an envelope into Cardona's hand. By the time the inspector looked around, the donator was gone; all Cardona saw was a quick, shambling figure making off through the heavy rain. Tearing the envelope open, Cardona read its contents by the scanty light about him.

That note, delivered by Hawkeye, was a message from The Shadow, who had posted Hawkeye in this area to give it to the right man at the right time. What Cardona read was something that caused a complete change in his personal plans. Leaving the capture of the warehouse to his subordinates, the ace inspector sprang into the nearest police car and ordered it to take him straight to the waterfront.

Deep beneath the corn warehouse was a scene even more extravagant than the one that Janice had viewed the night before. Here was no mere cellar with a shallow, slimy pool. Malmordo's men had reached a subcellar consisting of a succession of low brick arches through which gushed a broad stream of water flanked by stone paths that looked like shelves.

At the last arch in the line, four of Malmordo's reserves were prying at a huge grating that looked like a prison entrance. Once loose, that would give them exit to a channel leading out to the river. They would have to swim for it, because past the arch the outlet became no more than a rounded pipe, filled almost to capacity. But these human water rats were used to such methods of transit.

From somewhere far above came clangs and pounding sounds, indicating that police were crashing their way into the warehouse. Then, louder than those muffled beatings, the clatter of footsteps sounded on stone. From narrow openings on either side of the sullen stream, men appeared, arriving from old stairways that led down from the cellar.

These were the rest of Malmordo's depleted horde, the survivors from the lopsided fray at the Azalea Plaza, less a few who had been clipped by police bullets during flight, but plus a quota of reserves that had been stationed upstairs in the warehouse.

As the big grating wavered, Malmordo appeared from one pair of steps and snaked his way along the ledge, shouting to his men above the gush of the swollen stream. As they turned, the slinky men saw Malmordo point across the channel. There on the other side, another figure had arrived.

The Shadow!

If Malmordo's men could have found a better

Hoisted there, he was a struggling thing in the grip of the great anaconda.

footing on the ledges, they would have blasted their cloaked foe before he could have opened fire. But the slime handicapped even these creatures who loved it and being men who were quick with knives, they were naturally slower with guns. By the time they were taking aim, a snarl came from The Shadow's side and with it, he peeled off his cloak and hat, flinging them across the torrent.

The black regalia landed squarely at the feet of the other Malmordo!

Facts dawned suddenly in the ratty minds of the ugly men who saw this new change of affairs. They had been tricked at so many turns that they were ready to accept things in reverse.

There had been two Malmordos up at Bradford's. One had seized upon The Shadow's garb just as the police arrived.

Why not the real Malmordo?

As for the other, the one who had called upon surviving rats to follow him, why could he not be The Shadow? He had let the fugitives outrun him and in doing so, they had led him straight to Malmordo's own stronghold, the place that the real Malmordo could reach more swiftly as The Shadow!

And such was the real answer!

Two men were straightening on their respective ledges. The one who had come here as Malmordo revealed himself as Cranston. The other, who had just flung the hat and cloak to their real owner, showed the blunt, square-jawed features that went under the name of Stacey, Dubroc, or any of a dozen names that Malmordo chose to call himself, according to whatever nationality he needed to adopt.

And yet the question of identity was still in doubt among members of Malmordo's tribe who still had no way of telling their real chief from the false. The doubt might have persisted had The Shadow cared to let it. But, knowing the frantic mood of Malmordo's men, he foresaw a serious problem.

Malmordo was drawing a gun and The

Shadow, as Cranston, would have to do the same. Whichever fired first and surest would have the satisfaction of spilling his adversary into the flood. But in the minds of half the witnesses, the victim would be the real Malmordo. They would aim at the victor the moment that the vanquished fell.

Whatever the case, justice would be the winner, for Malmordo would perish. But The Shadow would be a loser too, from a personal standpoint. It would be better to declare himself and shoot it out with Malmordo's crew at large, before they had a chance to aim his way. It would mean avoiding Malmordo's own fire meanwhile, but that was the risk The Shadow took.

There were factors that decided The Shadow's choice. One was the topple of the grating, down there at the lower arch; a few more tugs and it would fall. The other was a peculiar swirl in the stream itself, a sign for which The Shadow looked and saw in the vague light of lanterns that Malmordo's men had brought with them.

Twisting skillfully along the slippery ledge, The Shadow scooped up the black hat and cloak, planting one upon his head, the other over his shoulders. With a challenging laugh that hurled back separate echoes from every arch, The Shadow opened rapid fire with his automatics.

Malmordo made a quick writhe along the opposite shelf and his men did the same to avoid the ricocheting bullets. The Shadow found it both hard to aim and difficult to tell if he scored a hit, the way his enemies acted. They were shooting back and wildly, but every blast was helpful to The Shadow.

For those shots, with their deafening detonation in these cramped quarters, were producing what The Shadow wanted, a strange, twisty commotion in the stream as though the water itself had begun to rise in protest. Then, from beneath his cloak, The Shadow flung the packet that he carried, ripping its end as it left his hand.

The missile struck the water down toward the final arch. There was a terrific burst of flame, for the packet contained a chunk of potassium. The rest of its contents consisted of a reddish dye, that spread like a gushing blot of blood amid the water. But the flame was the feature that counted at the moment.

Heaving itself from the water came a great shape more than twenty feet in length, a thing that outwrithed even Malmordo. The creature was an anaconda, a giant snake of the constrictor class, recently a dweller among the coastal lagoons of the South American jungle. As it swept its great head along the ledges, lashing its coils as if to encircle its tormentors, the anaconda created terror among Malmordo's crew.

The grating fell with a loud clang and toward the wide opening rushed the human rats, their leader Malmordo among them, all anxious to reach that outlet and escape the anaconda. After them trailed The Shadow's laugh, bidding them a bon voyage as they slipped and slid into the water, just as some of them had splashed overboard from the *Santander.*

This scene linked with that night.

It was then that The Shadow had recognized the presence of the anaconda. Only such a creature could have crushed the unlucky stowaway who had fled to the hold to hide among the mahogany logs. The giant snake had come aboard with that shipment in search of rats and birds as food.

Only something as powerful as an anaconda could have broken the hatch above the hold of the *Santander.* Once on deck, the snake had slithered overboard like the rats and stowaways that preceded it, finding the same pipeline that they used, leading in from the river to one of the warehouses.

The anaconda was the reason why rats vanished from each warehouse that Malmordo picked for his men to use as temporary headquarters. It went where they went, because they coaxed more rats to become their pets, which in turn meant more food for the snake.

And this anaconda was the thing that The Shadow alone had seen pluck one of Malmordo's men off the plank from which The Shadow had rescued Janice Bradford. That was the reason why The Shadow had expected the monstrous reptile to be around tonight, ready to act again if bothered.

It was turning now, this massive writhing foe that Malmordo's followers had so unwittingly harbored, and what disturbed it was the echoing clang from the grating. By then, Malmordo and his companions had been carried into the pipe beyond the final archway, so The Shadow had no reason to remain.

Blackness faded from the lantern light as The Shadow went up the stone steps leading from the ledge on his side of the underground channel.

Out in the river, Inspector Cardona had taken command of a police boat and had sent orders to all others to sweep their searchlights in among the piers. Finding human figures would have been difficult, almost impossible, in such sweeping style, but the police were looking for something else.

They saw it.

From beneath a pier came a great, spreading splotch of dark crimson that seemed to be reaching for the boats themselves. It was the dye that The Shadow had flung into the stream beneath the warehouse, the type of dye used by planes to mark large spots in the ocean.

The tremendous potency of that dye was proving itself as usual, but tonight its purpose was unique. Having preceded Malmordo's men in their last flight, it was marking their outlet into the river. Instead of continuing a blind search, the police boats were converging upon one spot.

This was Cardona's follow-up of the instructions he had received from The Shadow.

And now, as heads began to bob from beneath the fringes of a pier, revolver shots peppered at them while machine guns raked the bottom of the pier itself. Malmordo's water rats came out, waving their hands in wild surrender from amid the red-stained water. Some of them didn't wave, they merely floated, indicating that they had stopped some of the bullets. Nevertheless, the police hauled them into the boats too, just to make sure that they were dead.

Among the faces that he saw, Cardona was looking for one that would answer to either description of Malmordo, his twisted features or the blunt visage that enabled him to pose as Trent Stacey, the man with credentials that Cardona now knew had been forged.

Malmordo was not among any of the prisoners or dead men that Cardona's boat took on board.

Then came a shout from another police boat. Men were pointing out a figure that was doing a swift twist back toward shore, hoping to reach the concrete buttress of the pier, where bullets wouldn't count.

It was Malmordo, clear of The Shadow's vengeance and now eluding that of the law. Yet his fate was already sealed.

Something curled around the frantic swimmer. A horrible scream came from Malmordo's twisty lips as huge coils embraced him. Hoisted there, he was a struggling thing in the grip of the great anaconda, which had fled the warehouse last of all and had overtaken the one man who had made an effort to retrace his path.

Cardona could almost hear Malmordo's body crunch as it went beneath the surface, warped more grotesquely than Malmordo had ever managed to twist himself when faking the part of a human freak. Such was the fate of the evil genius who had followed the ruin of war to perpetrate crime and had met his match in a new land where he had dared defy the power of The Shadow.

Silence settled above the murky water where the great ruddy splotch spread upon the surface was thinning, as though its work were done. Silence, except for the beat of rain, the lap of waves, and something else that seemed to blend amid those natural sounds.

That something else was a weird laugh that Cardona heard from the shore beside the pier, telling that its author had arrived to witness the climax that he had arranged as an end to monstrous crime.

It faded into shivering echoes that the blanketing night absorbed, The Shadow's laugh of triumph!

THE END

Walter B. Gibson (1897-1985) was born in Germantown, Pennsylvania. His first published feature, a puzzle titled "Enigma," appeared in *St. Nicholas Magazine* when Walter was only 8 years old. In 1912, Gibson's second published piece won a literary prize, presented by former President Howard Taft who expressed the hope that this would be the beginning of a great literary career. Building upon a lifelong fascination with magic and sleight of hand, Gibson later became a frequent contributor to magic magazines and worked briefly as a carnival magician. He joined the reporting staff of the *Philadelphia North American* after graduating from Colgate University in 1920, moved over to the *Philadelphia Public Ledger* the following year and was soon producing a huge volume of syndicated features for NEA and the Ledger Syndicate, while also ghosting books for magicians Houdini, Thurston and Blackstone.

A 1930 visit to Street & Smith's offices led to his being hired to write novels featuring The Shadow, the mysterious host of CBS' *Detective Story Program*. Originally intended as a quarterly, *The Shadow Magazine* was promoted to monthly publication when the first two issues sold out and, a year later, began the unique twice-a-month frequency it would enjoy for the next decade. Working on a battery of three typewriters. Gibson often wrote his *Shadow* novels in four or five days, averaging a million and a half words a year. He pounded out twenty-four *Shadow* novels during the final ten months of 1932; he eventually wrote 283 *Shadow* novels totalling some 15 million words.

Gibson also scripted the lead features for *Shadow Comics* and *Super-Magician Comics,* and organized a Philadelphia-based comic art shop utilizing former *Evening Ledger* artists. He also found time for radio, plotting and co-scripting *The Return of Nick Carter, Chick Carter, The Avenger, Frank Merriwell* and *Blackstone, the Magic Detective*. He wrote hundreds of true crime articles for magazines and scripted numerous commercial, industrial and political comic books, pioneering the use of comics as an educational tool. In his book *Man of Magic and Mystery: a Guide to the Work of Walter B. Gibson,* bibliographer J. Randolph Cox documents more than 30-million words published in 150 books, some 500 magazine stories and articles, more than 3000 syndicated newspaper features and hundreds of radio and comic scripts.

Walter hosted ABC's *Strange* and wrote scores of books on magic and psychic phenomena, many co-authored with his wife, Litzka Raymond Gibson. Walter also wrote five *Biff Brewster* juvenile adventure novels for Grosset and Dunlap (as "Andy Adams"), a *Vicki Barr, Air Stewardess* book and a *Cherry Ames, Nurse* story (as "Helen Wells"), Rod Serling's *The Twilight Zone;* and such publishing staples as *Hoyle's Simplified Guide to the Popular Card Games* and *Fell's Official Guide to Knots and How to Tie Them.*

No one was happier than Gibson when The Shadow staged a revival in the sixties and seventies. Walter wrote *Return of The Shadow* in 1963 and three years later selected three vintage stories to appear in a hardcover anthology entitled *The Weird Adventures of The Shadow*. Several series of paperback and hardcover reprints followed and Walter wrote two new *Shadow* short stories, "The Riddle of the Rangoon Ruby" and "Blackmail Bay." A frequent guest at nostalgia, mystery, and comic conventions, Gibson attended the annual Pulpcon and Friends of Old-Time Radio conventions on a regular basis, always delighted to perform a few magic tricks and sign autographs as both Gibson and Grant, using his distinctive double-X signature. His last completed work of fiction, "The Batman Encounters—Gray Face," appeared as a text feature in the 500th issue of *Detective Comics*.

Walter Gibson died on December 6, 1985, a recently-begun *Shadow* novel sitting unfinished in his typewriter. "I always enjoyed writing the *Shadow* stories," he remarked to me a few years earlier. "There was never a time when I wasn't enjoying the story I was writing or looking forward to beginning the next one." Walter paused and then added, a touch of sadness in his voice, "I wish I was still writing the *Shadow* stories."

So do I, old friend. So do I.

—Anthony Tollin